"What is intriguing [about *Waiting in Vain*] is the assurance of the voice, the strength of characterization, and the clear redefinition of the Caribbean novel."

—*The Washington Post Book World*

"A lavish and lush read filled with spice, sass, and passion."

—DIANE MCKINNEY-WHETSTONE

"[*Waiting in Vain*] is what happens when a gifted writer decides to get romantic."

—*Time Out New York*

# SATISFY MY SOUL

"A stunning novel of extraordinary power . . . Highly recommended."

—*Quarterly Black Review*

"Sizzling . . . Wildly entertaining . . . A smoldering love story with tantalizing dialogue and gritty text . . . Channer's mastery of descriptive verse and strong voice are compelling."

—*Black Issues Book Review*

"Frances challenges Carey in ways that are both disturbing and satisfying. His struggles with spiritual convictions, love for this woman, rejection by his father, and haunting conflict with his friend leave him questioning himself and seeking peace of mind. After many weeks of seclusion and soul searching, Carey is finally satisfied—as is the reader."

—*Booklist*

ALSO BY COLIN CHANNER

*Waiting in Vain*

*Satisfy My Soul*

*Got to Be Real* (four novellas)

# PASSING THROUGH

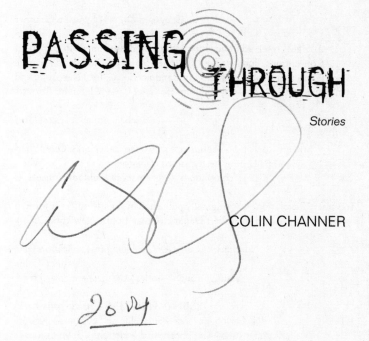

# PASSING THROUGH

*Stories*

COLIN CHANNER

ONE WORLD
BALLANTINE BOOKS • NEW YORK

Strivers Row
An Imprint of One World
Published by The Random House Publishing Group

Copyright © 2004 by Colin Channer

The story "Revolution" was originally published in slightly different form in *After Hours,* edited by Robert Fleming (Plume Books: New York, 2002).

Library of Congress Cataloging-in-Publication Data
Channer, Colin.
Passing through : stories / Colin Channer.— 1st ed.
         p.     cm.
ISBN 0-345-45334-4 (trade paperback)
1. Caribbean Area—Social life and customs—Fiction.
2. Americans—Caribbean Area—Fiction.　3. Volcanoes—
Fiction.　4. Islands—Fiction.　I. Title.
PS3553.H2735P37　2004
813'.54—dc22　　2004046935

ISBN 0-345-45334-4

Text design by Susan Turner

Manufactured in the United States of America

First Edition: May 2004

1　2　3　4　5　6　7　8　9

*For my mother Phyllis Grant, the Black Cinderella,*
*who was born Gordon, raised Thompson, and*
*married Channer before she found her name.*

# CONTENTS

I would like to thank the three editors who helped to shape this book—Anita Diggs, Dan Smetanka and Melody Guy. One bought it. One shaped it. One gave it its cover and gave it her heart. It took a lot of heart to get this book to you.

We're not here forever. We're all just passing through.

Dear Editor:

I'm writing to express a very grave concern. Specifically, someone needs to take the younger generation in hand. They need some straightening out.

When I was a young man, which was a long time ago—I am at present ninety-five and holding—young women cared about their undergarments. This is no longer so, it seems; and I'm highly disappointed. Two nights ago I had the exquisite pleasure of a frolic with a young American miss who was here on Spring Break, a lovely student of mathematics, who brought along a friend for good measure. I was quite excited, you see. I'm still fascinated by the range of expression afforded by the ménage. But I am not consistently able to provide enough exertive force, having overextended, so to speak, in the days of my youth.

However, I've been in good nick of late and so I looked forward to the challenge. So can you imagine my disappointment when my playmates showed themselves to be the wearers of undergarments that looked like men's briefs? And so great was my distress, that I was unable to perform.

It is clear to me that this is yet another example of what happens when children have been left alone to raise themselves. Certain crucial bits of information are not passed down.

Yours, etc.

St. William Rawle

# THE HIGH PRIEST OF LOVE

## I.

IN WHITE, AT DUSK, on the final day of all that he had known to be his life, Eddie Blackwell left Eugenia sleeping in a ball of naked flesh and made two strides across the planking to the open door.

He was broad-shouldered and compact with wavy, center-parted hair, and there was something in the way he slightly hunched and kept his pelvis taut that marked him as the kind of man who'd taken drinks in places where the patrons settled arguments by dropping in a crouch.

He was long-faced, with tight skin, and if you saw him in a quarter pose, even if your view was just a glance, you'd note the angle of his cheeks, the way they jutted then descended in a scoop along his jaw, how they tapered thinly from his eyes toward his ears as if they were designed to swim.

Eddie Blackwell's hut was built on stilts on marshy ground with pilings driven deeply in a natural bank of mud and sand along the sloping crescent where the River Janga made its final curve before it poured into the belly of a dark lagoon—a mangled mass of mangrove roots and hidden channels with a secret opening to the minty waters of the Caribbean Sea.

In the shadow of the mangroves, Eddie, an American who'd lived in the West Indies for the most fulfilling years of his chaotic life, could see a buzz of trembling lights.

An armada of canoes had come together overnight, and he could see now in the water right below him pink and yellow petals from the flowers that the people of New Lagos had released into the stream. On the other bank, a little string of boats constructed from banana leaves were tangled in the reeds.

A light emerged out of the pulsing mass of brightness and began to shimmer up the stream toward him. And, living as he did before the camera was a common object, he built a book of memories in his mind.

In deep focus, he looked east across the marsh toward the hills, which in the lifting darkness had begun to show their edges in the bluish-gray collage of earth and sky. Dark and undulating, they approached from either side, a gentle rise and fall that gathered force, congealing in the cratered cone of Mt. Diablo, the volcano that had caused implosions in his life.

Eugenia wasn't sleeping. This he knew. And as he thought again about the multistranded knotting of her complicated love, he panned now to the north. From his elevation he could see the marshland merging with repeated frames of cattle farms and cane.

Satisfied, he walked around the deck, which, like the roof was shaded by an overhang of thatch. He looked toward the south in the direction of Seville, where he'd lived for seven years. The little capital was shadowed. But even in the brightest light it would have been obscured by stands of trees.

From a wooden box below the window ledge, he took a pewter flask, poured a drink and gripped the rail a little tighter, waiting for the light.

He slowly drank until the darkness broke apart and he could

see the steeple of his church, a long white-shafted arrow pointed at the sky, and the school above the town that he'd built with funds obtained in secret from the father of the girl.

With his eyes, he drew a line from Mt. Diablo to the steeple of the church. A flow of superheated ash and rocks could swamp it very quickly. The year before, in Martinique, Mt. Pelée blew . . . nearly thirty thousand dead. Six months later, in St. Vincent, Soufrière surprised the world again . . . nearly sixteen hundred more.

Eugenia stirred behind him and temptation snaked along his guts. He heard the sheets against her shoulders, the crackle of the matting in the pallet when she turned. And he braced himself for an eruption of her young, volcanic love—vows of deep affection swirling with a mass of jagged taunts, since it had seemed unfair to her that he'd allowed his other obligations, which he didn't always keep, to leave her damp and longing.

Giving partial vent to his desires, he began to think of what would happen if he turned. In his mind, he pulled the parted shutters wide and reached inside the darkened room.

His breathing getting short, he saw his body leaning, the reaching of his arm, saw her lying on her side, her face toward the hairy wall, a hand beneath her face, the other clamped between her knees, and then his trembling hand now climbing up the gradient of her soft upslanted thigh, then sledding from her hip into the hollow of her waist, and now his fingers walking up the rung of bones along her ribs into the fatty dampness of her breasts as he wondered if she would forgive him if he showed some sign of willingness to try.

Another sip, he thought, would bring the courage to resist his fears and climb across the ledge into the room; there, he would disrobe himself of collar, cape and vestments. But that would not be right.

Antonio, his confidante and helper for the last four years, would be arriving soon, and Father Eddie's need for women— the reason that his flock had made a present of this nest above the marsh—was a fairly open secret guarded by a people who believed that chastity was not the most important talent of a priest. For them it was more crucial to be loyal and discreet.

When he heard Antonio call his name, the young priest made his way toward the front, where he could see the older man, who was standing upright in a striped canoe, thirty feet below, white-haired, dark and slender.

"Father, everything okay?"

The young priest raised his hand, commanding silence, and answered in a voice that was low but not a whisper that his trunks had been transported from the rectory to the wharf and that he had no other luggage.

He didn't want the man to see the girl.

Eugenia was young. Just seventeen. But already quite experienced. She was long-haired and full bodied, with an elongated nose that curved like a banana, and eyes with heavy lids. When you saw her naked from the side it always struck you that her breasts and buttocks were connected, that if you traced the undercarriage of her large, uptilted breasts and slanted with your eyes across her ribs you'd end up at the point at which her ass extruded from her body in a long, down-drafting line.

As Father Eddie fussled with the ladder, which was made of wood and rope, Eugenia slipped her hands beneath her head and crossed her ankles on the pallet, her eyes in hazy focus but directed at the steeply angled roof, disappointed after struggling in some way or other since the age of twelve to make her first appearance in this legendary bed.

Beside her on the pillow was an envelope. Money? Well, that wasn't why she came. She tossed the envelope. By accident it flew outside the window. Why she came was leaving. Why she came was on the verge of flight.

From outside and down below she heard Antonio's voice again, "Everything okay?"

And being petulant and disappointed, she replied, "Everything is not okay. I've been forsaken."

"That's not true," came the priest's reply, his smoky voice now tense but weary.

She wiped her face; but could not stop herself from crying.

"You haven't been forsaken," came his voice again, damp this time and sorry. "You're a wonderful girl. God loves you. God loves you."

"Not as much as I love you," she blurted with a force that drew her upright in the pallet.

"More. Much more. Much more," came his contemplative answer. "Much more. Much more than that."

"I don't believe you. Prove it. Prove it now. I asked you to prove it last night and what did you do? You did nothing. You smoked and drank and slept as if I had no bloody use. And instead of leaving you I stayed. I'm not a wonderful girl. I'm a bloody stupid girl because I let you make a fool of me."

She was resting on her elbows and, for the first time in their conversation, she allowed herself to look. At first she didn't want to see him, afraid of what she might have felt the urge to do. There were times at which her temper took control of her the way a body could be wracked with cramps and fevers. When this happened, her anger could remain aflame for days.

She'd expected him to leave more quickly. But he'd lingered; and, as she neared the limits of her self-control, she felt as if she'd been provoked.

Through the door she saw his forehead sinking, leaving her to stare into the emptiness between the planking and the overhanging thatch—two lines, one straight, one jagged, with nothing in between until his answer filled the space.

"If you don't believe, the fault is mine," he said with force so that his voice would carry, accepting that their privacy was gone.

"I hate you," she responded.

By this point she was sitting on the pallet with her back toward the window and her face toward the door.

Her body wilted and she placed her elbows on her knees, breasts tugging at her sternum with their weight. Her dark hair fell forward, the ends so long they touched the floor, and as she glanced up from behind the spray, he reappeared.

His incarnation struck her with the instant optimism of the gambler who decides to bet the world against a fleeting sign of luck. And although she couldn't see his features fully in the light, his skin of yellow-brown, which had deepened in the heat to somewhat of a reddish-gold, she imagined that his face was flushed with love.

"Please try and understand," he told her. "I didn't make this world. If I did, then this is not the way that things would be."

"How would they be?" she asked, convinced that he was speaking vaguely for Antonio's sake.

"If I answered that, I'd be putting myself in the place of God and that wouldn't be right."

"But I worship you."

"That is just a saying. I'm not worthy of worship. Neither am I worthy of your love."

"But you are."

She wanted to approach him, but she knew that this would not be right. And rightness was a thing he valued much.

"Good-bye, Eugenia."

"My love," she muttered, as her passions crystallized into a plan.

"Good-bye."

"I love you. Do you love me too?"

After a pause, he answered quickly as he disappeared, "I do."

She closed the door and shutters and lay down in the dark. Gray light seeped between the gaps along the hairy boards that made the walls. And in their stream now floated schools of dust and smoke—dust that he'd aroused with movement, smoke from his big cigars.

If he wouldn't have her, she thought, then she would have herself. She used her fingertips to make her rosy nipples hard and traced her nails across her arms and thighs to make her body flame with prickled flesh. And as she heard the splashing of the oars beneath her spurting breath, she continued to enjoy herself, each touch exciting her immensely. It felt to her as if the skin that formed her aureoles had been stretched across her length—upholstered tightly—and that her fingers had been dipped in mint. And as the splashing of the oars grew softer and the hum of blood inside her ears became a roar, she feather-touched herself along the shaft of muscle in her abdomen toward her arrowhead of pubic hair, wishing she were made of water, tightly focused on the image of his body leaving sperm and perspiration in its wake. "I'll find a way to follow you," she moaned and muttered. "You'll never get away."

## II.

HE WAS SET to leave that evening on a packet boat that had arrived the night before from Cartagena via Port of Spain. Officially, he'd only been recalled, but a secret letter brought him wind of circulated gossip—they were going to defrock him in New York.

After leaving San Carlos, the RMPS *Córdoba* would sail to Cuba. There, it would call at Havana before sailing up the North American coast. But if he had the courage to pursue his plan he wouldn't be aboard; instead he would be sailing on another ship to New Orleans.

As Antonio paddled down the Janga, Father Eddie focused on his plan. New Orleans was in every sense but geographic like a Caribbean town. In a place like that, he thought, a man like him could find a way to be himself.

He began to think about it more as old Antonio rowed . . . shuffled it with other places like a deck of cards . . . Boston, St. Louis, even Montreal . . . and it always reappeared . . . on top, face up . . .

the only place that could alleviate the damp malaise that would arrive like fever with his sepia-toned nostalgia for these islands . . . the humid towns and wooden houses . . . the porches trimmed in iron braids . . . the wantonness at carnival . . . the piety at Lent . . . the wonder of a Creole chorus cruising over music pocked with tribal accents . . . the acceptance of people with mixed blood.

From the prow of the canoe, he looked up from his thoughts and saw the shaggy hut retreating up the stream above Antonio's head, three stories tall on pilings set wide and braced with rough crossbeams. What was Eugenia doing? Did she read his note? He began to wonder if he should have left some money; but this was overwhelmed by other thoughts.

*For the love of money is the root of all evil: which while some coveted after, they have erred from the faith, and pierced themselves through with many sorrows.*

But what about the love of love? This would be the challenge of his coming life.

Father Eddie had approached the priesthood as a pragmatist, as many colored men had volunteered to go to war. The uniform itself was an advancement, elevation to a caste above the one to which the wearer had been born. If he was a Father he could never be a *boy*?

Although he'd joined the Jesuits fifteen years ago, Father Eddie, in the secret place in which he kept the names of all the things that he would like to see imprinted on his grave, was a teacher, not a priest.

He'd studied math and languages at Fordham, the beneficiary of a trust for orphaned boys, and had joined the priesthood, at the urging of a curate, Father Higgins, known by all his students as "The Blessed Uncle Auntie"—a drinker whose gin-wizened face retained a rosy femininity that didn't match the booming voice in which he lectured forth on theorems and their proofs.

As he often did while pondering his future, he reflected on

the late professor's sharp advice: "There's nothing here for you, my son. Join the priesthood. See the world."

If he couldn't be a teacher in New Orleans, Father Eddie thought—nodding with politeness to Antonio, who continued to apologize about "arriving while the Blessed Father purged vexation from that demon girl"—he could start a gym, a place where troubled boys would learn some discipline and vent their rage. In his teenage years, three of which were spent "away," he'd learned to box. At first he'd learned because he wanted to be fierce. But the ritual of taping and skipping and the intellectual challenge of perfecting techniques had made him calm. But then again, he thought, I've always been a drinker. Maybe I should start a saloon.

As Antonio rowed and jabbered, Father Eddie tried to see himself in different roles, in different places, doing different things, exploring each idea—examining its fit from different angles like a woman in a changing room with lots of blouses. Purposeful. Decisive. But compelled to look at options. Knowing he would always be a teacher. Teaching was his love.

In ten years in these islands he'd founded five schools, two of which, St. George's Boys and Holy Childhood Girls, were built above Seville in 1900. Each of them had boarding room for eighty-five, with thirty places set aside for children of the poor.

"Father, we going show them," said Antonio.

Like most Carlitos, the old fisherman didn't speak English, but a dialect of Spanish called *sancoche*. For although San Carlos was an English colony, it had a longer history under Spanish rule.

*Sancoche* was spoken in the rafters of the mouth with a barely moving tongue. And its natural pitch was low and rumbling, even in the mouths of little girls.

"When they see we, they go know," exclaimed Antonio. "They go know who shame and who ain't shame. They go know who smart and who ain't smart. They go know that they can't mash up our something with their strategy, that they can't do

God work if God ain't choose them to do it. Only God anointed can do God work. And is God anoint you, Father Eddie. Is God write the Book. Man could only type."

"Thank you," Father Eddie murmured. He was grateful, but embarrassed. And he made a note to speak more brightly, hoping that a bolder show of gratitude would make Antonio cease.

They were fifty yards away from the armada of canoes. Overhead, among the mangroves, monkeys skittered when the crowd began to cheer. At Antonio's urging, Father Eddie rose and faced the people, greeted them with open arms, thinking as he neared them, I have failed.

Father Eddie would have chosen to depart alone, to launch himself into infinity as self-contained and private as a message in a flask; but the people of New Lagos, the descendants of Yoruba slaves who'd run away and made a secret life among the manatees, desired a parade, and Antonio had organized an armada of the island's fishing people, a convoy of peasants in their Sunday bests that would circumnavigate the pear-shaped island, gathering force and numbers at each cove . . . each beach . . . each bay . . . each town . . . before entering the harbor in Seville, where they would come ashore beside the market with their red turbans and black jackets and white frocks, shoeless, slippered and unshod, and make their way along the foreshore road to the foot of the statue of Admiral Nelson where a band of drums and fifes and tambourines and two regiments of *jonkanoos*—some in masks of bulls and demons, others clad from head to toe in raffia that transformed their wearers into spectacles like bobbling mounds of hay—would lead a dance around the garden in the center of the flagstone plaza, chanting Hail Mary's that would echo through the archways of the old stone buildings with gables and columns that looked out on the square.

And if anyone should say they were disturbing the peace, they would say there was no peace to be disturbed, that there would never be no peace on this island till this man here on our shoulder, this first black priest we ever see, this man who make a school so we children could learn something, this man who save everybody on this island's life, because when the ground started to shake and a little smoke and bad odor start to seep out like Diablo was going to go *boo-doom* like them devil mountains in Martinique and St. Vincent last year, and everybody was getting frighten, and all who had the means to leave was packing up and sending off their wife and children to Jamaica and taking up with housekeeper 'cause they say if they go dead they want to dead happy, when both the Anglican and Catholic bishops and the governor pack up and leave, Father Eddie, call up clergy from all churches on this island and say, "Let we go up to the mountain and call upon the power of God."

And all of them was 'fraid, and he say he going to go alone. And they give him their blessing. They give him in truth. But when they find out that he keep a meeting with the *babalaos* to persuade the most powerful ones to go with him, they say Father Eddie mustn't go because them things is worshipping false gods and that if he go is blasphemy and promoting idol worship.

So Father Eddie didn't go, and the *babalaos* go alone and they was up in the mountain fourteen days and is more smoke and sulfur odor coming down. And when they do come back three of them dead, and then is more panic now. And all the people say the world was going to end.

So naturally, all who have feud with who decide to take it out. And all who was harboring ill feelings start to tell off who they ain't like. And one and two fellas who watching a girl long time start to terrorize the place with rape. Even down to police was involved.

And the only thing that stop all that was when the Lord put His hand across Diablo's mouth. And the man who God work through was Father Eddie. This man.

When all was lost, this man went up in the mountains one more time with the remnants of the *babalaos*. The last two left when the others get 'fraid and soft. And this man call down the power of God. And this man chant and pray and exorcise those demons from that mountain. And this is what the bishop want to run the man away for. This is what the bishop say he blaspheming for. This is what he say he worshipping false god for, that blasted Irish clown. Is this he want the Blessed Father to swear he not going and do again. And this is why the Blessed Father get defiant and say he ain't do nothing wrong and that if he do something wrong well that is between he and God, and that the *babalao* praise the same God as everybody else but only in a different way, and that if a Catholic can pray with a Protestant then a priest should be able to pray with a *babalao,* and that if the bishop would only take the time to learn some *sancoche* then he would understand, and that he, Eddie Blackwell, done work it out with God already. And that is when the bishop pass his place and call the man who save this place a little nigger boy. And that is when the Blessed Father look at him hard—with his hands behind his back—and the power of the Lord came down from heaven and drop the bishop hard.

And those wickeds went and make a story that the Blessed Father uppercut the man and knock him cold—those liars and cowards and thieves who wasn't even in the room to see what happen. Some even say they heard the Blessed Father tell the bishop kiss his ass before he lick him down.

Is lie they telling. Is scandal, slander, blasphemy and lie. For Father Eddie is a saint. And saints don't say bad words like that.


III.


"SHIT!"

The *Córdoba* was now at sea, and Father Eddie, hung over from the binge of drinking he'd prescribed himself to clot the pain of separation, had arisen from a dream in which he'd seen himself in bed with Eugenia at the moment that his name was called for judgment by the Lord and had rammed his head against the upper bunk.

The ample berth, cream with a barrel roof and panel work that ended midway up the walls, was on a middle deck and had a little porch. For furniture there was a pair of bunks in brass with railings, a writing table, dresser and a chair; and between the bunks, a vaguely Oriental rug, four feet wide, in a scheme of red and blue, a frame within a frame of floral patterns with a geometric border of abstracted blooms.

Groggy, Father Eddie stood between the beds and splashed his face with water at the sink—a slab of white ceramic with a pair of swan neck faucets mounted on a cabinet with double doors. In the mirror, which was oval with a heavy wooden frame, he finger-combed his hair and lit a fresh Cohiba, looking like the gangster many used to think he would become. Against the background of the walls in wood and cream, his skin a freshly plated gold from sailing round the island under pressure from the sun, he exuded all the lush immortal magic of a sepia tone.

In another generation—this is too ambitious—in another three or four, Eddie Blackwell could have been a movie star. But in the time in which he lived, his features were perceived as faults, the evidence of sin.

As a child, born of a frightened Irish girl in a home for wayward mothers, as a waif raised by nuns among orphans, he'd always felt untrue. As a boy, there was a way that people used to look at him—as if he were a griffin or a dragon or some other creature thrown together from ill-fitting parts, as if he were a thing that struck the mind with alternating wonderment and fear—that made him doubt himself, that made him see himself as odd, the camel in the beauty show for horses.

And now, as he smoked and posed before the mirror in his priestly robes, he felt again inside his guts the inter-knotted feelings of that complicated boy whose code of genes was not a language but a dialect, the boy who'd never heard or seen a single word of beauty that he felt that he could gather with assurance to create a wreath of interlocking images to crown himself. And he heard the taunts again. *Mongrel. Half-caste. Yellow. Nigger.* Nobody knows my name.

As he often did whenever he re-entered certain moments, he began to see another boy, the boy who teased him till he passed from shock to anger into rage, a rage through which he sank into a calming peace, the kind of peace that comes before you do the kinds of evil things that in their moment feel so right.

That boy knew my name, he thought. He knew my name was Ed. He was my friend. But he kept on saying those things, those really awful things. But he was my friend. He said my mother was a whore. Hesaidmymotherwasawhore. He said my mother was a . . . whore. And although I never knew her, well, my mother is my mother and you can't talk about my mother. Sure enough, I'd told him dirty things about his mother first. But that's because he said I was a mutt.

He punched and beat and stomped the boy. They sent him to another home. Labeled him "disturbed." Two years later, after months in isolation, he was sent away to be reformed.

With a twisted smile, the young priest raised his fists and dropped into a crouch, jabbed twice, ducked left and came back with a cross. They didn't change you, kid. They couldn't do it. You're damaged. Not broke. Keep your head up. Stick and move. Stick and move. Stick and move.

Still, he felt alone. And it was in this mode of alternating triumph and nostalgia that he felt the rising terror of his need for love, and made a plan to find a girl.

If he were a different man, he thought, as he removed his robes, and if Eugenia were a different girl, oh what they could do, his mind now worming through the fragments of the broken dream to lick the pulp.

But unbeknownst to him, there was no need to satisfy himself with dreams. Eugenia Campbell was already on the ship.

## IV.

EUGENIA CAMPBELL WAS a *chocoblanca,* which in *sancoche* meant "white chocolate," one of eighty-seven racial flavors recognized on San Carlos, an island fascinated by the subtleties of blood.

Looking at the people of this island you'd be tempted to believe the legend that they fornicated as a kind of art, that Carlitos chose their partners based on secret recipes for new eye-pleasing flesh.

Look. There goes a *Cuban coffee.* Over there, a murky *tamarind juice.* And standing by that column there is what you'd call a *Spanish rice.*

Since the end of slavery, the range of tones and textures had expanded. The Indians, Chinese and Arabs had infused the pot with new ingredients—the *rum masala,* the *sugar almond* and the *lychee-kola cream.*

Eugenia's father, William Campbell, had been born there on the island to a family of Scots, and managed an estate above Seville. Her mother, Emelia Raposo, was a seamstress, a Cuban émigré whose skin, in English, when translated from *sancoche* meant "finely sanded hardwood varnished with a lustrous blend of logwood honey strengthened with a wash of gold Antiguan rum."

Until the age of twelve, Eugenia had been raised in bourgeois comfort in an airy cottage on a shady lot between the great house and the barracks. Now she lived with her mother in a pair of crowded rooms above a shop in Woodley, the district of the artisans and traders near the market, walking distance from the wharf.

Now, instead of the accountant and the engineer, her peers and neighbors were the potter and the cook. Oh, how she'd come down.

After five years of boiling, her hatred for her mother had congealed to something hard; for it was Emelia who had caused the fall, Emelia who had caused their lives to shatter on the cobbles of the lower class, where no one had a tutor, or a room of their own, and you rarely found someone who understood the King's English, for no one had been to school—so all you heard around you was *sancoche*.

In Eugenia's estimation, Emelia had been careless—hadn't done the things that women did to get their futures guaranteed. Hadn't found a way to move from mistress into marriage. Thusly, she had dangled all their lives across the edge of shame. And how easy it had been for them to fall. How easy it had been for William Campbell's whispered words to blow them over. *Last month I met a woman on a trip to Edinburgh, and I'm afraid she's coming out* . . .

And thusly, Eugenia was damaged. Thusly she was left without a suitor with the right amount of suitability. Thusly, she became reduced from future wife to object, a thing of beauty to be ogled. Fingered. Rubbed. The temptation in the heart. The obsession in the dream. But in reality, the woman who would always be returned. The vase that slipped and shattered into powder, which, even after careful reconstruction, would always show against the porcelain, a web of darker lines.

Father Eddie was the one who had restored her. And this is why she'd given him her deepest love.

IN THOSE DAYS, when people weren't allowed to show their deepest feelings, society replied to shows of true emotion in the way it did to things defined as dark and savage. Suppress. Displace. Destroy.

The lasting meaning of her discharge; the shock of her abandonment; the regimental way that people she had thought of as her peers so quickly closed their ranks; the ridicule with which she and Emelia were saluted by the folks that had been left behind; all of these combined to crack Eugenia's will. All of this combined to break her down. And as soon as she arrived in Woodley she descended into what for all around her was a living hell.

She cried. She screamed. She cursed. She tried to run away. When they brought her back, she told them that she wouldn't eat. When they pried her jaws to force her, she began to piss and shit in bed.

Rumors raced. People whispered. Someone told another that Eugenia had been bitten by a rabid dog. Another whispered that the haughty seamstress was receiving payment for some evil done in Cuba. And crowds began to gather, first a little lingering, then a little loitering, then people bringing stools and chairs to catch the drama from a perch below the window. People sitting down.

The owner of the shop on top of which Eugenia lived, Khalid Salan, recently arrived from Lebanon, was deeply wounded by the efforts to restrain the girl. Still, he was excited that the *bangarang* had drawn expanding crowds, throngs of people sharing gossip in the heat, which made them great consumers of his Carling beer and Royal Standard rum.

On hearing from a worker that his daughter was insane, William Campbell wavered, tossed between competing loves.

After days had passed, he broached the subject with Sir Terrence Rawle, who owned the old estate. Over planter's punch and rum cake on Mt. Pleasant's tall veranda, sweating horses tethered just below, feet up on the carved, out-folded arms of wood-and-wicker chairs, they reasoned with the openness of men who shared a culture and a past—Campbells had been running businesses for Rawles for generations; had even bought and sold their slaves.

"You should not have started something that you couldn't finish," said the older man, whose voice was strongly English even though this was the house in which his father and his father's father had been born. "Why raise her up to let her down?"

"I loved her, Mr. Rawle," confessed the younger man, who gazed in the direction of his cottage with his heavy lidded eyes.

"Don't confuse yourself with love," replied his gruff adviser. "Don't even love your wife. There's admiration. Obligation. Idleness and lust. All of these will stroke the natural urges. Do you understand?"

"Yes sir," Eugenia's father answered feebly. "Yes. I think I do."

"Go where you need to go, and do what you need to do, but return alone with empty hands. Whatever you do, however you might feel, never bring them up. If you bring them up they'll bring you down. Stand your ground, young Campbell. Stand your ground. The woman you must marry is coming out. There will be no moping here. Manage."

Days later, a melancholic William Campbell went to see his priest, an ancient Presbyterian.

"From everything I've heard," the vicar told him, "from you . . . the help . . . this is all an open secret . . . what is done in darkness must come out to light . . . poor Eugenia isn't mad. She's demonic."

To punctuate, the vicar grabbed his robe with spotted hands and shook it out as if it harbored dirty secrets, then went on: "You don't need a doctor. Or ordinary prayers, for that matter. You need an exorcism by a priest. And if I were you, I'd get a Roman Catholic. I think they're regimented brutes in most respects. What's the big hurrah about a mass in Latin? What does it really prove? But again, I've always been the first to say the Roman Catholics are the most efficient exorcists. Practice, you see. Practice. Look at me, I'm seventy-seven and I haven't done a single exorcism in my life. They're tedious to do if you have to stop in middle spell. One has to memorize the formulas, you see. Speak to Father Eddie, an American who's just arrived from Jamaica. Or is it St. Lucia? He's been around. A good man, I've heard, but what his countrymen would call a 'colored,' blunt-edged in these matters as they are. I might as well inform you, considering"—he tipped his head and flexed his brows, which raised eight lines of ripples to the fringe of hair that ringed his glistening crown—"I'd suggest one of the others, the old hands, if you will, but it's my understanding that they're rummies. Every single one of them." He leaned forward and stage-whispered. "Why Roman Catholics drink so much is another story for another time—perhaps as fascinating as the reason demons have a preference for their souls. The two phenomena are related, obviously. Go see this Father Eddie fellow, then. Good luck."

And this is how Eugenia came to see a stranger in a habit by her bed one morning. He was seated on the only chair that wasn't broken, and before she could arouse her rage he handed her a note, which he said was from her father.

Knowing that he must have heard about her temper, and believing he would be afraid, Eugenia wrenched her face as tightly as a bud and jerked at her restraints, a rigging made of sailcloth, rope and stud-connected pieces of old bridles.

But instead of discipline, she got instead a parting of the lips, a smile whose backward peeling, like the skin that holds the life-sustaining pulp and nectar of a fruit, aroused an appetite, which in time to come would have a name.

His voice, its manly timbre—his accent—which, compared to the familiar tart expression of the English had an optimistic tone, triggered something in the fertile garden of her soul.

But the very thing that tenderized her caused an ache—a sudden crack, an elastic sear, and in the moment, this unstable mix of pain and pleasure made her feel unsure, and she began to see the man beside her as threat. In a gentle voice she asked him to untie her. Deceived, he obeyed, and she smashed her fist against his nose, which drew his blood, blessing the projected consummation of her newly propagated love.

Accustomed to brutality, Eugenia rolled into a ball and braced, her emotions changing form so many times they lost their meaning; but instead of hitting her, the one who had become the unsuspecting object of her deepest love attended to his nose and wiped his face and told her in his lowered, smoky voice, which had assumed the tone in which one shares a fact of real importance with a confidante, "I am here to comfort you. There is nothing wrong with you. The people in the street will never understand. Give your mother time. She will understand. Your father loves you. Read the letter. It will be hard. But try to understand. I know your hurt. I know your pain. I've felt that pain before. There's nothing wrong with you, Eugenia. I believe this. I know. I understand."

With this he called down to the crowd for liniments and bandage, and sat beside the girl. She tried to read the letter but she could not see the words beyond the curtain of her tears, and she asked him through her body language if he would kindly read it. And he said the words that he'd dictated to her father, who did not understand that children must be balmed with love.

When the liniments and bandages arrived, he washed her with a flannel in the bed, drawing cooling water from an earthen jar. Weeks of grime had settled in her creases. And when he turned her on her belly he could see her spine as clearly as the stem along a leaf.

Her skin was bruised in places, and he cooed at volumes louder than her cries in every moment that his actions made her wince. But there were so many wounds—scrapes incurred in tussles, scratches she'd induced herself, strap welts from her loving but frustrated mother—that they cooed and cried a symphony of love and pain.

He couldn't find her clothes in that shambolic place, and so he cut a length of cooling muslin from her mother's many bolts of cloth and made the girl a sort of shift, which he closed with knots along the sides. After this he called downstairs for bread and milk and took advantage of Eugenia's willingness to give him charge over her body, and administered some food. She took it slowly, sometimes pausing just to hear his deep, peculiar voice.

When she had been cleaned and fed, Father Eddie tidied up the room, then asked her nicely if she thought it would be good to send an answer to her father. After thirty minutes of persuasion, she obeyed.

Before leaving, Father Eddie blessed the room, Eugenia's body and the bed with sprinklings from his flask of holy water, dabbed her in the ritual places with his sacramental oil, handed her an aromatic rosary made of sandalwood—and just to entertain the people looking upward through the window, raised his voice and paraphrased in Latin all the portions of the formulas of exorcism that were floating like exploded fragments in his mind.

From that point onward, Father Eddie was the people's hero and what could only be described as a religious star. But to Eugenia he was nothing but the object of her deepest fascinations, and four years later, on her sixteenth birthday, she handed him a note:

*I gave you my heart on the first day that I saw you. Now my love has fructified. Pluck me at the peak of ripeness. I'm no innocent. I'm a harborer of secret urges that are relevant and pertinent to you. Please don't pray about this. Hurry. Make haste. If you don't, I am afraid, I will be spoiled.*

By the time of her ascension into Father Eddie's bed, twelve months after he'd received the note, her sexual juices were well fermented and she'd earned a reputation in some circles as a seamstress whose abilities surpassed her mother, and in others as a good expensive pour, the discrete decanter of a luscious, creamy love whose flavor in the mouth recalled a rounded Chardonnay that teased the palate with its pulsing notes of coconut and cloves.

## V.

IN A SOFT cream suit and a panama hat, the object of Eugenia's love, dressed according to his purpose, left his berth and went up on the forward deck—the open, tapered space toward the prow.

It was a lovely evening, cool with just a hint of breeze, and couples moved in streams.

They moved stiffly but with grace, as if on skates, their hands behind their backs in a reserved, Victorian way although the queen for whom the period had been named had passed away; in truth they were existing in Edwardian times. But like most things in the tropics, even time itself came late.

From a higher deck, there came the strains of music. A band was playing a waltz in which the trombones made a cloud of woolly notes that hovered in the air before it broke apart and showered all on deck with sentimental sounds.

The *Córdoba* was a steamer at a time when most vessels in the islands moved by sail. Compared to a sailboat, it was larger, rode higher in the waves and offered larger berths, but most importantly, its turbines had the power to create the magic of electric lights.

In those days, people in these islands weren't used to seeing farther than the range of candles, lamps and matches in the night. And as they walked around the deck, the strollers, most of whom were white, and based upon their clothes and accents, employed as overseers or mid-level civil servants, gazed upward at the glitter, eyes agape as if they were observing hives of fireflies.

Father Eddie, when he first arrived on deck, was caught up in the phosphorescent mood. Leaning on the rail and gazing back along the looming body of the ship, he felt the humming of a soft internal glow, as if the power of the engines circulated through his bones, which made him think about the times when he'd experienced God in close communion.

He glanced across his shoulders, upward at the sky and down toward the waves. All was black. Haze from the twin eruptions in the year before had left a veil across the stars that would exist for years to come. The darkness on the sea was so concrete that he could feel it pressing on the ship, holding back the glitter of the light from spilling out.

He began to think of what the ship in its magnificence would look like to a person on the shore. He'd left Seville at dusk; and as such he hadn't seen the *Córdoba* at night.

Perhaps, he thought, it would appear to be an isle of light, a piece of some important city set afloat. From this image there evolved a game. So if the vessel were a piece of an important city, then, he thought, the lights along the funnels would be buildings with a lot of floors . . . the lights along the decks would be the bulbs along a grand marquee. . . .

But as he entertained himself, while searching inconspicuously for single girls, he discovered something new: when he made himself the viewer on the shore he found it hard to see his actual, living self. The self he knew, the self he was, would bloom, then disappear. He could see the hull—from stem to stern a little shorter than a train. He could see the lights—green to starboard, red to port, the masthead all in white. People strolling. People talking. But he couldn't see himself.

He began to wonder if this was an illness, an affliction sent to warn him by the Lord. And in the vastness of the ocean, beyond the reach of heaven's brightest star, he felt the power of the Lord upon him in a different way.

He felt it not as something deep inside him but as something distant, something fading quickly into time. What if God no longer cared, he dared to think, breathing tightly as he felt the inward rush of ancient fears, fears that drew with them a swirl of recollections . . . of loneliness, of bully boys, of loving nuns, of conceding and rebelling in the dark.

He began to feel disoriented. His past had leaked into his future and had spoiled his mood. A briny sickness filled his throat as if he'd swallowed salty water thick with weeds.

Where would he go? What would he do? God was everywhere. In San Carlos. In New York. In New Orleans. *What is hidden in the dark must come out in the light. What is hidden from the wise and prudent shall be revealed to the babe and the suckling.*

He glanced around and saw among the couples now, a pair of single girls with older chaperones. They were pretty, yet they left his senses numb.

Once upon a time, he thought, I had a future. Now all I have are damp regrets. He watched the girls with rising hatred, as if it were their fault that he was feeling shipwrecked on a mermaid island, that he was feeling like the sailor who'd ignored the lighthouse for the splendor of the golden comb. *All that glitters is not gold. If thy right hand offend thee, cut it off. The wages of sin is death.*

Where? What? When? Who? The answers that had come to him all seemed so flimsy now, as weak against the darkness as the steamer's magic lights.

He went up to the dining room and learned that it was later than he'd thought, and it struck him that the people on the deck were on their after-dinner stroll.

"IS IT POSSIBLE to get any service?"

He was standing just outside a set of double doors, one of which had been ajar, and was speaking to a waiter, an older man from Malta in an ivory jacket with a silver-gray mustache.

In reply, the waiter stood aside, allowing him to glance inside so he could see the busy waiters cleaning up and prepping for the morning.

"Anything at all?"

"Not here, sir. No. You might try to see if they'll seat you up in upper class." Seeing a dour look on the gentleman's face, the waiter caught himself. "First class. Upper class. It's all the same. Their service goes a little late."

Seeing in the moment a distressing glimpse of what his future held, Father Eddie muttered, "If I were—"

Defensively, the waiter cut him off.

"We say the same to black or white, sir. Rules are rules, are rules."

"If I were a priest this f——ing devil would've let me in," said Father Eddie just beneath his breath.

"*If*," the waiter emphasized. "And maybe even then. But what's the point? We're closed. They're open. And you're not."

Father Eddie drew into himself. Across his inner vision passed an arcing revelation, a momentary glimmer like a leaping fish—he couldn't see himself upon the deck before because he had been looking for a priest. And he gained a greater confidence that he could be convincingly unpriestly, that in looks, at least, he could appear to be a natural man.

You're not a priest, he told himself. You're a man afloat. No one knows you. At Seville, you were the only person to get on.

Molding for himself a different image now, he felt his quest to find a girl renewed.

## VI.

IN THOSE DAYS, marriage was, for women, a profession, a serious occupation that required teams of coaches, grooms and scouts. If a woman was distinguished by a body built for breeding, and a character that showed a willingness to play a role and follow orders, she was poised to get a contract that could change her life.

As such, married women could afford to travel in the upper

decks; and single women traveled cheaply down below. The schism was so common that it could have been a rule—steerage was the place to find the single girl.

The least expensive class of berth, steerage, was adjacent to the mechanisms used to steer and move the ship—the rudder, the propellers, the gigantic boilers in the engine room—things that shook and growled and gave off heat.

Moving through the belly of the boat, the pleasures of his compact body hinted in the glimpse of shirt that flashed each time the panels of his open jacket swung, Father Eddie, smiling whitely from below his slanted hat as if he held a naughty secret, left the trembling air above and strode embracingly toward the smoky stillness that approached him from below, acknowledging the stolen stares and fluttery glances that applauded him with subtle pouts and nods, trying to clear his head of all his doubts.

It was hot below the decks, and he felt as if the hairs along his body had been set ablaze. Beads of perspiration formed a cloud against his skin. And as they burst and rolled he felt as if he had been set upon by fleas.

From the stern, the sound of music trickled forth, drums and something stringed, some kind of banjo or guitar pursued in circles by the shaking breasts of twin maracas. Along with music came the smell of food, of fried fish and boiled bananas, of different kinds of fritters—in their heightened state his nerves distinguished plantain, corn and black-eyed peas—pepper sauce with mustard, dasheen leaves and okra stewed in coconut milk, various kinds of roasted yams. Oranges and limes.

By a narrow corridor, lined on either side with tight-eyed couples kissing slowly, their eyelids flickering like the conjured wings with which their souls eloped, Father Eddie entered a fiesta.

The passengers in steerage were accommodated in a common room on either side of which were rows of iron bunks on an uncovered floor. On one side, a row of portholes which were never opened as they were too close against the waterline showed themselves as rimless, inky circles. And along the raftered ceiling was a row of weak electric lights.

From the rafters, the members of the servant class had hung their woven hammocks, as they would from branches of a tree. Between the bunks were mats with piles of sleeping children and wicker pails of clothes and food; but in the center of the smoky room there was a tight, encroaching circle of gyrating shoeless girls in shades of wood and brass.

They were dancing with abandon, but with purpose, tightening on a band of old musicians, all of them white-haired and old with puckered skin like salted meat.

The men were sitting back-to-back on crates that they had brought on board, dressed as if they still existed in the century that had gone, in blousy shirts and pantaloons, their faces tight like soldiers under siege as they barraged the throng of girls with music, shooting them with pellets that exploded in their wombs, playing with the pride of decommissioned men who'd boasted that their loss of vigor placed no limits on the skill with which they could inflame a gal to jerk like so, and spin like so, and hold her waist and sink like so, and spring like so, and bawl like so, and flutter like a hen like so although their cocks no longer crowed.

From overhearing conversations, Father Eddie knew that most of these young girls were going to Cuba, which was newly independent and afloat with *Yanquí* money since the Spanish-American War; and further, that the girls were going to try their luck at prostitution, which offered them, without a binding contract, the most important perk of marriage—money—which in Cuba was on offer in abundance, created by the presence of an occupying force.

It was hot inside the room, and Father Eddie held his jacket by a finger hooked behind his ear, the fabric draping like a cape along his back, and picked his way toward a corner, stepping over listing pails and mounds of tiny, sleeping forms to sit along the edge of a bunk, the hump of muscle flexed between his thighs now acting like a wedge to keep his legs apart.

Overhead, someone had strung a pair of hammocks horizontally across the upper bunks. The braided cotton sagged with snoring hulks that seeped the smell of rum.

From this low position, Father Eddie's point of view was like a dog's. He could no longer see the dancers individually, but as one vibrating shadowed mass engulfed in smoke, framed above the knees and just below the shoulders in the gap between the hammocks and the lower bunks, divided by the bedposts into strips.

But sometimes someone would strike a match to light a cheap cigar and he would glimpse the ruffle of a lifted skirt, and, just before the light would fall, of a flash of lower thigh.

Soon, his hand began to move toward his muscled hump, sideward like a crab along a beach. And he covered it to keep himself from caring.

To touch himself like this in public, he discovered, was an exquisite, tart delight. Perhaps "touching" isn't quite the proper word, because his hand was still, but the tender aching that was bulging on his resting palm was ringing with an intermittent pulse whose timing corresponded roughly to the times at which a dancer would erupt with, "Sweetness" and a voice responded like a digger, "Ugh."

Marinating in his secret bliss, he didn't notice when a shadow separated from the mass and made its way toward him in a sly approach.

"IS YOU PAY for this bed with me?"

He shuddered when he heard the voice. The woman's face was turned across her shoulder but her legs were on the other side.

He made out that she was dark, with a rounded forehead

drawn forth as if by tongs to make a shined, emerging globe. She wore a yellow turban, which was knotted in the front, and a red blouse worn just off her shoulders with a long blue skirt, over which there was an apron.

"What you have there playing with?" she teased, leaning over, with her elbow on his thigh, her concave mouth now open in a smile that showed the sparkle of a golden tooth. "Call me Margarita. Take me to your room."

Although he had experience with prostitutes, he'd always preferred if Antonio made the deal. So at first there was a hesitation. But his curiosity, which had begun to kick and rear, now bolted, and brought with it a confidence that trampled on his doubt.

"I'm having a good time already," was his answer. "Is this really your bed in truth? If it is, may I lie down?"

"Where you wife?" she asked, reaching in her bosom for a hand-rolled cigarette. The dampness from her perspiration made it hard to light; and, illuminated by the sparking fragments, she revealed herself to be attractive, maybe twenty . . . twenty-five, with brows that marched in file above two deeply settled eyes.

"I'm not married," he answered, suppressing the anxiety that always came whenever he was forced to tell a lie.

"Talk again."

She put her elbow on his shoulder and bounced herself across to him, tightening the space, until the outward curving muscle of his leg was pressing on her spreading thigh.

"What do you want me to say?"

"You is a Yankee?" she asked, her thin voice making yet a higher swoop.

"I'm American . . . yes."

"And what your name might be, sir?" she said, enunciating in a high-heeled voice that almost caused her tongue to trip.

"Ahh . . . Antonio."

"I could be a good wife to you, you know, Antonio." She

handed him the cigarette. "I was only testing you to see if you was any kinda careless man. I ain't looking no careless man, yes. You is the only loving man I meet since leaving Port of Spain. I can tell them things, you know. You're a tender, loving man. And a man with learning too. So as I see that, I thought me and you could run we little joke." She winked. "Is not my bed. And if I was you I woulda get off. It have some ignorant people on this *Córdoba.*"

Sensing his discomfort, she began to make him feel at ease with self-negating jokes that created the illusion of exposure, giving him the room in which to ask her, in the open-ended way in which one asks a fresh acquaintance, if she'd like to find a more secluded place to talk, obligating her to answer that she had a few more things to do and to ask him for the name of a convenient place to meet, at which point he appeared confused and gave directions, which she—of course—repeated with errors till he intervened and said: "Let's make it simple. Just meet me in my room. And here is some money. I haven't eaten. I'd appreciate it dearly if you brought me some food."

WITH HIGH ANTICIPATION, Roselyn Thompson took a washup in the bathroom from a bucket, taking special care to scrub the fatty pleats between her legs, removing all the odors and deposits from its most immediate use—a standing quickie with a steward in a storeroom for a pound—and wore to meet with the nice brown man, whom she found attractive and intriguing, an ensemble improvised from bolts of cloth because she had to lend her cousin Millicent her only other dress.

She had seen him as he came along the hallway from the decks above as she left the cubby with the steward, whom she hugged—but did not kiss—to hide her face. On instinct, she'd perceived the man she knew as Antonio as a moral man, and his very presence made her self-aware. But after trailing him and seeing for herself that his needs were base like hers, she felt a combination of sympathy and luck. And as they had so many times before, pity and a dream of better living drew her into unconsidered love. But apart from dreams and pity, there was something more. He'd treated her with dignity, had slipped her twenty pounds to bring him fifty shillings' worth of food, making what she was to him, unspoken, freeing her to think of his intentions as meaningful and true.

At the door, he greeted her warmly, in a bathrobe and slippers, and accepted with warmth the food that she'd brought him on a bamboo tray, the same tray on which she made a living selling homemade candies on the streets of Port of Spain to feed the children that were left now with her mother. To her delight, he seemed neither amused nor disappointed that she'd wrapped herself in muslin—a simple sheath that she'd caught beneath her arms and rolled across her shoulder blades and round again across her watery breasts and tucked. With another length of cloth she'd made a bandeau, which tightened flatly on her head, then bloomed out of a knot along her nape as if it were a giant rose.

True—he was not amused. Neither was he disappointed. He was slightly drunk.

On returning to his room, he'd begun to feel the tentative beginnings of the melancholia that always seemed to rise inside him on the eve of carnal love. Like the streams of birds that drift across the sky before the sun begins to fall, the melancholia always brought at first a dreamy lightness, a fragility that exposed the nerves and heightened sensitivity, bringing emphasis to textures previously ignored.

The first drink had been a celebration—of luck, of life, of love itself; the second one a drink to toast the first; the third and fourth were jaunty tosses—doubles just because, after which the glass began to feed him on its own, revolving like a bucket on a waterwheel, giving him the strength to crush the larger fragments of his memories into dust.

He led her through the other door onto the terrace; there, she hastily deflected his offer of a wicker chair and pressed him into sitting, pushing not as gently as she thought against his shoulders, and placed the tray against his lap.

She unfolded each delight, all of which were wrapped in either plantain leaves or kitchen cloths—a fragment of a dress or skirt used only for this purpose, hygiene being so important to the poor.

It was dark inside his body. The lights had gone out. And he felt as if his hollowed self were filling with a column of smoke. But being a man who was in love with love, pride and an inverted code of honor compelled him to create illusions.

"This is the most perfect thing that could've happened," he told her in a courtly way. "I found it very hard to wait for you. I thought you'd never come. I almost went to look for you. Is this what you always do—leave men dangling on the edge of broken hearts?"

If her skin were light she would've flushed.

"If I told you why it take so long you wouldn't believe," she answered, deciding as he paused to lean toward her that the story of her dress was neither funny nor romantic, poverty being, from everything that she'd experienced, a topic that depressed a mood.

"I would believe anything you tell me," he said in a partial confession whose truth he was unwilling to acknowledge or admit. "Tell me the story of your life. I want to know you deeply."

"I could kiss you?" she answered, her face unsmiling and unstable, sensing that the cue to move from where they were toward the gate of something deep could only come from her. Some men came to prostitutes because of a desire to be ruled.

"Are you sure you want to kiss?"

His surprise confirmed that this was not his first experience with this kind of love; and she stood, removed the tray and was direct.

"Come," she told him with a warmth that didn't go above politeness, as if she were an interviewer or a nurse. "Let we go into the bed."

With a twist he freed his hand from hers and held her just below the shoulders, as if he were about to lift her up.

"I know that many women find it hard to kiss a man they do not know," he said sincerely. The type of women being invoked was clearly understood. "I didn't want to make you feel as if you had to go ahead with something that you didn't want to do."

"If I like a man, then is a different thing," she told him as she flexed her feet to raise herself and pluck her kiss in twos. His upper lip had creases like a raisin; the other one as seamless as a grape.

In truth the kisses had been stolen. And although he didn't understand it, there was something in the hint of force that drew him taut, that called his muscles to attention like the members of a lax platoon.

He held her by the face and pressed her mouth with his and locked her tongue into a tussle, his passions rushing blindly onward while their bodies whispered in collusion, his pelvis skimming hers as if they were the leading dancers in opposing conga lines.

"Come we go to bed and done," she told him. Their mouths were still engaged and he thought he felt his tongue coordinating with her teeth and gums, as if they'd spoken with one voice.

"No. No. No. No," he said. "Kiss me some more."

"I feel I want to take you," she said, her fingers raking through his hair. Its softness filled her heart with joy and envy—envy that her hair was not as soft and loosely curled, and joy from idle dreams of walking down the streets of Port of Spain as mother of a brown-skinned child.

"Now is not the time," he told her.

"Come we go and done."

Inside the room, she stood between the beds, one ankle

crossed against the next, and in this pose unwrapped herself, beginning with her hair, which had been plaited and unloosed, and now sprung high from confinement in a palm-like spray of thick, down-curling fronds.

She held his gaze as he disrobed as well, but whereas her nakedness was complete, allowing him to see the golden streaks that marked the pull of children on her breasts, and the skin below her navel that was crinkled like his lip, and the mound of hair so tightly rolled it looked like pepper grains, he hadn't taken off his underwear—knee-length drawers according to the fashion of the times in soft linen with wood buttons and, to bind it, a drawstring in the waist.

He was leaning on the doorframe, and she saw the line that halved his body from his navel to his neck, and beneath his golden skin she saw his triceps turning downward like a pair of twisting roots. Like her, he wore a crucifix.

Turning back to look across her shoulder, she lay down on her stomach with her legs apart, and closed her eyes to make it seem as if she were asleep. There was a slackness in his drawers that showed a waning interest, which from experience she knew had come from fear.

"What you want me do?" she asked him when he cut the lights and crawled into the bed.

"I just want you to hold me," he said.

"What you mean by that?"

"Just put your arm around me. Just keep me close."

"I never felt a kiss like that before," she said as if arising from a dream.

"I've never kissed like that before," he admitted, surprised that the subject didn't resurrect the mood. "The way you kissed me made me want to kiss you in the most compelling way. I did it without thought. It just happened. I had to do it. I just had to do it. Do you know what I mean?"

At this their bodies closed as one, her darkness fitting tightly through his golden limbs, fastened like a belt.

"Something happened," she said, her voice trailing to a pause.

"Nothing happened," he responded.

"You change on me," she said. "You not feeling strong again?"

"Tired," he said. "Just tired. I didn't sleep a lot last night."

"You don't like me?"

"I do. You're nice. But I don't want to talk right now. I just want to go to sleep." He took a big draft of air, then said, "But I don't want to sleep by myself. It would be lovely if you stayed with me. That would make me very happy."

"Till in the morning?"

"Yes," he said. "Till then? Will they miss you? Your family? Your friends?"

"I want to stay with you," she said, evading. "I'll stay."

"That's good."

"I could read things, you know," she mentioned after they'd lain in silence for a while. "You not the kinda man that do this kinda thing."

"What kind of man am I?"

"You is a soft man."

"What's a soft man?" he asked a little sharply.

"It have two kinda man," she said in illustration. "It have hard man and soft man. Hard man is the regular kinda man that does do regular things like cuff woman and drink plenty rum and is always chopping with cutlass and could hunt wild meat and them things. Hard man is the type that from I walk in here woulda pull up my clothes one time and bend me over that rail out there and give me plenty talks while he bull me."

The description made him laugh.

"And soft man?"

She played at giving him a bite.

"Soft man is a kinda gentleman. He not a auntie man, but he kinda womanish, if you know what I mean. He's a man does do things with consideration. When a soft man want to bull you he does talk to you. He make it nice for you. He don't just bull you just so. I 'fraid hard man, you know. They inconsiderate, bad. The only feelings that don't get hurt is their own."

"I'm glad to be soft," he said, although it was a word he didn't like. "Now do me a favor and go to sleep."

"I can't sleep," she said. "When my blood does get hot it doesn't just cool down just so. It has to take a while. Is like tea." As if she heard a question in his silence, she continued to explain: "Just like how it have soft man and hard man, it have hot woman and it have cold woman, you know. Me? I naturally cold-blooded. But when I get hot I does get real hot and then it hard to cool me down."

"I don't like the word *soft*," he said. "Not in general. When you're talking about me."

"I is not the one who make the word," she said, feeling that her point had been ignored.

"I'm not a soft man," he told her. "I'm just me. I'm tired. And I want to go to sleep."

"All brown man is soft," she muttered.

He rose up on one elbow and looked down at her. She rolled onto her back and stared at what she could discern of him, her hands by instinct forming fists.

"You need to listen to me when I talk to you," he said coolly. "I don't like to be taunted. Don't talk about my skin. Don't call me soft. Don't call me brown. Shut up and go to sleep. I've got a lot on my mind right now."

"But you is a real nigger man, eh," she said, her encouragement disguised as a tease. "You is a hard man in truth, don't care how you pretty. Look how you ready to gimme a cuff."

Triggers pulled inside him as she talked.

"You is a hard man, in truth," she enunciated, smiling from behind the dour mask with which she watched his transformation. "You is a hard man. You see how I don't know a thing. You see how I lying down with a real hard man and talking nonsense. You know what? You should just cuff me one time."

"I don't want to do that," he answered, as his body trembled with the hidden urge.

She spread her legs. He slid over and between.

"So what you want to do?" she asked him. "What you want to do? You ain't want to cuff me, but you know I ain't right to talk to you like that. So you have to dish out some kinda blows or I won't take you serious."

His big c——k elongated from its buttoned coop and pecked her crinkled belly. She reached down low and felt it.

"If you talk I cannot do it," he said tensely and with doubt.

With her body taut against the bed, she launched her hips and held his c——k to help him make the plunge, but something in her smile uncoiled him. In the dark, the rest of her had all but disappeared completely; but when she spoke he saw her flashing tooth and his self-consciousness returned.

He collapsed on top of her, his limbs unglued as if he'd just ejaculated.

"I have never been with a woman," he mumbled. His face was buried in her neck. "I like you. I think you're very nice. But I just want to hold you. I don't want to make love with you. I just want you to stay here and love me. Just hold me like you love me. Just hold me like I'm precious, like I'm the smallest thing in the biggest world. Like if you let me go I'll blow away. Just don't ask me to do something I cannot do. You don't understand the fear."

"That is real poem you say there, you know, boy." She sighed, emotions brimming in her eyes. But she'd raised his face after he'd begun to speak and so had missed the most important part of his admission.

"Don't talk, love," he asked. "Just hold."

He slipped a palm beneath her head and sunk his fingers in her hair, which was damp with sweat but soft in its uncurling.

"You know how long I want a man to make me feel the love I have like when I hug my children?" she said. "You know how long? I have it hard, you know, sir. I have it hard." She turned her head as hot tears began to trail into her ears; but she couldn't bring herself to let him go. "Just now, I was giving you all sorta talks like I is a bad woman, sir; but I ain't no kinda bad woman you know, sir. I'm a Christian girl, sir. I grow in church, sir. I don't really do them things, sir. But is hard life, sir. Is tough life, sir. I ain't really want you to hit me, sir. But I find it have a lotta man that does get their strength when they cutting woman blows, sir. And I know it must be hard when you can't get your strength, sir. I ain't no kinda bad woman, sir. Times is really, really hard."

"I know," he said. "I know. I know."

"You don't know, sir. You don't know."

"If you're a Christian, you should pray to God."

"I tired pray. I tired pray. I say so many Hail Mary that I cannot count. And still I cannot find a way to help myself and my children. Is four. And is me alone."

"Hush."

"I can't hush, sir."

"Cry."

"I can't cry."

"Sleep."

"I will try that. And thanks for letting me stay."

"You're welcome."

"Don't say something if don't mean it," she said, as if this was the most important statement in her life.

"I mean it."

"What you mean?"

He stroked her like a pet.

"I really want you here. I don't want you to go. If you left me right now, I would be unhappy. You're making me happy and I'm glad."

"How am I making you happy?"

"Just by being."

"A man never tell me anything like that before."

"So there. You've heard it. Now it's time to go to sleep."

"Promise me something."

"Okay . . . well . . . it depends."

"Promise me you'll never treat me like a whore."

"But you're not."

"So why you gave me money then to come by you?"

"You're making this very hard."

"Just promise me."

"I promise you. And look, if I've done anything to make you feel any less than you should feel, I'm really sorry. Sometimes I have bad manners."

"Okay."

"Have I made you feel like anything less than you should feel?" he asked, breaking through a pause. "Be honest."

"No. You make me feel really nice. I swear to God."

"It's not good to say the Lord's name in vain."

"Is not in vain. I'm swearing to Him. He watching at us right now. And I saying it right before Him that you make me feel nice. Just like you made a promise to me before Him," she poked.

"I didn't."

"God is everywhere?" she asked him in a tone of gentle mischief.

"Where is all this going?" he replied with apprehension.

"Just answer me and stop being so."

"Yes," he conceded warily. "He's everywhere."

"So if you make a promise to me, you make a promise before God."

"I don't agree," he said flatly.

"Well, you don't have to agree. It ain't no big set o' something. Same way you make it before God you could break it before God. It ain't stop nobody before. Man is man."

"You're making me dizzy. Please stop."

"Kiss me and I'll stop."

When they kissed again, she asked him achingly, "I could stay the night with you for true?" It was a good, slow kiss accompanied by puffy exhalations that provided them the pleasure of a long cigar.

"You have to stay the night with me," he murmured.

"Promise me."

"Okay, I promise you. You can stay the night with me. That is a promise that I've promised to you as promised."

"They say a promise is a comfort to a fool," she giggled, enthralled that she was talking to a man who was not impatient like a brute.

He kissed her one more time and said, "You're the comfort. I am the fool. Now go to sleep."

"I could ask you something?" she interjected after they'd lain in fragile silence for a while. "I feel I want you."

"That wouldn't be right."

"You married," she said, as if something had been confirmed.

"You could say that. But I think I'm headed for a big divorce."

"Antonio, when you're in the mood to take a woman, what you like to do with her?"

She smiled on hearing that his heart accelerated when she called him by his name.

"I like to hold her and have her hold me and make me feel loved."

"And when your blood get really hot then what you like to do?"

"I like to think of things I know I cannot do," he secretly confessed. "I do a lot of things in my mind that I don't do anywhere."

"If you divorce from your wife I would marry you," she said

giddily, amused just by the thought. "The Church won't allow it, but maybe it could still happen."

"The Church has many rules."

"A lot of them is stupid."

"Yes, but don't blaspheme."

"Which is the worserer one you think? Blasphemy or fornication?"

"Blasphemy."

"So fornicate me then."

"I can't."

"Both o' we know you is a hard man," she attempted.

In a final tone he said, "Be that as it may, this is the farthest I can go."

She slid her hand along his side toward his belly.

"Don't touch me," he said firmly. "Don't touch me anymore. You can stay. I gave you my promise. But I'm sleeping in the other bed."

She held him as he tried to roll away and said, "I'm sorry."

"It's not your fault," he said as he twisted from her grasp. "It's mine. I led you on. I should have told you clearly. I've never had a woman." She didn't seem to understand, and so he was emphatic, "I'm a man who's like a virgin. I've only been close. It has gotten me in trouble many times, leading people on, then having to explain. Okay, I have explained it. You can go now. There's nothing here."

"Oh Jesus Christ, Antonio . . ."

This was not the time to tell her that his name was Ed.

"It's okay," he told her, feeling blessed that he was not alone. "It's okay. It's okay. It's okay."

"I don't want to go," she said with compassion. "I want to stay with you. I want to hold you. If you want me to hold you, I will hold you."

"We could touch a little," he suggested, for what he told himself would be her sake. "A little. Not a lot."

"Only if you want, *doux-doux*."

"Just touch, okay. Well, maybe. Touch, but nothing more. It's really, really hard for me. Really hard for me."

"God will help you, *doux-doux*. Never mind."

"Not with this," he answered through a yawn.

"You never know."

"I know. I know. I know."

The intimacy of his revelation, and the stealth with which she had to tease the pleasure from herself so that she wouldn't wake him, held her back from falling deeply into sleep; and so it was that she believed that she was dreaming when a tall white girl with thick long hair came creeping through the door to stand beside the bed with arms akimbo, expressing clear displeasure in a heavy, rumbling language that her wakened lover seemed to understand.

## VII.

A FIGHT WAS going on.

Although they weren't lovers; although they'd never kissed; although she'd seen him naked once—the night before—when she'd made her first appearance in his legendary bed, Eugenia felt betrayed, and on seeing the object of her deepest love enlaced with someone else, had rushed out on the terrace with determined speed as if she were about to jump.

It was an uncontrollable reaction, like a hiccup or a cough, or any kind of instance when a hormone takes an action on its own. Her first concern when Father Eddie flew toward her was her own importance—the other woman had to leave; otherwise she wouldn't entertain his explanation and would continue to subdue his protestations with a tuneless hum.

Father Eddie had closed the door between the terrace and the room, and had draped around himself a belted robe. It was white with a blue trim, and in the way in which he paced and twitched he called to mind a nervous fighter in a ring.

"I can't tell her to go," he was saying, pointing to the door as Eugenia crossed her arms as much in anger as against the oceanic cold. "I told her she could stay. And my word is my word."

"I'm not going to stay here with her," Eugenia said. "I will not be disgraced like that. I came here to see you. I didn't come here to see you and someone else—least of all a woman like that. Is this how you reward my love?"

"If you don't stay here, then where are you going to go? If they find you, you're going to be arrested. Stowaways are treated like thieves. They'll lock you up until they get to port, then they'll turn you over to the police, who will lock you up again. This is not a game, Eugenia. You can't just follow someone like this. You can't just turn up like this. No one knows where you are. Not even your mother. This isn't right, Eugenia. You're getting off at Cuba and you're going home."

"On whose authority?" she asked. "I answer only to the man who runs the ship."

He swallowed hard as he remembered what she'd told him when he'd asked her how she'd come aboard: "I went to Port of Spain a week before and f——ked the captain. While you were being heroic I was being transported on the launch."

At first, he'd thought that she was trying to hurt his feelings, by saying what she knew would spear his heart. But as he looked at her now, alluring in a silken dress in royal blue, her hair well combed, a shawl around her shoulders, smelling of lavender soap and what he knew by instinct was a French perfume, it was clear that she hadn't stowed away; and he accepted with guilt and a puzzling feeling he was yet to recognize as titillation that what she'd said was true, which directed him to wonder how their histories, being in many ways so much in tune, could have produced such different people, one indulgent, one chaste; one honest, one untrue; one natural, one forced; one a source of pleasure, and one a source of pain.

Receding into melancholia, he began to think of all the women that he'd led along and cast away; had seduced with promises of pleasures that he knew that he would never give; had bribed, making them evangelists of lies.

Was slavery not the transformation of a person to a thing? he thought. What does it mean to trick a woman with implicit words? To lure her to your house and then refuse to see in her the natural needs and feelings of a human being? To treat her like a piece of cloth, a blanket for your body, a bandage for your wounds, a hem to gather round you when you need a place to hide? How can that be charity? How can that be love?

"Is he nice?" he asked sarcastically.

"Very much a man."

"And you are such an unforgiving girl."

"On whose authority?" Eugenia poked again.

In his head, he said, *On mine*. Aloud, he was oblique and philosophical: "Let your conscience be your guide."

Ignoring what she thought was an attempt to be evasive, Eugenia flicked her head toward the door and asked, her sleepy eyes awakened by a lean, sarcastic smile, "Why is she so important to you?"

He shrugged and said, "She showed me kindness."

"I'm sure. Does that mean that now you're broke?"

He ran his fingers through his hair.

"It's nothing you'd understand."

"Why not?"

"Just go to bed."

"I have a headache," she declared, her body motionless but soft, as if in preparation for a hug.

Instead of holding her he slouched in a wicker chair and put his feet up on the rail, guilty and ashamed to the point of being oblivious that his robe had fallen open to reveal his trembling thighs. It was clear now that she hadn't read his note, in which he'd told her that his legend was untrue.

Should he tell her now? he thought. Or should he trust that she would read it later? Was it really his concern? The ship would be arriving in Havana in the morning, at which point they would all be going in their separate ways.

As he thought of what to do, he found himself in the position of the boy who could recite and use the theorems but could not provide the proofs.

After his experience with Roselyn, he suspected that his feelings were related to events that had been buried in his past. And although he knew that the unearthing would provide the proof, he didn't know what lay below the surface, neither did he have the tools with which to dig, for the idea of the unconscious mind, of a landscape on the other side of life, did not exist in those days outside a tiny circle of psychiatrists like Freud.

"It's nothing you would understand," he said again, although she hadn't asked. But how could she understand it when he really didn't understand himself.

"I need a smoke," Eugenia said.

Without looking he replied, "They're in the room."

"I'm not going in there," she answered. "The very sight of her just might provoke me into doing something that I will or won't regret."

"I'll go."

"Who would have thought," she asked, approaching now.

With her hips she nudged his legs along the rail and stood before him like a door. Annoyed, he sat up straight and crossed his legs, which shuddered with the repercussions of his penned emotions fighting for release.

"Who would have thought," she said again, pointing now and bending forward like a teacher speaking to a child. She lost her words and after hesitating, grabbed the tray of food and wheeled it overboard. "Last night you were so much the saint.

You couldn't do *this* because of your vows. You couldn't do *that* because of your vows. And look at you now? What is wrong with me, Eddie Blackwell? What is wrong with me? She looks as if she just walked out of a cane piece for Christ's sake? Is that the kind of woman that you want? Is that the only kind of woman you think you can get? Or is it the only kind you can get on a ship like this? I used to believe in you, Eddie Blackwell. I used to believe that you were a sophisticated man with sophisticated tastes. To me you were like God on earth. But you are such a bloody fool. You don't know anything, Eddie Blackwell. You don't know anything about heaven. You don't know anything for sure about earth. You don't know anything about anything. And because of that you ruined my life. I have been in love with you since I was twelve years old. I thought I would grow up to marry you. As stupid as it sounds, that's what I thought. But then I grew older and realized that I couldn't be your wife. But that didn't stop me from loving you. You were still God on earth to me because you raised me from the dead, Eddie Blackwell. You laid your hands on me and called me back, because God knows I was ready to die. God knows I wanted to be taken from this miserable earth and my miserable mother and those miserable people who spend all their miserable time talking about me. Before you I didn't know what it meant for a person to *really* love another person. You raised me up, Eddie Blackwell and then you let me down. You should have left me where I was. You should have let them kill me. Or let me kill myself. You should have just let me goddamn die than to do this to me. Than to reject me like this, in this way, for a woman like this. I saved myself for you. When I began to feel these fearsome urges in my heart I reached out to you. I would have been yours—yours only. Dutiful and faithful to you. I want to feel that, Eddie Blackwell. I want to feel what it's like to belong to someone. But now that's all gone. I can't control it. Do you understand? I can't control it. I am weak for men. I have a need for men. Sometimes I tell myself I love them, but when I think about it, that's not really true. I hate them. When I think of men, I hate them from the bottom of my heart. That's why I don't like to think about them. I just let my urges take me. They bed me, then ask me to make sheets and nightgowns for their wives. I am lower than a mistress. I'm a servant who cannot leave her boss. I am the slave who loves her master more than he could ever love himself. I'm nothing but a high-class whore. I was not born to be a whore. I was born to be a wife. But whore is what they see because of you. Because of you and my father I am everything I wasn't meant to be. Every single man I've ever loved and wanted has bloody let me down. I thought you were more than a man, Eddie Blackwell. I used to think you were like God on earth. But you don't know anything about heaven. You don't know anything about earth. You're worse than a man, Eddie Blackwell. You're as dumb and stupid as a girl."

"You're out of order," he replied, looking sideward at the floor as he squeezed his fists together and his knuckles cracked. "As a gentleman, speaking to a lady, I'm asking you to stop. You better, stop. Eugenia. You better stop. And don't *ever* call me a girl *ever* in your goddamn life."

She fanned his voice away and asked him loudly, "How many times did you f——k?"

The both of them were startled by the word. He rose quickly to his feet and she braced against the rail but didn't cower.

In defiance, she left him standing, pulled the door and saw her rival draw the sheets across her face as if she were asleep. Gazing at the floor to keep the object of her deepest love from reading her intent, Eugenia reached into her purse, which had been sitting on another chair, slipped a cigarillo from its wooden case and struck a light.

"Did you f——k?" she asked of no one in particular, her head surrounded for a moment in a cloud of smoke.

In the anxious silence, she began to chuckle, then addressed her rival in a courtly way: "One for you?"

Roselyn, who'd been lying with a pillow on her head, did not reply until Eugenia shouted.

"What are you getting out of this, Eugenia?" Father Eddie asked as he sat down again.

"Pleasure. Satisfaction. Something I could never get from you."

By then the one who'd shown him kindness was standing at the door. The sheets were drawn around her, reviving recollections of the bolt of cloth in which she'd wrapped herself for presentation. When she had arrived, he mused, he had been drinking in this very chair, thinking of this very girl, this very f——king angry girl. Be careful what you wish.

The one who had consoled him was right, he thought, although she'd made him angry. Sometimes he was too much of a soft man. But soft is what Eugenia needed. Her life had been so hard. And he reflected on the first time that he'd seen the angry girl tied to the bed with a combination of sailcloth, rope and stud-connected pieces of old bridles, bruises blotched across her meager body, which he'd washed and blessed with sacramental oil. He reflected also on the woman she'd become; and was suffused again with deep compassion, first for her, then for himself, and lastly for the one who had consoled him—for she had been impacted by his sorry life the least.

"I apologize," he said, standing up and turning as he spoke to them, an elbow on the rail. His hair was ruffled like a mess of feathers and his handsome features had a haggard, rummy look. "I've hurt the both of you, and I am sorry. I've used the both of you, and I'm ashamed. Neither one of you should feel as if I'm really worth it. You're really better off on your own."

Eugenia laughed. Roselyn struggled with the urge to hold him, but she was reluctant to do anything that would provoke the girl, and she knew this kind of girl, this kinda girl who think she white and can talk to anybody anyhow. If she just say the word I going to give she a cuff one time and whatever happen after that is up to God.

Roselyn took the offered cigarillo, leaned against the door-frame and watched with mild amusement and a rising irritation as Eugenia took a stance across from her against the matching upright of the metal frame and began to imitate her pose and movements—one foot forward, arms crossed below the breasts.

"Would you like a light?" Eugenia asked her, almost at a hush across the foot or so of space between them.

Roselyn sucked her teeth.

As Father Eddie watched, Eugenia took her rival by the head and fought and won a muted struggle as she brought their faces close. In her mouth, she firmly held a burning cigarillo, which she touched against the bobbling one that Roselyn held between her lips, an action that required that she turn her head from side to side, conveying the impression of a kiss.

Roselyn wiped her mouth when they were finished, angry but avowed that she'd ignore the girl. She had her children to support. And she couldn't do this if she went to jail.

But Father Eddie, who had seen the action as a blur, experienced deep internal shudders as he felt his lust renewed.

"I need to speak with you," Eugenia told him, while her rival smoked with gathered brows in front of her.

He answered, "Now is not the time."

"You think she doesn't know when she's intruding?" Eugenia asked him, pointing with her tone. "She knows. She doesn't care if you're sorry. She wants you to tell her what to do. She doesn't want to hear it from me. She needs to hear it from you. Okay, you're sorry. But what are you going to do? You need to talk to me. That's what you need to do. You need to talk to me when there's nobody else around. You need to give me some respect. You need to be a man."

"So is he nice?" he asked, his mind disturbed by thoughts of her cavorting with the captain, whom she'd praised for being *very much* a man.

"Speaking to me?"

"Who else could it be?"

"You have a point. For all intents we're the only persons here."

He'd renewed their earlier conversation without context for important reasons. It was a way to draw her back into their world of secrets, of a common past, of retrieving her away from any plan or impulse to align herself with her rival; for as allies, even of convenience, they would talk. And he'd decided that he didn't want Eugenia to know of certain revelations. She had no control of her emotions, and as such, could not be trusted.

To Eugenia, though, the murky nature of the conversation proved that Father Eddie and her rival had some things to hide.

If he wanted to speak to her in privacy, she reasoned, there were many choices. One, he could send the woman packing to whatever hole she came from. Two, he could speak in *sancoche.* Isn't that what she'd done—for him—when she'd entered the room and found him rolled up tightly with a strumpet like a bloody cigarette? And does he know what she'd really done to get aboard? Of course she didn't go to Port of Spain. She'd met the captain of the ship that very day, had used her brains to seek him out among the bars along the waterfront and, while the man she truly loved was gone around the island at the head of his armada—leaving her forsaken—she'd bribed a stranger with her body and he'd smuggled her aboard, but only till Havana, where he would be meeting yet another of his girls. There was already one—apart from her—on board. Disgrace. Disgrace. Disgrace.

The ship would be arriving in Havana in the morning, and would be leaving for New York in the early afternoon. She had no time to lose.

"So," the man who had forsaken her said vaguely.

"So what?" she snapped.

"Is he nice?"

"I don't know who you're talking about," Eugenia challenged. "Speak freely. If there're things you think we should get out in the open, let's do it. Let's talk. Let's be specific. Give details. Name names."

"Don't speak to me that way."

Like the sea on which they sailed, the calmness of his voice exuded menace, something unsettled that suggested the capacity for rapid change.

"How should I speak to you?" she lashed. "With reverence?"

His shoulders rolling as their blades began to shear, he warned again, "I'd stop if I were you. If I were you, I'd stop."

"Oh dear," she answered flipply. "Perhaps I should obey you like a sheep being led across a pastor. Does she know?"

Roselyn was rubbing one foot across the other—angry, nervous and cold. Spots of frigid perspiration had begun to stain the sheet in which she'd draped herself. When Father Eddie looked at her, she looked at him and tried to speak but changed her mind, and Eugenia, who'd read conspiracy in her rival's hesitation, grabbed her by the cloth and pressed her fists against her throat.

She spat away the cigarillo, plucked away the one that dangled from her rival's mouth, sucked it hard, filled her cheeks and blew a pall of smoke across the darker woman's face.

"Before I throw you overboard this f——king boat," she said as Roselyn did her best to gasp with pride, "tell me—is he nice? Was he good? Tell the truth. Was he of any use? What did he do to you? What did you do to him?"

Father Eddie grabbed Eugenia as she pushed her rival through the open door.

"She taking advantage," Roselyn managed as she caught her breath. Her hands were at her side, slightly forward with the palms turned out, her shoulders heaving. And as she talked, her fingers gathered into fists. In her mind she held a machete and a jagged bottle. "Antonio, you acting like a soft man? What the ass is this? How you could make she do me that? If you was any kinda man you woulda give she a cuff one time and make she shut she mouth. But you is a soft man. Don't care what you want to say. You show me two times tonight that you is a soft man. I can't take a f——king soft man."

"Don't call me soft," he said. "I said don't call me soft."

She took a forward step and pointed with an open hand.

"Well, you acting like soft man, Antonio. You want me to lie? In fact you acting even worse. You acting like a little auntie man. A little sissy. How you could make she go on so? If you was any kinda hard man you woulda give she what she want. A cuff in she *rass*."

"My name is not Antonio."

He'd conceived it as a whisper, but it came out like a bark.

With Father Eddie holding her, Eugenia sent a kick toward her rival, the vigor of the action pulling off her shoe.

"Is one thing why I don't grab this shoe and beat you," Roselyn threatened as she skipped the blow. "Is because if anything, nobody ain't go take my side because o' color. You see this black here," she added, using two fingers to rub across her cheek. "It curse."

She fell to her knees with her hands across her face and cried. The sound of her pain reminded Father Eddie that he was a person with a mission, that in times like these he had to find a way to rise above his earthly troubles to fulfill his obligations as a priest.

"Look at what you did," he told Eugenia, pushing her a little as he let her go. "The woman is in tears."

He strode inside the room and squatted on his haunches; there, he took the one who'd shown him kindness by the head and consoled her in the smoky voice in which he'd given comfort many times to strangers he had met in jail.

"I am very sorry for what has happened," he said softly. "The fault isn't yours or hers. It's mine. I have a problem. A very big problem that I can't work out. In my selfishness I've made that problem into something other people need to solve. But it's something that can only be solved by God."

Then he told her what he'd said before, with added information: "My name is not Antonio. It's Edward . . . Eddie . . . Ed."

He was about to tell her more, but stopped, on realizing that a part of the confession was self-serving, a way to guarantee forgiveness by revealing that he was a priest.

"Come," she whispered. "I want to say something to you. And I don't want her to hear."

He glanced over his shoulder at Eugenia, who was outside on the terrace, leaning on the rail. She'd rolled her sleeves above her forearms, which loomed brightly, like her face, which was in profile, allowing him to see the inward curving beauty of her long banana nose, her eyes so sharply turned toward the side to watch him that she brought to mind the paintings of the old Egyptians.

"Come," Roselyn said again. Father Eddie turned to face her, and set himself so as to shield this interaction from the angry girl. "I don't want she to hear. Come. Come. Thanks. You keep your promise. You never treat me like a whore."

She kept calling him and he kept going closer. When their foreheads touched, they kissed.

He didn't want to kiss her, but if he jerked or showed evasion in some other way, Eugenia would have seen. So, for the sake of peace, he allowed the intimate to happen—he silently allowed her tongue to swim inside his mouth, to penetrate his body, to come in contact with his succulence, the tender membranes in the lining of his jaw—although he knew it wasn't right.

Her simple action filled him with a complicated pleasure. In itself, the kiss was nice, but beyond the kiss itself was something more dynamic, a tingling in the mind that made his neurons glow. It was the pleasure of eluding his tormentor with deceit, right and wrong in unison creating in his body a unique effect, like piano keys of different colors struck to make a chord.

"I'm going to bed," he said across his shoulder.

"Good night Eugenia," Roselyn said with resignation, her secret victory tucked between her breasts.

"Good night," Eugenia muttered, her face as fragile as her voice. "Tell him that I need to speak with him."

Father Eddie overheard and answered, "No. I'm going to bed," as Roselyn held her rival's shoes.

"Have it," Eugenia taunted, as she made another plan. "You'll never get the prince."

## VIII.

FATHER EDDIE LAY down in a lower bunk, aware of love and consolation lying feet away from him across the rug.

Staring at the slats along the undercarriage of the bunk above his head, he knitted details from the strands of sound unspooling from the darker woman's bed—the untucking of the sheet in which she'd tied herself; the splatter of her breasts against her body when she sat upright to spread the sheet with evenness across her legs; the grinding of the pubic naps that spread along her inner thighs whenever she would rub her feet.

Alone, he would have touched himself and thought of her and warmly gone to sleep. Cool air was coming through the door, and he felt it on his body as he lay there in the bed, limbs in slack alignment as if he had collapsed. Though limp in all extremities, he felt a presence in his c——k, a muted sense of action, an awareness of its eagerness to change.

As the pleasure of the secret kiss began to flow throughout him, Eugenia came inside the room.

She stood at the foot of the bed, her face awash with indecision. Aware that he was watching her, she made a turn toward the outer door, placed her hand against the knob, daring him to let her go. But although he was aware that she was twisting his emotions, Father Eddie also knew her hurt was true, and further, that he was obliged to stop her from returning to the captain's bedroom as a whore.

The girl had sold herself for him. He was the one at fault. And now she must be saved.

"Where are you going?" he asked, still lying in the bed.

"For a walk. For a dip into the ocean for a swim. I don't know."

"It doesn't make any sense to leave," he told her as he raised his head. "Stay here."

"He's not nice," she offered, knowing what burdens rested on the Blessed Father's mind. "He isn't nice to me at all."

"Come," he said, firmly but with warmth. "Come. Forget it all and come."

She began to move toward him, then she paused, unsure if she'd received an invitation to his bed.

"Up there," he said, while pointing to the bunk above her rival's head. He did not want Eugenia to be close.

As she began to answer him he closed his eyes and turned his face toward the wall and listened as the nicely built, voluptuous girl undid her clothes, a fugue of snaps, and clicks and cracks that worked against the background of a constant rustle, all of which was followed by the flap of various undergarments— chemise, drawers, socks, corset, petticoat, underskirt—on the lustrous crumple of her dress.

Eugenia had not lain quietly for five minutes before renewing her torment.

"Cinderella, can you please turn out the lights."

"I'll get it," Father Eddie intervened.

"Are you sure you want to do that?" said Eugenia. "When you're ready, you'll find it hard to sneak some loving in the dark."

He chuckled as the thought aroused him . . . slipping from one bed into the next . . . getting love and consolation right beneath her undeserving nose.

He cut the lights and lay down in the dark, his body as unsettled as his mind.

"Tossing and turning. Mark of the guilty conscience," said Eugenia, as if she were reciting from a book.

"It's the mark of a man who's dumb enough to sleep in a room with a child who doesn't mind her manners," Father Eddie said impatiently, aware from her voice that she was lying on her side on the edge of the bunk, but oblivious that she'd insinuated fingers in the gap between her fleshy legs as she addressed him, seeking to infuse her fantasizing with the sound of rage—anger being at least a form of passion.

"My mother was right," she baited.

"Sure."

"I'm very sure."

"Sure."

"You think this is a joke, don't you? You don't think we talk? We talk about a lot of things, including you. You know what she said?" She waited for a while for him to answer, then continued when it struck her that he might have gone to sleep. "She said that you're a fraud. She said that when you went up to Diablo that you didn't do a thing except just sit and wonder what the hell was going on, hoping God would take you from your miserable life."

"Your mother knows a lot."

She was bluffing, he knew; but what she said was right. He had gone up to the mountain out of duty, out of an understanding of the symbol of his effort to the people who had even greater faith.

"Antonio."

He didn't answer. Eugenia called out to him again.

"What?" he said sharply.

He pressed his cheek against the wall and softly ground it.

"Why does Cinderella call you by the name of the old fart who finds your whores?"

"Don't talk about a man behind his back," he warned.

"But I'm talking about you."

"Well, don't talk about me. Don't talk to me or don't talk *about* me."

"Let me speak to Cinderella, then." She leaned over the rail, the brass of which was cold against her skin. "Cinderella, can I talk to you?"

Roselyn rolled one way and then the next before she answered.

"Miss, if I was you, I would leave me."

"Don't threaten, me." Eugenia laughed. "I'm not afraid of you."

Roselyn crossed herself and looked across the aisle.

"You need to discipline this child, you hear me. You need to discipline this child. I ain't know what she is to you, or what she want from you, or what you owe to she. But I know one thing. I'm a big woman and as a child to me she ain't have the right to talk to me like that. I ain't trouble nobody. Why she coming to harass me for? I ain't taking this kinda thing from she no more. You need to deal with this as a kinda man."

"Eugenia," he said harshly, spurred on by the woman's speech and its unspoken taunts.

Eugenia didn't answer. He called her name again. He sat on the edge of the bed with his feet against the floor and shouted: "I am getting sick of you. You're making me so goddamn sick. Do you think that you're the only person in this world to have a shit of a life? I have my own shit to deal with. She has her own shit to deal with. Why are you putting your shit on us? Keep your shit to yourself."

"How could you forsake me so," Eugenia murmured as she rolled into a ball and cried. "How could you leave me after saying that you loved me? You told me that you loved me. If you don't really love someone, you shouldn't lie. All of you are just the same. You're just like my father. You tell me things. You make promises. But everything's a lie."

Roselyn sat up, facing Father Eddie, whom she was afraid was going to melt.

"White people," she said casually, but at a volume that the

girl could hear. "My children don't see they father either, but they ain't go on like so. You know why? 'Cause I does grow them with manners. I does give them discipline. I ain't grow them to be soft. I grow them to be hard. This world is a hard world and if you raise children to be soft you raising them to suffer. I raise my children to do without. If they ain't have they ain't complain. They ain't break down. They ain't act spoil and want to carry on as if they ain't have no manners nor training." She paused and tossed her head with its crown of newly matted hair. "When you see them growing that way you have to straighten them out. You ever see the blacksmith with iron in the furnace how he beat it? Is so you does have to beat them to make them take their shape and get hard. Otherwise they get soft like this one here. Bawling for she daddy like is he make her so. Like she is the only one in this world with problems. I glad you tell she the truth. I glad you stand up and talk. Because the way she talk to you is like she think you is a soft man. But you and me know you ain't no kinda soft man. You have some soft ways. You is a brown man. I could see you have the white in you. But you is a black man to the core. You have the white flesh but the black seed. The tough black seed. I know them hard seed that you have. I know what the hardness feel like. She ain't know. And is that killing she."

Father Eddie smiled at her and shook his head. Eugenia wailed.

"How could you bring me so low, Eddie Blackwell?"

She swung around and now her feet were dangling off the edge. He was thinking now, the older, darker woman rightly sensed, that it was he who had produced Eugenia's state, trying to justify the way she was. But there ain't no justification for behavior like that. It have sadness. It have pain. But there's a thing called courtesy, consideration and manners. *Buckra massa* days done. Don't make white people give you talks like that. Don't lemme see that—somebody who ain't have like me. When I see a brown man like you who wear suit taking talks like that from white people and ain't do nothing it make me feel like there ain't no hope for my children. Man up yourself, boy. Man up yourself and deal with this situation, before I have to jump in and deal with it myself.

"You can't bring a woman low," she said, although in truth she disagreed. "She have to born low. And still yet it have people who born low and reach up to the highest height."

"Why is she even here?" Eugenia shouted, pointing with a foot.

"Throw her out," Roselyn ordered, losing patience now. "Bust she ass and throw she out. Spare the rod and spoil the child."

Eugenia sprang off the bed and landed on the clothes on the rug between the beds and gave herself a stinging slap that sounded soft and wet.

"You seem to know a lot about this kind of thing," she answered Roselyn. Father Eddie tried to stand up, but she timed his move and shoved him down. "Well, Miss Cinderella, your prince has neither heart nor prick. So maybe you should bust my ass yourself."

On instinct, Father Eddie grabbed Eugenia from behind and Roselyn rose before her slowly. As Eugenia wrestled, Roselyn wiped her face against her hands, and in the moment that it took her palms to pass along her face, she found a fragment of compassion in her heart. And so the girl was spared.

"You see what hard ears cause?" she told the heaving girl. "Remember how you grab me and had your fist up in my throat? Suppose I was to grab you now."

"Release me."

In the dark, the angry girl could barely see her rival's face. However, she could feel her bottom pressed against the body of the object of her deepest love, and the sweat-oiled confinement inflamed her even more. And she began to fantasize that he was not restraining her, that he was grasping her to take her from behind, right here standing up, giving her the victory in her rival's face. Wouldn't that be the best revenge?

"Are you going to listen?" Father Eddie asked.

"I'm calling the police."

"Cuban police ain't care about this," the older answered as she placed her hands against the younger woman's shoulders.

"Put your nigger hands on me again," Eugenia hissed, "and I'll kill you."

Roselyn grabbed her by the hair, but Father Eddie yanked the girl away.

"You have to go," he told Eugenia. Roselyn lunged at her, but Father Eddie used his leg to block her path. Frustrated, Roselyn grabbed her sheet and went out on the terrace, where she curled into a chair.

Eugenia climbed the ladder to her bed and sat there with her white legs dangling. To Father Eddie, who was sitting with his shoulders rounded on his lower bunk, she said, "I don't want to go. If I say I'm sorry, can I stay?"

As Roselyn entered the room again, complaining of the cold, he answered, "No."

"I want to speak to you," said Eugenia, who'd misread the quiet gathering of his fury as complaisance, and had no hint of what his hormones were directing him to do.

He rose. She asked him to come closer, and he stood before her with her shins against his body, pressing where his chest and shoulders cleaved.

"What do you want to talk about, Eugenia?"

"How could you treat me that way?" she asked, with disbelief.

"Life is hard," he answered. "Living is the hardest thing you'll ever endure, Eugenia."

"That's all you have to say."

"You should tell her that you're sorry, Eugenia."

Lovingly, she ran her hands along his face and said, "I won't."

"Stop," he barked, as Roselyn tried to take him in her mouth from down below. The action made him stiff, but he was too distracted, too deeply hurt to continue the deceit that had begun with their clandestine kiss.

"Stop what?" Eugenia asked, unaware of what was happening in her presence. "Stop touching you?"

"Yes," he said, as Roselyn draped herself around his thigh.

Expecting it to be a source of sympathetic feelings, Father Eddie brought to mind again the memory of the first time that he'd seen the angry girl, tried again to see her as the shackled child; but the memory, instead of being warm and vital, was as cold and rigid as a sculpture carved in stone.

To Eugenia, Father Eddie's silence meant that he'd achieved the pause at which he'd make the turn, like a ship about to find its way to port, and she began to savor visions of revenge, when her rival would be forced to listen as she shared devotion with the object of her deepest love.

"You know if she's a nigger, I'm a nigger too," he said, hoping now to hear something redemptive from her mouth.

"That is not the way I see you," she apologized.

"You have no idea of the hurt," he said. "No idea of the hurt."

"You shouldn't be hurt," she reasoned. "I wasn't talking about you. I was angry. She wanted to fight me. People say bad things when they're about to go to war."

"Some things you never say, especially around some people. How do you see me, Eugenia? What am I?"

She reached between her legs and touched him lightly on his temples like a dabbing with the oil of chrism.

She paused to think, perceiving that her answer could affect her fate.

"I see you as a priest."

"I'm not a priest," he said obliquely. "I might be something different in the morning. But right now, I'm just a man."

With this he reached below and placed his hands on Roselyn's head and used the remnants of his faith to bless her womb so that no child of hers would grow up to be like him or this unruly child, ghosts in search of love.

"I'm not a priest at my core," he mumbled. "At my core I'm something else, something more"—he couldn't find the word—"fundamental and long lasting."

Realizing from his voice how much she'd hurt him, Eugenia tried to speak, but he placed his hands across her mouth.

"Wait," he said. "Close your eyes. There's no need to be afraid. I'm here. This is my room. Nothing can happen here unless I say so."

She obeyed.

Father Eddie went inside the little cupboard, where he kept his suitcase, on top of which he'd thrown his crumpled suit. His face serene as if his mind was focused on a thing of great importance in another place, he unbuttoned the suspenders, which he gave to Roselyn with a stealth that told her how it must be used.

"Can I look now?" Eugenia asked him, when she felt his palms against her legs. They were warm but covered with a film of icy perspiration.

"There is nothing to hide. I'm going to give you what you asked for," he said with resolution. "But first, I need a drink."

He went out to the terrace with a quart of rum. With a single tilt he drank it straight, smarting from the burn as if it were a rush of salty water and his mouth were a gigantic wound.

"She has to leave the room," Eugenia whispered, turning on the light.

"Just pretend she isn't there."

They lay together in his bed and Roselyn, suppressing her emotions like a sentinel, tried to think of other things as Edward, Ed or Eddie kissed her rival and tormentor for the very first time—a fact that was delivered in a moan—and ran his hands along the firm but densely fatty length of her and slipped his tongue between the narrow cleft between her breasts, which stood erect and did not fall in muddy puddles like her own.

And she was sad because she didn't know that it was not the younger woman's body that inflamed him, but the echo of her brute enticements. *But you is a real nigger man, eh. You is a hard man in truth, don't care how you pretty. Look how you ready to gimme a cuff.*

Although he was inexperienced, Father Eddie knew of all the things that men could do to weaken women, having heard so many details in confession, which he duly plagiarized.

"I have waited so long for you to take me," said Eugenia in a stream of words that had the steady slowness of a seep. She placed his head against her neck and she could feel his cheekbones pressing on the tender skin that lined the dip between her collarbones.

Toying with herself beneath the sheets, Roselyn felt vexation mounting with her envy, and she found it hard to keep herself from spitting on the girl.

Father Eddie rolled onto the carpet from the bed and Eugenia rolled on top of him, her body in a straddle on the woolen fibers, which began to burn her knees.

"It is time," Eugenia uttered, as Father Eddie beamed an urgent but regretful look toward his confidante, who used the length of cloth with which she'd wrapped her head to bind the girl across her mouth and—as Father Eddie held her strongly from below—administered the strokes, at first with lashes of the heavy brown suspenders, then later, as the girl appeared to draw a heightened pleasure from the sting, she beat her bluntly on the back and shoulders with the shoe.

In Havana, without any monumental show of sentiment, they went their separate ways.

"There is nothing left," Eugenia said to Father Eddie after Roselyn was gone.

"That's not true," he answered. They were standing on the terrace and could see the forts on the bluffs above the harbor and the curving elongation of the promenade the Cubans called the Malecón.

"What's left?" Eugenia asked, her body scarred and bruised beneath her clothes. Her understanding of herself and the dimension of her urges had changed in ways that left her satiated but confused, and her question was in truth directed at herself.

"Money, glory, freedom, love and power. There are some things that people always want."

"What about salvation?"

"Salvation will come on earth when we find a way to bring these things to all the people known as niggers in this world. Without salvation there'll be war."

"It's a really awful word," she said, drawing weakly on her well of indignation. What had been done to her was wrong, she knew; but the intensity of the pleasure, the shock of discovering this capacity in herself, had seduced her; and, being a woman of defiance, she did not complain, did not protest. She managed.

Like her rival, Eugenia carried seed inside her as her secret shame. In time it would be public. What would happen then? Should she tell him? Had he been too drunk to know?

With her thumb, she peeled a film of perspiration from his brow. He took her face; and for the first time since she'd known him she saw that he was scared.

The sun was warm through Father Eddie's cassock and he surrendered to the tightness of his collar with the resignation of a man who'd undergone conversion and believed that he deserved the noose.

"I'm going to a country where they say it every day," he said. "I no longer have protection. I used to be a priest."

Dear Editor:

There are times at which I think that I succumb to the expectations of my own cliché by complaining about every decision that the government makes. Today, I am happy to say that I am writing in praise. The repeal of the bastard laws is the most important legislation in the history of this nation and—permit me a moment to complain—it is an indication of this government's overemphasis on economic development that so many people on this island had to wait until the twenty-first century for this benefit to come. I am one of them.

It is an old secret in my family. I am a bastard. I was born out of wedlock. I am not my father's son. This fact was revealed to me on the night before my first marriage, the date and time of which had been determined in a state of duress. My wife to be was, in the parlance of the day, "with child."

My parents were opposed to the marriage for many reasons, the most obvious of which was that my wife to be was Arab and not white, a distinction—on this island, at least—that does not exist today. But on the night before my wedding, my mother called me to her chambers while my father was out and gave me an additional explanation.

Knitting as she rocked, a blanket spread across her lap, she told me that my father was a priest. At first I didn't understand. At first I thought that she was being redundant, that she'd said, "Your father is a beast." I listened. She explained.

When my mother married my father, she was pregnant with somebody else's child. About him she would only say, "He was a priest." The dates of her marriage and my age were incongruent. When I challenged her on this she informed me that the child was stillborn. Seven years later she was pregnant with me. When I asked her if she and my father had been separated or divorced, she raised a brow and said, "Oh, no."

More than seventy years have passed since that revelation, and now it's time to talk. My father's name is Edward Blackwell. My mother, Eugenia Rawle—née Campbell—was not his wife. He was her lover before she was married, and they remained as such until the end of her life. The details of conception will remain with me. I am trying to illustrate a point about the bastard laws and I regret having to besmirch the dead with scandal and disgrace.

The point I'm trying to make is this: from now on, when I use the word "bastard" in relation to the leader of this country, who is my flesh and blood, I point with one finger with four more pointing back at me.

Yours, etc.

St. William Rawle

# THE GIRL WITH THE GOLDEN SHOES

I.

THEY WERE SITTING on old buckets, scaling fish beneath an almond tree when someone pointed to the water and they all began to shout.

They were hardy children who'd been raised in isolation on a crescent beach below a cliff and had experienced many horrors—drownings, stabbings, births and storms. But when they saw a one-eyed monster rising from the deep, they dropped their tools and dashed toward the clump of shacks in which they lived, a blur of skirts and faded tunics raising clouds of sand as white as salt.

The eldest girl, Estrella Thompson, would be fifteen soon, and thought herself mature. She'd recently begun to read, which had created an awareness of a world beyond San Carlos. So, unlike her friends, she was interested in the war.

The war was taking place in Europe, a place that she'd only heard about the year before. Poland. Antwerp. Riga. Spain. The names were sparkling gems of sound that shimmered with a range of possibilities that went beyond the dreams of any of her neighbors in the cove. So on the rare occasions that she had the chance to travel into town, she'd steal away to loiter in the little shops in Woodley, the district of the artisans adjacent to the port, and listen to the intonations of the BBC announcer on the redifusion box, transported like a person who had gone to see a medium for a glimpse of life across the void into the other world.

On these nights more than others, as she curled up in the hammock that she shared with other girls beneath a shed beside her old grandmother's hut, she'd gaze outside the window as she fingered old newspapers and her cache of stolen books, dreaming of the day when she'd be rescued from this place where nothing happened.

So while the others ran, she hid behind the tree, and watched in fearful fascination as the creature loomed.

It was not until the mask had been removed that Estrella, who'd never been to school or traveled widely on her tiny island, understood that what she thought had been a monster was a human being—a scuba diver in a rubber suit.

She stepped out from behind the tree and walked toward him in an old blue frock with eyelet lace around the hem, hips moving widely underneath the faded fabric, giving insight to the marvel of her shape. She was tall and big-boned with mannish shoulders and a long face with sharp cheeks. Her eyes were bright and slanted, and although her skin was darker than a Coca-Cola, she had a length of wavy hair.

"What are you wearing?" she asked in English, which she rarely had the need to use, since everyone around her spoke *sancoche.*

"It lets me breathe beneath the water."

They talked for several minutes, during which he explained some of his duties, then he disappeared below the surf.

In *sancoche,* her native dialect, Estrella kept repeating as the ripples disappeared, "I never even thought to dream of seeing a thing like that."

## II.

"You can go on with your stupidness."

Two days had passed, and Tucker Ross had heard the story many times from many people, but most often from the girl, his granddaughter by the common law.

"Big Tuck," she said, insistently, "is true."

He fanned as if her words were buzzing insects.

"A man can't breathe underwater no matter what he put on his body or his head, Estrella. I really think is a mermaid you see. It have different kinds, you know. And I heard it have some that look like man, in truth."

They'd just completed dinner, and Estrella, who'd replayed her visitation many times, had told the story once again, with every detail in its place—the fellow was a blue-eyed Yankee soldier, and he'd told her that he was a part of something called "man hoovers," which meant that he and other men were practicing a thing they had to do. And the thing they had to practice was to stick a thing like dynamite on German boats below the waterline and blow them up.

The night was hot, and she was sitting on a woven mat beneath the hut in which she lived with Big Tuck and her grandmother, Roselyn—a dark, thick-featured woman with a golden tooth that twinkled when she talked.

She'd arrived in San Carlos in the 1920s from Havana, where she'd gone to work. And after living on the island for many years, she was forced to go to Cuba when her daughter died while birthing Estrella, who was sick and dying when she came into the world. Now, she was overgrown.

Like the other dwellings in the camp, the hut was roofed in

thatch and set at shoulder height on wooden stilts. And on the hottest evenings, they would eat below it on the shaded sand that had been shielded from the heat.

"Is not stupidness," Estrella offered in the rumbling cadence of *sancoche.* "It have a lot of things going on in this world that we ain't know 'bout up here down this coast. Even in town things going on. Is only we don't know nothing. All we know is fish. Catch fish. Scale fish. Eat fish. Fry fish."

Big Tuck sat with his belly pressing on his dark brown shirt. He was squat and hairy, with skin the orange-brown of rum; and his chest and arms were bulky still from rowing boats and pulling nets for almost all his eighty years.

"I ain't disbelieve you when you say you see what you say you see," he told her in a silly voice that made her younger cousins giggle and her old grandmother laugh. "But all I know is that a man can't breathe underwater no matter what he put on. I ain't have to go no school to know that."

"You know from the other day she start to read she getting different," Roselyn added in a gentle tease. "She start to know everything—even things that nobody ain't suppose to know until they dead. Because is only when you dead that you can see certain things. I ain't think it was a mermaid, at all. I think she dead in truth and see a ghost."

"When she tell me that she teach herself to read, I frighten," said Big Tuck with admiration. He tapped her leg and handed her a cigarillo and his flask of rum.

"Tuck, she is a child, you know. She ain't suppose to drink no rum. It ain't have any beer?"

"Rose, you ain't see she's a woman? Leave the blasted child alone."

"Tuck," implored Estrella, smiling at him warmly, as she smoked and took a swig. "Look how long I tell you send me to school. But you only want keep me here to fish."

"Estrella," he replied, easing Roselyn from his lap and taking on a more attentive pose, "if you was in town right now, and the boss man come and ask you what kinda work you want to do, what would you tell him, in truth?"

"I ain't know what kinda work there is," Estrella answered promptly. "But I could work in a shop or in the bank. As long as you could count you could do them kinda things. How hard them work could be more than selling fish? Things is things. If you could sell one thing you could sell another thing, as long as you know how it measure, and how much a measure is the price. And most things they sell in these shops ain't have to measure. They just sell off a shelf one by one. All I would have to do is put them in a bag, make sure I give the right change, and don't insult nobody. Which to me might be the hardest part. Because in truth it have some people who will agitate your nerves."

"Is where you getting these thoughts?" her grandmother asked. A tone of slight concern had seeped into her voice.

"I have it in my head long time to do something, Grandma. But I just ain't get the chance to even know what I could do. How I going to know? Who going tell me? Them people here?" She gestured broadly. "I ask the fellow that was doing man hoovers what I could do if I leave here, and he tell me I could do anything if I only put my mind."

"So," her grandmother said, "you let a stranger tell you what to do with your life?"

"You know it have a lot of educated dunces in this world," Big Tuck replied in illustration. "Take Rawle boy. They send he away to university in the mother country and I hear he ain't pass no exam. I hear is bare zero he getting up at the place there." He paused to find the word. "Camron or Campton or Cam Ditch or some *rass*. That and Oxfam is the two biggest school they have in England, they say. What kinda man get opportunity like that and come back with two long hand and no qualification . . . no doctor . . . no engineer . . . no barrister? That is why I keep myself right here. Rawle ain't know the white man school hard like brick or he wouldn't gone and fail. And he a white man too. Me? I stick with what I know. The fish in my blood. And Estrella, it in your blood too. If you let that go is death."

"If I stay here and don't do nothing with myself then that would kill me worse," she blurted, adding childish frills along her intonation. For although Big Tuck was funny, he was quick to take offense. And when he was upset he could be cruel.

They ain't understanding what I trying to say, Estrella thought. But maybe I should keep it to myself.

She had not been led to reading by a great ambition—that was something reading had produced. But this wasn't easy to explain.

A year before, in 1941, on a market trip to Seville, she'd wandered off while running errands, and had taken up a spot across the street from La Sala de Amor to watch the cars arriving with the idle wives of businessmen and English civil servants.

La Sala, as Carlitos knew it, was the first of many mansions on the Queensway to be sold for business use, and was large, and white, with thick limestone columns; and between the columns ran a lacy banister whose loops and swirls in black conferred a lingerie allure to anyone who dined on the veranda, basking in the currents driven by the celebrated fan, an engineering marvel that was bolted to the ceiling and whose giant wings, which had been woven in the previous century from a fiber that grew only in the Yucatán, made slow, gigantic swoops.

The Queens, as people called it, was an upward sloping mile that started at a square beside the harbor and ended at the governor's imposing gate.

In Spanish times it had been known as the Paseo, and was the site of much parading by the rich. In its center was a flowered median lined with rows of royal palms and curving paths with benches made of heavy wood and gas-illuminated globes that seeped a misty sentimental light.

That day, as she watched the wives arriving for their lunch,

Estrella recognized a chauffeur as a man who bought his fish from her grandmother, and she tried to make a sale.

"Oyi," she shouted from a bench beneath a tree. "It have some good jack and parrot today. Nice bonito too. I save up some for you. When you finish you should come."

With his finger quickly brought across his lip, the man, whose job was marked by nothing more official than a visor, tossed his head, inviting her to cross the street. There, he introduced her to another driver as "the smartest little girl you'll ever meet."

"What kinda woman you calling child?" the man replied.

He wore a pith helmet and an ivory jacket with a scarlet sash.

"She overgrow," the man she knew remarked. "Overgrow and overripe."

"Is the fish she eating make her bottom juicy so?"

As the drivers talked about her as if she wasn't there, and other people passed along the road, Estrella watched the people on the grand veranda, dreaming, and by accident observed something designed to be unseen.

When a husband moved toward the door to greet his friend, the waiter slipped his wife a note that had been scribbled by her lover, who was seated by himself across the aisle.

The reaction to the written word was something that the girl had never seen. In an instant, the lady's face, which before the note had been as plain and inexpressive as an egg, was crackled with a smile.

It was a kind of smile the girl had never seen before—one that wasn't triggered by the mouth, that only ended there. That looked as if it started somewhere deep inside her liquid core. And that is when she knew that writing was an elemental force, like hurricanes and floods, and began to visualize the stream of words that she would like to share with someone that she loved.

That very day, she stole the first of many books, a primer slid beneath the skirt along an aisle in McSweeney's Stationery Shop, followed by a lesson here and there in phonics for a penny, which she took on credit from the eight-year-old who worked behind the counter in her father's Chinese shop.

However, in the weeks that followed her encounter with the diver, Estrella's greatest problem wasn't books. It was the *Star*.

Before she had begun to read, the daily paper was a *thing*—a thing a mother used to line the box she turned into a cradle; a thing a child would fold to make a hat when it would rain; a thing that everybody used to wipe their ass; some yellow things you picked out of the garbage when you went to town; a thing for everyone to use.

But in the weeks that followed her encounter, Estrella had begun to keep some for herself.

Because no one believed her story, she began to read the papers with the single-minded effort of a lawyer on the quest for vindicating proof. And to her family and neighbors, it seemed as if she'd pulled away.

It unsettled them to watch her reading . . . smiling to herself . . . whispering fancy words . . . her finger pointing all the time . . . her head bowed like she praying to the damn *rass* thing.

If you play your drum or pluck your *cuatro* when the gal was reading one, she'd walk away. What kinda thing is that? And when she come back after she done walk away and you ask her what it really have inside that thing, she only want to tell you things 'bout other places—like where we from ain't place.

So although they were amazed that one of them had learned to read, they also felt as if she'd put them under siege, a sense that if they didn't act, then history would remember them as people who'd watched and waited while their way of life was slowly laid to waste.

As days turned into weeks, the girl began to find herself preparing fish beneath the almond tree alone. People whispered.

When they had too much to drink sometimes, they'd throw their blunt words.

Is them things you reading in them papers have your head so tie up. You think we born big so that we ain't know how children can be devious? If is your dead mother telling you things to come and confuse us, well is a good thing that she dead.

Intimidated by their parents and confused, the other children who'd been there when the diver waded from the surf began to doubt what they'd seen. Under pressure from his parents, a boy began to spread the rumor that Estrella had confided that the story was a hoax. Two girls swore on the Bible that they'd seen the mermaid flopping on the shore. Long hair, gold comb and all. But most just shook their heads when asked and mumbled that they didn't know, that they were there, but didn't see, that so much time had passed.

Through all of this, Estrella found a way to manage. And when her younger cousins, candid children, told her that it might be better if she went away, she left the hammock where she slept with them and made a bed inside the body of an old canoe that had been beached outside a cave, a hundred yards beyond the almond tree.

While this was happening in San Carlos, a tepid winter in the North Atlantic caused a shift in ocean streams around the world. And the swimming patterns of the fish in the West Indies were disrupted for six weeks.

Every island had its range of local explanations. But in this corner of this island, there was one. And after forty days of empty nets, the elders called a meeting on a desert cay.

"Big Tuck," the meeting started, "there's a problem in your house and as a man you have to fix it."

They were sitting in a circle by a sea grape tree, whose twisted branches formed a dome.

"Is not your flesh," they argued when he told them that he couldn't do what they were asking him to do. "Everybody else who live here in some way or other is blood. The fish in we blood and it not in hers. And you is the very one that say she look you in your face and tell you right in front o' Rose that if she stay here she going dead?"

"Well, that ain't what she say exactly," said Big Tuck, who had true, natural feelings for the girl.

"Tuck, what the *rass* you talking 'bout? This is forty days of judgment. Forty days of blight. The only time I see people round here holding they head like they ain't know if they coming or going was that long time when Diablo look like it was going to blow. Tuck, when you old like we you have to accept that we could see the signs. And every man in this place here seeing the signs right now. And you is one o' we Tuck, so you bound to see them too."

"You ain't have to say nothing like that," Big Tuck replied. He took another drink, but couldn't keep it down. "You ain't have to test me if I is one o' you. I is one o' you in truth."

He wiped the trace of spit and vomit from his mouth.

"Is you bring Rose here to live," someone accused. "And is Rose bring she there. And Rose own story is a mix-up too. She born in Trinidad then she gone and live in Cuba, then she come her with a baby saying the mother die in childbirth and no father ain't there. Tuck, how so much mix-up going on in your house?"

"You see sign?" the one who'd mentioned the volcano pointed out. "The gal kill she own mother. What she would do to we?"

"Tuck, if you get the feeling that you ain't able to manage," said the oldest one among them, "put the pressure 'pon your wife."

ON THE MORNING that she had to ask the girl to leave, Roselyn passed the line of huts belonging to her neighbors and walked into the water till it caught her at her knees. She was dressed in white, a flowing dress with puffed sleeves and a turban, and in her ears there was a pair of silver hoops.

In a calabash gourd lined with a swatch of gingham cloth in white and blue, she'd placed some silver coins, red flowers, a watermelon slice, and molasses in a jar. And as it bobbled on the waves she sang hymns to Yemoja asking the *orisha* for prosperity and safety for the girl.

The neighbors watched her furtively, peering through their barely open shutters and the cracks between the boards that made their doors, unhappy but relieved as she heaved her heavy body past the anchored, striped canoes, which came before the almond tree, where she stopped and ran into the sea and put her silver earrings in the gourd.

"My heart feel like it going to burst," she told Estrella when the deed was done. "But since you curse the fish is only blight. Why you had to spit in God face? Now, he giving everybody bad eye."

Sitting on the edge of the canoe with her elbows on her knees, Estrella answered with a quiet pledge: "One day I going to come back here and all of you going look at me and frighten. That's all I have to say."

Square-jawed and trembling, Roselyn put her hands across her ears and heaved away.

"I not going live and dead in no shack in no place where nothing don't happen," said Estrella, standing up to shout. "Mark my words. Something big going happen to me. And you lucky you even find me anyway. You lucky you find me here this morning. I already made up my mind to leave this place . . . to go my own damn way. And that ain't no jest. That's the gospel truth."

In the hut, Roselyn did as she'd promised Tuck the night before. She lay down in the bed beside him, listened to his snores and took a dose of poison that would kill her in her sleep.

Later, during the hour of siesta, while Big Tuck and all the neighbors found it hard to sleep, Estrella sat beneath the hut to pack her things. She didn't have a lot, but she couldn't take it all, because she didn't have a bag. So she packed what she could carry in a basket, which she slung across her body with a length of rope, unaware, like Big Tuck and all the neighbors, that Roselyn was dead.

As she walked along the empty beach, Estrella felt the glare of eyes, which encouraged her to fortify her walk with more authority and grace, and she pulled back her shoulders and stuck out her ass and used a hand to dab at any hairs that might have loosened in her plaits, which fell to her shoulders from a grid of squares.

When she came upon the almond tree, unsure of what would happen and wondering what to do, for she'd never seen this happen in her life, she saw two fellows sitting in a red canoe.

"Hey, Estrella. How're you doing? Come here. I want to talk to you."

The fellow said this with the artificial warmth that West Indians generate today when speaking with a tourist.

"Come where?" she answered them with a knowing look.

She was standing, arms folded, with the water lapping at her shins.

"Well, it just look like you going out," said one of them, hoping that there wouldn't be an argument and that her leaving would be easy and discreet. "I just said lemme ask you if you want a ride."

"Don't fret 'bout me, Alston. I could take care on my own."

She spat in punctuation, cut her slanted eyes and stomped away.

"Estrella. Where you going? Come back here. It ain't have no other way."

"Leave me alone."

"You have to come, Estrella. Make it simple. Don't make it turn a fuss."

She spun around.

"If I had my own boat is one thing. But I ain't going nowhere with the likes o' you. I would rather climb a cliff."

"Well go, nuh. See nuh. Climb the cliff and break your neck and dead."

"You is a blasted dog."

As she walked in the direction of the cliffs, she thought, How I could sit in a boat with Alston and Perry and act like nothing ain't happen? Them is fellows I know all my life. I know them men children. Them men even put talks to me a few times when their wife wasn't about. And in truth, I even do a little feel up with that Alston there, one time. Man is man, eh. After all o' that, he expect me to go with him in a boat so he could carry me 'way like I is some piece o' filth. Before I go with them, I'd rather climb this cliff and get my death. Then what they going to say?

The limestone cliff was high and sheer, a little under ninety feet, and flecked with blinking crystals that at certain angles caught the light. In certain spots, the roots of hardy plants came dangling out of fissures in the rock, and as she climbed, Estrella Thompson, who was too scared to look below, felt around with shoeless feet for little gaps or sills to hold her weight.

Hand over hand, her body taut with dogged anger, her sweating face so deep in focus that it was serene, slipping once or twice, she reached the top.

Without looking down to see the depth from which she'd come, or stare in triumph at her neighbors, who'd spilled out from their huts across the sand, the tall, strong-bodied girl began to sprint across a field of guinea grass toward the world that she believed contained her future, moving through the gulf of green as swiftly as a marlin that had snapped a line.

She wore a purple dress with long sleeves and puffed shoulders that were fraying at the seams. In its large and deep patch pockets bounced her gutting knife and some money that she'd stolen from Old Tuck.

With the money—fifteen pounds and fifty pence—she planned to buy a pair of shoes, the first ones in her life; after this she would present herself correctly for a job.

## III.

LIKE A BEETLE on a trail of gum, the stubby, silver bus was crawling north along the wild, Atlantic coast. Estrella stared outside the window, a strong out-pointed cheekbone pressed against the dusty windowpane.

From the cliff, she'd walked and run eight miles through grass and scrub and climbed through woodlands strung with vines where little monkeys skittered on the limbs of trees with overlapping leaves that blocked the light and heat.

When the forest opened up, she'd seen a narrow road below her, curling in a double bend then gathered in the grip of interlocking slopes.

She began to sweat profusely as she left the cooler, denser woods behind and picked her way through lighter ones with smaller, thinner trees that came advancing from the road. She took the road, which she didn't realize was the one that ran in other places on the coast, and came upon the Indian reservation.

The Indians were *Caribes;* not *madrasitos,* the local name for workers who were brought from India in the 1800s to replace the slaves. These were the remnants of the people who'd seen Columbus when he stumbled on their shores and had fought the Spanish for a hundred years. But like most Carlitos, they were now impure.

Apart from a tin sign hammered to a shoulder-level post, nothing marked the reservation as important or unique. It was like any other village—a little road that cut a little shop in two; little lanes that led to little huts and little fields; little, ribby dogs and little naked children; women selling things nobody wanted by the road, and the dominating mass of old Diablo, the volcano that had rumbled forty years before, rising high above the other peaks.

The *Caribes* were so small, that at first Estrella thought that all of them were children. And she found herself staring at their flat cheeks and straight hair, which most of them cut bluntly, as they looked on with a mix of allure and suspicion through dark eyes that were so tiny that at times she thought that they were closed.

She went inside a bar—a dim square in coral pink with a zinc roof stretching past the door to shade a porch supported by unshaven posts, where a pair of women sat on stools surrounded by displays of woven objects. One wore a bonnet and the other jazzed a yellow cowboy hat, and when the tall *negrita* passed to go inside the bar, they turned around to look.

"Excuse me, what it have to eat?" Estrella asked across the counter. Two men were drinking and the barmaid looked as if she hadn't fully gotten over a debilitating sleep.

"It have opossum and iguana. Fried and stewed."

"No. I ain't feeling that today," she said politely as a grimace flashed across her face.

One of the men who'd been drinking pushed a plate of bones with knots of meat attached along the bar toward her. "It have some chicken too."

"Yes, please. I would rather take a plate of that."

She took a table by the door so she could look outside, and the barmaid brought the food.

"This is chicken?" she asked when she'd sniffed it. "It smell kinda different to me."

As soon as she'd said this she remembered there was another kind of chicken here—a giant frog that lived in mountain forests and whose hind legs had the shape and juicy texture of a duck.

But you pay your money already, she thought. So you might as well eat it. Is not as if you have money to waste. You ain't eat from this morning. If you eat it and pretend is something else, like octopus, then your stomach would be full. And Seville must be at least a hour or two by bus, so you should really eat. But what if this thing make you vomit. You can't look for work if you sick.

"If you don't want it, I can eat it," said the drunk from his position at the bar.

"Gimme thirty pence for it."

He wobbled off his stool.

"What? You trying to make a profit?"

"Is fifty pence I pay for it. You're saving twenty pence. Is almost half price." She tossed her head toward the barmaid. "It cheaper than you would get it from she. And apart from a little piece I break off, you can't really say I even touch it. Is almost brand new."

"Well, she's my wife," the drunkard said. "And I'm the owner of the bar. So, if I want some more I can just take it."

The woman and the other drunk began to laugh. Estrella went outside and asked the woman in the bonnet for directions to the bus. With a wrinkled thumb she pointed to the shop across the street, where a man with shoes was standing with a suitcase in his hand.

"What kinda food they have in there," Estrella asked.

"Chicken. Nice, nice chicken from right up in them hills."

"Oh."

FROM THE RESERVATION, the bus descended through the empty, wooded hills then moved along the coast. Before, in a landscape that was strange, the girl had felt a sense of turgid peace, but here, moving through landscapes that were familiar in some ways—

she'd glimpsed them by boat—she felt a need to double-check her orientation, to challenge her understanding of some things that she'd accepted all her life.

Whole villages existed where she'd only seen the steeple of a church. The gaps between some hills were larger than she'd known. Half a mile from where she lived there was a district with a school. Buses rode higher than a boat, and when you were inside them you couldn't see the wheels.

She kept her sense of orientation by relating everything she saw to an imagined bearing on the sea. It was as if she had another, greater self out there, allowing her to see her journey from a seagull's point of view.

But when the driver turned into the northern hills to cross the island, ten miles before the rough Atlantic coast would taper to a neck and turn to swell again into the body of an avocado on the smooth Caribbean shore, Estrella—miles from home—began to lose her sense of place, and tears began to trickle from her eyes.

Where I going? she thought. To who? To do what? All my relatives in country. What I going to do?

As the old bus labored up and down the steep volcanic slopes, which were planted thickly with bananas, Estrella felt a knot of hunger harden into bone.

"What time we reaching town?" she asked across the aisle. The man who'd been waiting for the bus in shoes looked upward from his paper, which he'd gripped as if its pages were a thief's lapels.

"This bus isn't going to town," he said. "You wouldn't get another bus directly into town until the morning, I don't think. This one going down Speyside and turn back."

SEEN FROM THE bus, which beetled downward, Speyside was a floral accent in a plaid of greens, an embroidered rose of wood and brick in low relief against a quilt of sugarcane.

The fields were separated by a grid of roads, along which mule trains pulling wooden carts of purple canes went inching by like centipedes, raising puffs of pinkish dust.

All of this—the town, the fields, the carts—was contained by a corolla, a serrated crown of hills that gave no vision of the coast. There was about the place the sense of something continental, the sense of being in a place where life extended to the limits of ambition, a place where there existed no continuous barriers like a shore.

It was late afternoon, and the streets were waiting to be filled by workers from the factory and the fields. It was the island's second largest town, but ten times smaller than Seville, and the buildings had the modesty and grace that had replaced the Spanish flair discouraged under British rule. Unlike Seville, the streets were laid out in a grid, as would be expected in a town that had been chartered as the most important base for English soldiers on the hunt for black maroons. On Estrella, the empty streets conferred an eerie feeling. She'd never seen a quiet town before.

When the driver parked the bus beside the market, the hungry girl got off. Her mind was like a fist of dice, a dark and clammy place where thoughts and choices tumbled. Decisions came. Decisions went. None of them would hold.

With her basket on her head to help her hide her face, she made a scouting trip along the cobbled streets that formed a square around the market, throwing furtive glances through the fence.

The old fence was brick to the height of her knees, then rose in a stockade of iron stakes above her head. Where the stakes were anchored in the brick there was a ledge where groups of people sat to watch the day, leaning forward with their elbows on their knees, the pose of age and unemployment.

It was a smaller market than the one beside the harbor in Seville, she saw. Smaller. More subdued. But like the one where she'd worked for two-thirds of her life, it was covered—but not in any fancy way—a shingled roof supported by cast-iron beams; but unlike her market, this one didn't spill its banks and flood the streets; also, things like pots and pans and nails were sold here. In Seville, these kinds of things were sold in shops.

But the thing that struck her most was that the people in the market, like the people in the town, were mainly *madrasitos*. And in her life she'd only seen a few.

She found them strange and fascinating, and through the iron fence she looked at them like they were creatures in a zoo. There were different types, she saw. One type wore turbans, and another wore what looked to her like small, inverted bowls of cloth. And she observed as she watched intently that the *madrasitos* bought and sold according to their type. Nearly half the men, she saw, wore clothes that she'd describe as "normal," but all the women dressed in brightly colored silk and, unlike *negritas*, seemed to live in awe of men.

Estrella sat against the ledge. On either side of her were groups of *madrasitos* roosting. They were speaking in a language that she didn't understand, and eating something with an odor that disturbed her nose.

Across the narrow street, above a white, imposing fence, she saw a high, extended roof with missing shingles. And from behind the heavy wooden gate there came the sound of voices, buzzing saws and the bangs and scrapes of lumber being moved.

From down the lane, a long cart filled with timbers rumbled round a bend. The cart was drawn by oxen, heavy things whose skins recalled the grubby whiteness of a butcher's coat, and the two of them without the cart were almost wide enough to block the street.

Behind the cart there came a band of little children shorter than the wheels. They were brown and thin and spread across the road like envelopes or fallen leaves disturbed by wind; and from feet to ankle they were covered in the pinkish dust.

When the tall, green gate was opened, Estrella looked inside the rutted yard and saw gangs of sweating men aligned on either side of heavy logs like ants about to move a turkey bone.

As he turned into the lumberyard the driver uttered something that Estrella didn't grasp, and the men on either side of her began to laugh. The laughter spread among the children, and, being the only one who didn't get the joke, she decided she would leave.

Them people is not my people, she reflected as she sucked her teeth and crossed her arms and walked away. They could say anything 'bout me right in front my face and I wouldn't even know. Plus, I ain't trust what they eating. And people who like to talk things so you don't understand them is the kind of people that does like to thief.

On returning to the entrance, where she'd gotten off the bus, she eased up on the ledge again, annoyed and apprehensive now, and gazed out on the empty street, trying to bring some order to her thoughts.

Down the sidewalk, there were women hawking trays of homemade sweets. But so great was her annoyance that she convinced herself, without investigating, that the *madrasitas* sold a kind of candy that *negritas* wouldn't like.

Across the street, a bull whose shape and color matched a rusty engine block began to bellow at the entrance of a bar. As she thought of what to do, a man who from his looks was only partly *madrasito* lurched out through the swinging doors and slumped against the steps and sang the bull a sweet bolero. She understood the lyrics, for he was singing in *sancoche,* and as she floated in the story being carried by the words—a man lamenting for a girl who ran away—her mind began to sail.

If it could be hard to live with strangers on a little island? What it going be like when time come to live in Europe? I wonder if I could really cope with that. But it shouldn't be so hard. It only have white people in them places. And I never have no trouble with white people yet.

In her mind she saw herself in Paris. Although she'd seen pictures of the city in the *Star,* she was unable to imagine it the way it was—a gray metropolis of stone.

In her mind she saw it as a vast agglomeration of the kinds of buildings that she knew, like the nicer ones that she'd seen as she'd ridden into town—wooden with glass windows framed by shutters set with mini louvers, verandas framed with latticework and bougainvillea frothing over decorative railings, and shingled roofs with peaks like hills. A few would have an upper floor, and those that did, especially the shops, would have their stairs outside, beneath a roof of painted zinc. It was as if her imagination had an accent, and came out of her as would the lyrics of European song—reshaped by her experience.

After she'd thought about Paris for a very long time, she composed herself and asked a passerby about the schedule of the bus that went to town. Like her, he was a young *negrito.* He wore a denim cap whose brim was low.

"Not till six o'clock," he said, with what she thought of as a useless grin. "London say that petrol short, so the buses get cut back. You ain't notice that you ain't see any cars?"

"I ain't see any people with sense either. What London saying 'bout that?"

"Why you so cantankerous."

"Mind your business. If I have to reach town before that, what is there for me to do?"

He shrugged and put a fist against his chin and tapped his nose.

"You could go by the main road and beg a ride. But you ain't going get no ride right now. You have to wait until they blow the whistle over there by Royal Standard and them big trucks taking people up the hill."

"And how I would get to town from there?" she asked him as she drummed her heels against the wall.

He shrugged.

"Beg another ride . . . or walk . . . or take the same bus you would take if you waited here till six."

"But it ain't have other buses that ain't stop here that go to town? It have one you could take from the *Caribes* straight to town they say. I take one from there that bring me here this afternoon. But is the wrong one I did take."

"I only know the bus that come there," the man replied. "Them other buses that go other places I ain't really business with them."

Live in a place and don't know a blasted thing, she thought as she watched him walk away. Damn head tough like concrete. Not even water can soak it much less learning. That's why I can't live here. That's why I have to leave. Nobody ain't care to know 'bout nothing. All they care to know 'bout is their self.

In the central square, located in the nest of streets behind the bar, the town clock began to chime and Estrella felt a lightness in her head. Along her spinal cord there ran a soft reverberation, a rising force that made her feel as if her body were the tower of the clock.

It was the force of recollection. She'd been here once before.

She was four . . . or five . . . and she'd come with Big Tuck and her grandmother. They were visiting his younger brother, a chubby man who liked to laugh. He was kind, she remembered . . . and when they were ready to leave he'd offered her a tin whistle and a piece of boiled corn.

And as she sat there feeling stranded, she thought, That man ain't know 'bout a thing that happen with me and Big Tuck. And seeing that he's a nice man, I could tell him that Big Tuck send me for a borrows, that since the fish not coming, times hard. And who knows? He might give it to me. If I tell him that they turn me out he going take their side, for sure. For blood is blood and Big Tuck ain't my blood. But first I have to find him. I know the last name and I know the pet name but I ain't know the first name. But I ain't bound to know the first name to find him, because everybody know each other by their pet name in this place, just like my friends know me as Pepper, 'cause when I cuss, my words is very hot. But lemme watch these *madrasitos*, yes. I heard they could thief milk out your coffee and is only when you drink it you would know.

She reached to hold her basket as she jumped down off the ledge and found to her surprise that it was gone.

## IV.

"THIEF! THIEF!"

The little naked madman dropped the broom and dashed off through the market with her basket on his shoulder, pumping with his only arm. The other one was amputated at the elbow, and he held it at the ready like a club.

He was a knobbly *yam masala,* a mix of black and Indian bloods, with ribs like an accordion and a fibrous beard that broomed his chest.

"Thief. Thief. You goddamn thief."

The group of children who'd been following the lumber cart appeared and chanted: "Run, Professor. Run."

Estrella hopped up on the ledge and hooked her toes between the staves and climbed. It was a gut reaction. She was right beside the gate.

The staves were topped with ornamental arrows made of brass, and they were sharp enough to gore her if she slipped. At the top, before the final leap, she glanced away to check her hands, but when she looked again the man was gone.

On landing on her toes inside the market, she fell into a crouch and ran with doubled fists along the cobbles from the heat into the coolness of the shade.

"You see a naked fellow running with my things?" Estrella shouted as she sprinted through the aisles. They were lined with makeshift counters piled with multicolored fruit and lumpy tubers. And she spoke while making sweeping glances like a tommy gun.

When no one had answered, and she'd listened to the way the shoppers laughed and seen the way the vendors shook their heads, she realized that she wasn't strictly speaking what you'd call a victim. Instead, she was the object of a local joke; and as she stood there with her hands against her hips, she guessed correctly that they'd communicated with each other using signs and gestures, giggling as they waited for the drama to unfold.

They think they have me going, Estrella thought. They think I ain't know what's going on. They ain't know I sell in market too. I do this to people before—laugh and carry on like I ain't see nothing. Is only sport. Is only sport. Calm yourself, Pepper. Is only sport. And if you get vex they going laugh even more. Calm yourself, Pepper. I know is wasting time. But calm yourself. You ain't know these people. And this ain't your place. You getting vex. But calm yourself. Make a sport of it. Don't take it on.

"What is *your* name?" she asked a butcher, who was smiling broadly with two rows of perfect teeth.

"They call me Asif," he said, his machete pausing then descending in a chop against a shank of beef.

"Asif," she said sweetly. "You see where the fellow with my basket gone? Tell me and I catch him for you."

"Catch him for me?" the butcher said, with mischief. "He ain't have nothing for me. He have something for you?"

"He might."

He leaned across the shank, which was lying on the counter, and quickly looked Estrella up and down.

"So you might have something for me, too?"

"If you see anything you could use," she told him in a flirty voice that made him blush, "then tell me. Maybe we could talk."

Charmed, he cupped his mouth and shouted so that everyone could hear: "If anybody find a basket in this market please let this young lady know because it look as if it might have been misplaced."

He said it in a language that she didn't understand and she tried to read the message in the lines above his brow.

"Is what you tell them?" she asked him in *sancoche* as she heard what sounded like the thing he said relayed from stall to stall.

"I tell them not to help the Professor to hide."

"*Professor?* That's a name?"

"That's what we call him."

She said the word inside her head. She liked the sound of it.

"So what that really mean?" she asked.

"I ain't exactly sure myself. But is a thing they call a man of great knowledge. And that is what he is, in truth. Don't matter how you see him there, he is a bright fellow. One of the brightest you will ever meet. Sometimes he will straighten out and you will see him here in the market dress nicely in his shirt and trousers and a shine-up shoe. And if he come here three or four days straight like that, people will come and ask him for advice— to read letters and write letters and things like that. Because as simple as you see him now, that man went away to study doctor. And he pass all the white man exam and was supposed to come back home. But then he make a bad, bad choice. Instead of coming home say he want to stay a little longer. Why? To specialize. Now some people say is pride cause him to fall. And I agree. Because when a little man get opportunity to reach far, he must be grateful and know when he suppose to stop. But who knows? He must be see them white boys specializing and say he must reach there too. But puss and dog ain't have the same luck. A man must know when to satisfy. He couldn't satisfy. He go on and on till he burn out his brain. And it ain't lie or joke I telling you. Is my brother."

Estrella glanced across her shoulder out of instinct, looking for proof in other eyes. Was he telling her the truth? In the stall beside him, another butcher looked at her and raised his brows.

"You have to watch how you approach him," warned Asif. "He don't mean no harm and is a mad fellow after all. But mark you—if he catch you with the nub is like somebody beat you with a pickax stick."

On knees and elbows now, Estrella made her way along the aisle. Although she was in many ways mature, she was still an adolescent, young enough to make decisions on a dare. Through her dress, which had begun to cling with perspiration, the butchers watched her body shifting shape, marveled at the way her muscles bunched then breathed into a slither, the rhythmic crest and falling of her curves.

At the end of the aisle, she slipped beneath the burlap skirting of an empty stall and scouted up and down the broader corridor that striped the selling floor in two.

Her position made her think about the stories that she'd heard from men who said they'd hunted savage boars along the high volcanic slopes. They were most dangerous when cornered. So stealth—not bravery—was the best approach. Which is why I like to fish. With fish you always have the upper hand. If he going to overpower you, you let him go.

She was shocked by this admission. Her chin was pressing on her folded arms, and she turned her head so that her arms were flat against her face. What did it mean that all her thoughts of fishing hadn't frozen into hate?

You have to harden your heart, she told herself. Otherwise, you might go back. And things ain't looking too bright. A day ain't pass and look at you. Flat on your face. Bamboozled by a fellow who ain't have all his brain. People taking you for joke. If you know what you was doing you would reach Seville already. But you ain't really know what you're doing. You ain't have no blasted use. When you see that man come out the sea, you shoulda run and shut your mouth.

Her mind began to squall with all the things that had occurred because she'd spoken to the diver. Thoughts leaped up and disappeared like waves. Trying to explain herself to Big Tuck and her grandmother underneath the hut. Dreaming of escape at night. Scaling fish alone. Sleeping in the old canoe. Hearing people whispering. The cliff. The bus. The reservation. Her own grandmother asking her to leave. And what was Roselyn thinking now? And what had she been thinking then? Did she really think she'd cursed the fish?

You can't curse anything, Estrella thought. Only God and the *orishas* could do that. Everybody know that. If is one thing I sure of is that. Maybe all of this is punishment. 'Cause I was thinking like a liar and a thief and then—Bam!—my basket gone. I ain't even know if what I think I might remember is true. As I think about it now, I ain't even sure if Big Tuck even have a younger brother in this place, or if this is the place where I come that time. I was only four or five. But what happen already happen. If I lose that basket I lose everything except my money and my knife. My only toy. My best books. My blanket. My only change of clothes. If I lose them things what I going to do? 'Cause I can't go back. Knowing them they wouldn't even take me. And to go back to let them put me out again would be a disgrace.

As she often did when she found herself in situations where she felt as if she'd lost control, Estrella felt the absence of her mother.

Her name had been Edwina. But Estrella didn't know that she had died.

What she look like? How old she is? What kinda work she do? What kinda mood she have? Quiet . . . bossy . . . jokey . . . tough? She have a husband? Other children? Or is me alone?

Whenever she'd asked these questions, she reflected, Rose-lyn would answer with evasion or a grunt. Some things were not discussed. Like why she move from Trinidad to Cuba? Or if she had a trade when she was young? Or why she move from Cuba to San Carlos? Or who her husband was before she meet Big Tuck?

To Estrella, the absence of her mother, in and of itself, didn't make her feel alone. Relations in the cove were so close. All children more or less belonged to all adults—which didn't mean that they were drenched with love. They were supervised and overseen, disciplined and watched, but when it came to close attention, children were ignored. They had no special place. There was no myth of them as warm, big-hearted beings. They were simply small adults. They worked.

The communal role of parents was encouraged by the fact that some forms of incest were allowed. It was not uncommon for cousins or half-siblings to marry or mate—or even fall in love. And marriage was a matter of the common law.

If a woman cooked your food and washed your clothes, and if you slept with her and didn't try to leave in secret in the morning, and if this went on for what was understood to be a while, then you were known as man and wife.

This idea also ruled the ownership of land. If you found a beach and built a shack on it, and went to sea from it, and fixed your nets on it, and beached your boat on it, there was a common understanding that the beach belonged to you.

However, people didn't move, didn't branch away to live alone—for in the deepest part of their collective understanding, they could only understand themselves as part of something that they vaguely knew as "one."

To be a fragment or a fraction was the greatest fear. So exile was the harshest form of retribution—the thing reserved for those whose thoughts and actions undermined the fundamental meaning of their lives.

When she'd thought of all these things, Estrella rolled away from underneath the skirting and began to move with purpose down the aisles. Her steps were heavy, and from a distance, even with the sound of other voices, you could hear the thudding of her heels against the floor.

Her face was blank, but tight with concentration, the look of a gambler who's taken full account of what he's lost and what he's going to lose unless he sinks this ball or draws this card; who can't quit, because quitting means it's over; who can't just walk away because walking is what losers do. When you lose like that it's not the same as losing fair and square. Losing fair and square will sharpen you, will give you edge, will make you whatever it takes to win again; but when you walk away you don't just lose the game, you lose a little bit of nerve; and when that starts to happen then your gambling days are done—they'll look at you and call your bluff, and you'll look at them and worry, then you'll always lose. And winning is for winners and losing isn't nice. And as she walked, Estrella slipped a hand into the pocket with the blade.

"Where's the fellow with my things," she asked Asif, when she'd covered all the aisles.

"I have no idea," he said with a laugh. "When I see you lying down I think you gone to cry."

She put her hands down on the counter, slowly but with force, and glared from way beneath her brows.

"I look like the person that cry easy?"

"I ain't say nothing like that?"

"Because you see I black you think I fool?"

"I never say you was no fool," he said carefully.

"Well, you talking in the way I talk to idiot people."

Her glare began to affect him and he raised his hands to shoulder height and told her, "Look, I ain't want no fuss with you. Better you just go your way."

"Well, I ain't want none either," she answered, in a louder

voice. "I just want my things. I just want to go." She spoke quietly again. "I asking you another time, sir. You see the fellow with my things?"

"It ain't necessary to come to this," he told her in a voice that made aggressive use of overdone restraint. "Just wait a little while, and don't make no fuss and everything will be okay. If you make a fuss, things mightn't go the way you want them. And I want things to work for you. Nobody here ain't thief."

"You ain't really know who you playing with," she answered, backing off. She spread her arms at shoulder height and spun around. "I will break up this place until somebody talk to me." She leaned down on his counter once again as crowds began to shuffle down the aisle. "It ain't funny. It ain't funny at all. You ain't know where I coming from or where I going. You ain't know me from Adam. You ain't know me at all. You ain't know what I will do." She sprung back and straightened up and pointed now. "I will mash up everything in this goddamn place until I get my things, Asif. You hear me? Not because you see me black so. I ain't no simpleton. I ain't have no mother supervising me. I ain't no goddamn child."

From a stall behind her, Estrella grabbed a hairy coconut, and smashed it on the floor. The juice sprayed in a silver fizz. A woman shrieked as jagged chips began to fly.

"Take time," said Asif. "Take time."

"I can't take what I ain't have. I want to go about my business, and here you is, interfering with my life. I laugh already. I give you that, Asif. I give that to all o' you. And I ain't going laugh no more. I ain't come here to turn into nobody clown. I give you entertainment. I give you a show. So, coolie man, gimme my damn things now."

"Who she calling, 'coolie,'" someone shouted over mutterings in a language that she didn't understand. "What? She want somebody cut her ass?"

"I will mash somebody skull," Estrella answered. Her neck

was so taut she felt that she would break it if she turned to look. "You watching me? You follow? Just like how you see that coconut, I'll mash a skull like that. You don't know where I coming from and you don't know where I going. Don't push me no more."

She sensed someone approaching from behind and turned around to see a hefty woman in a sari stealing sideward.

"If you trouble one you trouble all," the woman warned. "You can't come here and break up people things like this and think you could just go."

"Same way you shouldn't let your people take my things and don't say nothing. So is even. One for one."

As Estrella grabbed another coconut, a butcher with a turban rushed her from the side and as she drew her knife she took his arm and turned him off her hip.

"Stop it," said Asif when his *compadre*'s head and back had slammed against the floor. "Everybody stop."

The groaning man was barely moving. But they saw no sign of blood.

And as Estrella backed away, suddenly aware now of the danger to her life, Asif came from behind his counter with her basket in his hand. One leg was withered, and he had a limp that made him waddle like a seal.

"Take it and go," he said, while barking orders in his enigmatic tongue. "Take it and go. It ain't have to come to this. Just take your things and go."

"Where you get it from?" she asked him as her heart began to pound. Another person lunged toward her, and Asif, displaying great fighting skill, used his arms and chest to block the blow.

"Spare your life," Asif advised her as he gave the sign to have the man who had attacked her hauled off for a smack-up down the aisle. "Listen what I say and go. Don't turn back. Run. Don't walk. That man you throw down is the most ignorant man I ever see. And the fellow I had to rough up was his son. Listen what I tell you. Go! Pick up your life in your hand and go! And learn to take a joke!"

## V.

ESTRELLA RAN OUT of the market and stampeded past the rusty bull that had been sung to sleep outside the bar.

Knees pumping, almost navel high, she took a bend that led her through an alleyway with doors that opened straight into the street and swerved around a group of men in undershirts who'd set up stools around a table on the cobbles for their game of dominoes.

Emerging from the alleyway, she squinted as she took a path that led her past the finger-pointing tower of the spired clock, and slanted in a wheeling semicircle round a little park where children played a game of cricket with a two-by-four, then veered around the courthouse with its large, imposing columns and its curving marble stairs and took the road by which the bus had brought her into town.

Raised with clannish people, she knew of all the things that could occur. So although she didn't hear the sound of feet behind her, or get the sense that all the people who were laughing as she ran were going to gather in a mob, she sprinted, as she'd later tell her children, "like I heard a rumor that a rich old auntie come to visit from abroad."

As she came upon the steep ascent, she cursed and tensed her middle as she hunched her shoulders forward, giving greater power to her legs, which labored with the challenge of the slope; and for a half a mile, she grunted onward till the band of muscles in her middle, which resembled little squares, began to soften like a bar of chocolate in the heat.

Tired and hungry, she began to walk. They ain't coming, she thought and put her hands against her hips. She glanced across her shoulder down the steeply rising road, which disappeared around a bend into the bush. They have better things to do. But a coward man keep sound bones as them old people say. I ain't able for anybody to gimme a chop or a cuff right now. But anyways, is a good thing it happen, in a way, 'cause you had to get outta that damn town. You was only loitering and wasting time when you have important things to do. You have to get to town. And town way, way far away. And you have to get there before night come. 'Cause by seven-thirty all them big stores going be closed. And that is the first place you have to go—a store where they sell shoes. 'Cause ain't nobody giving any sensible job where you ain't have to wear no shoes. And you have to get a job before tomorrow. 'Cause you ain't have a soul in town.

As she spiraled up the lonely road she fantasized about her coming life and saw an older version of herself creating stares and whispers of excitement when her driver brought her to Salan's, the island's most elite department store—two floors, a wooden escalator, a soda fountain and a cafeteria with a balcony that overlooked the Queens.

Smiling with a puckered mouth as if she held a secret, Estrella saw herself among the aisles in yellow satin pumps—shoes that had the bag and dress to match, accented by her husband's breezy black fedora, and behind her, waiting, a clerk whose arms were filled with boxes, calling her "Madame."

The main cross-island road was seven miles away, and Estrella worked toward it at a slow but steady pace. From time to time, small herds of goats would trickle down the road or drip in ones and twos out of the dark, encroaching woods, which at certain points would form a roof of shade.

Later, after she'd noticed that the goats were coming down the mountain in a heavy stream—groups of ten and twelve—she came upon a clump of leaning houses. To her mind they were the poorest houses that she'd ever seen. They were made of cracked, ill-fitting timbers that had not been planed, and between some of the timbers there were spaces large enough to slip a hand.

The shaggy homes were built on stilts to keep them level, and with their brown walls and dry roofs they looked like herds of animals reduced to skin and bone from drought, and in their shadows lingered clouds of little children, their heads as round and dark as lice.

As she looked, an old *negrita* standing in the shadow of a doorway wiped her hands against her dress, which was a flour sack, and asked her with a mouth that had collapsed against its gums, "You hungry, sweetheart? You want a little something?"

And in a moment of illumination, Estrella knew that these were not the poorest houses that she'd ever seen. The people of the cove had homes like these.

Looking at the dirt she hadn't dusted from her clothes, her hands entangled in her fraying hair, feeling dust transforming into mud along her sweaty feet and shins, glancing as she passed the woman, Estrella held her basket and began to run again, her breathing dry and cracked with effort, like someone waking from nightmarish dreams.

SHE WAS AT a height now where the intermittent grunts and groans of vehicles on the main cross-island road began to filter through the net of translucent sounds that caught and held the chirrups of the woods.

Her soles were budding with the early pain of blisters, whispered pangs that felt like they were giving birth to cleats. And although the pain had not emerged completely, she began to hobble, balanced on the outer lines that marked the point at which her soles were fused against the uppers of her leather-colored feet.

Eventually, she came upon a bridge. It was old and white, with small columns at each end and parapets of stone. On approaching it, she saw a path that led into a bamboo grove and heard the sizzle of a stream. After taking minutes to decide, she took the path, and inched her way toward the water, holding on to creaking stems to keep herself from falling, watching out for razor-pointed stumps.

It was a narrow stream, forty yards across, and she came out of the thick, steep-sided forest onto rugged grass that grew along its wide embankment.

She sat against the edge of the embankment with her feet above the flow and lay back in the furry hotness of the grass, the sun against her pressing like a lover who'd waited long for them to be alone.

When she'd rested for a while and her skin was clammy with an oily perspiration, she stripped and lay there thinking, her body smooth as wood without the bark, then slipped into the olive water.

She cavorted with amphibian ease, turned on her back and stroked froglike with her forceful legs then twisted sharply in a shallow dive, head down, toes long, strong arms along her side, tadpoling over stones and grass along the muddy bed.

In the middle of the stream there was a scattered line of oval rocks that had been sanded by erosion to an eggy whiteness, and she played at leaping on their warm, protruding tops although the landing sometimes stung her feet.

After she'd played, she used a hunk of soap to wash her purple dress and underwear and laid them on the grass, then swam against the current to the point at which the river swung beneath an arch of overhanging trees and fell in baby steps.

She sat against the broad, flat stone that she'd felt for with her hands beneath the current, and braced her feet against two upright ones and let the falling water pound her neck and back. Although the stream was moving slowly and the drop was from a shallow height, the water had the power of a solid force, and as it hammered her, she felt old fears dispersing and the hairs that formed her brows untwining from their knit. And she closed her eyes and smiled out of her diamond face while spitting plastered hair out of her mouth.

I is the luckiest girl in the world, right now, she thought. It might have people with more money and thing. But right now, as I feeling this water on me and hear them birds how they make sweet sounds, it ain't have nobody with more luck than me.

She returned downstream to bathe. With lazy strokes, she used a scrap of cloth to cream her body in a slop of suds, and the whiteness of the soap against her dark complexion made it seem as if she were about to hide herself in snow.

Her waist was tightly tapered, and her breasts were little banks of mud with twig nipples. She had no cleavage, and standing up, her bosom looked the same as when she was lying down; but her hips were matriarchal and her buttocks had deep clefts, and when she sank into the stream to rinse, emerging from the slick of suds to walk toward the bank, she was the vision of a goddess coming through the clouds.

On the bank, she wrung her hair as if it were a towel and lay down on her stomach in the grass beside her dress. With her face against her folded arms she listened to the sloshing water and, above her head, the flap of lifting wings. And for the first time in her life, she experienced what it meant to have the privacy in which to read.

From her basket, which was placed beside her head, she took her only toy, a wooden doll with missing arms that she'd never named, and read the story of another girl who'd led an awful life. Her reading voice was mumbled and self-conscious, and she didn't fully understand what punctuation meant, as such she ran periods and rear-ended sentence openings like a granny at the wheel.

As she read she overlaid her life against the tale of Cinderella and felt a smoky joy, a kind of bluesy satisfaction, which, in *sancoche*, was called *memweh*, for which there is no good translation. In English, the closest feeling is nostalgia. But this is not enough. *Memweh* is nostalgia for a person or a thing that might have existed in another life, a vital kind of sadness experienced as a grope, like swimming upward from deep water into light and breaking through the surface only to be covered by wave, then sinking with a glimpse of something beautiful that propels you to grope upward once again, a lament for the amnesia of the middle passage, a search for a suspected loss that only *negritos* fully understand.

How I never meet nobody like a prince? Estrella thought, caught up in the tidal cycle of *memweh*. I wonder if it have men like that in truth? It would shock them if a man like that come sweep me off my feet, I tell you. Old Tuck and my grandmother would lose their mind. That would shame them, boy. I tell you. They think I ain't going to come to nothing in this life. But watch me. When I get to town and get my shoes and get a job and work and save my money and put myself together with my shoes that match my bag and my bag that match my frock I going meet a man who going make me feel like that white lady at La Sala that day. Me and my husband, all we going do all day is write each other notes. Even when I see him face-to-face, I going slip one in his pocket, so he can read it later. For no reason. Just for so.

But in nearly fifteen years on earth, she'd never seen a man who looked like her do anything that anyone considered princely, had never seen a woman of her color being treated in a way that made her think of queens.

She'd seen *negritos* giving women what Carlitos knew as "talks," frilly conversation on a sheet of innuendo, seen fellows making women tremble with their bluff. But she'd never heard a loving word from a *negrito,* if it wasn't in a song, or witnessed a *negrito* read a book, or heard about *negritos* who would do these things. Not even in a rumor or a tale.

When she'd thought of all these things, she gave herself an

explanation—like fashion, all things go in and out of style, and maybe, long ago, before her time, *negritos* did the kinds of things that people knew as white; so, one day, when styles had changed, they'd do these things again.

She curled up on her side, then stretched out on her back and crossed her arms beneath her head, and pursed her lips as if she'd tasted something that was sweet although acidic.

Of all the men that she had slept with, she was thinking, which had come the closest to a prince? There had been a few, for she'd lost her hymen at the age of twelve when a game of wrestling accidentally put her and a playmate in a pose that inspired the desire to explore. With this kind of introduction, sex for her was something rugged—a game in which she liked to have the upper hand. She must win and he must lose. He must like it more than me. I ain't want to be no woman who exchange rum for man. I ain't want to be no cockaholic.

With a finger on her nipple, she began to stroke her tender parts until the air was crackled by a tiny scream. And she lay there half-smiling till her strength returned.

## VI.

On the bridge, she leaned against the parapet and waited. Her purple dress was not completely dry, but she'd packed it and was wearing now her only change of clothes—a dark blue skirt and a green-striped blouse, both of which were old.

With her hair down to her shoulders, her face seemed more mature; and features that had not revealed themselves began to be pronounced. She had a small nose with a low bridge that ended in a smooth, compacted mound, and nostrils that you couldn't see unless she raised her head.

Her mouth was small and oval like a circle cut in two; and

the upper lip was shiny, with a reddish tone, and from its corners ran an upward slanting seam that made it look as if her mouth and cheeks were linked beneath the skin with little guitar strings. The space between her nose and mouth was close, as if her lips were slightly resting on a sheet of glass; and where the hair along her temples grew toward her brow, there was a scar, a little crescent moon, whose ridge of smoothness you could follow with your thumb.

She heard the sound of diesel engines and looked with expectation down the road, and stood up when she saw the tall, imposing grillwork of a truck.

It lurched around the bend and rumbled by so closely that she could've stretched her hand and touched it. It was filled with *madrasitos,* workers from the factory and the fields, and their limbs protruded through the gaps between the slatted sides that formed the bed like stalks of cane. Some sat on the cab as if it were an elephant's head. Those who found a ledge to hook their toes and fingers rode along the side; and she watched the driver take the curves without regard, coming close against the bush, as if the people holding on were fleas.

I ain't able for them people, thought Estrella, as the *madrasitos* called to her and waved. They run me out their town already. I ain't want to get inside no truck with them. Worse of all, they have machete. I ain't going nowhere with them. The fellow by the market said it have a bus. I prefer to wait for that. Plus is only dirty people I seeing in them trucks. And I now just bathe myself.

The trucks were coming close together in a convoy like an army in retreat, and she kept her eyes engaged by reading so she didn't have to look.

But when another thirty minutes passed and she hadn't seen the bus and the gaps between the trucks began to lengthen to the point where she would hear one engine fade before another grunted up the hill, she changed her mind.

## VII.

THE TRUCK WAS crowded, but not as crowded as the ones that went before. No one clung against the side or rode the cab. But those who had a seat were stacked with someone else, like jars of pickled pork. With their backs against the cab, their hats aligned in humps below the glass, some were sitting on the floor with their hands around their ankles and their chins against their knees, gazing at their toes. The others stood and held on to the ribbing of the missing canvas sheet.

The old blue truck groaned upward. It was an old Pierce-Arrow from the twenties, with an upright cab like a telephone booth, and light external fenders of the type you see on motorbikes today. It was older than the other trucks, and smaller, and rode like a carriage on weak leaf springs that creaked.

With the engine under stress, they passed a scrappy settlement and turned onto the main cross-island road.

They came upon a string of solid villages with paved streets and good houses: verandas, hedges, lattice trim and then a pond below the wreckage of a white great house, then for miles, on rolling land, long rows of young banana trees just planted by United Fruit, whose guards rode up and down the verge on horses—some of them with guns.

From there the road was like a lashing whip, and the old truck rose and fell along its dips and rises flanked by humps of land in terraced cultivation—tenant farms of beans and cabbage next to ample citrus groves with cars and concrete houses.

The truck made frequent stops, and Estrella dropped her head each time so that she wouldn't feel compelled to wave.

Although she was grateful that they'd slapped their hands against the truck to make the driver stop, and had gripped her arm and helped her in, she held the workers in contempt. They'd failed. They were dirty and poor and wore their tattered clothes on bodies in decay.

In their company she felt as if her bath had been a waste. Above them was a tender stink that slipped inside her body when she sighed and made a sharp intake of breath—as she did on seeing a man unearth a booger from his nose and crush it on his sleeve.

The stores would be closed when she got to Seville, which meant that she'd be going to bed without a job and waking up without a future in the morning, after sleeping who-knows-where.

"Which part you going?" somebody asked.

Without looking she replied, "I going town."

By now she was the only person standing, and was staring at the road behind her as it faded into dusk.

She felt the heat of eyes on her, and when she looked she saw a woman leaning forward to reveal the man who'd asked. He was in his twenties, with a handsome face that had been spoiled in places by a rash, and as she looked at him she wondered why he didn't hide it with a beard.

"Which part you coming from?" he asked.

The leaning woman put her elbows on her knees, and now the man looked like a toilet.

Estrella answered, "Far."

"Far like far where? Every far has a name."

"Farther than you'd want to go."

"How you know that?"

"I ain't know that. And I ain't care that you know I ain't know that. Worse, I ain't care what you want to know for."

"Suppose I have important reasons?"

"I'd say good for you."

"Well, it must be good for me. Because I want to know so I could go and see your mother and thank her. For she made a lovely girl like you."

When the laughter in the truck had died, he pointed at the woman in his lap and said, "Don't worry. Me and her ain't nothing. When she gone I'll take you."

"If you know where I want to go you wouldn't say that."

"How you know for sure?"

"Well, you're old enough. If you did want to go you'd be gone already."

"Maybe I was waiting for you."

"Some kinda things can't cook in the same pot," she said, annoyed but quite amused. "Some things together is poison. Like cornmeal and rum. You ever drink that?"

"No."

"Next time I see you remind me, and I promise to make it for you."

The people in the truck began to laugh again.

"Your hair pretty," he said almost shyly. "You have Indian in you?"

"No."

"You want some?"

"You're a blasted fool. You know that?"

"Stop acting like you vex. I can see you want to laugh."

"It have children just like you, you know. They fill they eye before they fill their belly. They always asking for big plate o' food and when they get it they choke."

"I never hear a truer word," a woman in a red bandanna said. She tapped Estrella on the arm and offered her a lighted cigarette.

Estrella sat against the gate, held on to the frame and crossed her legs and smoked, the slow wind picking on her still damp hair.

She had the nature of a gambler, and as she smoked, her lips began to clamp more tightly as she replayed the conversation. She felt as if she'd lost.

"Which part you want to take me to?" she asked the man directly.

"Well . . ."

"Don't play jackass now. I'm interested. Tell me where you

want me and you to go? Where this place is where they giving people Indian blood?" She took her deepest drag, then added, "Or is Indian baby you did say?"

As the *madrasito* women chuckled, Estrella laughed and settled down to smoke again.

"Vashti, you can't have them woman laughing so," a man began to tease.

"What you want me do? Beat her?"

"No. It ain't call for that. A man like you so full of argument should have the strength to give her back some talks."

"You're right. I going take your advice. So," he started, looking at Estrella now, "you want to know where I going to take you? That is what you want to know, right. Well, hear now where I going to take you. Listen good and—"

"Vashti, cut the shit and talk, nuh man."

"You want to know where I going to take you?" he began again. "That is what I was going to tell you before this eunuch interrupted me. Well, hear now where I going to take you. Listen good. I going to take you to a place where you're not going to know yourself. Where you going to see yourself and wonder if is you because you never see yourself like that before . . . looking happy like you just finish eating a plate of goat stew with white yam . . . like when the goat stew finish and you make a belch and cut a fart you best friend give you back the money that he borrow thirty years ago . . . with interest . . . and take you down the bar and put your drinks on *his* tab. But it ain't done yet. Because after you leave the bar, you go to church and find out that Jesus tell the pastor to forgive all them rudeness I could look at you and tell you like to do." He paused to add a bite of intrigue and excitement. "You is a bad girl. I can tell. An experienced Indian ever take the time to light a fire on your tail?"

She sucked her teeth and didn't answer.

"Eh?" he prompted.

"Sister, what you have in the basket?" someone asked Estrella from a corner by the cab. "It have anything to eat?"

"It ain't have no food," she said, smirking in the dark. "It have book though. And soap. But if you look like your friend here who just tell me all this stupidness, then book and soap ain't make for you."

"Boy, the country girl have words, eh?" Vashti said.

"And you're from which part?" Estrella answered. "Paris? You acting like you come from town. Man, don't try me this evening. All you make for is one thing."

The woman in the red bandanna opened up: "And that's to burn and throw away."

THEY WERE EASING down into the flats now, where the central mountains stuttered in a taper to the Caribbean coast. Now, only four of them remained—three *madrasitos* and Estrella, who by now knew all their names.

The naughty banter had evolved into an easy conversation, during which she'd shared with them a little of her life, and they had shown a new regard for the *negrita* when she lit a match and grabbed a book and showed that she could read.

When the truck had reached its final stop, four miles before the intersection with the coastal road, the man who'd tried to give her talks, said, "Wait here while we see what we can do."

The *madrasitos* gathered by the driver's door, and Vashti, the one who'd tried to Estrella her talks, said, "Do me a favor, boss, and take her down the road?"

"She who?" came the sharp reply.

"The girl we pick up by the Sandy River Bridge. She going town."

"That's what you telling me now," the driver said impatiently. "But I ain't business with that. This ain't even my truck. Rambana drive my truck and crash it last week and now I have to drive this skeleton they dig up from the boneyard. I ain't even know if it can take them hills it have to go back home."

"It can take it, man. It can take it. Have faith. Is a old truck, but it good. Look how it carry all o' we from clear down Speyside to here."

"Vashti, you can't even drive a cow out your yard, but you want to give me advice?"

"Is far she coming from, you know, Joseph. Is not just from the bridge. Is far. From way down the Atlantic side. I ain't asking you to take her all the way. Just down to the coast road. You ain't even have to run the engine. You could just make it glide."

"Have a heart, no Joseph," said the woman with the red bandanna, who'd been silent all this time. "Have a heart. Do it, nuh. God will bless you."

The driver cleared his throat.

"I have a heart," he said. "I have a heart, in truth. But I want to have a job too. So tell her get out of my truck."

The woman in the red bandanna stepped away and looked up at the disappointed girl.

"Your people is a funny people," she said, enraged. "They say everybody fight them, but they love to fight themselves."

As Estrella bit her lip and thought of what to say, the woman stepped up on the running board and shouted in the driver's face.

"Joseph, you is a worthless nigger man. A worthless nigger man. The child trying to reach somewhere and you is the only body who could help her, and look how you going on? Down by the estate you like to talk your tripe about unionize, and work to-gether, and black and Indian must help each other. And here it is now, you wouldn't even try to help your own kind. We is Indian and we care more than you. You is a disgrace to your blasted race. You is a damn disgrace. Listen—the next time you see me don't tell me nothing 'bout Marcus Garvey and all them tripe.

Just don't tell me nothing. As a matter of fact, don't even drive me in your blasted truck again. If you see me in your way and you driving your truck, Joseph, just run over me to *rass*. Just run right over my head. And run over me from behind, because I ain't want see your blasted ugly face no more."

With this she tramped away.

"In thirty-five when we strike," the driver answered. His voice was low but poised to grow into a bulging force. "I take bullet in my ass and baton in my head for ungrateful *rasses*, like you. Damn coolie! You is a blight on the black man. You is a lice. They bring you here so we couldn't get our proper pay when free paper come, 'cause the white man know your kind would work for rum and a bowl o' curry rice. But when I call the strike, you wouldn't stand with me. That's why we don't have any blasted union in San Carlos today, and Rawle could pay we what he want to pay we. Because of folks like you. Everybody in the West Indies striking those times . . . St. Kitts, Jamaica, St. Vincent, St. Lucia . . . and all o' them get their union from that, except we. Why? Because of people like you. That's why we ain't have nothing in this country." He paused to catch his breath. "I is a old man, trying to live out my days. And you want to pressure me to prove myself to you. To bow down to you? To do what you want me to do just because you say so? Why I should follow you? You name Gandhi?"

I ain't want no *bangarang* because of me, Estrella thought. Lemme just take my things and go.

"Hey," she called to Vashti. "Let him go. His conscience going jam him tonight."

She came down from the truck and stood beside him. With a hand against her head, he mumbled, "Sorry."

"It ain't nothing to sorry 'bout," she said with disappointment. "It ain't nothing to sorry about at all. I come further than a lot of people think I could go. But thank you anyway."

"You know as long as we talking, I ain't know your name?"

"Listen it good."

She told him with her lips against his ear and he tapped her on her shoulder with a disenchanted look on his disfigured face and said, "Don't make anything happen to you," and walked into the bush toward a bobbling light.

"IS NOT MY fault," the driver said when they were left alone. "If it was up to me, I would take you. But I ain't even think it have enough petrol in this thing. And if it stop with me out here on the road, how anybody going to know? Plus my wife and children waiting at my home."

With her chin against her chest, Estrella placed her back against the door.

"Is not me you have to tell," she said as she thought of what to do. "I ain't ask you for a thing. Is they ask you. I ain't ask them to ask you. Is them is your friend. Is them you let down. It ain't me."

She slammed her hands against the door and walked away. "So don't say a goddamn thing to me."

"I ain't supposed to do this," said the driver, leaning from the cab. "If they find me out is *rass*."

With a hand across her brows, her body silvered by the bright high beams, she heard the driver crunching down the grade, slowly coming into view.

When he was beside her, she saw that he was short and stocky and wore glasses on a peanut-colored face. His silver hair receded sharply, and he'd shaved his mustache in a pencil line.

"Let me take the basket, come."

When she'd climbed into the cab and they were coasting down the road, she asked him, "Who's Mr. Rawle?"

The windshield had a set of hinges where it met the roof, and he'd opened it so that it formed an awning, and the wind was blowing straight against her face.

"On this island," he began, "it have three families that count.

It have Rawle. It have Campbell. It have Salan. Rawle and Campbell is like one because of marriage. And soon it going be Rawle alone since Salan young daughter married Rawle big boy. Rawle own sugar on this island. Rawle own cattle on this island. Rawle own coconuts. And although he get a blow with the coconut blight, and although he had to sell of most o' the estates so that he only have this Speyside now, and although nobody buying beef now because the war, Rawle is still the sheriff in this town. You see Salan?" He glanced at her to see if she was attuned. "He's coming up fast. And I like him more, because he is a man that start out poor, and he deal with people with manners. But you have to watch him, 'cause them Jews and Lebanese is tricky like *rass*." He tapped her shoulder. "I watching this scene long time, you know. I know what's going on. I bet you a thousand pounds that before I dead Salan going richer than Rawle. I don't know exactly how. But I know it going happen. Lemme show you how the man full o' tricks. Just when the war broke out and Rawle get lick with the coconut blight, Salan go to Rawle and said, 'Lemme take some swampland off you hands.' Well, Rawle like a fool go and sell him. Well, guess what? Before you know it, the Americans leasing this land from Salan to make a airbase. Now why would anybody build a airbase on a swamp? Because they need plenty land that is flat near the sea, and this place is only mountains. So the Americans use their big machine and dig down a hill and use that dirt to fill up a swamp. But guess whose hill? Salan. And guess what again? Salan want to flatten that hill long, long time, but he couldn't find a way to do it cheap. And guess whose land they dump?"

"Salan," she said distractedly, while thinking, *I hear he also sell the nicest shoes.*

"You're a brains. You hear what I telling you?" He beat his hands against the steering wheel. "You *get* what I saying. You *understand* my point. So, the Americans spend their money to fill up this land with soil and then the next thing you know they not building no base again. And the next thing after that you hear is that Salan take that land that was swampland and planting acres and acres of cane. Miles and miles of cane. You see how the man smart?"

"He should open a school."

"But it ain't book smart that man have," the driver emphasized. "It ain't book smart at all. That man have common sense because he's a common man. And that is why I like him. He's a common man. Rawle act too high and mighty, like his shit come from Nova Scotia in a tin like sardine. And the only thing that is making him ride high right now is that Royal Standard Rum. That is the best rum it have in the world. I hear people talking 'bout Bacardi and Appleton and Havana Club like them rum is anything to talk about. Listen to what I saying tonight. I take them rum and wash my glass before I tip the best. And is one place grow the cane for that rum and that is Speyside. That's where grow the finest cane. And that's why they build that factory there in that bowl that so hard to get to. You lose the quality if you make that rum from them fields it have near the sea. And that is why it burn me when them lice head coolie never stand by me when we make that strike in thirty-eight. Because if it had union in this country we could boil down Rawle and all them *rasses* till they reach the bottom o' the pot. A lotta people vex that the Americans taking over . . . talking all kinda *rass* 'bout how they ain't trust United Fruit. But in a sense I glad. One man beating my ass all my life. I say let another man come and lick me and see how it sweet."

"You would be vex if I tell you I ain't feel like to talk?" she asked him dryly.

"If I would mind?" he asked, offended. "If I would mind? Of course I would blasted mind. I giving you a blasted ride . . . you better talk to me. Them people I work with ain't talk to me. They think I talk too much. And some say I must be a spy because how I could cuss Mr. Rawle so much and he ain't fire me yet. But I ain't stupid. I ain't cuss the man to him face. I cuss him to his back. I old now. I do my time. This job to drive this truck here is the only thing I have name pension. When I was cutting and leaf was slicing up my flesh was a long, long time ago. When I born it still had slaves in Cuba. Brazil too. A lotta people ain't know those things. But they ain't read books, you see. They ain't read books. So they ain't know what's going on."

"I like to read," she said, interested now.

"For true?"

"Yes. I like it more than anything it have in the world."

"So how you can read but you talk like you ain't go to school?" he asked, amazed.

"I can speak English," she said, switching from *sancoche*. "But I have never been to school. I taught myself and I received a little help from a Chinese girl whose father owns a shop."

"You are a prize," he said, pulling over. "A real, fantastic prize. What is your name?"

"Why you want to know?" she asked defensively.

"So I could present you with a proper compliment."

She leaned over her basket, which she carried in her lap.

"I ain't want nobody to tie up my head right now," she said, reverting to *sancoche*. "I ain't want nobody compliment me or anything like that 'cause that is only talks. I going about my business, you see me here. And that is all I want to do."

When they'd begun to coast again, he asked, "Why you going to town so late?"

"I have business down there."

"When I leave you off," he asked with genuine concern, "how you going to reach?"

She shrugged.

"Girl, it going be real hard to get a vehicle going that way, you know. Unless is a emergency, you shouldn't try to go."

"Is a emergency in truth for me. I sick. I real sick. I real sick of this place."

She turned so that her back was partly pressing on the door and placed a thigh against his seat. "Mister, you would never imagine what happen to me."

"Tell me."

But how I could trust a man who only cuss his boss behind his back? she thought. A man like that is a two-face man. You're suppose to say what you feel. 'Cause talk is what make a man greater than a beast. And when you say behind a man what you want to say to his face, you're showing him something. You're showing him that he's a man and you is some kinda mule for him to ride, or some kinda dog for him to kick around. And people who take so much kick and ride, they mind weak. And they will talk your business when the pressure start to come. That's exactly what happen to me. My own friends who was there when that man come out the waves, tell lie and spread rumor 'pon me. They 'fraid o' what come out their parents' mouth.

"Let it rest," she told him. "Let it rest. But something happen to me that make me sick down to my soul."

In his head he said, *This subject need a change.*

"I hear that fire burning down in Black Well."

"Which part is that?" she asked.

"On the way to town."

"I never hear about no place name so. Which part is that? When you say, burning, what kinda burning you mean?"

"I ain't really know. A man tell me today that they was burning down there again. You ain't know which part Black Well is?"

She shook her head and made a grunt.

"That is where Salan get the Yankee them to fill up the swamp so he could plant the cane. The same place we old people call New Lagos is the same place name Black Well now. When I was a young man a Yankee priest name Father Eddie . . . Eddie Blackwell was his name . . . use to do some things out there. Have woman and all, I hear. Maybe that's why they call it so. But still, it have some o' the blackest nigger man you ever see out there. So maybe that's why they call it so."

"You mean where it have some houses in the water on the poles?" she asked. "And sometimes out there you could catch manatee?"

"Same one."

"Yes. I know out there."

After they'd driven for a mile in silence, which Estrella used to prep her mind to walk, the driver took a hand from off the wheel.

Looking at the girl, her tousled hair, her diamond face, her upper lip, which was encroaching on her nose, he began to use his palm to rub the leather knob that crowned the long gear stick that slanted from the floor.

I ain't able for this *rass,* Estrella thought. I ain't able for this *rass* right now. But you're almost there. It can't turn into nothing big. If he try to force you then it have to be a fight.

"You have a boyfriend?" he began.

"I might," she said flatly.

"You do or you don't?"

"Why you want to know?"

"I have a son," he said nobly. "A nice boy. The youngest one. Nineteen years old with a good trade. He's a mechanic down at Royal Standard. He's a man can fix anything that break. But is only Indian girls he like. That woman in the red bandanna who just cuss me off, she carrying bad feelings for me. Why? It have a rumor that my son fooling with her girl. But that ain't true. My son have taste. My son know better than that. My son is an educated boy. Can read and write. And her daughter would see her name on a envelope with money and use it to wipe her ass. By the way, how old you be?"

"Old enough," she said, smiling.

"I ain't want none of them town girls for my son. Them girls have too much guile. He need a nice country girl with ambition.

A girl who could read and write." He raised his hand to make the point. "And she must be pretty too. What man want a bright, ambitious monkey in the bed?"

Estrella laughed.

"I ain't making joke," he said. "Is a serious thing. Just like no woman ain't have no use for no fat man. No man ain't have no use for no ugly woman. And that is fat or slim! When you wake up in the morning and your head ain't settle yet, you ain't want to turn and see a face that could stop your heart."

"So you think I pretty or you making talks?"

"Baby, if I make talks to you, you'd ask me to marry you right now. My talks is like a sweet rum punch. It nice you when it going down, but when you're done you feel regret, 'cause it will drunk you and make you give away your life."

She felt her doubt receding.

"So I pretty then."

"Like the moon right there."

She leaned forward and craned her head and saw the moon. It was bright and almost full, and as she felt it pulling at romantic feelings in her liquid depths, the driver asked her faintly, "Could I touch your leg?"

"I don't think so?" she said, then, on thinking that she might have sounded indecisive, fired: "Touch my leg for what?"

Respectfully, he answered, "So I could give a good accounting to my son."

The moon illuminated certain passions; she was grateful for the ride; and flattered that he'd choose her for his son. Plus the cab felt oddly safe, safe in the way of a studio, a place in which to probe around. Try new things. Test limits. Rehearse.

"But don't go too far," she said, and dropped her forearm in the crevice where her pelvis met her thigh. His touch was quick and light, and was more a test of ripeness than a fondle or caress, and she took his hand and held it and they rode in swollen silence.

\* \* \*

WHEN THEY REACHED the intersection with the coastal road he came around to help her from the cab.

"You're a beautiful girl," he told her. "My son deserves a girl like you. Some men ain't like a girl with lip, but I like a little lip. Is the ones who ain't like to talk I can't take. See . . . if they ain't like to talk they like to brood. I can't take a woman who just stare at you over breakfast when she vex. When they look at you that brooding way, you lose the taste for food. When a woman gimme lip I take it, smile, then eat my blasted food. But when they stare at me like that, oh god." He felt that he'd said too much and tapped her on the chin. "But look. I running. God bless you. I glad you make me change my mind."

"A man never tell me that I beautiful, you know, so I don't know what to say."

Across the street she saw the orange light of bottle torches glowing in the stalls where old *negritas* dressed in skirts and turbans sold small fritters made from black-eyed peas and eaten with a pepper sauce and shark steaks fried brown. She could also see the silhouettes of dogs and milling people, and smell the garlic marinade in which the steaks were left to soak all day before the old *negritas* dipped them in the cornmeal batter, turning them so that the batter creamed the meat, which they would slide into the iron pots that had been used by their grandmothers, and the battered meat would settle in the oily depths where all the salty flavor lurked and gain a brittle shell.

Beneath the smell of fish there was the wheaty fragrance of the heavy bread the fat *negritas* baked in ovens that they'd built from lime and brick right there beside the road, round loaves that came out bronzed and dusty with the smoky taste of coals.

She was warmed by all of this—the smell of food, her conversation, and the sound of happy voices crackling like the splash of water dripping in hot oil.

And her head began to sink toward her shoulder when the

driver stepped up on the running board and sat alone inside the cab, which now seemed unbalanced.

"If you ever pass again come by the distillery gate and ask for me," he said. "Xavier Joseph. Everybody know me down there. Just call my name."

She wanted to say something romantic, but all the words she thought about did not feel true.

"If you ever get a message that a girl name Cinderella by the gate," she said, believing that the meaning would be secret, "then you'll bound to know is me."

They looked at each other the way that people do when time begins to curl and stretch as if it were a lazy cat.

"Come," he said, and slapped the door. "Let me take you further down."

THEY QUICKLY LEFT the stalls behind, and moved along a flat, unpopulated coast. The road held closely to the water, which she heard above the engine, breaking on the reef.

It was a long, straight beach with hardly any curves, and the water was so clear that in the daytime you could see the shadows of the fish against the ocean's rippled floor. The sand was so white that on the coolest days you had to squint to see it, and so dry that people said it had been blown there by a desert wind.

She wanted him to try to hold her hand again, and was disappointed that he didn't reach.

Suppose he was just holding my hand to make me feel good? she thought. Suppose he ain't even have no son. But nothing ain't wrong with that. Nothing ain't wrong if a person tell a little lie to make another person feel okay. I do it all the time. Maybe he was asking for himself. Sometimes them old man have some crafty ways. But it felt good all the same. He touch me nice. I was feeling little wetty when he touch my leg in truth. But you know what? I ain't want to tie up my head with no stupidness. I have important things to do.

But she was young and disappointed and couldn't help herself.

"Why you being so nice to me?"

"You know if they catch me with my headlights on they lock me up?"

"So why you ain't turn back?"

"Is blackout time now, you know. If they catch me now is grief."

"So why you going so far out of your way to do something for me? You ain't know me. And I ain't know you. And I ain't make no kinda promise to you."

"Sometimes in life you shouldn't ask so much," he said. "Sometimes you should just take the drive."

"I think you say you like woman with lip?"

In his mind he said, *With hip and ass as well.*

Aloud, he said: "How old are you, Miss Cinderella? In truth how old are you?"

"Old enough," she softly taunted.

"Girl talk to me in a serious fashion. How old are you?"

"Pick a number."

"Okay, let's call it sixteen. When you turn into a big woman and have children and all that, you going to realize something. When you is a pretty woman, you could get man to do all kinda things. You could get man to work all their money and come and give you like your name is bank."

"You so full o' talks," she said. With an elbow on the door she'd begun to stroke her hair.

"Well, I is a old man. What you expect?"

"They say is better to be an old man darling than to be a young boy slave," she offered, playing at being adult.

"Well, is who full of talks now, me or you?"

"That ain't talks, man. That is truth."

"You know what is true?" he tested, as the tires crushed a

mob of crabs caught crawling in the road. "Maybe I shouldn't tell you anything about my son. Maybe I should keep you for myself."

"But how you could keep what you ain't have?"

She resettled herself in the seat.

"So what it take?"

He reached for her. She eased way, but let him hold her hand.

"I ain't know," she answered as she squeezed it. "Nobody ain't catch me yet."

"So what it would take?"

His foot had left the pedal and the truck began to slow.

"I ain't know," she said, and shook him loose. "Drive up. Drive up, fast."

"Tell me," he said sincerely, "and I promise to do it for you."

When she realized that she'd broken him, her skin began to tingle with the warm electric current of a thrill.

And she told him in a slightly bossy way, "Well, take me into town."

"I can't do that," he mumbled with regret. "I ain't have the petrol in the tank."

"But you care for me?" she said, the bossiness receding from her voice.

"I ain't know you long. But in this short, short time, I do."

"Don't make it spoil then." There was a part of her that wasn't sure that what he'd said about his tank was true. "Here's what you do. Stop the truck right here, and touch me 'pon my leg again and call me beautiful. Don't do one then do the next. Don't touch then talk. Do the two of them together. And when you finish, put me out and wish me luck. I'll do the same to you." She kissed her palm and pressed it to his cheek. "You make me feel real nice, yes. And I ain't want that niceness to spoil. 'Cause it always spoil. It always spoil. Thank you very much."

## VIII.

THE ROAD WAS dark and silent and she focused on the slapping of her feet against the asphalt as she walked. In the distance, she could hear the engine fading and the short compression that would come before the elongation of the gears, a pattern like a snore. And she hummed to help it fade, to help her rinse the loss before it stained.

There was grass along the verge, and as her eyes adjusted to the moonlight, she could see a narrow path.

But I ain't know what in them grass, she thought, standing in the road. Them grass could have all kind *macka* to jam you in your foot. And it have some that worse than snakebite I hear. Those, when they jam you, make your foot swell so much you feel like you walking with a ball and chain. The road hard, and my foot feel soft, but I ain't able for no swell foot tonight—especially how my driver gone.

Her conversation with Joseph had left her feeling sentimental, and now, as she'd never been before, she felt uneasy in the dark. Like a novice in a boat caught in big waves, she couldn't find a way to put herself along an even keel. And her skin began to prickle as she grudgingly admitted that she, Estrella Thompson, a girl who had been cast away, was something precious that someone could lose. Her life was not her own. It belonged to all who showed her love. Like the woman in the red bandanna and Vashti, the handsome man who had the rash along his face. Like Joseph. Even Asif!

It would matter if they woke up in the morning and heard that something awful had happened . . . that she'd been robbed or killed or raped. If something awful happened it would count. And she began to feel now that she should have talked to Joseph more to find out what it would have cost to take her into town. If it had come to it . . . if he'd said he'd do it but her body was the price, she would have paid it, would have found a way to make it work. Maybe she would have asked him to repeat that she was pretty while he touched her leg as if it were a length of rich, imported cloth. Maybe she would have touched herself while he was sliding in on top of her and thought of someone else . . . just so she wouldn't have to be alone . . . just so that she wouldn't be the one in charge of making sure that nothing awful happened, of making sure that sadness didn't flood these people's lives.

One mile. Two miles. Three miles. Four. She walked without seeing a soul. Sometimes she saw dim flickers and heard voices, and knew that she was passing by a hut set back into the bush. Sometimes a shadow in a larger clump beside the verge would break away and she would recognize the blotchy outline of a moving thing. When she thought it was a human she would say good night. If she thought it was a ghost she'd cross herself and say novenas.

Eventually, the beach gave way to cattle country and the road began to swerve. As it swerved, it drifted and began to change its course, and she found herself being pressed on either side by humps of aromatic pasture tipped with chimneyed houses and long fences of stacked stone.

I see where I going now, she thought, on seeing the houses, which were silhouetted on the lighter sky. When I make it, that's the kind of house I going to buy. Far away on top of a hill where nobody ain't have to know my business, and I could see if anybody coming to interfere with me and send my dog to bite them. You getting to town soon. Not soon like *soon*. But soon. You moving. You not staying behind. When you see things like a fence it mean you're close to people who know that things can't just be wild like that, that you have to set them so that they have a proper look like lines you see in books. And you only find them kinda people in town.

As Estrella walked, a sour taste began to creep into her

throat and she sat against a stone. She had eaten some mangoes as she'd waited on the bridge, and now the juice had fermented, and the acid had begun to burn her stomach walls.

I tell you . . . sand ain't easy when it hot, Estrella thought as she rubbed her aching feet. But if you put your mind against it you could bear it. But them paved roads that it have here ain't easy—hot or cold. This town thing going take some getting used to. To live in town . . . even if you only manage to get a simple job . . . even if you don't get to reach your ambition . . . even if all you going get to do is walk around and sell peanut or newspaper, you going have to get a pair of shoes.

As she'd done when she'd been traveling on the bus, she took her bearings by projecting out to sea and gathered that she was a little under thirteen miles from town.

As she began to walk again, her nostrils caught a trace of smoke. It was too dark to see it in the sky. And in truth it could have come from someone cooking late at night or burning coal. But there were disturbances in Black Well, which was directly on the way.

As she wondered if there was another route, she heard the clop and scrape of iron shoes behind her, and turned around to see the shadow of a rider on a horse.

"Begging a ride," she asked from thirty yards away. "Please, if you could help me. I'm begging you a ride."

The rider waited till he'd drawn his horse beside her.

"Who is that?" he asked in Spanish. "How do I know you're not a thief?"

She was standing by a tree that overgrew a fence, and although he was ten feet from her she couldn't see his face. But from his voice, which had a rasp as if his vocal cords were made from rope, and from the fact that he spoke Spanish—which she understood but didn't speak—Estrella knew he was *criollo* from the South Atlantic coast, a descendant of the early Spanish settlers who'd accepted British rule.

"I ain't no thief," she said in *sancoche*. "If I was a thief I wouldn't call you from afar. I would bide my time and wait until you're passing easy, like everything is fine and then I'd knock you off your horse."

She imagined that he had a tapered face and skin that was the color of the waterpots his people made from clay, and she was right. His hair was dark, and he wore it in a *cola*—a lengthy ponytail—that was partly hidden by his black fedora.

"I know the horse tired," she persisted. "But my feet is tired more, and they ain't stony like your horse's foot that wearing iron shoes."

The horse stomped. The movement scared her. And she jumped away.

"How old are you?" the horseman asked in Spanish, leaning over.

"Old enough."

"Old enough for what? It's very late," he told her in a curt, officious way. "I'm sure you know that there's a curfew. Where's your mother? A girl your age should be at home."

"I ain't no child," she said. "And I ain't live with my mother for a long, long time."

He got off his horse and tied it to a limb of the overhanging tree and leaned against the long stone fence.

He was an experienced seducer, who understood that women fell in love through words, and when he met a prospect, he would take the time to find out what she liked to talk about, and was famous in his district for saying, "If you listen, you will learn."

"Nice night," he said matter-of-factly. "Look at that beautiful moon."

"I been watching at it all night."

"What do you think of when you see a moon like this?"

"That night is darker than day."

"You don't like to talk about the moon?"

"It have other things I like to talk about more."

"Like what?" he asked indulgently.

"Nothing I can bring my mind to think about right now. Right now, all I can think about is getting into town while the moon is in the sky. Because when sun come is morning."

"Did the horse frighten you?" he asked in a considerate way.

"I frighten, yes. I think I see about four ghosts on this road tonight. My nerves ain't able for no excitement."

Oh, he told himself, she's afraid.

"I am very sorry," he told her. "He is a strange horse, you know. A faithful one too. Whenever he gets a feeling that I might be in danger he tries to warn me that I should escape."

"Horse have so much sense?" she said, her intellect aroused.

He eased up from the fence and paced the verge with his long, slim legs. He was short, but high-waisted, and wore a denim workshirt and tan trousers, which were tucked into his knee-length riding boots.

"This is not an ordinary horse," he told her, improvising on a story that he'd often told before. "First of all he is a police horse. He was trained by the police. All my family is police, you know. And this horse was a good police horse. Strong horse. Faithful horse. But he got a damage to his foot."

He heard Estrella laugh with recognition as he shifted from Spanish to *sancoche*.

"You smell smoke?" he asked, sniffing loudly.

"A little bit," she said.

"Trouble," he said mysteriously.

"What kinda trouble?"

"Black Well hot tonight. That is a place that I can't understand. They always having some excitement." He shook his head. "You see that same Black Well where the smoke coming from? Right down in there. That's where it happened. This horse took a policeman down in there when they had a disturbance and one of those wild people—'cause they *wild*, you know—just all of a sudden jump up and swing a machete. The edge was going to take his head. But at the last moment, the horse rear up and took the chop on his front leg. Bam! And you know that after all those years of service the police was going to shoot him? But I was there at the time. And I jump up and say, 'No! You shouldn't do that. This is a good horse and a faithful horse, a horse you can always trust.' And I told them I would keep the horse and care the horse. And look at the horse now." As if apologizing, he paused and said, "Well, if it was day you could really see what I talking 'bout. A damn fine horse as you would ever see."

The passion. The engagement. The details. The drama. The way he told the story made her think of Joseph, and she felt as if she knew him better than she did, and because of this, she suspended disbelief.

"When you go through a lot and people help you, you have to be grateful," she said in deep reflection. "Even a horse could know that. But it have some people in this world, you know, sir, that never learn that lesson in their life."

"You are one of those?"

"No sir. Not at all."

"What kinda person you is?"

"Oh. It hard to say. I never have to answer any question like that in my life before." Then after she'd thought about her day she said, "Unlucky."

"Well your luck might change tonight."

"Gimme a ride and maybe I'll believe."

He made a noncommittal exclamation.

"Well, it was nice to meet you," he said, in Spanish again. "All the best and good luck."

He began to untie the horse.

"Which part you going?" she asked in mild panic.

"Town," he said, as if from deep inside a thought. "Seville."

"Then I could get a ride?" She held him by the arm. "I thought you was stopping because you was going to give me a ride."

"He's an old horse," he said with false compassion. "And his leg is still not very good. And I'm not sure if he likes you." He paused as if to think. "No . . . I don't think he can take the weight."

Nervous, she began to stroke the horse along the neck to show that she was liked.

"See there. He ain't mind me at all."

"But the weight . . . the weight . . . the weight."

"I don't weigh plenty," she said. "Come. Weigh me."

He reached for her and held her close and ran his hand along the length of her, pretending that he couldn't find a grip. She was firm and tight with even curves and as he lifted her, he paused and dipped her twice so that her little breasts would brush against his nose.

But although she was smooth and had a subtle give, the girl was densely muscled, and the man began to struggle with her weight. While wobbling, he softly slapped her flank, which signaled her to wrap her legs around him, giving both of them the pleasure of a quick embrace.

"Okay," he murmured when he'd set her down. "Okay. You can come."

With this, he lifted her as one would lift a bride and placed her on the horse.

Accustomed to a kind of easy gruffness all her life, and feeling tender in the dark, she assented when he used his hand to draw her back into the armchair comfort of his chest.

The horse had not been covered with a saddle, and she found it hard to keep her balance on the padding made of sugar sacks.

"You okay?" he asked her when the horse began to move. "You 'fraid?"

"I feel high," she said, too scared to turn her head in case the movement made her fall.

"You want me to hold you?"

"I feeling okay for a while."

"When he start to trot it going be kinda rough. And the way you was talking I think you want to reach town really quick."

"When you talk about trot and all that it have me a little nervous," she confessed. "He could see where he going? How he know where he going in the dark. Next thing something frighten him and he throw we off."

He slipped an arm around her waist and used one hand to hold the rope.

"This horse is a good horse," he said. "As long as he don't think you want to fight me or nothing, he will do the best for you."

When he felt as if she'd settled on the brawny colt, he asked, "So what you going to town to do?"

She answered brightly, "Improve myself and find a work."

"What kind of work you can do?"

"I could do any kind of work," she said. "I ain't 'fraid hard work, you know. As long as people ain't try to bamboozle me, and get me in any kinda tug-of-war, I could do anything."

"Whoa! Whoa! Whoa!"

He startled her.

"What happen?"

"Take your time. Slow down. Everybody ain't from the countryside. I know *sancoche,* but when you give it that backward twang you throw me."

"Not because you gimme a ride, you could insult me, you know, sir. I begging you a ride and I grateful for it, but I could walk my walk and reach where I going. I ain't take insult."

But when all this had left her mouth, she thought, You need to learn to hold your tongue. Suppose the man get vex and put you off, what you going to do? The road hard. The way long. *Bangarang* down in Black Well. Tell the man you're sorry. As old-time people say, when you hand in the lion mouth, take your time and pull it out.

"Mister," she began before he interrupted with, "I'm sorry."

He said it in a way designed to touch her heart . . . mannish in his voice but childish in his tone. "I don't mean to insult you."

"It was an ungrateful thing to say. And I am not ungrateful. Believe me. I just tired."

"I'm tired too," he said and placed his chin beside her neck. "We're two tired people. We're both sorry that we're tired. We have so much in common that we'd make such good friends. Let's do that. That's what I want to do. I just want to ride with you and be your friend, and talk to you and get to know you. I want to know the way you think."

She smiled. The movement of the horse beneath her was a mounting pleasure; but more importantly, the man had made her feel that he'd perceived her as a person with a mind.

"What you want to know?"

She squeezed a shoulder to her ear.

"I want to know about . . . you," he half-stuttered. "About how you feel in general . . . about life."

In English, the language of all things important and bright, Estrella said, "I think to be boring is one of the most awful things that could happen in life" when in truth she meant "bored."

"Are you an exciting person?" he asked in English more fluent than hers.

"I think so. But I just haven't got the chance to do a lot of things I really want to do."

"Like what?" he asked warmly.

"Like to go to Europe."

Her mind began to drift. And while she saw herself arriving in a car at La Sala and working in a store, and eating only beef and chicken at her meals and feeding fish and lobsters to her dog, the rider gripped the stallion tightly with his knees, and ground against her flanks.

Getting no resistance, he slid a hand along her leg, which felt damp and firm beneath her long blue skirt, and outward curved with strength. And with his thumb, he traced it where it had a solid crease along the side, where down below, he knew, there lurked the heavy bone.

"How much is for a pair of shoes in town?" she asked, distracted, returning to *sancoche*.

He quickly moved his hands as she began to shift her weight as if she'd just awoken from a dream.

"Are you comfy?" he asked. "You seem unsettled."

"I don't know," she told him. "Maybe is because I know that Black Well coming up."

"Oh. I thought you'd leaned against my pistol."

"Oh. You have a gun?"

"Not that we'll need to use it. I could walk through Black Well anytime."

He leaned away from her and fussed around his waist and made a mental count, then uttered, "There."

"That feels better," she told him when he eased her back to lean on him again.

"Now what kind of shoes would you like?"

She paused to think.

"The kind you wear to work in a office or a shop."

Accustomed to the horse by now, she'd turned her head to speak.

"I ain't mean to be rude," he said. "But you have money to buy shoes?"

He tapped her with his boots against her heel.

"I might," she answered in a way she thought of as *mysteriously* but was in fact, "vague as if she had no clue at all."

"You ain't really know town, do you?" he told her in a sympathetic voice.

"What are you trying to say? Of course."

He didn't challenge her, but proceeded in a tone that said that any difference of opinion when it came to town had little consequence. Because his perspective was right.

"I ain't mean to disappoint you but them f——kers—excuse my language—ain't like to give *negritas* certain jobs, you know . . . in banks and office and shops. But you know this already of course."

"I ain't care what they like to do," she said. "I just want to know what shoes you have to have to work there."

"Well, being that I used to own a store," he said, in English now, "I know a thing or two. Everybody else in my family are po-lice as I told you. That is one of the ways how I was able to get this thirty-eight. But be that as it may, I am the only one who had the head for business. But that too is for another day. Back to your question about shoes. You can't just wear any shoes when you work in a place of business, you know. You have to wear the finest shoes. And the finest shoes in the world are English shoes. You can't go for the kind of job you're talking about in say Span-ish shoes or American shoes." He slapped his thigh for empha-sis. "No way. Wear one of those and the boss will take one look at you and say you don't know what you're doing."

"For true?"

"Absolutely. Now why would I lie to you?"

"No. I'm not saying you is a liar, sir. Is just a phrase."

"I know it's just a phrase, sweetheart. But so is, 'Why would I lie to you?' "

"Oh."

"I know about English shoes, you know. I know so much I could write a book. I know the English very well. I met a lot of them when I lived in Europe."

"Really!"

She was so excited that she tried to turn around to face him. She lost her balance and he held her waist, then found and squeezed her hand.

With his fingers playing on her palm, he said: "I used to live there for a very long time."

He said this in the kind of breathy tone in which a singer introduces certain kinds of sentimental songs, and she reacted with the gush of people who attend those certain kinds of shows.

"Where?" she asked him. "Which part? Tell me."

"Paris," he said. "Then after I had lived in Paris, I moved . . ."

"To where?"

"Oh, after Paris . . . let me see . . . I lived in so many different places. Oh . . . after Paris, I moved to France."

"And what about the war?" she asked. It struck her that she hadn't read the news. "You see the war?"

"*See* the war?" he chortled. "*See* the war? My love, I *fought* the war?"

"Oh Jesus Christ."

"That's why you need to listen when I talk. That's why when I tell you about shoes you should never doubt me. You need English shoes, my friend, and those shoes are expensive. How much money do you have on you right now? How much could you put down on a counter for a pair of top-class English shoes?"

"Five pounds," she said with force.

The man exploded in deep-throated laughter.

"That can't buy it?" she asked with doubt, unwittingly revealing that she was unaware that she was right.

More excited now, he laughed again.

"Okay then . . . fourteen pounds. I could walk into one of them stores and fling down fourteen pounds on that counter and say, 'Gimme your best pair of goddamn English shoes. I have fourteen pounds on me right now.'"

He stopped the horse, and put both arms around the girl.

"Good shoes like that cost forty pounds," he took a lot of time to say. "With fourteen pounds you couldn't even buy a single foot."

Estrella Thompson raised her head to calm herself, then dropped her chin and cried.

"But it's not the end of the world," he said in a fatherly way. "Oh, hush."

"It ain't you feeling pain. So you can say what you want."

"I know pain," he improvised. "I know a kind of pain I hope you'll never understand. Look . . ."

He allowed his voice to fade.

"What happen to you?" she asked him, working to control her breath.

"I don't want to talk."

"What happen?"

"I . . . just don't want . . ."

"Tell me?"

Her voice was creamy like a soft eruption.

"I want to. But I can't."

"Yes, you can. You have to try."

"I know but . . ."

She told him sternly: "Do you know how many times I want someone to hear and it ain't nobody there?" She held his arms and used her weight to rock them. "I thought you said you wanted me and you to be good friends?"

He sighed. He hummed. He moaned. Then said, "When they shoot me in the war, you don't think it hurt? It hurt so bad. It hurt so bad. It hurt so goddamn bad. As I talk about it now, I feel the pain as if it was happening again." She felt him shiver. "I thought I was going to die. Death is not a easy thing. When it stare you in the face, you ain't want to see it close again. And that's how it feel when you talk about it."

"I know it hard to talk about but . . . what happened?"

"Three Japanese ambushed me in Berlin. But I got them, though. They thought I was dead. But I saw them running in the dark. And as I lie down there, thinking that was it, I shoot them down like birds."

"In the dark?"

"In the dark. Dark night just like this. Well, not so dark, but noisy. Fighting is a cantankerous thing."

With this, he got off the horse and walked away.

"Where you going?" she cried. "I ain't want this horse to run away with me . . . and . . . and how you doing down there?"

She couldn't see him in the dark, and she imagined rightly that his arms were raised toward the gods.

"I am a damn disgrace," he screamed toward the sky. "I am nothing but a big disgrace."

"What you mean? No. That ain't true."

"Of course, I am. I should be taking care of you to *rass* and instead of doing that I'm crying like a baby. Oh, lord. This thing called war is hell."

She stumbled off the horse and groped toward his voice.

"You can't leave the horse alone," he called out as he took a path toward a spot he often used.

She led the horse toward his heavy breathing till she felt his hand against hers in the dark, and followed.

She left him with the horse and went to stand some yards away, allowing him the privacy to cry. Her whole being felt exposed and tender, and her fourteen-year-old heart was full of sympathy and awe for this traveler, this soldier, this stranger who'd come to her rescue, this gentleman who'd lifted her and placed her on his brave and faithful horse and had tried to get to know her as he rode her to the place where she'd have a chance to fix her damn unlucky life.

"What is your name?" she heard him asking from behind.

"Estrella," she said. "Estrella Thompson is my name. And what is yours?"

"Simón," he said. "Simón . . . Simón . . . Bolívar."

She said in English, "That's a wonderful, beautiful name."

"And you, my love, are a beautiful, beautiful girl."

"How do you know? You've never seen me?"

"Because . . . beautiful people have beautiful . . . they're just beautiful all over. Come here. I want to use my hands to know your beautiful, lovely face."

"Do you find me interesting?" she asked.

He sat on a stone emplaced at the foot of a tree.

"Of course," he said. "Of course."

He placed a cheek against her stomach, and touched and stroked her face, then slid his hands across her body, from her shoulders to her thighs, as she removed his hat and rubbed his head as if he were her nameless wooden dolly come to life.

"I'm so sorry about what happened in the war," she said, delighting in the texture of his silken hair.

As if he were in mental pain, he stood and shrugged and slouched around the tree, knowing she would follow, and she slipped her arms around his neck and felt his body stiffen in her tight embrace. There was a near maternal softness to his middle, an endearing strangeness in a slender man.

She pressed her diamond face against his chest. He smelled of rum and cedar shavings and carbolic soap, but none of them intensely. And when she squeezed herself between his arms she felt secure, as if her tender feelings grew a shell.

He was a man of patience, and he held her without moving, till he was certain that her feelings wouldn't change; then he sent his strong hands sliding down her sides and up again as potters do with clay.

"Why you touching me like you want something?" she asked him in her awkward country way.

They'd been kissing slowly for a very long time and he'd placed her hand against his pants and she'd stroked the thing she found there till it felt as solid as an ear of corn.

"If you offered me something, I would take it," he said as she stroked him. "But I would never ask."

"Beg me the right way and maybe I give you."

His hands were masters exercising their control. One was

sweeping down along her side, around her back, swooping with her spine. The other one had reached beneath her skirt and was touching her so lightly that it felt as if he meant to finely sand the rims of muscle slanting from the cleavage in her bottom to her thighs.

"You are so finely made," he whispered. "So finely fashioned. Jesus was a carpenter. He made you out of wood."

"But look how your mouth full o' sweet talks," she said. "And still you won't come out and tell me what you want."

"You know what I want," he told her.

"Well touch it then. If you're dumb, you're dumb. Come on, dummy. Touch it. Show Mama what you want."

He paused, overwhelmed. He was accustomed to women who were coy.

"You 'fraid?" she softly taunted. "Like how your big horse scare me, my little catty make you scared? Big man like you who fight war and thing? Who kill man and thing? A little catty ain't supposed to frighten you."

"Put my hand on it."

As she led his hand into the clenching hump of fur between her legs he used the other one to pull her buttons, starting from her neck.

When the blouse had been undone, he ran his hands along the curving, rising length of her sea-strengthened smoothness and, amazed by its perfection, laughed.

"What sweet you?" she asked.

"I just don't know what else to do."

He unhooked her frayed brassiere.

She told him: "Take care. Mind the pins."

He obeyed and she slipped out of her skirt and hung it with her blouse and undergarments on a limb above her head.

"But we have to make haste," she told him as she turned around and gripped the tree, and hoisted up a leg.

"No, no, darling. Take your time and face me."

When she'd placed her back against the tree, he knelt before her with his trousers tucked into his long black boots, held her by the hips and swept his tongue across the rosy droplet barely sagging from her pubic hairs, and she sputtered like he'd thrown her overboard while she was sleeping.

"Did I frighten you?"

His head was clamped between her knees.

If Simón take his hands from me right now, Estrella thought, I going fall down in a pile.

I never feel nothing like this before. It feel like he pull out all my bones. Or like my body was a shaky tooth and that he just play with it until almost turn to pain.

If you frighten me? Yes, you frighten me, yes. Because any man who could do this to me could wreck my blasted life. Could have me thinking 'bout this and nothing else. Make me stay home instead of going to work in the morning. And I ain't want nobody rule me like that. I ain't want nobody to rule me with nothing at all. And how the *rass* I come to this? How it go from talking to something like this? This ain't what I out for—taking man in bush.

"I have to put on my clothes," she said, reaching for the limb. The faucet of emotion was turned off. "You okay?"

"Is this some kind of joke?"

He staggered to his feet in disbelief.

She couldn't find the pin for her brassiere and she grumbled as she looked, talking to herself, cursing just beneath her breath as if he weren't there. She gave up trying to find the pin in the dark and slipped on her skirt before she stepped inside her bloomers—a habit that had started when she and a boy were nearly caught by Roselyn and Old Tuck.

Dressed, she stuffed the bra in the pocket with her money and her knife.

"How long till we reach town?"

"Walking," he said, "a very, very, very long time."

"Don't get sulky and contrary now," she said across her shoulder as she walked toward the horse. "Come visit me tomorrow at my place in town."

Estrella wasn't being dishonest. She was playing at being adult—reaching forward into what she wished to be her coming life, a life in which she'd have the means to live alone and have the privacy to entertain whenever she might please.

"Don't play me for a fool," the rider said.

With long strides, he overtook her. His voice was soft but stiff in tone; his shoulders taut and hunched.

"I'm not trying to bamboozle, you," she reassured him. "But time is going fast."

"We can do it very quickly," he insisted. "Why start and stop like this? Why tomorrow? We're here right now."

This is what I can't take, she thought. Now everything gone and spoil. I have to work out where I going to sleep and all he want to do is f——k. If he could wait a while I might give him a little thing. But I have to see where I laying my head tonight. It have a few place down by the waterfront that them sailors use. I wonder how much for those. It can't be too much. And I only need it for the night. But anything you spend to get a room, she told herself, is taking money from your shoes. Now what going happen with that?

"Simón," she asked, "how much for the English ones again?"

"I really don't care anymore. I hope you get to where you're going safely. I'm gone."

"Listen, Simón," Estrella bluffed. "Since you ride me on that horse and my feet get to relax, I could march with Mr. Hitler army from Tokyo to Japan and ain't care. You hear me? So don't talk to me 'bout how you going to ride away and leave me. Everything have its time. And every time have its thing. And this is not the time for no more thing. You understand?"

"I have a thing," he said, and took her by the arm. "Does it have a time as well?"

"I ain't know," she answered as she tried to pull away. She was separated from her basket. If she didn't have it then she couldn't run away.

"Simón," she reasoned, as she felt her back against the heavy body of the horse, "you was going somewhere. Wherever you was going you have to get there. You ain't have no time for this. I tell you tomorrow. Then let it be tomorrow, nuh. Why so much of a haste?"

"If we're going to f——k, let's f——k," he muttered. "Are we going to f——k?"

"I ain't like that kinda language, Simón. I really ain't like it at all. A nice man like you shouldn't say those things, Simón. They ain't suit a gentleman like you."

His breath was hot against her face. The horse was firm against her back. A presence like a wall. She was about to bite him, then remembered that he'd talked about a gun.

If you take the knife and stab him you could get away, she thought. But what going happen after that? All his family is police. They going lock you up. You is a outcast. Ain't nobody coming to talk for you. And even so, what your grandmother and Big Tuck could do? I born unlucky. I born f——king unlucky to *rass*. Lemme rub my thighs and see. I still a little wetty. I could turn my mind to something else.

"Come," she said, abruptly. "Since you have to f——k me, let's f——k. But don't take too damn long."

She reached under her skirt and tugged away her bloomers and grumbled as he kissed her on the neck.

"Baby, can you just pretend?" he asked her in a whining way.

"Simón, pretend that what?"

"That . . . that you like this. That you like me."

"But after this I won't like you no more. Because everything have to be how you want it. You don't give me any consideration.

I really have to get to town. I tell you we can do this tomorrow. But your tomorrow have to come and mash up my today. I wish I could say I ain't like you, Simón. If it was so, this wouldn't be so bad."

"Look . . . I'm sorry."

"Don't confuse me. Just be quick."

She stomped across the grass toward the tree.

"Maybe we should lie down in the grass," he told her sweetly. "I want to lie on you and touch you. I don't want to be like no beast."

"Look, I wash my hair today and all sort of things on that ground, and I don't have no more change of clothes. I ain't do this because I want to do this, Simón. Is because this is how it have to be. Push it in. Do it now so we can go."

"Don't be savage."

She was resisting his control and he'd begun to worry that she was about to change her mind—slam it like a door. And in the anonymity of the darkness, in the isolated wildness of the bush, with the feel and taste of her distinct—like voices egging him on, he accepted that he didn't have the nerve to pry her open, although he had a coiled emotion that he thought might be the urge. The discordant echo of these clashing feelings rang and hummed along his bones, feeding back distortion to his moral core, amplifying everything till all that he could hear inside his head was one gigantic, primal roar of shame.

"Don't insult me, Simón, or I going to stop right now."

"Can't you just be nice?"

"To who?"

"Stop talking. You're making this worse."

As she leaned against the tree she thought, Look at what I come to? I really born unlucky. Look. I have the proof.

She didn't fight him when he hooked one thigh beneath the knee, and the truth is that he didn't do it in a forceful way.

They proceeded with the strained cooperation of a pair of

office clerks. She did what she could but nothing more, moving every now and then; and when he tried to kiss her she would turn so that his lips would skid across her cheeks. When he dipped and tried to put her knee across his shoulder, she didn't let her body help him with the weight, and grumbled when he sucked his teeth and clamped her thigh against his ribs. Her resistance was unnerving, and he found himself existing in a dim suspended state of neither pleasure nor disgust, and suffered through a kind of stultifying rote, wishing he could come . . . in and out . . . out and in . . . like sorting bags of mail.

Half an hour later when he wasn't done, she reached into her pocket for her knife and pressed the point behind his ear.

"Simón, is either I put down my leg or you done right now."

"One more. Don't kill me. Two more. Please wait."

"Stop it, Simón. Stop it. You ain't feeling how I dry?"

The danger of the knife against him brought his feelings to an edge, and when she told him that she'd slit his throat he felt the vertigo of tumbling over and he wanted to give her anything she wanted in the world.

"You want the shoes?"

"Just finish now."

"Reach around the back into my wallet. It have ten or twenty pounds."

IT WAS A little after midnight when they rode into town, which was as dark and unreflective as a glass of port. Under blackout orders, all lights were off, all curtains drawn, and the smoke that blew from Black Well dimmed the glitter of the moon.

The balance of the journey had been passed in silence. Their lips were sealed by shame. When they had remounted he'd let her sit behind him so he wouldn't have to face the fact that she was there.

Estrella wasn't sure if she'd been raped. He'd overpowered

her, she knew, but not with anything she knew as force; after all, she'd been the one to pull the knife.

Maybe I just worthless, in truth, she'd told herself. I like to say I unlucky. But maybe I just worthless in truth. So you have a knife and he ain't beat you. He ain't put no gun to you. He ain't put you on the ground. And then he give you money and you take it. That ain't sound like rape when you put it like that. That sound like whore to me.

Maybe I ain't really know myself in truth. Maybe them people at the cove know me better than I really know myself. Maybe them old people see things in me I ain't really see. Them dirty parts. Them nasty parts. Them worthless parts.

If I never take the money, I wonder if I'd feel a different way? I ain't know. I ain't know. But I can't give it back. It ain't make no sense. If I give it back, I going feel like nothing never come from it. Like I ain't get nothing for my pain. 'Cause what I feeling right now is pain. Which one carry more shame? A prostitute or a careless girl that get rape? I ain't really know . . .

She spent the balance of the journey in a deep deliberation. Either way the people of the cove would say that she'd gotten everything that she deserved, and her name would be a watermark for years to come. *Continue on your ways and end up like Estrella. Go on. Continue. You will see.*

When they'd come across the iron bridge that led into the town, she felt a gradual lightening of her mood, and she consoled herself by saying that everything between the cove and town were sacrificial acts, and paid homage to all the powers that she knew . . . God, the *orishas,* the abstract unseen . . . and told herself that she was not alone, that Vashti and Joseph and the woman with the red bandanna would be sad if they knew what had happened . . . that she was beautiful and precious . . . that she'd be missed if she were taken from this world.

"I'm sorry," said the rider when he'd helped her off the horse before the statue of Horatio Nelson. Behind her was the lapping harbor. Across the street, behind him, were rows of old buildings on Nelson Square.

"I have it in my heart to forgive you," she said, "but I ain't going to lie—it going be harder to forgive myself."

"I don't know what to do."

"I ain't ask you for nothing," she said blankly, scooping sand over the fragile memories, hiding them like turtle eggs. "I have twenty extra pounds. I ask for a ride and you gimme a ride. At the time, I just ain't know the price."

"I hope you get your shoes," he said. "I hope they're strong. I hope they fit you good."

"And I hope you get what you deserve. I get my share tonight."

He touched her hand, and for reasons that she didn't fully comprehend, she drew him close and kissed him quickly, hoping that he'd do something to make her think that what she thought of him was wrong—unsure of what she'd take as proof.

She squinted hard to watch him mount the horse, but she didn't watch him ride away.

It began to drizzle, and she made her way across the street into the square. In the dark, she picked her way along a cobbled path that sprayed out from the fountain, and sheltered on a bench beneath a tree.

When the rain began to pour, she dashed into the portal of a colonnaded building on the square.

Nelson Square, the oldest part of the town, was a collection of fine buildings, some in marble, some in coral stone, constructed in the sixteen hundreds—in San Carlos, a period of excess at the height of Spanish rule. Many of them had colonnades, stained glass, and Moorish courtyards, evoking larger, grander squares in Old Havana.

One side was open to the sea; two sides were closed and the

third was dominated by a large brick building with a grand archway that opened on the Queens, the boulevard that rose along the row of former mansions to the governor's gate, the address of Salan's and La Sala—the restaurant and store of her dreams.

In her blue skirt and striped blouse that was damp with man smell, sweat and rain, Estrella Thompson found a spot beside the high stone steps of the court. Before she fell asleep she took her brassiere from her pocket and tickled her nose, grateful that her day was done.

## IX.

"GET UP, YOU."

"What the devil is she doing here?"

"She's sleeping. Take your time."

At a little after four in the morning, Estrella was awakened from a dream in which she'd been walking through the battlefields of Europe in a pair of English shoes with Tuck and her grandmother, when she felt a pair of hands against her limbs and sat up to be blinded by a light. In the glare, she saw what looked like effigies . . . or ghosts . . . ghosts with heads like turtle shells.

They were home guards, Carlitos on patrol, and they were dressed like English soldiers. But not like English soldiers in India or Egypt, who sported khaki drill and light slouch hats to keep their bodies cool. These fellows were colonials in an unimportant place, and as such were issued surplus kit from World War I—heavy olive wool designed to hold the body's heat.

So they were Carlitos, but Carlitos of a special kind—local whites, irregulars who'd volunteered for duty as they'd been raised to do. The impulse wasn't bravery or valor or anything that would be lauded at their graves. They'd volunteered for reasons that were hormonal, a part of an old, established cycle of blood—it was better to stop a bullet than to give the people with the most to gain a taste of what it meant to organize and kill with guns.

"Hands up. Don't move. Are you deaf? I said don't move."

Estrella dipped and cowered with an arm above her brows to save her pupils from the light. When her eyes adjusted she observed that there were three.

"Declare your business," said the one who held the lantern. Of the other two, one rubbed a billy club against his palm. The other held a wooden rifle with the muzzle pointing down.

Declare your business, she repeated to herself. What he really mean to say by that?

Although she spoke English, it was sometimes hard for her to understand official speech. The gun was frightening in itself, but it also made her think of Simón; and she stood stiffly, a nervous grin across her face, trying to look polite, wondering if her understanding was correct.

"Bloody insubordinate," the lantern bearer said. "She's trying to be difficult and I'm running out of patience and time. I'm tired and I'm hot. The shift is almost done. Just make it simple. Lock her up."

"But I ain't do nothing wrong," Estrella said in disbelief. "Lock me up for what?"

"Well, declare your bloody business, then," the lantern bearer said.

"But what you mean by that?"

The one who held the rifle leaned toward the lantern bearer's ear.

"But according to the proper regulations, you're supposed to ask her name and age and where she lives."

The lantern bearer shouted, "Who the hell put you in charge?"

"It's not about being in charge. It's about correct procedure. Is this how you'd interrogate a spy?"

"Which she is—obviously. Another German in disguise."

The one who had the billy club began to laugh.

Now that is what you call a boof, Estrella thought. When he tell him that is like he stun him with a uppercut. Which part of me could be a spy? I thought it ain't have nobody who could boof like me, but I meet my match tonight.

"Are you mocking me, you little shit?" the lantern bearer asked.

The one who held the rifle stepped in front of her and cut him off.

"Little darling, what's your name? We're out on duty. There's a curfew going on. Do you understand me? Okay. Let me say it in *sancoche*."

When she'd heard his explanation, she was irritated with herself. For her, the war was an important thing, and from what the rifleman had told her, she'd wasted their time.

"You're not allowed to sleep out here," he added. "Everybody must be off the street. If you want we can give you a ride."

"I live real far from here, sir."

"How far?" the lantern bearer asked in English, stepping forward as he tugged the rifle holder to the rear.

"Way up in a far place, sir?"

The one who had the billy club began to whisper to the rifleman, who sucked his teeth and tramped away.

"And what's that far place called?"

He brought the lantern close against her face and she could feel and smell the heat.

Carefully, she said, "That kinda place, sir, ain't have no name."

"If you don't have a place to go," he told her in a change of voice, "I could arrange for you to have one for the night. I think a night would help you to get over whatever's put you in this mood. What do you think? I could make that happen. Is that what you want?"

The subtlety had missed her, and she shrugged and said, "Okay."

He took her answer for a taunt and led her down the steps across the square, which had been puddled by the rain.

On the street, adjacent to the statue where Simón had left her, was a car, which in daylight would reveal itself to be a white-walled Buick Century—silver, with a running board and bug-eyed headlamps on its elongated nose.

As she felt the plush interior pressing on her back, Estrella felt relieved. Not a horse. Not a truck. But a f——king motorcar. On top of that, a bed in which to sleep.

The lantern bearer sat behind the wheel and asked the one who had the billy club to sit beside him. The rifle holder sat beside Estrella in the back. Someone pressed a button and a motor whirred the iron roof away, and she slouched with deep amazement in the toffee-colored seat.

When they'd driven up and down the foreshore road, completing their patrol, she sat up suddenly and turned toward the rifleman, and introduced herself in her most formal English: "I'm sorry. I'm Estrella. Nice to meet you. I didn't catch your name?"

He nodded, lit a cigarette and stuck it in his young, impassive face.

The driver tossed his head and ordered, "Stub that bloody light."

The rifle holder answered: "Go to hell," and clamped the gun between his knees.

"You don't listen. That's your problem."

"Daddy, I'm a grown man with a family, for Jesus' sake. I'm not a child anymore."

The father tapped the shoulder of his younger son, who rode beside him.

"Your brother told me he's a grown man. What do you think of that? The words were his, not mine. A grown man who can't do a bloody thing. You would think a grown man raised by good parents would have his own car by now. It's his turn to do transportation on patrol and he shows up in his father-in-law's big American car, which he can't even drive because the steering wheel is on the other bloody side. You would think a grown man would be able to prevent his wife from running around like a common whore. You would think a grown man would stop having bastard tadpole children all over this bloody island without having any practical means of their support. You would think a grown man who had strings pulled so he could get into Cambridge would have paid attention and come back to this place with some damn respect. So he fails at everything and you pull more strings, and he gets appointed head of one of the island's finest schools. But did he hold on to the job? No! He goes off be some kind of artist, like a bloody fag. You would think a grown man would realize that you can't build a business or a future or respectability from painting like a fairy or writing stupid books. Paint a house, for God's sake. Or be whatever you call the people who serve the books in the library . . . those ill-tempered spinsters. You would think a grown man would, by now, have taken stock . . ."

"I get the point," the younger son objected. "People are different, Daddy. Everybody can't be the same. Will just needs a little bit of time."

They'd gone around the park and had passed beneath the arch that opened on the Queens, and the six cylinders pulled them smoothly up the grade between the former mansions and the median with the flowers and the trees.

"Time?" the father shouted. "Who has a lot of that these days? None of us have time. Black Well is a mess. They rioted again. Over what, who bloody knows. We have no bloody coconuts. They've all got bloody blight. The frigging Germans just might win the war. And the Chinese and the Lebanese are so deceitful and underhanded, they're making wads of money trading while we sit on sugar that nobody wants, while we feed cows that can't bring you ten pounds at the abattoir."

"We're part Irish," said the older son, who had just turned thirty-two. "Once upon a time they were new here too. But I know it's not the same. The rules have changed. Now we make them."

"Trying be sarcastic?"

"No. More along the lines of sardonic."

"The Lebanese are saints. Of course. Of course. But of course you know this. Your wife is one of them." He stopped the car and leaned across his seat. "Where is she now? Do you know? How do you know she hasn't left your house while you're out here risking life and limb for King and country? The little bitch. Knowing her, she's leaving footprints in your ceiling. Giggling in your bed."

The man who held the rifle wiped his face. The car began to move again.

Estrella couldn't see for certain, but she knew that there were tears, and she felt obliged to take his hand and reassure him that he'd be okay, that she knew what it was like to hear that what you loved was wrong and that your passions were just careless dreams, that she'd bought from Lebanese people and everything was nice, and that the Chinese them was nice ones too, and that a Chinese girl had helped her with her books, that you had to be a bright, bright man to be headmaster, that you shouldn't listen when your family tried to put you down, 'cause that is all they do—try to give you bad eye and bad mouth and blight your ambition and bring down your will, that if your wife is out of order then is up to you to ask her why she always fooling round, 'cause woman ain't just wicked so, that they're wicked when they feel that something wicked is the only thing that's left to do . . . like how she, Estrella Thompson, had to pinch a little money when she had to buy a book because she ain't grow with people who understand that books is things that people have to have.

I have to thief from them when I run away, because I need to get a start in life and they ain't want me reach nowhere. But they should see me now. In a motorcar . . . in a motorcar like those that bring the fancy English ladies to La Sala . . . see there, we just pass it now . . . the place where I see the man send the woman the note that make her face turn red like blood.

Look at me now. Driving in that kinda car. And look how the car just pulling smooth like them boat that have engine. And look how it feel nice when the breeze blowing right past my face. And look how my life turn interesting already, and I ain't fully even reach where I going in life . . . and look now . . . I just pass Salan's, where I going to get my shoes.

Where you is, Grandma? And where you is, Big Tuck? Nowhere where nobody who have anything to think 'bout even care. A place that ain't even have no name. A place that even other fishermen refer to as "back so" or "over so" or "under the cliff." How somebody can be happy when they come from a place that ain't have no name?

But I have a name. My name is Estrella Roselyn Maria Eugenia Thompson, and you see how I black so? And you see how my foot bare so? Is white man driving me, though, like how black men drive them English ladies. And I take that as a sign.

When I go back and see my grandmother and Big Tuck, people going to know my name, and they will hear other people call my name and they will want to say, "That's my granddaughter." But how you could bring yourself to say, "That's my granddaughter" when is you tell me to leave? When is you turn me out like Joseph in the Bible?

And I ain't really want to run away. And when I think about it now, I wasn't going to really run away. But I have my pride. And when my own grandmother come to me and tell me that I have to leave, and when none of my friends come to me and say, "Here, take this sixpence that I saving up," or "Don't worry, I talk to my mother and she say you could come stay by we," or "I praying for you. I praying for you. You know if I was a big person I would put down my foot," I had to make a move.

And if some of them had done that . . . if some o' them had done what they bound to do as friends, then them evil people couldn't go on with their stupidness. They couldn't go on with their wickedness. They couldn't do something as ignorant, worthless, ungodly and savage like turning out a child.

I ain't plan to tell nobody I was going to leave. Because I wasn't going to leave. But they test my pride. They question my ambition. They put a dare to me.

But is jealous they jealous like Joseph brothers. And one day, one day—it might take a while, but is sure to come—a blight going to take this island, and they going to have to come to Seville. And they going see me and ain't even know is me until I tell them. That is how much I going change.

"Mister, don't mind," she whispered to the rifleman beside her as she tapped his shoulder through the heavy wool. "Mister, don't you mind."

Without looking, he removed her hand and gently squeezed it with condolence. For her. For him. For history. For life.

"I'm sorry, miss," he muttered.

His father and his brother laughed.

"Is okay," she said. "Is awright."

AT THE GOVERNOR'S gate they made a left and took the rising stretch of road that led to an exclusive area called Savanna Ridge.

The governor's tall brick fence was on their right, and in the thinning darkness she could see the shadow of the town becoming smaller, shrinking like a drought-afflicted lake. Out to sea, a golden razor sliced along the dark horizon line.

She felt a nudge and looked at Will, the one beside her with the gun, who wrestled with a hook along his belt and handed her his water can. It was made of tin and dented, with a body like a wheel, and had a short, thick neck with a big, wide mouth.

Around the neck there was a collar, with a chain that held the cap. And as Estrella tipped her head and sucked and gulped and swallowed, making loud barbaric sounds, the cap began to beat against the tin.

The water had a bad metallic taste, and on the rim there was the been-up-late-all-night aroma of a soldier's mouth. But she drank it with a grateful throat, and sloshed it round her teeth and gums and heard its falling change in pitch as it began to fill her stomach, rising from a bellow to a gurgle that was shrill, like a spigot spewing beer into a mug.

"It have more, please?"

She used her sleeve to wipe her lips.

Will leaned against the seat in front of him.

"Are you finished with your water?"

His brother and his father passed him their cans and he gave them to the girl, who began to drink in spurts, tossing back her head and guzzling, then pausing to breathe deeply and think.

Ahead of them she saw the fork that led along Savanna Ridge, whose lovely homes she knew from all the times that she'd been sent by her grandmother with deliveries from the market—times at which she'd trotted up the Queens with trays of snappers packed in ice and wrapped in plantain leaves and sugar sacks upon her head, and idle by a kitchen door and gaze down at the grand savanna—an imposing sward behind the governor's house—while she waited to be paid.

As they came upon the fork, she felt that they were taking her to one of these, a house that she imagined would be owned by one of them, because the owners of these houses on Savanna Ridge were white. She began to wonder if she'd ever seen their wives at La Sala, but she didn't linger on this thought, which faded quickly as she thought of how and where she'd sleep . . . on a cot perhaps, or on the floor . . . or squeezed into a wicker chair out on the porch.

As if how and where she'd sleep had been decided, she began to think about the coming morning. Then, she planned to go to town to buy her shoes. And if she didn't have enough to buy an English pair, she'd buy whatever pair she could afford. Is not like the shoes would come with *England* stamp on it, she thought. And if *England* stamp on it, it must have something you could use to rub it off.

That decided, she began to think about the coming morning once again, and saw herself behind a house with a veranda as grand as the deck of a ship, sitting in the grass and gazing through the mist at the sward.

Her brows drew tight and wrinkled as she summoned all the details of the view—the little zoo and garden in the corner by the bridge across the Abuelito River . . . in the center, clouds reflecting off the pond, which was encircled by a ring of palms . . . at the racetrack, Queen Victoria Park, grooms and jockeys exercising horses, wheeling them round the final bend and easing as they came into the straight, the trainers in the grandstand watching through field glasses . . . beside the track, the cricket pitch, the Nelson Oval, where herons floated just above the grass like laundry, flopping on the stones that made a loop to mark the boundary line . . . and above it all the smooth, unbroken rise of Mt. Diablo's cone . . . and in its foothills, old estates.

If it was up to me, Estrella thought, the way I feeling now, there wouldn't be another sea. If is me alone in this world I would dry up every sea it have and put the fishes in another place . . . like a river or a pond . . . so it would still have fish to eat. But there wouldn't be a single piece for me. I ain't going eat fish or nothing from the sea no more. Only chicken and meat and goat. Chicken back and cow foot and goat head for me. I done with the sea. And when it dry up, if it have anybody who have somewhere far to go they could build a train along the seabed where the water used to be. I ain't want to wake up and see no goddamn blue tomorrow morning. All I want to see is green.

When they continued up the hill and didn't take the branching road a mood of apprehension fell upon the car. Unconsciously, Estrella placed a hand against the lock and scratched her feet against the mat, her instincts dulled by lack of sleep.

"I thought we was going to a place that have a bed?" she said.

"Oh," the father answered, drumming on the wheel and glancing at his younger son. "They have beds there, don't they?"

"Where?" Estrella asked.

They didn't answer, and she crossed her arms and wondered what to do.

"Where we going?" she asked the one beside her, as she kneeled against the seat. "Why nobody ain't talking?" She put her hand against his shoulder. "Somebody talk to me."

With a heavy sigh he mumbled, "We're going up to Thunder Hill."

## X.

IT WAS A citadel constructed in the 1800s by the British on a ridge a thousand feet above the town. There were many buildings there. Among them were the prison and the island's oldest working fort.

"Will," she said in disbelief, sinking in her seat, "is there you really taking me?"

"Hold her," said the father.

Will looked at her and didn't move.

"Will, I gave you an order."

"Father, go to bloody hell."

"You," he shouted at his younger son. "Get in the back right now."

"This is really stupid," said the younger son, who did as he was told.

I lose, Estrella thought. I lose. I f——king gamble and I lose.

I ain't do nothing wrong. I ain't trouble nobody. But look how everything was going good. They even give me water and let me drink. They ask me if I want a ride. I say yes. They ask me if I want a bed. I say yes. Is because I laugh? They ain't still vex 'bout that? If is that, then I sorry. But it can't be that. Maybe they change they mind and think I is a spy for true. But a spy for who? Maybe they telling lie. Maybe they ain't even going where they say. Maybe they carrying me away to take advantage. I think is that you know. I think is that. In fact I know is that. I wonder if is that? What else they could want to do me but rape me off? 'Cause I ain't do nothing.

Calm yourself, Estrella. Calm yourself. Don't act like Pepper now. Is three of them and one of them is holding you. If you try to fight them with your body they will win. Play fool to catch the wise. Go on like you going to sleep. And when you feel his hand ease up, then that is when you bolt. One man take advantage already and you had the chance to use the knife. But what you do? You acted like a fool.

Jesus Christ come off your cross and witness this today—if I get the chance again I ain't thinking what to do. I ain't guessing what to do. I know what I going to do. I going jam them with this knife. And who dead—dead. And who live—live. Because I tired. Everything I touch is like I wrong. Everybody want to advantage me. From my grandmother and Big Tuck and them coolie people down by Speyside. Is what wrong with me so? Is what they see in me so that make them think they could do that? Even Joseph. He nice and thing, but he just couldn't gimme a blasted ride without wanting to feel me on my leg. And that Simón Bolívar. He's another thing. He going to go down in history. I wonder if he know? He going to go down in history as the last f——king man who advantage me. Every rope have a end. And every hook have a point. And I at the end of my hook right now. And somebody going to get hurt.

Thunder Hill had always seemed foreboding to the girl. She'd seen it many times by boat and had always thought it had an evil look.

Up close it was larger than she'd thought. It was not a single building, but many buildings carefully emplaced on different heights, and every level had a scheme of thick retaining walls— some of them as thick as seven feet.

After coiling upward with the thick retaining walls for three miles, passing many ruins on the slopes below, they parked on the parade ground, which was grassy, and in width and length a little smaller than a soccer field.

"You're not going to jail," Will, the older brother said. He pointed to another building on an upper hill. "We're going over there."

*There* was the citadel, a massive installation with an inner courtyard large enough to hold five thousand troops. It was sunk into the hill and surrounded by a trench, which had made it hard to hit in war. Beside the prison, it was the only portion of the complex that was still in use, and below the ramp that led toward it they could see platoons of U.S. soldiers doing calisthenics on a grassy rise.

"Dad, why're we stopping?" asked the younger son, annoyed.

The father answered, "Just to let her walk."

"With all due respect, Dad, I don't have time for this. We're the last ones back, I'm sure. We should've been here hours ago. You and Will can sort this out. Let's go."

The father cleared his throat and put the car in the gear, and they drove along a ramp toward the citadel, where at the gate, the father mumbled, "Rawle."

On hearing this, the guard, who'd come on duty after they'd gone on their patrol, saluted them although they wore no signs of rank, and begged them for a chance to wash the car.

*　　*　　*

INSIDE, THEY PARKED adjacent to a line of trucks and armored cars with canons and machine guns. The younger son still holding her, the four of them got out.

To Estrella, her real hope as she saw it was the diver. Would he remember me? she wondered, after all this time. And if he did, would he talk on her behalf? Was he one of the men out there in undershirt and trousers exercising?

She was standing with her back against the car and the men who'd detained her were standing in a semicircle, touching length away. Their faces had expressions that she couldn't read.

"So, smarty," the father said, taking off his helmet, which he clamped beneath his arm, "what should we do with you now?"

He was tired, and he shook his head to make himself alert. Like his sons, who'd taken off their helmets as well, his hair was blonde with streaks of sandy brown.

"I have a friend," she said. "A soldier man who do man hoovers in the sea . . ."

As she spoke to them she slyly watched the gate. From here to there, she estimated, was a hundred yards. She also paid attention to their stance, how they moved their weight, how sometimes they'd lean apart to stretch or gesture, creating accidental gaps between them, tempting her to drop her head and run. And each time that she thought of this and waited for a better time, her desperation grew and she felt the urge to bet her life as would a gambler in the hole.

If I just run just like so, they could just shoot me, she thought. And I'd be too far to fight them with my knife. But if I have that gun, I could protect myself, and if that guard boy who salute them try to stop me, I would shoot that f——ker too. I would shoot every last f——king o' of them. Whatever amount o' bullet it could have in this gun . . . how I feeling now . . . I ain't 'fraid to use it.

Dawn had begun to break by now and Estrella had an understanding of each face. Will, the older son, who was in his early thirties, had clear blue eyes. The father had a slim mustache. The younger son had freckles and a dimple in his chin. They were all of average build, and she could see from their faces that their heavy uniforms had given them some added stock; but from their eyes, which were fatigued, she perceived them to be worn, and doubted that they'd have the strength to give pursuit.

"What's your name again?" the older brother asked.

He leaned against the gun as if it were a walking stick, with the stock against the damp stone floor.

"Estrella," she said, blinking sleep out of her eyes. "I told you once before."

His body heaved, his mouth opened, then he stopped. And he did this five more times, heaving then stopping, and changing his mind like a discus thrower warming up. Then finally, as everybody stared at him, he let it go.

"Look," he said, embarrassed. "Just get out of here. Go home."

She began to walk in circles. The sudden shift in circumstances was a lot for her to bear, the lack of plot disorienting. There was no clear pattern. No clear link between action and reaction. Cause and effect. It didn't feel like life.

"Just go home just like so?" she asked when she had settled.

He shook his head, excused himself and yawned.

"So what all this was about?" she asked, looking at each man in turn. "You must have a reason why you do me what you do?"

The father said, "One day it will soak in."

She shrugged and thought, One day in truth, but not right now. I ain't want to talk no more. I ain't care 'bout nothing no more. I just want to go my way and never see these people face again.

"So how I get back to town from here?" she asked.

They looked at her in silence. They hadn't thought that far.

"If I have to walk then I have to walk," she said, holding back her rage. Then speaking in a clear, respectful tone she asked, "Well, may I kindly have my things?"

They craned their necks and cocked their heads, confused.

"What things?" the father asked.

"That I bring from home." Her brows and voice were raised. "My basket with my blankets and my books . . . my clothes . . . my dolly . . . my soap . . ."

The father turned toward the younger son, the one who had the freckled face, raised his hands indifferently and shrugged.

"Sir, where are my things?" Estrella asked again. She rolled her fists and bit her lips, squeezing back the other words.

The father answered, "Must be where you left them, I suppose."

"Sir, you is the one who told me I had to come. Not that I want to make a big thing out o' this. But when you hold my arm and told me to come on and you bring me to the car I think one of you was going to bring my basket. You leave it? You sure? I ain't mean to take up your time, but we could look in the car?"

She began to walk around the Buick, peering inside, as they watched as if inebriated by a cocktail mix of surprise, regret and indifference, brows half-raised . . . skin softly tingling from a mild attack of nerves . . . something fearful, but not quite paranoia, an awareness that they might have hounded her so much that they had crossed the line and entered places that they didn't understand and therefore not equipped to rule.

"They were not my things," the father pointed out. "They were yours. What? Am I supposed to be your servant now? Same thing down at Speyside. Nobody wants to work on this damn island anymore. Everything is on the boss. Boss do this. Boss do that. Well, boss is tired now and boss wants to go home."

"You know all my money is in there, sir?" she droned, astounded by the loss. "I had it in my pocket but I move it. I wrap it up and put it in my basket right under my head in case it drop out of my pocket in the night. You know all my clothes in there, sir? You know that if I ain't get back my things I don't have nothing in this world, sir? When you answer me the way you answer me . . .

as if I ain't really lose nothing . . . like this is a simple thing . . .
you did know how much it had in there, sir?"

"I was only doing my job," he said glibly. "You weren't supposed to be there. If you had obeyed the law, then none of this
would have happened."

Desperate, Estrella trampled her pride and went down on one
knee. "I begging you for a drive into town to get my things, sir.
Please, sir, before somebody take my things away. I didn't mean
to talk fresh, sir. I didn't mean to offend you, sir. Sometimes I can
get carried away, sir, and talk like I don't have no sense or no up-
bringing, sir. But I am not a hooligan or virago, sir. Please, can
you carry me so I can go and get my things?"

"No, I can't," replied the man who owned the truck that took
her from the bridge across the island to the Caribbean coast.
"Carry you? I'm off duty now. But you're free to go on your own.
The lesson has been learned. That's what's most important. The
lesson has been learned."

Through the open gates of the gigantic fort, the broken-
hearted girl could see the eastern sky becoming filled with
shades of red. And in her head she thought she heard a creaking
as her heart began to fall.

Dazed, she made a step toward them, half-expecting them to
tell her not to move.

"I ain't know what to say no more," she said, when she'd
used her hands to part them. "But what you do to me is a sin. I
will take this lesson to my grave. It have some wicked people in
this world."

And as the father forced himself to laugh, so he could drown
his feelings of regret, Estrella Thompson ran toward the morning
on her blisters, hoping that the one who held the gun would raise
it, aim it and draw a breath, ensuring that the bullet that would
free her from this life would hit her clean between the shoulder
blades. This way she'd go home in a coffin instead of in disgrace.

## XI.

St. William Rawle—the older son—was driving down the hill. The car was big and the road was small with many twisting turns, and with the steering wheel on what Carlitos called the "other side" he found it hard to judge the curves, forcing him to stop at every corner just to calculate the angle of bend. Sometimes he stepped outside the car to look.

Considered from an unexpected point of view, the turns disoriented, made him question where he sat. In this way they called to mind the girl.

The last time that he'd felt this way was when he'd first encountered Graham Greene's *The Power and the Glory,* and had felt a sense of urgency to write about someone as complicated as the whisky priest.

Compassion, he'd thought. This is what writing is about—having compassion for the people on "the other side." And that's no easy thing to do.

So, he'd written and still wrote—without support or glory—publishing his efforts at his own expense.

It was hot and he'd raised the roof to shield him from the sun, and he used a yellow handkerchief to dab his neck as he perspired in his crushed white suit.

Alone in the car—his father and his brother had been taken in the Jag—he turned off the main when he'd passed the parade ground and drove along a lower rampart that led him to the wide, stone deck of a bastion.

The mighty stones had fallen over time, and what was left looked like a jaw with blackened teeth, and he could see the footprints of the various buildings that had crumbled—barracks, cisterns, storage rooms.

The bastion had been built like an arrow, a two-hundred-meter flying wedge lined on either side with cannons, some of which remained.

He wandered through the ruins in deep contemplation and went inside the old munitions building, which was larger than a parish church. It was cool and shaded there and he sat against a window ledge, his back to the outdoors, and thought about the girl, the whiteness of his suit intense against the gray, volcanic stone and beautiful against the ocean blue that filled the empty arches of the missing windows and doors.

He knew the girl, he thought. He knew her without knowing. But he'd like to know her more.

When he was headmaster he would meet this kind of girl. You'd be in your office on a Monday morning and one of your father's cronies—some member of the opera society or the yacht club, or some member of some board—would bring her in and introduce her as a Christian girl with sense and morals who deserved a chance, and you'd look at him and think, Okay, you've got an outside daughter and you went to church and got a case of guilt. Or if she's not your daughter, then she's the object of some kind of complicated love. And you would do what you could—which was a hell of a lot, and the girl would get in.

But these were not the circumstances of this girl . . . Estrella. She didn't think in English, but she spoke the kind we speak here fairly well—which tells you that she's been to school but not for many years. If she'd gone to school for longer, then her English vowels wouldn't be so short, or as she'd say it, "shot."

She could be a farm girl. She had that kind of ruggedness and strength. But if she were a farm girl then her hands would be as rough but in a different way. No . . . she didn't farm. She fished.

When you held her hand or when she held yours, you were stunned by the feeling that infused you—you don't even remember what happened. Only that she made you feel good . . . so good that for the rest of the ride you found it hard to talk. You know what farm girls feel like. No, she isn't one of them. Her calluses were in a line that ran along the inside of her thumbs to where they joined the fullness of her hand, and you could feel them climbing like a set of rungs along the outside of her pointer. You got those kinds of calluses from pulling on a line. No . . . she didn't farm. She didn't farm at all. She fished.

So Estrella is a fishing girl. From her voice, I'd say from down the wild Atlantic coast. She hadn't been in town for very long, because word like that would get around. And she surely didn't live in Black Well, where you went to find the young *negritas* that you pay to pose for you so you could paint them in the nude.

This is such a funny backward place, this island. It's okay to get young girls to stand around for hours in the flesh. But tell them that you want to write and paint for the rest of your life and they think you need to be committed.

But what is really weird is that this girl was sleeping in the street. Why would she have to do that? What could she have done? You get the sense that she's a warm and loving soul. What did she do?

Your family's your pride. You're nothing if you're not your blood. If someone kicks you out you just go somewhere else. A relative. A friend. Or you stay and make amends. Because to leave your household is a big disgrace. And you know this very well. Because your wife just told you that she wants a damn divorce and that's why you're here, marking time. You don't want to go home.

He walked outside across the flat expanse of stone, and stood there in the open thinking of Rebecca . . . Rebecca Salan . . . Rebecca Salan his wife, then walked toward the point at which the walls converged into a prow, and saw the land below him sheer away.

On the lower slopes, the lines of other ruins and the edges of the sweeping thick retaining walls were overlapping like the kind of waves that cause an undertow, and St. William Rawle, who'd gone away to Cambridge in the years before the war and had flunked out in disgrace, put his hands behind his back and dropped his chin, sorry, lonely and ashamed—at thirty-two, the unevacuated captain of a ship that had been wrecked against a reef, and thought about his wife and wondered what had happened to the girl.

After she'd run away he'd argued with his father, who'd insisted that he'd actually been nice. His younger brother listened, but he didn't intervene and only talked about it when his father went to change.

"Will, we know that he's an ass."

They were moving through the courtyard to the storeroom with their weapons and their clothes. "But you've got to understand . . . he's disappointed."

"Albert, what he did was wrong."

"True, but in a way she brought it on herself."

"How?"

He tapped his brother's shoulder, sorry for the shout.

"Insubordination. If you let them get away with that there's nothing left."

"Insubordination? She was frightened. She's a simple country girl."

"Don't get too high-minded now. You've screwed a lot of them."

"Why're we straying from the point?"

"But that *is* the point. You want to screw this girl and so you're getting sentimental."

"You're getting out of order now. Please stop it."

"Everybody likes to burn a little diesel now and then, but you've let this crossing overrule your life. What's this painting all about? Have you ever sold or shown a painting of a naked ass?"

"You just don't understand."

"Well . . ."

"Albert Rawle, you *are* your father's child."

"That's good. He gets respect."

"No. He gets castrated hate."

"Listen, Will, and listen good. England is at war. There's a madman in Berlin. There's an emperor in Japan who thinks he's God on earth. There are brutes in Italy and Spain who think their backward countries have a reason to exist beyond our need to have their women and their wine. And you want me to waste time on a spat about a little girl I hardly f——ing know? Go home to Rebecca. Whatever she might be, she's your wife. Do you hear me? Get some sleep. In the morning everything will be okay. Drive safely. Everything is dodgy from the other side."

## XII.

As St. William contemplated all these things, Estrella watched him from the shadow of a ruined barrack on a grassy ramp of earth, the length of her against the ground, her knife sideways across her mouth, stalking.

When they didn't shoot her, she had sped along the ramp and veered across the grass away from where she'd seen the Yankee soldiers and took refuge in a crumbled building where she hid and watched the fort to see if she was being pursued. After thirty nervous minutes, she began to execute her slow escape, moving down the hill on trails, staying off the main.

She was hiding in the bushes when she saw the car, and at first she wasn't going to give pursuit. But when she realized that the one who had the gun was now alone, an idea came to mind.

It might not have come to mind if the car had been driven by any of the other two, but his timid driving made her think of him as soft. He sat close against the wheel and craned his neck across the dash so he could see the nose; and seeing this and thinking of the way that almost everything he'd said was overruled, she chose him as the object of a lesson in revenge.

At one point she was sure that he'd seen her when she tried to dash across the main before he came around a bend. But he was focused on his inner life and didn't notice when she spun around and dived into the bush.

Lying on her side, she said while watching him go by: "You would die in war in Europe. You're so careless and so soft." As soon as she said this, an image came to mind, an image that was instantly translated to a thought. It was an image of a knife against a throat, which was translated as, "I have to get him in the car." After that there were no other thoughts. Just actions. Running. Hiding. Jumping. Rolling. Scaling. Shunting. Creeping. Crawling. Darting . . . until now.

As she watched him walking back and forth across the lonely open deck, two truckloads of soldiers rumbled down the hill. If I going to do it then I have to do it now, she thought.

That man ain't going stand up there all morning. Any minute now he going to go about his business. And if he goes before you do what you're suppose to do, then your plan get spoil.

If he could just frighten, she thought, as she disciplined her nerves. If he could just frighten when he come and see me in the car, and don't try to wrestle . . . then it would be awright. Because as I lying here I ain't want to cut nobody anymore. Them things easy to think 'bout, but they hard to do unless you have them kinda mind. And I ain't have them kinda mind.

I have it sometimes, but I ain't have it right now. That's why it ain't good to talk out your intentions, even to yourself. 'Cause if you talk them is like you do them already, and you ain't going have the feeling to do them again.

Is like when somebody tell you the last part of a joke. You ain't bother want to hear the joke again. You know the whole joke now. Same way, I lie down here thinking what I going to do, and now I ain't feel to do it.

I want to do it, but I ain't *feel* to do it. And that is two different things. Is like when a person want you to do something, and you want to do it just because that person ask you, especially when they ask you in a forcing way.

Well, something inside me *want* me to do this thing. Want me to shuffle down this hillside and hide in that car and jump up when that man pull that door and drag him by the arm inside and tell him, "Shut your mouth. Shut your mouth. Shut your goddamn mouth and listen to me right now before I open up your f——king gills and gut you. I going take you for a ride just like how you take me for a ride. I going take you outta your way and mash up whatever business you have, just like how you mash up mine. How that feel now? How that feel? This is what you going to do. You going to take me back where you find me so I can find my things. And just in case we don't find it, you going have to gimme a hundred . . . no . . . a thousand pounds as pay for what I lose and for how much you make me go through. For all the suffer I suffer. For all the pain I feel. And as a matter of fact, gimme that money right now 'cause I ain't trust you. I ain't trust you at all. I used to trust you one time. But I ain't trust you again. You grow up and hear all kinda thing 'bout all kinda people how they thief. But nobody ever tell you white man thief too. You hear how everybody thief. And they always say we nigger is the worst. And I myself use to think so too. But I see for myself now. All man is man. All flesh is flesh. Drive this f——king car right now and drive it fast. I lose too much time already. I have a lot of catching up to do. You ain't going to hold me back no more."

That's what I *want* to do, she thought. But that ain't what I *feel* to do. Maybe I is a coward or something. But that ain't what I feel to do. And I ain't really know what I feel to do. All I know is that I want back my things and my money. And I ain't want to fuss no more.

Her head was heavy with combusting thoughts, and the heat was as solid as a piston pumping downward in its case, and she stood up as the man began to move toward the car.

Something was about to happen. What, she wasn't sure. And she felt it was important to look at her surroundings. As if she might be seeing them for the final time.

Down the coast, and to her left, she saw the hooking headlands of the harbor in Seville, but a spur came angling down across her line of sight and she couldn't see the town. In the sky, beyond the spur, there was a stack of piling clouds. It would rain.

It would rain. But she would have known this even if she hadn't seen the clouds. She would have known this even if she'd only seen the water, which was frilled with waves, or if she'd simply closed her eyes and concentrated as she breathed, for as a daughter of the sea she'd learned to smell the rain from miles away, for sharks were born to catch the faintest scent of blood.

"Hey."

She withdrew behind the column with her back against the stone.

"Hey."

She put away the knife. The voice had been hers.

"Who's there?" St. William called.

From her hiding place, she saw him cock his head, trying to find the sound.

"Come."

"Who's there?"

"Come."

"Come where?"

"Up here."

He put his hands against his hips.

"Is it who I think it is?"

"I can't read your mind."

"Is it . . . is it you?"

"Is me . . . yes . . . is me."

He pointed at the ramp.

"What are you doing there?"

"I don't know."

"Well . . . what do you want?"

She swallowed.

"I don't know. Just come."

"There's no one here. Just me. They're gone."

"I know."

"So come."

"Why I should come to you?"

"The ramp is very steep."

She sucked her teeth and thought, I ain't able for all this *rass* right now.

"You know what? Just forget it. Just go your way. I ain't want no worries anymore."

"I don't want trouble either. If you want, let's talk."

"Where?"

He looked around and dabbed his brows.

"Let's do it in the car."

She drummed her fingers on the wall.

"No. If you want to talk to me, you have to come here."

He was too far away for her to hear his footsteps growing closer, but close enough for her to hear the fact of leather crunching over the ground.

In the middle of the floor there was a pool where rain had settled. When she went to wash her feet she saw reflections of her face and thought, You ain't look like nothing, And you have to look like something when you meet this man. He have to look at you and judge you as a person that is talking sense. And he ain't going to hear what you saying proper if you looking like a tramp.

Yesterday you look like something. When you bathe off and you was riding in the back o' Joseph truck, every man was looking hard. Now you look like chew-up-and-spit-out. Who would find you interesting now? Who would give you a job? You could go to the Chinese shop and beg a little alms from the girl who help you with your books. But where you would go from there? Back to your grandmother and Big Tuck and plead with them to take you in . . . looking mash up so, and ragged so, and smelling so? So they could ask you what you was doing and what happen to the things you leave with? Eh-eh, you gone with high pride and big ambition and come right back with two long hands like . . . Rawle!

The skin along her body prickled when it struck her that the man who was approaching was the one who'd gone away to England and returned with two long hands, the legendary failure invoked by Big Tuck.

She could hear the forward motion of his footsteps now and with a greater urgency began to slap the dirt out of her clothes.

Tuck might be a wicked f———ker; but this time I taking what he say, 'cause I hear the father cuss him 'bout the same damn thing . . . how he gone to big school in England and ain't come back with nought. Well, is a good thing you never stick him with you knife, because now you have a better chance to get what you want. Because that man brain ain't sharp like yours. You could outbrain him. He's a dunce.

Don't care how he was headmaster. The man is a blasted dunce. His own father say so. And no dunce man going outbrain me. I going talk to him like a barrister. I going make my case. And if he is solider man or a policeman or whatever he suppose to be then he suppose to know the law. And I read 'bout them big barrister how they persecute they case when people thief and dirty other people name. And I hear it on the rediffusion box as well. Well if this dunce man is the law then I going persecute my case against him and win. 'Cause what they do me wasn't right.

They take advantage. And I tired of people taking advantage of me. Because of people taking advantage why I ain't wearing my shoes now, and going about the place to find my job. And no way under the sun that could be right.

She spat into her hands and smoothed her hair and scooped

it into one, while she used one foot to scrub the other in the dirty pool. Deciding that her clothes were too dirty, she turned them inside out. The colors on the inside had a richer tone. They were not as badly bleached. And she rolled her cuffs above her elbow, for the buttons had been lost, and swung out from behind the column—solid in her presence as a door.

"Mr. Rawle," she said in her most formal English, swinging her arms the way a pitcher does while warming up, "I need to speak with you."

He paused along the ramp, some thirty yards away, and eased his hat off his wet brow, leaning with his forearms on his forward knee, frozen in a stride.

"Mr. Rawle," Estrella called again. She raised her voice and placed her hands against her hips. "Mr. Rawle, you need to come right now. I need to talk to you."

The seams that lined her face from mouth to cheek were pulsing as she walked, and when her shadow striped his shoulders and his back he looked away and winced as if he thought he would be caned, which unleashed a brutal instinct from her core, urging her to hook him in the collarbone, use his hat to slap his face and give him what the British called "a proper straightening out."

"Mr. Rawle," she said. "I come to talk to you because—as a soldier man or policeman or whatever kinda man you is—you are the law. My name as I told you before is Estrella Thompson, and I have come to persecute my case in front of you. Yesterday afternoon, I left my home to come to town to buy a pair of shoes because I want to get a decent job so I could improve myself in life. I will be honest with you—my grandparents put me out. They are ignorant people. They don't want to learn and they don't want me to learn, and I want to learn. And because I want to learn, it caused a problem. Because I like to read, the people that I live with stop talking to me. Even my own blood. So I left my house and went to sleep in a old canoe. Then the people on my beach began to say that I'm the reason why fish stop coming.

I took a bus to come to town and by accident I took the wrong bus, which drop me off in Speyside. And after I waited for a long time I began to walk until I got a lift in a truck. I began to walk again until I got a ride from a man on a horse. I came off downtown right by the statue, but then the rain began to fall and I went in the park. The rain came more so I left the park to sleep by the building. And then you came and saw me and thought I was a troublemaker. Mr. Rawle, I am not making any trouble, sir. I am not like the people from Black Well that I heard your father saying make a lot of trouble all the time. I am not the best girl. But everybody have faults. But my head is good and I want to be something in life. Now as I told you before—that bag that I had with me had all my belongings in this world, including all my money. I have no money now, sir. Not a penny in the world. Which simply means I cannot go home."

As she looked at him, awaiting his response, he closed each eye to look at her from slightly different angles, and saw that one of his suspicious had been right—her face had perfect lines. If you halved it right along her nose, and took away the crescent scar, both sides would be the same. No part of it was deviated, or uneven, or of a different height.

"We were wrong," he said, exhaling, "but there is nothing I can do."

"I'm not asking you for money, sir. I need a ride go to town."

She slipped her hand inside her pocket.

At least you'll clear your chest, he thought. Do this thing and then it will be done. You'll never have to see her for the rest of your life.


## XIII.

THEY DROVE IN an electric silence. Between them was a soundless hum until she asked, when they'd passed the last retaining wall that led to Thunder Hill: "You think that what you do me could be right?"

"It is not a matter of right and wrong," he told her, stopping as they came upon a curve.

"Is just wrong," she said.

Her arms were crossed; her back against the door.

"It is not as simple as that. It's not a simple thing at all."

"You're a headmaster. I've never been to school. Explain me what you mean."

"We're all faced with hard choices every day," he said with reservation. "And sometimes doing one thing for right will make you to do another thing for wrong. I always try to do the right thing. But sometimes in doing the right thing people get hurt. It has nothing to do with you."

"I am very disappointed, Mr. Rawle. You don't know how disappointed I am. Stop the car and let me out."

They had gotten to a place where she could see the turnoff to Savanna Ridge, the place where she'd thought she would be taken. And the memory relit the fire under what had been a third degree of pain.

In the tense, unmoving car she looked away from him toward the sea and held her stomach as she felt the mass of something dark and sleek inside her rushing upward from her depths, driving with the power of a whale. She held the dashboard and addressed him quickly, rushing all her words before the monster in her depths erupted, making waves. At which point, words wouldn't matter any more.

"Mr. Rawle," she told him in *sancoche*, "the way I heard your father curse you is just how my grandmother curse me. When I saw you wipe your face in the back of this same car here I feel so sorry for you, because I know the pain you was feeling in your heart, because I feel that same pain too . . . anger, shame and heartbreak knot up in one. And when I tell you I vex with my grandmother and grandfather, you know Mr. Rawle, believe me.

I vex. But I can't vex with you. You ain't owe me nothing. Them is my grandmother and my grandfather. You ain't own me nothing. But truthfully, Mr. Rawle, you make me lose my faith. I used to think that all I had was to do was to try, that all I had to do was to give it everything and the rest would just be ambition and luck. I born unlucky. But ambition is not something you can have by yourself. Other people have to have it for you too. Because if they ain't want you to be nothing, and if they ain't give you a chance to be nothing, nothing going to come of you. You teach me something, Headmaster. You teach me a lesson I will keep in my head all my life."

With this she pushed against the door and sprinted down the road, and when she reached the spot at which Savanna Ridge branched off to her left and she could see the loop of white-washed stones around the cricket ground, and the flutter of the royal palms around the pond, she drew the knife and flung it in the bush and howled.

After this, she straightened up and walked again.

Mingled with the mist of sound suspended in the air above Seville she heard the slapping of her feet against the rain-slick road and the drumming of the blood inside her ears.

To the market was a fifty-minute walk, she thought and it had people there she could ask for something, a little money, a little water, a little *choops* of food to eat.

Your granny ain't suppose to come to town for days, and although them market people bound to know that is you your people blame for all the fishing blight, they ain't go know they turn you out.

But what they going to think when they see you with your clothes turn inside out, and smell your sour breath and hear the failure in your voice? They going want to know. And what hide in darkness must come out to light. So even if you ain't going tell them. In time they bound to know.

She was deep in these thoughts and about to cross the road

and take the Queens toward the harbor from the governor's gate when she saw a movement from the corner of her eye and skipped up on the verge.

With the steering of the Buick on the "other side," St. William's face was just a foot away. Speaking in *sancoche*, he said, "You ain't even know your size, I'm sure."

His eyes were red as if he had been crying, and his nostrils quivered as he tried to stop his running nose.

"I ain't wear no shoes before," she told him curtly and began to walk again.

He caught up to her and stopped again as horns began to honk, and other drivers cursed and ordered him to move.

Standing on the grassy verge, Estrella leaned against the car and put her elbows on the roof and waved the cars behind him to go on. With her belly inches from his face, he stole a little of her smell and, feeling sentimental, wished to God that human beings were born with special pockets in the nose for keeping special scents.

When the cars had passed she crossed the street. He scrambled from the car and chased her and she felt a secret pleasure when she heard his footsteps coming close.

"My wife have a lotta shoes at home," he said, and took her by the arm. "Dress too. Blouse too. Skirt too. And I sure she have too much of anything a girl like you might want. You were right. You *are* right. What we did was wrong."

"Thank you, Mr. Rawle," she said, twisting from his grasp. "But I want you look at me and look at me good."

"Okay . . ."

"I ain't come to town to beg no alms. I come to get a job. And I might be doing the wrongest thing in the world, but I am going to ask you a favor. And if you can't do it, you should tell me you can't do it. Don't make no false promise to me."

"Okay . . ."

With a smile, she said in English, "F——k off and leave me alone."

"What?"

"I came to town to get a job, Mr. Rawle. I didn't come to ask for charity from the likes of you."

"You want a work?" he shouted as he grabbed her blouse.

"Let me go," she said between her teeth. "Let me go. You f——king let me go."

She grabbed him by the neck and they began to grapple, breathing hotly in each other's face until he used his tennis grip to twist her arm, which made her lose her balance and she fell against the ground.

"If you want a job, then ask," he told her as he held her in a pin. "Who the f——k are you that I should plead?"

She spat at him and freed a hand and reached into her pocket. But the f——king knife was gone.

From all angles, people rushed toward them, and he stood and waved them off. They hushed but didn't move. They wanted to observe the drama as it turned.

"Just who do you think you are?" he shouted as he rose. "Tell me. Tell me now."

He stood there feeling helpless but it came across as rage. The girl had spat his compassion in his face. And he needed her to see him as he knew himself to be—a man who wanted her to live in a different island from the one in which they lived today, a Mr. Rawle who was nothing like his dad.

"I ain't going to beg you for a thing," Estrella said when she was on her feet.

"You can cook?" he asked.

She brushed the grit from her elbows as she watched his blue eyes.

"All poor people can do them things."

"You can cook?" he asked her, glancing at his dirty clothes.

"Anything you want. Except fish."

"And clean?"

"*That* and wash and press."

Two policemen jostled through the crowd, and St. William told them all was well, and after making whispered inquiries, they left him with the girl.

"And if you want," he said, avoiding what he thought of as her *damn man-breaking stare,* "you could live in. It's a big place. You could have your own room."

Chewing on her pride, she told him, "But I would need to start today."

"You can."

"And I would like to start right now before anything else happen and nothing don't work out."

"You can start when we get home."

When they reached the car, she asked him, "Could you teach me how to read and write the proper way? Even if you take it from my pay."

He shook his head and offered her a cigarette. She took it and they smoked.

When they'd begun to drive again he took the road that led along the big savanna, and she looked out at the horses exercising on the track, their sharp hooves lifting dirt, and up above, the lovely houses on the ridge, until he turned along an avenue that led away from all of this.

They began to pass some newer houses, which were even larger than the ones along the ridge, and they privately acknowledged in their separate ways that something had been started when they grappled that would always complicate their lives.

"Wake me when we reach," she said, and closed her slanted eyes. "I going to catch some sleep."

She hadn't fallen fully into sleep when she began to feel the vehicle slowing down. When it stopped, she sat up lazily, awakened by the sound of conversation. Beside St. William's window was a man. Grazing on the verge, there was a horse.

"Who's that?" she asked him when the car began to move again, although she knew the answer by the accent and the smell. He'd tipped his hat politely, but it didn't seem as if he recognized her; but she knew him by his scent. He smelled of rum and cedar shavings and carbolic soap, but none of them intensely, and, also, she believed, a little bit of her.

He was red like new pottery with a long straight nose, and his tight cream pants were stained with grass and dirt.

"That's Wilfredo Dominguez," said her new employer, with suspicion, "and he's coming from my house. My wife is there. You'll meet her. My little son as well. Wilfredo is the finest carpenter you'll ever meet. In fact he made our matrimonial bed."

"I'm glad to know his name."

"Are you okay?"

"No, Mr. Rawle. I'm not okay at all."

"What's the matter?"

She closed her eyes, hoping to reclaim the peace of sleep.

"I ain't want wear your wife old shoes, Mr. Rawle. I walk too far from country for that. I need a ride to Salan's. I need to buy my own."

"I thought you didn't have any money."

"I lost it. But is your fault. So you going have to give me back. Fourteen pounds and fifty pence." Then she remembered the money from Wilfredo, whom she thought of as Simón, "Plus twenty pounds on that."

"That's a lot."

"That was my point."

"I don't know if I have that."

"If you ain't have it, put me out."

"Okay. You'll get it when we're home."

"As soon as we get the money then we're going to Salan's."

"Well, you can't go there like that. Maybe you should wait until you've had a bath and tried on something that you could wear."

"No, sir. I ain't have that kinda time."

"Well, I can't go like this. And to get there you'll need a car."

She touched his shoulder.

"Listen me now, and listen me well. When we bathe and change our clothes, we're going out."

Dear Editor:

I fail to see the reason for the undue excitement surrounding the fiftieth anniversary of the Institute of Science and Engineering. Where is our equivalent for the arts?

When the ISU was established shortly after self-government in 1959, I was a member of the steering committee that developed the plan for tertiary education, and I can assure you that a commitment to a school of the arts was there. Despite numerous promises over the years, that school has not been built; as such, the very foundation of our society is at risk.

As a society, we've grown increasingly unromantic over the years. The young fellows of today are simply romantically inept. They look at women as gadgets to be deciphered and improved, measured and critiqued, and as such our women have been making secret trips to foreign shores. No! They are not going to Miami to shop!

When I was a young man, I understood a woman to be a mystery, the product of a great imagination like a book of verse. We boast of being another Singapore, but have you ever heard of any woman salivating over Singaporean men? However, Singaporean women have a reputation for embarking on extremely lengthy shopping trips abroad.

Yours, etc.

St. William Rawle

# PASSING THROUGH

**I.**

ALL SEX INVOLVES perversion. It's a matter of degree. One day, on the island of San Carlos, when interracial marriage was illegal in the States, Lowell and Cornelia left their room and went downstairs for lunch.

They were staying at Grande Vue, a small hotel that had been built up on Savanna Ridge in 1800 as a house and office by a doctor who'd fled the Haitian Revolution, and were speaking to each other in a tart, sarcastic mood.

"So, you're sticking to your story?"

He waited for her answer but she passed him on the wooden stairs and flitted down a sunny hallway to the narrow dining room, a slender woman in a denim skirt and gauzy peasant blouse.

"There's no story," she told him through a deep exhale. "Believe it if you want to. It's the truth."

They were the only guests—there were few tourists in San

Carlos in those days—still, they glanced around before they took their seats.

"Look, I'm not accusing you," he told her as he rolled his sleeves. It was a light blue shirt with flap pockets, and he wore it with chinos and beige desert boots.

She stretched her neck from side to side and drew her frazzled hair into an uncommitted bun, leaning forward with her elbows on the woven mat, which stamped a waffle pattern in her skin.

"Aren't you tired of scolding me?" she asked him as she filled his glass with water from a cream, tight-waisted jug. "Doesn't it wear you out?"

"You've been really thoughtless," he remarked. "These people have been used."

"Look, I need a smoke."

He slapped his shirt and said, "I guess they're in the room."

Lowell Mason had the stirrings of a double chin, which hinted at a weakness for desserts. But he was tall and lean and fit. He was an independent publisher of independent means who summered on the Cape and had a cluttered office underneath a tavern in the Village, a liberal who'd passed on Brown for Vanderbilt to live his father's dream.

The owner of a large apartment overlooking Central Park, he'd moved from Nashville to Manhattan in the thirties to become a poet and, while foundering, had abandoned the craft; but after serving as a navy pilot in the war he'd drawn some money from his trust account and started Blue Line Press. He was a simple man, with simple tastes—equally at leisure with a pencil or a gun—who argued for his love of jazz and other forms of negro music through the titles that he carried on his list.

Cornelia Ward was twenty-four, and young enough to risk her savings on a dream. At her own expense, which wasn't much, she'd been traveling through the Caribbean shooting moody stills of fishing people for a speculative essay called "The Beach."

She was raised in Philadelphia and had studied art at Penn, but made her living as a stringer for the *Times*.

Before leaving for her trip, she'd told him as they lay beneath his desk, exhausted, that she'd come to see him for a week before she sailed from Montserrat to Martinique; but instead, she sent a note:

LM
*Not coming. New plan. Meet me. San Carlos. 5 wks.*
CW

In those days, calling the West Indies was a project undertaken with the help of skilled technicians—like changing the plugs on a car.

He wrote her daily but his letters often crossed her short replies, and against his better instincts, he began to sense the presence of a man.

If she'd been staying in hotels, he would have seen somebody like himself; but Cornelia had immersed herself in island life. Her letters spoke of shacks, of going to sea with fishermen and spending days and nights alone with them on far, deserted cays. Of roughing it. Roughing it. Roughing it with whom? What if all her letters were dictated by a brute. Big neck. Thick limbs. A mallet for a nose. That would stop his heart.

The waiter came. And as she ordered for the both of them he gazed outside the door. The house had been constructed on a ridge that opened on the broad savanna on the lower part of town—a disc of green so large that in the previous year's election there were rumors that the PPP had plans to sell it for a million dollars to a wealthy Texan who was going to close the racetrack and the cricket ground and raze the public garden then re-flag the people's park in the imperial name of golf.

Pulling backward like a camera now, he saw old houses with steep gables rising quickly in a mist of trees and shrubs that

melted at the garden gate through which a climbing path meandered fifty feet along an easy but uneven slope of weedy grass
toward the back veranda, where, on checkered tiles of white and
blue, a khaki mongrel rolled from underneath a table and began
to sun itself against a slab of silver light.

In what at first was nothing but an ordinary glance, he
caught the way the dog's complexion seemed to change against
the light. But in the moment that his mind had been distracted,
some hidden thoughts escaped and scattered out—in New York
he'd never seen Cornelia darker than a scone. But after three
months in the tropics her complexion had been deepened to the
will-erasing golden-brown of buns.

Her new complexion made his whiteness seem forsaken, like
something oddly fixed and absolute, the zero on the scale—the
point from which her love had moved.

Her laughter broke his spell, and he dropped his head and
gazed at her conversing with the waiter from beneath his furry
brows. From her slanging body he suspected that their talk had
gone beyond the food. They were speaking in *sancoche,* the local
Spanish dialect, which a month in Puerto Rico and her gift for
language allowed her to pick up.

"I get jealous," he said coolly, as if speaking to himself.
"Why's that so hard to understand."

"Look, I'm speaking."

"Who's your boyfriend?" Lowell asked her as the waiter
crossed his arms and eyed her with a dreamy look. "Him or me?"

She tugged the waiter's arm reluctantly, and tossed her chin
to signal him to leave.

"It's a natural thing," said Lowell. "And before you interrupt me
now, allow me to explain. You've been gone for a very long time.
Twelve weeks. A quarter of a year. All winter. I miss you, that's all."
She tried to interrupt him but he raised his hand to make her cease.
"We make a plan . . . a great plan. In fact *we* didn't make it—*you*
did. You said you'd come home for a week. I believed you. I got ex-

cited. You raised my hopes. Then after weeks of lovely letters back and forth, I got this awful, cryptic note. It was so different that at first I didn't think it had come from you." He raised his hand again as she leaned forward to cut in. "I had to change my life around to come to see you. And you know I have a complicated life. But I did it because I missed you. I did it all for you." She unsealed her lips to answer, but he cleared his throat to pause her once again. "When I arrived two days ago, there was this awful feeling. You looked at me as if I were a heavy bag you had to lift. You didn't kiss me. We hugged. After three whole months—we hugged. I felt as if I wasn't missed. I wondered. I wondered for a day. Then last night while slipping something in your case to tide you over, I discovered something that was such an awful disappointment—found these really awful things." He took a sip of water, shook his head, then drained the glass. "I'm sure you understand."

"No I *don't*," she answered, leaning sideward with an elbow on the table and a shoulder pressing close against her ear. "And where are the cigarettes? I thought you were gonna get them in the room. Lowell, this is bullshit. You see some contact sheets of naked men and I'm a wild, unfaithful whore? No, I *don't*, Lowell. I *don't*. Sometimes you really piss me off."

She glanced around the room on recognizing that her voice had boomed against the walls, which were white and chipped in places and festooned with garish oils of sunsets and ripe fruit.

He put his elbows on the table and approached her in a different way: "If you found a picture of a naked girl in my apartment, how'd you feel?"

"Amazed that I'd received the invitation."

"This is not the time for childish answers."

"Okay. It wouldn't be the same."

"Sometimes I just don't know with you," he said, frustrated. "Nothing ever seems to work. You have this way about you where you close your mind and lock out everything except your own concocted truth."

"They swim naked here," she told him. "They take their showers in streams. This is what they do. This is not the Waldorf, man. They don't give you slippers at the waterfall or bathrobes at the beach. You get freaked out about the weirdest things."

"I was raised with negro people," Lowell told her in a tight commanding voice. "You've come to *really* know that part of you a little late in life. They're real to me."

"They labored in your pappy's fields. Of course."

"Don't gimme that, Cornelia. It's nothing that I claim."

"You don't have to. It's yours."

"Look. I respect colored people. And the ones I know respect themselves. Would you even dare to say to Mingus, 'Hey man, don't get excited, I just wanna take a picture of your naked ass'? No, you wouldn't. He'd tell you where to stick it—well, a little more than that."

"Stop trying to be my father, Lowell. Do you want a drink?"

Her posture slackened as she gazed outside the door, and thought about her dad, a married man who never left his wife. As a child she'd see him once a month, when he'd take the train to see her from his home in Queens, a red-bone from New Haven who'd met her Turkish mother when she waited tables at a diner close to Temple, where he'd studied for his law degree.

She drank some water though she wasn't thirsty—just to hide her face—and when the glass was drained she gazed outside a window, dodging Lowell's eyes.

Watching her in profile, Lowell marveled at the wavy gather of her hair, her steep, aggressive forehead, which was edged above her eyebrows with a gentle ridge of bone. She had a long, side-drafting nose, which slightly overhung a pair of fatty lips, and at the corner of her mouth there was a tuck from which a crease erupted in a high out-pointed cheekbone that descended and dissolved behind her ear.

"I've missed you very much," he mumbled. "Are you ever coming home?"

"I don't have a date," she answered pensively, while staring at her hands. "I'm working. I don't dictate the pace. I don't know what to tell you. I just don't know, man. I really don't know. I love you, Lowell. But loving you is not my life. It can't be my life. You've got too many lives right now. I don't want this love to be a heavy thing, man. I don't want this love to be a ball and chain. And that's the way you make me feel sometimes—like I shouldn't have a life away from you. You got your dreams, Lowell. I've got to make my own. And that's what I'm doing out here. Making my dreams. Seeing where they'll take me. It doesn't mean I don't want you. It doesn't mean I don't love you. It just means I'm getting close to other people, connecting with their souls. That is how I shoot. To shoot, I must connect. Maybe I'm becoming something else. I don't know. Maybe I'll return to being me when this is done. But right now I don't need you or anybody telling me what to do. Or how to be. Or where to go. I just need to be alone."

"I'm sorry if I hurt your feelings."

"No," she said, and shook her head. "My feelings hurt themselves."

"I love you more than anything," he told her, working hard to hide his oddly braided sense of disappointment and relief. He took her hand and stroked her palm, happy that he understood the sense of distance in her notes . . . but hurt.

"You don't love me," she mumbled, playing with his fingers absentmindedly, as children play with food.

"I do."

"You don't."

"I really don't," he said in error.

"There you go."

"Cornelia, I'm here. I came to see you. I'm feeling sick inside because you just told me that you need to be alone. What do you want as proof?"

"Marry me," she answered blithely, making silly faces that reminded him how young she was. "You've known me long enough. We've had some good years. You've kicked my tires and had your spins. Checked my hooves and seen my teeth. What do you say?"

He took her lead and answered in a flippant way.

"When do you wanna do it? Now? Later? On the next full moon? Halloween? Me dressed like a gorilla and you in a chicken suit?"

"Let's do it today," she answered in the breathy intonation of a movie femme fatale. "Let's do it soon. I wanna get some pictures with a sunset right behind."

"Sure. But first I've got to get a monkey suit."

Lowell had misread her mood. And with each exchange, each failure to appreciate the irony in which she'd dressed her voice, Cornelia's eyes became more radiant and her silly faces formed themselves into a smile that slowly spread, her mind already living in the moment when his face would be contorted by the shock.

"When you get your suit, will you also get a frock for me?" she asked. "Or should I wear the chicken suit."

"Either way, you'll make a lovely bride."

"Can I be a princess bride or do I have to choose?"

"But that could mean I'd have to be a prince. And princes aren't old."

"Well, be the king then."

"And you would be my queen. And I'd parade you all around the world in a golden carriage that could fly and—"

"Oh, can we stop this stupid shit. Let's just stop this cruel game. What's my move? I say six months from now, so you can tell me that you've got a wife, and that your kids would find it hard to deal with—even though they're grown—and all the shit about your dad?"

She grabbed her napkin and began to twist it like a rope.

"I'm fifty-four," he stated coolly. "No one tells me what to do."

"I could get a dress embroidered with a burning cross," she answered in the slow, molasses cadence of a southern belle.

"No one tells me what to do," he grumbled, rolling down his sleeves.

"Lowell, if you marry me your life will turn to shit. I'm a bastard and a concubine. I know my place. Sometimes I act like I don't know it. But I do."

"The grass is always greener on the other side, you know."

"Baby, mine is old and brown."

He began to tell her something, then he changed his mind— he wasn't married anymore. He'd divorced his wife, the playwright Gilly Rhone, a year ago, but little in his outer life had changed. They maintained the same apartment, slept in the same room, and made the same missteps while stumbling through the rote of making love, wooden like a pair of uninspired students conjugating Latin verbs . . . amo . . . amas . . . amat.

Gilly was older—well, she'd seemed that way in 1932, when they were young. Now the seven years between them was compressed, as were some disks along her spine, which made it hard for her to walk. So when they ventured out these days, he had to link her arm, or hold her hand and grin and bear it like a boy caught out in public with his mom.

Gilly had been carrying on a long affair with A. Delmonte Brown, a poet that he liked to call "a tassel on the fringes of the Beats." The affair was not a secret, neither was it known; rather, it was something that vibrated in the gap between *unnoticed* and *ignored.*

"If Delmonte knows I'm single, he'll leave me." This is what she'd told him on the day that they were granted their divorce. "Without you in the picture he'll think I'll really need him, then he'll go. I'm frightened, Lo. I'm frightened. I'm too old to be alone."

Sitting with his elbows on the table now, his lover staring back at him with misty eyes, Lowell really wished he had a drink. Without a gin or two, he thought, he wouldn't have the strength to raise the heavy things that rested on his mind—that although he lived with Gilly, that while nothing big had changed, it mattered that they weren't man and wife; that being a husband was a job he'd never choose again; that if someone chose him he would have to fight or run away; that married people were a pack of savages who raped and pillaged love.

He must have loved Gilly. He must have, he thought. But somehow, even when he looked at pictures where his face and body were aflush with care, he found it easy to recall the moment but impossible to feel the mood.

What he and Gilly had today did not remind him of the love they must have built. What they had was sanded like the writing on a tablet of pharaonic stone. How did they lose so much so fast? Or were the changes slow?

And how do you say, "I love you too much to marry you" to a girl who wants to be your wife, without looking like the biggest jerk in the world? Like the heavyweight champ of jerks? Like you thought she was a lightweight and a fool?

How do you tell her that whatever happy thing she'd ever heard about it was a piece of propaganda; that if marriage was love, then war was valor. And that although you don't know shit about valor, they gave you two medals in the war. That war's about not getting shot and making sure you make it home with all your limbs on straight and praying for some heroes in your squad.

When he'd thought of all of this he said, "It's not all it's meant to be, you know."

"If it's good for her, it's good as hell for me."

"But it's not."

"But it is."

"No. It's not."

"Yes. It is."

"You've never done it. Don't do it. Take my advice. It's not for you."

"I understand," she said primly.

"No. You don't."

"Yes. My father likes to tell the story of the teacher who advised him he should stick to woodwork and forget his dreams of going to Yale."

"That was so unfair, Cornelia. That was so unfair. It has shit to do with that at all."

"Don't lecture me about what's fair or not. I live it every day."

"If it weren't for Gilly, though—"

"Forget Gilly," said Cornelia, probing Lowell with a stare. "Let's talk about me? Do you want me?"

"Yes, of course," he said. "Do you ever need to ask that? That's why I'm here." He swallowed hard and scratched the sudden itch that crept along his temple from his brow. "Of course I do."

She cut her eyes and said, "You're gonna miss me when I'm gone."

"Okay. Marry me," he told her in a huff. "Everybody wants to be happy, but no one gives a shit about me? You wanna get married, Cornelia? Fine. Let's do it. Let's do it. I tried to warn you. But you'll see what I mean. Oh damn you, Cornelia. Damn Gilly. Damn the both of you. Don't say I didn't warn you, though. Don't blame me when it all goes wrong."

She threw her napkin in his face and walked away, kicking at her chair, which fell over. And he sat there feeling like the biggest jerk in the world.

As he tossed the napkin on the wooden floor, the waiter sauntered from the kitchen with their food. With his able hand he brought Cornelia to a halt, his face and body angled in a way that said, "What happened? I'm concerned."

Lowell poured another glass of water as he watched her talking to the younger man, pausing with his glass suspended as she gestured warmly, wincing as he tried to understand, for they were switching back and forth from English to their rude, exclusive tongue.

Signing with her hands, she asked the waiter for a smoke and he obliged by leaning closer, prompting her to pluck the one that dangled from his lips. On instinct, Lowell tapped his pockets as he watched her slip the man's saliva-coated Camel in her mouth.

On the night that he'd met her, he'd observed her dancing with a man like this.

It was a rainy autumn evening at a party in a ballet studio overlooking Union Square. She was twenty and had just released the book for which she'd earned a little fame—portraits of share-croppers in the south: simple people standing up in front of simple houses, washed in simple light, the awkward angles of their limbs articulating shame and loss.

Before this moment, he'd believed that love by definition was a process, a thing that took time. But when Cornelia slipped out of her poncho, and began to dance, her hair pulled back, her silver earrings swinging like gymnastic hoops, he learned that love could happen in an instant, could be stunning like a flash.

She was a woman with a presence. In a red suede dress drawn tight with a belt, her pelvis making calligraphic figure eights, she stood across the room and held her arms apart in open invitation and A. Delmonte Brown, whose turtleneck was barely blacker than his face, excused himself from Gilly and approached. The Contours were singing "Do You Love Me?"

With confidence, Cornelia placed her face against his shoulder on the hazy, shaking floor, and clutched his fist against her breast, and when she realized that he couldn't dance she took the lead, drew him in, pressed the rhythm tight between his legs, turning all his charges off her hip with ease, twirling him in circles like a girl.

"Sorry . . . for the time," the waiter said in halting English as he served the food.

The mongrel padded through the door from the veranda and began to bark. The neck. The limbs. The nose. The brute. The rage. The fear. The blow.

## II.

THE NEW CHIEF minister was lying in his hammock the next morning when his mother told him that a wild American had killed her sister's dog.

Arriving in a rush, she scattered goats and chickens as she drove her silver Aston Martin down the dusty lanes that trickled through the shantyscape of Black Well, a squatter camp that sprawled along the edge of a lagoon. Waving at the children who'd gathered by the car, she left the engine running as they tumbled in the seats and slapped away the sawdust from her clothing as she pushed the bamboo gate, confirming what had been suspected—she'd returned to sleeping with the man who'd made her matrimonial bed.

She was forty-seven, and her son, the island's only surgeon, lived with two dogs in a one-room hut although he owned a villa in a newly subdivided area on the steep, volcanic slopes above Seville. But in the previous year's election he'd promised to "reside among the poorest people of this island for a year if they gave the PPP the privilege of leading them like Moses to the promised land of independence, the first stop of which is internal self-government, otherwise known as home rule, which will bring in the first two years, food for all, and light for all, and a bed for every single child at night."

Thick-haired and small-bodied, with his mother's girlish overbite, he was only thirty-one, a populist whose public speeches were ornate and operatic, who in person spoke softly, with contemplative pauses, during which he slowly smoked.

"Your aunt's hysterical," she told him as she put her face against his chest and curled against him. He was wearing nothing but a pair of khakis, rumpled ones in which he'd slept the night before, and he smiled with satisfaction as he ran his hand along her fatty haunches as they passed a Dunhill back and forth.

Their unnatural closeness had begun the day that he was pulled out of her womb and drawn along her stomach, wet with blood and mucus to her nipple and she'd noticed how he suckled like his dad—who was not her husband, something that was never talked about.

The doctor harbored feelings for his mother that he didn't give himself a chance to know. And whenever they unnerved him, he would distract himself with cigarettes, masking his desires with a screen of heavy smoke.

"I need to go," he muttered as he squeezed a pinch of softness on her arm. "Your crazy sister has a gun."

SLUMPING IN THE back of his finned Chevrolet, the whitewalls rousing dust along the narrow lanes, the doctor gazed out through the open windows at the rippled fences caked with rust, his nostrils now so used to smelling rotting fish and sewage stewing in the heat that he detected no aroma but his mother's soft perfume.

He saw his face at every turn—on metal posters nailed to trees, on the T-shirts of the sweaty people who began to jog beside the car, asking for a favor, seeking blessings for a child, describing complicated pains, stretching through the window just to touch his cheek, misting spit into the folds of skin beneath his eyes; and always, he responded with a promise and a smile.

At a wide acacia tree, the driver left the rutted track and took the coastal road, which had had been paved for the elections at the doctor's own expense, and the Chevy powered through a sea of cane and cattle ranches that were owned by his grandfather Khalid Salan.

Aunt Naila, who'd never married, lived alone in a rambling house in Mayfair Gardens, a gated enclave built on land southeast of the savanna during the final stages of the war. To an American it would have felt like southern California. The roads were wide and made to intersect at perfect angles. There were sidewalks—where the standard for the island was a verge; and many of the houses were designed with arches and columns and terra-cotta roofs to "give that Spanish look."

In a black homburg and a navy suit, the doctor passed into the quiet house. As always, the door had not been locked. Inside, the rooms were dark and very English, lots of heirloom chintz; and the scalloped walls were barnacled with paintings of its owner's favorite subjects—sunsets and ripe fruit.

Before he passed into the courtyard through a sliding door, the doctor kneeled and crossed himself, for standing on the diving board, arms above her head displaying pits in need of shaving, was his mother's only sister, his fifty-year-old aunt, the owner of Grande Vue. Without her tapered limbs the rest of her could be mistaken for a breast, for she was formless, fat and round.

Outside now, he shuttled back and forth along the thirty-meter pool, back bent as if he'd lost his wallet, talking slowly with a lot of repetition to his wheezing aunt who had prescribed herself a dozen laps to ease her mental pain.

Through it all—her splashing, her garbling, her digressions and the heat—he gathered that her dog had not been killed, but had been knocked unconscious. And further, that the man who'd kicked the dog was not a brute, that in fact he was a gentleman who'd shown his deep regret by asking her forgiveness in a hand-presented note.

"But that's not why I didn't shoot him," she remarked, pausing halfway up the ladder in her yellow bathing suit. Rolls of fat were stacked in rings along her neck. "His wife kinda looks like your mum."

In the car, on the way to see the woman on a fuzzy pretext whose details he trusted would arrive in time, the doctor asked his driver, "Ever done it with a woman who resembled your mum?"

"No," the driver answered, "but don't ask me if I've thought of doing it with one who looks like yours."

As they laughed, the car was overtaken by a motorcycle cop, who gave them urgent news—Fidel had sent Camilo from the hills to take Havana, and the doctor had to go to parliament at once.

## III.

DAYS LATER, ON Concordia, her father's wedding gift, the doctor's mother left her husband writing longhand in their little beach house and meandered down a path that curled beneath a roof of palms toward the turning sea.

The elongated cay was one of many scattered off the *back beyond,* the shaggy neck of land that jutted from the island's northern coast where there were neither homes nor roads, but many butterflies and monkeys in the humid forests from whose limbs birds lifted in the evenings in great flocks as dense as swarms of bees.

While she swam, St. William came to watch her from the covered deck of the unpainted house. Made of planks and bamboo, with a steeply angled roof, it was raised above the tree line on a set of logwood timbers driven deeply into coral through an overlay of grassy dunes.

It was the only thing of permanence throughout the cays, and sometimes when they came to visit there was evidence that fishermen had used it, which they didn't really mind, as long as they cleaned their mess and didn't desecrate their bed, a pallet made of sailcloth stuffed with rags and fibers that they thought of as the sacramental birthplace of their love. This was not a fact; but every marriage needs a myth, some way of explaining its illogic to the people who, against their better judgment and objective proof, continue to believe.

One such person was the doctor, who'd been told by Aunt

Nalia that, "Your father has confronted your mother about some foolishness about an old affair and now she's threatened him to leave." And partly as a way to get the time to focus on the news and rumors streaming out of Cuba, he'd prescribed a weekend of seclusion in the cays.

Concordia sat across a channel from a smaller cay with palms compacted like the bristles on a brush, and, sipping from a glass of gin, St. William watched Rebecca swimming to and from it as he turned a lot of feelings in his mind.

He was forty-nine, with short blonde hair and blue eyes in good condition. He had a lanky body and a tennis player's legs, but whenever he would bend to keep her in the frame created by the roof, a momentary belly would occur.

With every lap he thought about the many times she'd left him and returned, her red suit like a warning, her red suit like a rose, her red suit like a spreading drop of blood, and beneath the red, her shadow sliding on the ridges in the creamy sand, the way perhaps her body slid across her lover's abs.

In a wide straw hat and a blue camp shirt, his face arranged in what he thought of as a taut, phlegmatic look, he walked down to the beach along the shady corridor created by the palms, some of which had trunks as rough as pineapples and others that were rifle-smooth.

With the house up on the dunes behind him, higher than the trees, and the bristled cay ahead, and other cays at different angles scattered all around, he shifted through a range of postures, trying to find the one that she would read as "cool."

When Rebecca made a sudden dive toward the sand and came up to the surface on her back and spread her limbs to float, St. William cupped his mouth and shouted, "What's the use of coming if you're never going to talk?"

She was drifting off their runabout—a low, sleek boat with a long, brown hull and a deck inset with lighter planks that alternated with the darker ones to make a set of stripes. There were two cockpits and two engines and a windshield that was raked and curved.

"What is there to talk about?" she asked with irritation as the current spun her slowly. "You know everything there is to know about everything."

He rolled his dungarees and stepped into the surf.

"But I want to hear from you."

"I don't speak to spies," she answered, splashing with her feet. "I hate spying. If you wanted to know, you should've asked. Don't spy on me."

"I didn't."

"Okay. You got somebody else to do your dirty work."

He began to walk toward her. With the weight against his legs, his steps created muffled roars that made crosscutting waves.

"You're disturbing me," she warned him as she craned her neck.

"No. I'm not," he told her, now submerged below his waist. "You're disturbed in your blasted head."

"So what's the point of talking, then? It's just a waste of time."

"What's so hard about admitting to your dirty deeds, Rebecca? By now you should be versed."

"Apologize."

"For what?"

"You're out of order."

"How?"

"How dare you make it seem like I'm some regular old whore?"

He stretched both arms behind him as it crossed his mind to heave a ridge of water in her face.

"You're right," he said. "I'm sorry."

"As you ought to be."

"You're a woman of extremes."

He left the beach frustrated. And when he was inside the house again, he changed into pajamas and poured two more drinks and lay down in the pallet on his back and tried to sleep.

The walls were punched with big windows, which had shutters and no panes. The one above the pallet threw a sheet of light against him. And he crossed his arms beneath it while the gin began to roll around his throbbing head.

He lay there for a long time, staring at the ceiling, at the pattern of the vines and wires that he'd used to hold the thatch against the ribbing of the roof, which was supported by a mighty center beam that kept the house from falling down, wishing that he could be just as strong.

He turned on his side with his back toward the window the lumpy padding pressing on his ribs. The room was sparsely furnished and almost all the pieces there were bolted to the floor so that the fishermen would find them hard to move.

But everything he saw reminded him of her—the stools, the bench, the hammock, his desk, the cupboard lined with cans of food. The gin had brought on him a rainy, pessimistic mood, and he rolled onto his stomach, clamped a pillow to his head and closed his eyes.

If he told Rebecca who had told him, he knew she would confess. For although she was deceitful, she was principled in certain ways. But telling her would open up another conversation—for he'd heard it from his mistress, who was their live-in maid.

He sat up now, and thought of her. Estrella was her name, a *negrita* of uncommon beauty with a lust for learning like he'd never seen. She was beautiful, and dark, and every part of her was well proportioned, well scooped, and well turned. When he looked at her he thought of wood. When he touched her, though, he thought of silk. But when he was inside her he could only think of cream.

The gin had made him drowsy and he crossed his legs and

gave his body to the hairy wall behind him as the house was shaken by a breeze that blew his papers all across the floor, which didn't bother him because the writing wasn't good that day, nothing had been good that day, for he'd awoken with a woman who would not admit that she was sleeping with another man. But there was something else. He'd made a promise to Estrella, the one who loved him more, and he didn't have the heart to follow through.

In his head he heard her voice, an unrelenting force that gusted like the wind: "Get off my breast and be a f——king man. She's your blasted wife. Don't plead with her. Take your balls in your hand and confront her right in front of that shit of a carpenter who built this shit of a bed and ask her if she has the guts to be an honest wife. Because that is what it really takes—guts. What you got when she left you all them times was a public shame. What you have to get from her is public praise. It don't matter what happen when doors close and who say what to who. You have to make that bitch of a useless woman humble herself in public to you. You can't be my man no more if you ain't make that woman bow to you. I take too much bad look from that woman. I take too much bad talk from that woman. The first time I take you was when she leave you. All them times you want me and I say I ain't do them things. I take two rounds of it and I ain't going take no more, Willy Boy. I'd love to get the chance to manage her myself. But I can't do it. So if you love me, so if you want me, manage her for me. If she ain't confess to you, then beat her ass for me."

St. William dragged his body like a broom and stood before the window that the wind was blowing through and braced there with his mouth agape, taking jabs and crosses from the wind as he thought of his *negrita,* feeling queasy as his guts were filled with air.

In more than thirty years of marriage his wife had left him many times. Two of them had ended in divorce and somehow she'd always found a way to make him take her back. Each time had been hard, for she'd never left to live alone. It had always been to live with someone else.

But as much as it was hard for him, he knew, it was harder for the one who loved him more, the one who would devote herself to him until the one who always left returned. After this, the one who loved him more would do as she had always done—cook the food and wash the clothes and clean the rooms, spitting on the linen every time she made the bed.

The most painful of her devastations must have been the second time, he thought, four years ago, in 1955, when they'd been left together for a year and had begun to venture out, and she'd shown how smart she was, how much better read she was than all the women who'd been picked for wives. He'd tutored her and given her great piles of books, and she'd read them, absorbed them, kept the knowledge in her head, but discussed them in her natural voice that blew in gusts. It was scandalous, of course; but shame was nothing new. But what do you expect from people who are worried that their money might become extinct? They hoard the genes. Control the blood. The eggs don't come from Europe anymore along with butter, cheese and condensed milk. You work with what you have. You cluster like a ball of desert snakes. Everybody f——ks each other over and over. The white must never spill. We just don't have enough to go around.

He stood in the doorway with his arm against the frame until he saw Rebecca come out of the water in her scarlet bathing suit, then he lurched out on the deck to watch her coming up the path between the trees.

"Would you like a drink?" he called out.

"That's more like it," she shouted back. Her voice was warm but guarded, as if his absence or the water had placed her in a better mood.

"Well, hurry up."

"What time is it?" she asked when she'd made it up the steps. Her face and limbs were deeply tanned and though she was approaching fifty, she filled her suit with curves.

"Ten-thirty."

"Oh. A drink might make me sleepy. Then we'll never talk."

When she passed into the room, he turned to watch and saw her tug and snap the suit to hide her quarter moons.

"We have to talk," he said, while standing on the deck.

"Oh, what's the use?" she said. "You've heard from everybody else."

"I need to hear from you," he told her gravely, when he'd followed her inside.

"What do you want from me?" she asked him as she stepped out of her suit. The movement made her body jiggle and she quickly drew a towel round herself.

"A little decency, Rebecca. I'm not saying I'm a saint."

"Who told you?" she demanded.

"Everybody knows."

"But who told you?"

"Evidence was everywhere."

"What did Estrella say?"

"What does she have to do with this?"

"She has everything to do with this."

"Is that why you went back to him? Is that the case? Because of her?"

"I have no idea who you're talking about?"

"In which case, who's Estrella?"

While St. William gathered all the papers that the wind had blown across the room, Rebecca changed into a yellow dress, and dried her hair while sitting on the bed. Seated at his desk, which faced a wall, St. William made some furtive glances, cracked a tin of mints and slipped one in his mouth, then held the tin against his body just a little short of shoulder height and used his thumb to flip it open. In secret, while pretending that his mind was miles away, he watched in admiration as her likeness shimmered in the frosted panel on the inside of the lid.

When they were introduced she was fourteen, he recalled, and had just come back from six years of convent school in Cuba.

Their one-year courtship was formal, but enchanted, as she was a virgin with experience. At nights he would meet her in the garden of her parents' house up on Savanna Ridge, where she would feed him on her fatty breasts, which he would take into his mouth with awe as if they were a pair of sacramental offerings. And every time he sucked them he would feel a deepening of his yearning and his faith—his conviction that she held the key to his salvation from disgrace.

She'd always believed in him, it seemed. Unlike the other women that he'd known and loved, she didn't giggle when he told her of the time his father's boat capsized and mysterious currents took him to the outskirts of Atlantis; or that his first ejaculations had been inside a goat; didn't laugh when he confided that his ultimate ambition was to publish the Bible, the Koran, the Bhagavad Gita and the collected works of Buster Keaton, Shakespeare and Aristotle in *sancoche*.

And this is why he'd asked no questions when she named him as the father of Octavio, whose conception was the reason that they'd first exchanged a marriage vow.

She was bending with her head between her knees now with her hair swept over, puckered feet against the floor; and the towel was so white and her action was so languid that it seemed as if her hair were foaming with shampoo. When she straightened up, her face was flushed from bending. She raised her arms to knot the towel in a turban and he saw the shadow of her rosy nipples tapping on the inside of the dress. The movement caused her fleshy arms to shake, and he swallowed quickly as he noted to himself that fleshy women must be nice to beat.

While waiting for more wetness to be drawn into the cloth,

Rebecca glanced in his direction, and before he slammed the tin he saw her cut her eyes then look again, her upper lip about to stretch into a smile.

Without a word, he crawled into the bed and lay behind her on his side, his face toward her, breathing hotly on her spine, accidentally at first, but when he saw the way in which her muscles focused on the jets, he did it with control . . . pursing to streamline it, flaring to create a light spring morning blow . . . dropping, raising, teasing, braking . . . coming back with force . . .

She undid the turban with a deep exhale, rolled her hem above her thighs and draped the towel on her knees, and without admitting any kind of weakness, drew an arm of his around her waist.

When she pulled his arm, he felt a slip inside the knotted ball of feelings in his chest. With a look of satisfaction, like a cat who'd just been fed, he curled around her tightly, and it looked as if she'd come along and squeezed into the curve created by his torso and his legs.

"You need her," said Rebecca as he softly spanked her spongy thighs, small pats that sounded like a spoon engaged in belly flopping on a pad of porridge. "I need him too. It's hard."

When her hair was fully greased, Rebecca halved it with a silver comb and leaned her head to braid it. Her face was hushed as it had been when she was floating on the sea, and when she closed her eyes a nervous flutter shook her lids.

There had evolved between them over more than thirty years a set of rituals that had kept the boredom out of making love, and one of them was set in motion when he rolled onto his back, his arms and legs spread open, feigning sleep.

With her knees on either side of him, she took him at a cautious pace with no exchange of words. She teased his ears with licks and murmurs while unbuttoning his shirt and circled his pink nipples with her tongue.

Sitting up, she reached behind her back and pulled the buttons on her dress and eased it to her waist and heavy breasts came down. They'd sagged with age but still had their essential form although the rings around her nipples, which were thick as bolts, had slackened into shapes that had an arc on top but something like a rounded point below. Still, they were her pride, and when she leaned toward St. William once again she hung them bulbously above his head and traced their nipples on his brows. And when he turned his face, she pressed their milky warmth against his cheek, which reddened as it took their spreading weight.

Like all rituals, this one had its rules. She had to give her pleasure silently, and he was duty bound to take this pleasure while maintaining the illusion of sleep. But most importantly, she had to secretly imagine that he was another person or a thing, the name of which she would reveal to him in subtle hints as she controlled his penetration—ring by slick contracting ring—leading him in circles as he probed.

With her forehead resting on his thigh now, she used the end of one braid as a pencil and, reaching, wrote confessions all across his stomach and his chest as if his body were an empty page at the beginning of a book.

With her teeth, she pulled the string that threaded through the waist of his pajamas and began to tremble as she always would before she did the thing she was about to do—a thing she only did with him.

The pajamas had been tugged across his thighs now, and he lay there, still unmoving, head flopped toward the window. Wind was coming through it and he felt it blowing warmly on his face as she touched him lightly with her lips and tongue, glazing him with gentle brushes, taking little sips. He was long and hard, but frail like ice, and she kept her heat in reservation, breathing through her nostrils, not her mouth.

When she did this thing with him, she felt pacific, and her

body had a pose of ease. Lying with him now, the weight of him a stabilizing force against her jaw, she began to daydream that her fortunes had changed, that she'd won the battle with the thing she called her darkness, the constant threat that forced her to maintain a standing troop of men.

Feeling peaceful, as she'd only felt in church, she imagined that St. William was her secret saint, St. Peter made of ice, and in her head she whispered soft novenas as she lit a ring of kisses on his pedestal of stones. In the glow of this imagined light, she felt a bravery that she'd rarely felt before, and dared to face the thing she called her darkness, which she'd only glimpsed before, flinching as she watched it looking back at her with fierce, obsessive eyes.

It was naked, stripped of all its manly affectations, and she saw it plainly as a tree against a field of grass. And as she'd long suspected but had struggled to deny, her need for men was feminine. Her darkness was a girl.

When St. William thawed, and his long, warm hands were playing slow melodic strokes along her nape, she lay there longing for the thing that she'd assigned Wilfredo to do. With hesitation, she used a finger dampened by her mouth to see if he'd allow her to explore the little navel in the shadow of his balls; but he grunted, flinched and twisted.

Hushing him to make it seem as if she'd made a grave mistake, she reached behind and slid her hand between her sweating cheeks, sighing as three fingers were sucked in.

AFTER NAPPING IN each other's arms, they made some sandwiches from lettuce and some fish that he'd caught and smoked, and set out for a picnic in a dome of sea grapes half a mile away along the windward coast.

In the afterglow of love they felt a warm assurance that seduced them into putting off the search for answers and they left the house in a refreshing, optimistic mood.

"What am I going to do with you?" he asked her as they came out on a curving beach that glinted like a cutlass in the light. They'd crossed the narrow cay along a path that led them through a glade of tall Australian pines that whistled when the wind came through.

"Keep me loved and happy and no matter what I tell you, never let me go."

She wore her yellow dress with sandals and he wore a crushed white suit, and through their floppy hats they felt the sun against their heads, a round and focused presence like a bun.

In the distance, down the beach, they could see where constant wind had raised a line of dunes, a caravan of sand with humps like white camels sailing down the coast. The dunes took a shallow swing toward a point then made a sharper inward wheel to form a cove, a small hoofprint of water in a bright Islamic blue.

The wind began to whip the sand into their faces as they climbed the dunes, and they held hands and pulled the brims of their hats low across their brows and plunged knee high into the drifts.

When they'd almost reached the top, St. William raised Rebecca's chin and pointed down the grade. In his other hand he held the basket with their lunch.

In the middle of the bay they saw a sloop at anchor, and along the beach a line of clothes and footprints leading from the water to the clump of trees where they'd planned to have their lunch.

"Well, what do you think that means?" St. William asked.

"Oh, I think we've lost our reservation," said Rebecca in an airy voice. "Should we march right in and see the maître d'? Or should we slink away and go home?"

"Do you own this island, ma'am?"

"I think I do. Well, partly. The other half of it belongs to the man that owns me."

"And that would be *moi*."

"*Vraiment*."

"As part owner then, I'm going to pronounce. I think we should go and speak to the maître d'. But we shouldn't barge in. That would be really out of order . . . might upset the guests. I think we should make our way down there as quietly as we can. We shouldn't rush to judgment. We should take a minute . . ."

"Or a few . . ."

"In secret . . ."

"To observe."

The high dunes made a banked descent toward the beach, and they made their way toward the clump of trees with exaggerated movements like a pair of children playing elves.

When they were close enough to hear the sounds of love, St. William placed the basket on the slanting sand and entertained Rebecca with a naughty puppet show in which he placed his thumb between two fingers that he hoisted at the knuckles like a pair of legs.

With this, Rebecca tipped and kissed him, grateful for the simple pleasures that he'd brought into her life, the early part of which was spent with old, astringent nuns.

By the time that they'd come upon the trees, she was draped against his shoulder. Above the steady sizzle of the sea they overheard the bodies crashing in a suite of soft explosions like the flurries of a boxer working close against a bag, and, underneath it all, a clotted groan stagnating in a tender throat.

The open twisted branches of the sea grapes formed a dome whose upper leaves were spread along the lower ridges of the sand the way a tree would grow against the shingles of a roof.

Peering through an opening in the leaves they saw the lovers coupled on a towel in the dappled shade.

The woman was beneath the man, and all that could be seen of her were golden legs out-angled from beneath his arms like wings. Her lover's undulating back was broad and white with subtle muscles that would surge and disappear each time he stroked. And as Rebecca listened to the woman's groaning she was drawn into the mystery of the female body's power to withstand in times of passion hours of the most cyclonic force.

"Do I look like that?" St. William whispered from behind her with his chin against her shoulder and his lips against her ear.

Thinking of the many times that she'd given up her body to this kind of pulverizing in the hope that it would smash the darkness till it disappeared like smoke, Rebecca answered tartly.

"If I had a camera when I caught you and your mistress in our bedroom, maybe I would know."

"We'd separated. You'd abandoned me. You'd moved away."

"She still lives in our house."

"Well . . ."

"That was just so sick of you."

"At least I never lie."

She closed her eyes, receding to her inner depths, but before she settled she was startled by a grunt; and when she looked again she saw a complicated set of actions passing in a blur. Now the woman was on top, leaning backward with her arms behind her, fingers anchored in the sand.

And although she couldn't see her face because her head was carried low, Rebecca froze. The woman's hair, and skin, and breasts, and hips, and thighs were hers—but not as they were. As they used to be. And as she watched this incarnation of her younger self gyrating with a slipperiness that made it seem as if her pores secreted grease, Rebecca sniffled as she faced the unrepentant truth of age, the brutal forward march of time that plunders everything of beauty in its way. And when the woman raised her chin, eyes closed, a smile vibrating down her face, Rebecca's eyes began to darken with a deep destructive love.

## IV.

REBECCA AND ST. WILLIAM lived at Mt. Pleasant, an old estate along the rich volcanic slopes above Seville; there, five generations of Rawles had been born. And that night, as they undressed in their room, a high-ceilinged chamber of dark wood and beige caning, St. William said: "Be honest. What do you *really* think of them?"

"Oh, they seem quite ordinary to me," she said of Lowell and Cornelia. "Rather bland."

She was appraising herself in the heavy standing mirror, feet together on the spot where she'd caught him with Estrella, wincing as she pictured all the ghosts of all her previous selves aligned in raucous laughter. How horrific. She was old.

"They'd make a pair of fascinating spies," St. William joked, as he slid into a pair of silk pajamas. "That's all I can say."

"Yes," she answered without looking, brows abandoned in a shocked, emphatic lift. "Our man and . . . woman in San Carlos. You need to wean yourself from Graham Greene."

"Well, you said she had a camera."

"Which people utilize to take a photograph."

Dressed in full panties and a luxe embroidered bra, she swiveled, first one way and then the next, examining her back across her shoulder.

Her body was smooth and well contoured, but her muscles had gone soft. And on seeing a subtle line of rimpled fat appearing in a slant from just below her ribs, which were completely spackled over, she began to pat the little pouch of wrinkled skin below her navel that she'd tried to lose for more than thirty years with corsets, sports and herbal rubs.

Rebecca was vain, but not arrogant. In the company of other women she carried herself with cool assurance and was known as one who answered compliments with grace and perfect timing as she handled tennis serves. But an encounter with her younger self had scared her, had pulled her up with doubt.

As she reflected on her looks and thought about her conversation with Cornelia, whom she'd eventually approached, Rebecca vaguely heard St. William say, "But what if what you thought had been a camera was in fact a gun?"

"Yes. A gun," she said distractedly, then shook in dim surprise.

St. William's lips were pressing on her shoulder, and a moment passed before she comprehended that the man who stood behind her in the mirror was the one who'd kissed her from behind.

"So your little foolish game is finished, then," he asked her in a puckish way and slid his hand along her flanks, which sparkled with the embers of a slow, dissolving burn.

The way in which she lusted for the girl had made her panic. An abstract fear had come to life, appearing in the flesh; now perhaps the battle would be waged outside her soul.

She'd been fighting with her feelings since her early teens, and had been successful through the use of overwhelming force—straight-ahead assaults by waves of tough conscripted men who forced the darkness to retreat each time it reared its head.

In his youth Wilfredo had been one of them, but now he was a special unit of his own, the cool assassin who was dropped behind the lines to open up another front along her rear.

Pulled in two directions, it had seemed as if the darkness was about to face surrender or defeat. Now all of this had changed. And feeling threatened, as she'd never been before, she began to look at marriage as a stabilizing force. So, on reaching home that evening she'd confessed that she had once again begun to see Wilfredo and had asked St. William to forgive her; but he offered her a choice—apologize in public or be flogged.

With her assent, he stripped her down and tied her to the turned-and-chiseled posters of the jacaranda bed, and sucked her toes and sang to her then poured into her spinal groove a stream of almond oil that he allowed to overflow and trickle warmly down her ribs before he spread it evenly across her back, and up her neck, and down her thighs, behind her knees and past her calves, then up between the cleft that halved her bottom into loaves then used a wooden spatula to spank her firmly, driven by the secret knowledge that his mistress was observing through a crack between the swollen timbers of the door, fully unaware though that his wife was thinking of Cornelia as she writhed against the soft chenille and grunted that she was his slave, his ungrateful f——king heathen slave, his property, his beast, a swine whose soul had been invaded by a sinful spirit and who needed all her evil trampled out.

"Is it done?" he asked again, his voice upswinging slightly in a subtle boast.

"It's done," she said with dull emotion. In the mirror she could see a look of triumph in his eyes and added in a voice of rote, "I lost my way. You brought me back. I'm good and straightened out."

"Do you think you'll ever change?" he asked her sentimentally.

"I have. I have." Then switching to an urgent voice she asked him, "Did I tell you that they're coming for a meal?"

"No. You told me everything about going back to see them but that."

"Is that okay with you?" she said sweetly.

"Absolutely. When?"

"Tomorrow."

"Just her or both of them?"

She twisted from his hug and muttered, "Let me go."

"Hey. Hey. Hey."

He trapped her arms and chuckled while she tried to stomp his toes, thinking this was just a game. She pushed and tugged against him, doubling over, and, realizing that she was upset, he let her go.

She grabbed his shirt and threatened softly, "Try to f——k her and you'll die."

## V.

PERHAPS IT WAS the news of escalating war in Cuba; perhaps it was the guilt that she'd obliquely hurt the dog; perhaps it was the sense of weakness and exposure that had washed her on admitting that she was a member of a lower caste. But hours after walking out on Lowell's gruff proposal, Cornelia asked him if he'd really leave his wife, and he'd cleared his throat and told her yes from love and guilt and what he thought of as a social obligation.

He sent a telegram to Gilly with a made-up explanation, gave himself two weeks in which to change his mind and launched himself into a great adventure with his mistress, secretly believing that his daily presence would annoy her, and that marriage would surrender its appeal.

But from that point their trip became a joy. In the mornings they went sailing in a little rented sloop along the shore, putting in at wide deserted beaches.

When they landed, she would drift away to shoot romantic photographs of shells and rocks and he would find a spot of shade, a pencil tucked behind his ear, and edit books, glancing up from time to time to gaze at her—the boxy Bronica held just above her waist, her shoulders round, her hem updrawn and tucked between her knees.

Sometimes as he watched her, she would fade into the woods and reemerge some hours later as a shadow fluttering on a distant rise, and he'd feel his body welling with excitement at the thought of her return, when with relish they would dive into the surf and float naked on their backs and discuss what they'd read and seen, then make warm love on dunes made cool by tree shade and wake up nice and toasty after drifting into sleep, their creases lined with sand that they would softly slap and brush into the wind.

In the evenings they'd go drinking in the bars along the harbor front, and either take a cab or stagger home along the Queens and make more love and sleep enraptured with each other in their big sleigh bed that smelled of sweat and lemon oil, rising only when their stomachs rang like bells, assured and optimistic, believing that with love, all things could be achieved.

It was in a mood like this that they departed for their dinner with the Rawles in clothes that they'd selected at Salan's, a brand that had expanded to include the brewery, the tannery, the Coca-Cola plant, and factories for producing textiles, acid, paint and cigarettes.

Lowell wore a navy blazer with cream pants and buckled shoes; Cornelia wore a sleeveless dress in beige, and for an accent wore a purple shawl. Her hair was up and gathered in a sort of nest; and in her ears were simple pearls.

Their hosts had sent a car, a whitewalled Buick Century that Rebecca's dad, Khalid Salan, had purchased in Detroit and shipped before the war. It was silver, with a running board and bug-eyed headlamps on its elongated nose, the grille of which was tall and sloped.

Although the car was old, it had been kept in good condition, and the driver drove with pep, and so they quickly left the town behind and rose into the hills.

The eight-cylinder pulled them smoothly on the narrow road, which swerved through bush and stands of timber like a salmon moves along a stream, and they felt the humid evening breeze rush over them like water as they settled in the softness of the leather seat as darkness came with flaming hues that lit the sky.

"So you're family?" asked the driver, who wore an ivory shirt without a jacket.

The roof was down and with the wind he had to twist his neck to speak, which at first the lovers found unnerving. But as they saw how well he knew the road, how true he matched the whitewalls to the tightness of the turns, their misgivings mellowed to an awe-inspired glow.

"So you are relatives?" the driver asked them in another way. He was a fat old man with short brown hair and wrinkles like a pack of franks along his nape.

Lowell said with mischief, "We just met the other day."

The driver cocked his head in slight confusion.

"Why?" Cornelia asked.

The driver said, "You could pass for Miss Rebecca's daughter."

"Me?" she answered, pointing at herself, struggling to recall Rebecca's face.

"I didn't think about it when I met her," Lowell offered. "But I think our friend here might be right."

They'd been dozing in the shadow of the sea grapes when they'd heard the engine of the boat, Cornelia now recalled, and with a towel wrapped about her she'd emerged into the glare.

At first the conversation had been awkward. From the cockpit of the boat, Rebecca told her in a flat officious tone that she'd trespassed on a private island, that perhaps it might be time to leave, and she'd apologized and told her of her book on beaches as she glanced toward the sea grapes, where the line of scattered clothing hinted that the island had a lot of sex appeal.

When she heard about the book, Rebecca, who'd worn a scarf to hold her hair, smiled from underneath her black sunglasses and informed her that her husband, who was dozing in their cottage half a mile away, was a writer of great style if not renown, and that it would be good for him if they should meet. At this point Lowell sauntered out and she began to share interesting little facts about the island, which then led to a discussion of the lovely view of the savanna from their bedroom on the sec-

ond story of a small hotel that used to house a doctor who'd fled
the Haitian Revolution, and Rebecca told her that she knew the
house extremely well because it was her childhood home, and
that the room in which they slept was rather special, for it was
the one in which she and her sister had been born.

"Is miss lady pretty?" asked Cornelia as she tried to bring the
details of Rebecca's face to mind.

"The most beautiful I've ever seen."

"Don't look back," said Lowell, complimenting her. "You'll
change your view."

"You're a very lucky man," the driver answered as they
crossed a bridge above a stream.

Lowell drew Cornelia close and said in expectation, "Why's
that?"

"She's very beautiful, your daughter. I have a son who's not
yet married. If it is okay with you, perhaps we could arrange for
them to carry on a correspondence."

"I'm very sorry but I think she'll be married soon."

"Oh, but can I meet him, Daddy, please?" said Cornelia,
playing with the joke. "Nothing may come out of it. But then you
never know. What's his name, mister driver man? Will you tell
me please?"

"Raymond," said the driver. "A lovely boy. Raised with good
manners. He is away at the moment, studying the law. The doctor sent him as part of our Future Sons Brigade. Our new chief
minister and great leader, Dr. Octavio Reynoso Ardiles Rawle—
who is Miss Rebecca's son—sent a hundred young men on
scholarships overseas to study medicine, engineering and eco-
nomics so that our nation will be prepared for total independence. Now we only have internal rule."

"And your young ladies?" teased Cornelia. "Will they get to
go away as well?"

"Well . . . no," the driver answered brightly. "They'll get one
hundred men with future prospects."

"Where'd he send them?" Lowell asked, impressed.

"Canada. He didn't want to send them to London; he wanted our Future Sons to come back with independent minds. And that would be hard to do if he sent them to the mother country. And he didn't want to send them to the States."

Lowell said, perhaps a little tightly, "Too lowbrow for you?"

"I don't mean to offend you or your country, sir," the driver answered cautiously.

"I'm not offended," said Lowell. "Curious . . . though."

"Most Yankees . . . well . . . Americans . . . sir . . . they're not like you."

Lowell shifted in his seat.

"Thanks," he said. "That's kind of you. But what do you mean?"

"I can see from your daughter's beauty that you have a colored wife. The doctor knows about the troubles that your *negritos* face, sir. And he didn't want our Future Sons to be afflicted with that kind of doubt and shame. Here, in San Carlos, there's no shame in being *concoco*."

"What's that?" asked Cornelia, breaking in. She slipped away from Lowell's arm and slid forward on her seat so that her mouth was close against the driver's ear.

"A woman like you," he said haltingly, unsure if he'd upset the girl. "The real word is *café con coco,* but nowadays we just say *concoco.* The *café con coco* is a woman with the body of a *negrita* but the skin of someone somewhat like the white—but not as much as, say, a *chocoblanca.* It is hard to explain. Once there was an illness here that killed off all the cows, and people had to drink their tea and coffee with coconut milk. It had a peculiar taste and color, which was different from *café con leche.* It's a compliment I'm paying you. The *concoco* is a woman of great attraction in San Carlos. They used to make them in the slavery time. The doctor told us during one of his many public lectures that producing *concocos* used to be a meticulous calculation—

very much like breeding orchids. My son would treat you like a queen."

Lowell sensed Cornelia's shock and intervened.

"I've never quite heard it put that way," he said, and drew Cornelia close. He could feel and hear her breathing getting short.

The driver noted, "But it's true."

THEY'D LEFT THE road now and were moving on a path between a corridor of trees with interwoven branches. They were cotton trees, monumental things with the giant height and spread of oaks, and from their boughs hung clotted beards of Spanish moss. It was almost dark; and very cool, and from a branch above the car, an owl with yellow irises took whispered flight.

The land on either side of them, Cornelia saw, was lined with rows and rows of withered coconut palms, frondless, fruitless victims of an ancient blight. And as she looked at them, she felt a chill as if her body had been splashed with rum.

In all her travels through these islands, she'd rarely left the beach, where it seemed that time had been suspended, history washed away; where the ocean with its constant flux had fooled her into thinking of these colonies as places on the fringe of natural law—forgotten havens where a woman like herself could have the luxury of a life without the weight of choices, of committing, of claiming, of taking sides.

But this journey to the center of San Carlos had reminded her that each island was a complicated world, that history was alive, that the boundaries of the past existed but in ways that weren't apparent to the stranger's eye. And for a woman whose very birth had been a crime, this was now a journey into doubt. We should not have come, she told herself. We should've stayed at home.

Lowell passed his hand along her arm.

"You're shivering," he said. "It's colder than we thought. We should've gotten you a thicker shawl."

"The trees," she answered distantly. "The trees."

While he waited for an explanation, her mind was drifting off.

The headless palms reminded her of something that she'd never seen, of which she'd only heard. And as they came around a bend and saw the large white house ahead of them, substantial on a flat commanding height, her mind began to cloud with memories of the year she'd spent in Mississippi picking photos of sharecroppers for inclusion in her book . . . memories of peeling shacks and passing cars cycloning dust on country roads, of cotton fields as white as foam, of meeting whole clans of negro people who'd never learned to read, but mostly of the shy old man who'd told her that he didn't like to read, that every time he tried to read his eyes would tighten up because of something that had happened to a friend of his who got a little learning and began to speak to them as if he thought he was some kinda man . . . and how they lynched that boy . . . how they took that boy one night and did him as they do . . . left him on a pole so everyone could see . . . twisting in the wind . . . his manhood in his mouth. If one day someone gathered all them lynching poles, I tell you, Miss Cornelia, all across the south, and put 'em all together in a single field, it would look just like the woods when winter comes. Like this, she thought. Like this.

Cornelia felt the tires skidding slightly as the driver made the turn around the ring of stones that framed the wedge of thick uplifted roots that held in place the hundred-year-old cotton tree that stood before the house, and opened dampened eyes.

It was a tall house roofed in shingle with high windows framed on either side with strips of louver blades. The ground floor, which was made of stone, was widened by a porch that swept around the sides and out of view. The second floor was made of wood.

Lowell asked Cornelia, "Are we fine?"

"Some things are hard to say," she answered as they passed into the shadow of the overhanging eaves and heard footsteps growing louder on the inside of the double doors, whose frosted panels glowed with light. He put his arm around her and she didn't move. Something inside her had changed.

## VI.

TWO LONG TABLES had been joined and draped in white and lit by silver candlesticks that spread a creamy light across the heavy plates. As the handprinted place cards showed, the couples had been separated and positioned far apart.

Although she was surprised at this, Cornelia felt a sense of mild relief, for Lowell had been seated six chairs over, sandwiched by a banker and a Presbyterian priest, which meant she could avoid his look.

As soon as St. William said the grace, Dean O'Connor leaned across the table as Estrella served a chunky turtle soup. Dean was in his fifties, and his red nose showed him truly as a man who liked to drink. He had a gravelly voice and a heavy jaw and spoke in sentences that had a strong attack as if his mouth had been embedded with a horn—which suited the commissioner of police.

"So, Cornelia," he began, a local accent rising through his brogue. "Tell us what you think of our place."

"I think it's beautiful," she answered shrewdly. "Romantic in a lot of ways."

At the other end, reclining from the light, Rebecca, who'd missed the cocktails by the pool on purpose and had come down from her bedroom just before Estrella rang the bell, was hiding from the light. She'd placed herself across the table from Cornelia, down toward the farthest end, way off to the side. This way she could watch her and no one would see.

Sitting on Cornelia's right, the balding lawyer, David Campbell, asked, "Romantic? Romantic? Romantic in what way?"

"I'm not sure I said what I meant," Cornelia said.

As he did with women that he found attractive, he began to hound.

"You meant we act as if we're living in a dream," he said. "Impractical, aren't we? Anyone who's read the *Star* of late would say the same."

"I haven't read the papers since I've been here," she replied politely, though she felt the urge to hit him with her spoon. "I meant romantic like a poem, like a song."

"Our young chief minister has been mouthing off about the Cuban situation," the commissioner intoned. "And it's making all of us a bit uneasy."

From the other side, the lawyer's wife began to whisper in a voice intended to amuse: "One less would mean some more for me. So keep talking, David, till your hostess throws you out."

"So it's your informed opinion that a poem is romantic?" David asked Cornelia, his questioning resumed.

Distracted as she thought about the conversation in the car, Cornelia tried to speak but couldn't find the words, and soup drained off her spoon and splattered on the table and the floor.

"I'm sorry," she apologized.

Someone called Estrella, who began to huff and groan while cleaning up in her expensive English shoes.

"I do this kind of thing to everyone," the lawyer said, and softly bumped her shoulder. "Welcome to the club."

While Cornelia joined the table in a knowing laugh, Rebecca said from out of view, "Oh give the girl a chance. She'll find out soon enough that you're depraved."

"That's right," said Mrs. Chang, whose round phlegmatic face was now enlivened with a grin. "Expose him."

"Cornelia," said St. William, in the kind of sober air with which a journalist begins a serious interview, "how did you get started with your hobby?"

Rebecca further eased herself out of the light.

"Well, it's a little more than that," Cornelia answered, craning, eyes narrowed in a squint. From her seat, St. William was positioned in the glare behind a candle's light, so everything around him was in silhouette.

"I stand corrected then," he said warmly. "But I know there must be more."

Gazing from beneath her brows while sipping from her spoon, she said, "I'm working on a book."

His warmth had drawn her out.

"Come," he said with vim and wit. "We're bored colonials. Excite us. Give us more."

"It's about beaches," she said brightly.

"A novel?" someone asked.

"Photos," joked St. William with a comic snort.

"Beaches?" asked Rebecca as the table shimmered with guffaws. "Out of everything—why that?"

"I find them fascinating," said Cornelia, in a well-projected voice. She didn't see who'd asked the question and she panned around the table as she spoke so that the person who'd asked would not believe that she was rude. "They're the place where land and water meet, where one thing washes over the next. The borders there are always shifting. There's no equivalent where the earth meets the sky or the sky meets the earth. Beaches are . . . interesting . . . for lots of reasons . . . none of which are easy to say in words. I'm more articulate with film."

"Well, we don't speak film here," the commissioner joked. "Just a bit of *sancoche*."

"Beaches are the color of the people who are neither black or white," Cornelia said in further explanation.

"Also where a lot of them are made."

She didn't see who said this; but the voice had the effect of passing angels—a hush descended on the room.

Fiona, Dean O'Connor's red-haired wife, who wore a tiny rosary on a double-stranded string of pearls, took it on herself to float the grounded conversation.

"I think it's silly of us to worry about what's happening in Cuba," she said in a voice that quaked then settled as it gathered speed and took a new direction. "In fact we should be happy if the rebels win. I trust Camilo. Castro is a man of honor. Guevara is the one that worries me a bit if anything. But that is not the point. If the rebels win, what are the Yankees going to do? As our guest of honor said, beaches are"—she gestured blithely—"oh, everything. We have a lot of beaches on this island, a sprinkle of villas and just one real hotel—if you would dare to call it that. No offense to present company. Until now the Cubans have been getting all the tourists. We can't stay rich off cows and farms forever. Disease completely wiped out coconuts. I think our future is the tourist trade. I hope the rebels win."

"Perhaps your Dean should send a squad to help," St. William answered. "But I hardly think tourism is the point."

The lawyer snapped, "Enlighten me."

"The point is that in Cuba there's decay of law and order," Dean O'Connor thundered as Estrella cleared the bowls.

"Oh shut up, Dean," St. William shot. "He wasn't asking you. We think that our Carlitos will begin to get ideas from Havana. We think that revolution is a kind of illness, some disease that will destroy our wealth the way that blight completely decimated every head of coconut my grandfather planted on these fifteen hundred acres. With people there are ways to vaccinate against disease. Housing. Education. Jobs and health." As other guests began to roll their eyes, Cornelia listened, rapt. "There are sixty thousand people on this island. And one hospital with fifty beds and eleven doctors, only one of which—my son—is qualified to operate. But we have two hundred thousand cows and twenty vets. We have four high schools and one teachers college. People are satisfied now because they don't know any better. Don't forget what happened to the Romanovs . . ."

"Oh, get a sense of scale," the lawyer joked.

"There's no need to have a revolution," offered Mr. Chang,

who Cornelia noticed had a voice whose pitch was higher than his wife's. "They have the vote."

"And look who they elected," came a quip.

"What do you mean?" Cornelia asked.

"The other candidate," St. William said, "was older. More experienced."

Someone added, "Oh, come out and say it. He's black like tar."

There were murmurs, and Cornelia heard the name Xavier Joseph Jr. and gathered that he was the man who'd lost. The older, more experienced man. The black.

"The negro man is not a fool," Dean O'Connor boomed. "Given a choice he chooses what he thinks is best. Xavier Joseph had just one agenda—to finish what his father started. So he formed a sugar workers' union. So he's been advocating all the things that people like to hear, minimum wage and blah, blah, blah. But the bloody man's afflicted with a stutter. Who can throw their vote behind a leader who can't move them with a talk? Not me, for sure. Not that he would ever get my vote. But be that as it may—with all respect accorded to our gracious hosts—the doctor is a charlatan."

"No, he's not," Rebecca challenged, leaning forward in the light. "He's charismatic."

Cornelia saw her face and smiled with recognition as she matched it with the voice that had been making clever comments all along.

"What's charisma?" David Campbell asked.

Rebecca answered, "Wouldn't you like to know?"

"Yes, in fact. I would," he dared.

"Well, ask your wife."

With irritation, he responded, "Well, I'm asking you."

"It's different things to different people."

"Well, what is it to you?"

"A charismatic man?"

"No. A paris patic pan."

"Oh. A charismatic man?"

"I see the message to the moon has been delivered."

In a slow, seductive voice designed to pique Cornelia's interest, Rebecca cleared her throat and said, "A man who can make *any* woman feel like a *negrita*." She paused until the nervous giggles tapered off. "And that's a special skill."

"And what is that supposed to mean?" asked Mrs. Chang.

Cornelia drank some water to conceal her blushing face.

"Ask my husband," said Rebecca blithely.

St. William quipped, "My juicy lips are sealed."

"Let me explain what I'm trying to say for the sake of our guests," began Rebecca in a prim, scholastic tone. "Caribbean people like to have a leader with the reputation of a stud. And lemme tell you, if a man can talk the drawers off a woman he can talk the vote out of a man. It's the same principle at play. When you see my son on a platform, you see a man who has the skill of touching all the common feelings in the common man. But that is not the proof of his charisma. The proof of his charisma is his skill at finding the *negrita* in the most sophisticated girls. His ability to find that ambition in a woman is his skill. We all want to be the *negrita,* you know, and that is what our husbands want too. But it's the very thing we're not supposed to be. Ladies, don't they love it when we whisper some *sancoche* to them in bed? Oh, let's not get embarrassed now. We're friends here. Old and new. I've never heard of anybody with a mistress who is white. They want a woman with at least a touch of sugar. We're as dull as milk and flour. They're looking for the sweet."

Cornelia tapped her feet against the creaking floor as she considered this, stunned . . . enraged . . . amused.

With a grunt Estrella placed a leg of pork before St. William, who dropped his arm and stroked her leg to show her that he cared. With aplomb he trimmed the cone of meat, creating frills that curled.

The table buzzed with shifting conversations as the guests

began to find their natural interest groups. And during all of this Cornelia felt a bit estranged. Wine was being popped and poured and the characters and stories all around her kept her fascinated and bemused, but mostly bored—and she found herself being drawn toward Rebecca, wishing they'd been seated close.

When the meat was ready and the wine completely poured, Rebecca raised a toast.

"To charismatic men, especially my husband and my son, and to Lowell and Cornelia, who've graced us with their presence at such short notice and have brought a spark of insight to this dull and dreary room."

"Hip-hip."

"Hooray!"

"Hip-hip."

"Hooray!"

As she sipped the heavy Spanish wine Cornelia noticed that St. William and Rebecca were divided by a space.

"Who's missing?" she asked.

Pointing with his chin, the lawyer answered, "No one anymore."

In white shirtsleeves and dark blue pants, the doctor tipped his homburg, which he put away himself. With arms outstretched, he called St. William for a hug and gave Rebecca a bouquet, then paused to light a cigarette before he sat down.

Like a cowboy in a tough saloon, he put his elbows on the table with his fingers doubled in a fist and placed his chin on top, then swept the faces looking outward from the shadows all around him with a civil but suspicious look, speaking in a dialect of nods and smiles and glances that required not a word.

While waving everyone to eat, he called Estrella with a finger while he whispered to his mom, who rose and in a warm endearing voice informed her guests that there would be a momentary darkness as the candles were blown out.

There were awkward chuckles when the flickers were snuffed,

and of course a comic shriek that sparked a cheeky accusation and a quick exchange of dirty jokes. After this their eyes were dazzled by the glitter of a crystal chandelier.

"You're killing us," St. William sputtered.

"I'm doing this for Dean," the doctor joked. "This way he won't trip and cut himself when he attacks me from behind."

As Cornelia watched the doctor's interaction with his mother, sensing something strange, he turned to her and said with interest, "You're the photographer, I'm told."

Rebecca reached around and took the Dunhill from his lips.

Cornelia said, "I am one of them . . . I guess. There must be many more . . . I suppose."

He put his hand against his ear to make it seem as if he had to strain to listen through the haze of voices hanging like a smog below the lights. She cupped her mouth and answered brightly, "One of them, I guess."

Leaving her to stew in her own juices, he turned to Lowell, who was facing him and warmed him with a droll stage whisper: "I know who you are. You're the man who's being seduced by my father. You don't know it but you're destined to publish his books."

"That would be me, then," Lowell answered in a bright, good-natured way.

"I hope you know that all of this has been arranged for you. If I were you I'd be careful. When the offer comes to go up to his study, man, your life as you know it will be done."

As Lowell laughed, Cornelia watched the doctor while she ate, and thought she felt it when he reached behind his mother's chair to softly rub her neck.

Once while she was chewing absentmindedly, he looked across and caught her stare.

"Did I tell you I was sorry for my lateness?" he asked, softly shrugging while Rebecca tried to curl beneath his arm.

"You must have," she said. "I think so. You might."

"I'm very sorry."

"It's okay."

"If things had gone a little differently, we might have met before. But that's another story. Things happen in their time."

1. The way he talked
   (*slow, with nothing of a British affectation*)
2. The way he smoked
   (*squinting, like a sniper taking aim*)
3. The way he moved his knife and fork
   (*careless, like a child*)
4. The way he laughed
   (*inward, like he had a private joke*)
5. The way he flirted with his mother
   (*boldly, like he didn't care about established borders and taboos*)
6. The sweetness of the wine
   (*which had seduced her into having many drinks*)

Having made this list of possibilities, Cornelia tried to focus on the source of his appeal. Her life had been disturbed. A pebble had been flung into her pond.

## VII.

AFTER DINNER—THERE was almond cake and honey-flavored ice cream for dessert—they herded to the drawing room to dance. It was a large room with soft chairs in chintz and plush Mongolian rugs. It smelled of old smoke and wood polish, under which there was the tender scent of grapefruits and wet stone.

Other people had arrived for aperitifs, which Rebecca and St. William served themselves on bamboo trays. Groups and cliques had formed. And for a moment Lowell and Cornelia found themselves alone beside each other on a floral sofa with a pleated skirt. Before them was a grainy coffee table, whose center was inlaid with mother-of-pearl.

"Are we fine?" he asked.

"Yes," she answered, with a taut self-conscious grin that told him that her feelings were confused.

"I love you quite a bit, you know," he said with apprehension as he slowly turned his glass of iced vermouth.

"I know," she said, while thinking, *But less than your daddy or your wife.*

"The guy was out of order," he said, referring to the awkward moment in the car. "I should have said something. I didn't. You're disappointed. I know."

She shrugged and said, "I'm fine," and drank some more Lillet.

"No, you're not."

"No, really," she said and tapped his leg. "I'm fine."

"Tired?"

"Yes. Tired. I'm sorry I'm tired. When I'm tired I get too sensitive sometimes."

He withdrew into a brittle silence while she slowly sipped her drink and gazed between the moving bodies at the lovely objects in the nicely furnished room. She thought she saw some paintings of the maid among the many on the wall.

"Do you mind if I refer to you as my fiancée?" he probed.

"No," she said quickly. "No. Not at all."

"There's no ring yet and I didn't want to put you in any awkward situations or make anybody confused."

"It's more important for me to know what I am to you. Don't you think?"

"Yes. But I was just wondering why you didn't say anything to the guy in the car."

"Anything like what?" she said, aware now that his feelings had been hurt. She put her arm around his waist and shook him hard to cheer him up.

"Anything like, *He's my future husband, not my dad.*"

"Did I hurt your feelings?" she asked and kissed him quickly on the cheek. "I'm sorry, hon. How rude of me."

"It's okay," he answered, feeling that he'd been dismissed. "Look, St. William wants to meet with me. Are you sure you'll be all right?"

She stood and stretched her arm. He took her hand though feeling slighted that she'd cut him off.

"Thanks for caring," she said. "I'll be okay. Don't worry. I'll be fine."

"You're just tired," he said. "I'm sure that's what it is."

"Very tired."

"Then I won't be long."

"Okay."

He turned to go then sat again; he held her by the elbow and eased her down.

"Strange mix," he said, with barely moving lips.

"What do you mean?"

"Ssshhhhhhhh."

"Okay. Okay."

"There were nineteen people at that table—twenty when the doctor came and not a single negro one among them."

"Apart from me, you mean?"

"You know what I mean," he answered, shaking her as she'd done to him.

"I'm not good at thinking now," she told him flatly. "Maybe it's the drinks."

"I've never seen it worse in Tennessee. Take a look around. There must be thirty, maybe forty people here . . . and nothing's changed."

"Don't try to understand it, man. And more than anything, don't make it worse. Don't explain it or try to figure it out. It's the way things are and how they'll be."

"I'm not explaining," he said tightly.

To change the mood, she tapped his leg and said, "I'm really tired, hon. Forgive me if I'm short."

"So, tell me," he whispered in a roguish way, "what do you *really* think of them."

"Rebecca and St. William or the rest?"

Chuckling, he said, "You choose."

"They seem okay to me," she said vaguely.

"But what about us?" he asked. "Are we okay?"

"Of course we are. Why do you keep asking?"

"I just want to be sure."

She took another drink and framed her thoughts.

"Lowell, if you're not sure, you can always change your mind, you know. Nobody knows but the two of us. We don't even have a ring."

"When you talk like that it breaks my heart," he said and hooked her with his arm.

"Gilly has a heart as well. Look, St. William wants to meet with you. Go meet with him. While you're gone I'll just sit here guarding Gilly's heart."

He fumbled for a good response, but, "Gilly is okay," was all that tumbled out.

She looked at him and shook her head in a smug, superior way and said, "Me too."

"Do you need some time to think?" he asked.

"Uh-huh."

He stood and slipped his hands inside his pockets.

"Well . . . honestly . . . me too."

By the wooden record changer, with its sliding door and single speaker cased in mesh, St. William tore the plastic from a stack of new LPs. Groups splintered into couples with the crack of a timbale and the guests began to waltz. Someone dimmed the lights, and Cornelia watched the doctor dancing with his mother to a lush bolero sung in English with a set of lustrous sentimental chords.

When Lowell walked away, Cornelia was approached by Mrs. Chang, who'd been watching from across the room.

"Our chief minister is something, isn't he?" she said.

"Is he really charismatic, then?" Cornelia asked her pensively.

"Based on what his mother said, I wouldn't know."

Her humor was parading in the absence of her husband, who was dancing with the lawyer's uncoordinated wife.

"Publicly, I mean."

Mrs. Chang drew closer and unwrapped her Matterhorns. She was short and fat-armed, with sloped shoulders that conveyed the wrong impression—that she was a dud at sports. On the tennis courts they knew her as The Iron Ballerina.

"Octavio is a man of great passion and with an even greater mind," she told Cornelia through her teeth. "His weakness is his mother, whom I've known since my eyes were at my knees. Our parents were just-comes. Her father was from the Middle East and mine was from Hong Kong. And lemme tell you, in their time they never thought that one of them would ever see the inside of this house. But that is not the point. What I'm trying to say to you is that Rebecca and her son are very close. If they changed the law and she could marry him she'd divorce poor Willy in the morning. She's obsessed. And that worries me. These are early days. But very soon she'll find a way to take the power from Octavio's hand. That day will be hell for all of us."

"Because?"

"Because she knows that every woman in this room has screwed her husband at some point and she's a creature of revenge." She waited for the fading of Cornelia's nervous laugh. "I'm serious. Even the maid . . . Estrella . . . she learned to read in the back of my father's shop. My baby sister used to teach her. But all this gossip must be boring. I heard you're getting hooked."

Cornelia drained her glass and answered drolly, "Like a mule."

"He's nice enough, it seems."

"He is."

"Older. Settled. More mature."

"That sounds like him."

"Rich?"

"But that's not it."

"Love?"

"Well, of course."

"Your answer was too quick, so let's pretend I didn't ask."

"I will."

Mrs. Chang drew closer now and took Cornelia's arm. "Here's a little secret. Take it how you want. Even give it away. But it is something of some worth. Marriage is not about love or money. It's about embarrassment. Shame is a very sticky thing. You make each other bleed so much the scabs begin to bind."

Cornelia drew her arm away and closed her eyes to ponder this. Pulling deeply on the Matterhorn, she felt the flaring heat against her nose, the mentholated smoke diffusing warmly through her lungs, which felt so huge behind her large uptilted breasts, contrasting with the empty tingle in her mouth.

Did she really love him? Did he love her? Did he love his wife? Did he love his wife more than her? Could he really handle the disgrace?

Her thoughts began to haunt her. The darkness underneath her lids began to feel unsafe, and so she blinked, her face illuminated by a guilty smile. The doctor was directly in her focus, staring, his mother's body hiding everything except his arms and face.

As she looked at him, he drew his hand along Rebecca's back, a languid stroke that started just above the rump and ended at the shoulder, and looking on, Cornelia felt as if she'd just experienced all the pleasure of a slow caress.

Reaching round his mother's neck, the doctor slid the Dunhill in his mouth, his fingers pausing in a slanted line across his lips now as he squinted and inhaled, which made Cornelia feel that she'd been asked to keep a secret, that she was a partner in an act of great collusion, that she'd been entrusted with important information that required her to hush.

Pretending that she hadn't seen him, Cornelia looked away, her face expressing nonchalance. But when she squinted as she smoked, she realized that she'd given her assent, had answered yes before he'd asked the question—and she quickly left the room.

Rebecca saw and slyly gave pursuit.

## VIII.

OUTSIDE, BEHIND THE house, the sky was softly shaking with the time-release explosions of a thousand stars. The windows and the doors that opened on the back veranda hummed with warm vibrations from the music, and their gauzy panes were sifting powdered talk and laughter on the lawn.

The lawn sloped down to the pool, on the other side of which there was a wooden bar, which was blue and curved, and had a shingled roof that had a heavy overhang along the front and sides. Anything below the overhang was hard to see—unless you looked.

Leaning with her back against the counter, wedged between a pair of wooden stools, Cornelia closed her eyes to block the world so she could focus on her feelings. From her belly button waves of strange emotions rippled out. She was angry and disappointed, confused and turned on, fragile and brave all at once.

There was something sexy in being the exotic, in being the *concoco* so desired and beloved. Rebecca's definition of charisma and its proof that had arrived without a jacket had intrigued her to the point where she was damp. And Lowell, didn't want her . . . really. She could hear it in his voice.

While Cornelia closed her eyes to block the world and think

of all these things, Rebecca watched her from behind a clump of bushes near a corner of the back veranda, forty yards away.

Anticipation made her slick between the lips and legs while envy stoked her pulse. Looking at my son like that. How dare that f——king girl.

By the time Cornelia saw her, she was standing by the pool, ten or fifteen yards away, her arms behind her back, one leg thrown forward in a thrust. Her fitted dress, which was navy blue and had a neckline with a plunge, was pulling sideways tightly at the hip, and there was sheen along the fabric where the forward-thrusted thigh exerted force.

For a hazy moment, Cornelia didn't recognize her. She'd been so deep inside her thoughts. And her reaction, when it came, expressed her disappointment—the mother not the son.

"Oh," she said, "it's you."

"Bored or boring?" asked Rebecca.

"Neither."

"Why'd you disappear?" Her voice was quilted with a homey softness crafted to create a tranquil mood. "I haven't really had a chance to speak with you. You were such a hit the hostess had to wait her turn."

Rebecca's gentle manner contradicted everything Cornelia saw and heard all evening. And she remembered now their meeting on the beach, which had opened tightly then progressed in graceful elongation to a give-and-take that left her feeling touched as if they'd danced.

As she watched Rebecca smiling now, she wanted to revive their lively interaction but was thinking forward to the ways in which their friendship would be complicated by her feelings for her son.

"I'm sorry that dinner was so overwhelming," said Rebecca, trying to draw her out. "I'm even sorrier that the conversations on this island are so stale. There's nothing like being the object of attention at a boring table. All the boring people want to talk to you. But that's what we need here in San Carlos. New blood. New ideas. Our thoughts are so inbred that our David Campbells are considered intellectuals. Can you believe it? That mongoloid."

"I didn't leave because I was bored or anything," said Cornelia, who'd begun to wonder if her exit and her table etiquette had made her seem uncouth. "Was I rude?"

"No. Not at all. You were fine."

"Thank you. I'm relieved."

"But I must be honest," said Rebecca, taking furtive glances up the grade before she took some quick but measured steps toward the bar so that the both of them were covered by the overhanging roof. "I like you very much. You're always welcome here."

"But?"

Rebecca took some time to calm her passions, which were rushing into war.

"But you cannot have my son."

The answer stripped Cornelia of the chance to contradict her or pretend, and she placed her elbows on the counter and began to stare with vacant eyes toward the pool—exposed and flabbergasted.

"I'm not speaking as his mother now," Rebecca said, her arm against the counter, closer to the girl. "I'm speaking as your friend. He has attachments and commitments of the kind you'd never understand. He's a wonderful man; but he'd mash up your life and give you pure grief. You're not the only woman who's in love with him, you know. There are hundreds on this island alone. And a woman like you should never put herself in any situation where she has to fight. Don't let anybody bring you low, my love. Keep your head on straight. But I understand your feelings, though. The boy is charismatic. He'll make you think of doing all sorts of *maddy-maddy* things."

"I understand," Cornelia answered, thinking now of what she'd seen at dinner and comparing it with all that Mrs. Chang had said.

"Do you?" asked Rebecca, inching closer down the bar—so close that she could smell Cornelia's natural salty fragrance underneath the woodsy glazing of a French perfume. "Are you really sure?"

"I'm sure," Cornelia answered quickly, just before she took the conversation on a different turn. "Can I ask a question?"

"Certainly. Of course."

Cornelia said what came to mind.

"I didn't notice any photographs of you in the house. Is there a reason?"

"There are a few," replied Rebecca, sitting as she felt her effort stall. "They're in my room."

"Of recent vintage?" asked Cornelia, sitting too.

"No," Rebecca answered, feeling grateful that the darkness veiled her form. "I don't pose for pictures anymore. You don't do that kind of thing when you're old."

"How old are you?" Cornelia asked with true interest. She swiveled on her stool to face Rebecca and didn't flinch or feel discomfort when their knees began to touch.

"Don't ask me," said Rebecca. "Please."

Cornelia thought her anxious answer was a joke and held her chin and leaned in very close, peering like a jeweler with an interest in a stone, swiveling the older woman's face at different angles, straining in the flaccid light.

Leaning back, she crossed her arms and made a grand announcement as Rebecca slowly caught her breath: "I want to shoot you, Mrs. Rawle."

The offer made Rebecca feel self-conscious; but she saw how she could use it as a door. Standing now, she placed her hands against Cornelia's shoulder, finding places that were loosely covered by the purple shawl and slipped her fingers underneath, taking private pleasure in the soft reverberations that began to stream along her arms, fuzzy tingles like a mild electric shock.

"So what crime have I committed, comandante," she joked. "Why do I deserve this execution? Who did I betray?"

"I want to martyr you," Cornelia pressed, irreverently. "Make you the patron saint of dinner tables all over the world."

"I don't want to be a saint," Rebecca answered, gesturing with flair. "I want my own religion."

"Okay. I'll give you that."

"Only if you'll be my pope."

"High priestess," said Cornelia. "Ironically, you need to have a peter if you wanna to be the pope."

Rebecca answered: "Women can be anything they want."

"Have you ever been shot by a woman before?"

"No."

"I want to be the first."

"Why?"

"In many parts of the world people hide from cameras because they think the lens will steal their souls," said Cornelia in a breathy philosophical tone as she became impassioned with the thought. In Rebecca she had glimpsed a little of the woman that she hoped to be—sensual, amusing, daring and bright. "And to some degree they're right. I don't shoot things or people. I shoot spirits—the unseen. Do you know how I want people to feel about my work? I want them to feel like they had a glimpse into the moment just before God waved his wand and turned a spirit or idea into a person or a thing. I know you've heard this lots of times before, but you've got a dynamic spirit. Will you do it? I have my equipment in my room. It could be fun."

"For you, perhaps," Rebecca answered coyly, feeling flattered, stimulated and a little ill at ease. "I'd have to figure what to wear. Someone would have to do my hair. It could end up being—please excuse me—just a lot of useless work."

"We can do it any way you'd like, you know."

"It always seems to be a fuss, though."

"I'll make it easy for you. There are many ways to make things easy. Sometimes we like to make a lot of things so stupidly involved. Sometimes all we need to do is to strip away the baggage."

"If there is an easy way . . . well no . . . not even then."

"You seemed really bold at dinner. Now I'm seeing the part of you that's shy. That's very intriguing."

"Well . . ."

"Which is why I was thinking that maybe we could do it . . . oh forget it."

"What?"

"I just thought of a way that could make it really simple for you. What if we did it really simply. Would that be okay with you?"

"What are you talking about?"

"I think we could get some really good shots if we made everything simple, if we did it in a way that would make your natural beauty come through. There is a lot of it. Your hair would be just washed and dried and left alone. And the rest is even simpler. Nude."

"I'll have to think about your offer," said Rebecca in the plucky timbre that she'd sought and found. Her smile was like a fire on a windy day. When she thought of how their naked bodies would compare when standing side by side, it dimmed; and when she thought of braiding limbs with her it blazed anew.

"I would do it in a tasteful way, of course . . ."

"Oh, I'd need two years of living at the tennis court before I'd think of doing anything like that. Which is so distressing. I used to be . . . well, everybody used to be. There you go, Miss Cornelia, making old ladies feel their age. That says a lot about you."

Cornelia felt a little guilty now, and wondered if she'd pushed a bit too hard.

"Mrs. Rawle, I didn't mean to twist your arm."

"You got away with it—which says a lot. I must like you more than anybody else I've met in years."

"Thank you," said Cornelia. "That was very nice."

"I only speak the truth. But before we're interrupted we should have a drink."

"No thanks. I've had a few."

"How many?"

"Wine? Maybe four or five at dinner—and three or four Lillets."

With a glancing kiss delivered to the temple in a warm maternal way, Rebecca said, "There must be rum behind this bar."

ROYAL STANDARD MADE three kinds of rum. All of them were aromatic. But one of them was over proof, a potent, concentrated force. Rebecca made the drinks from this—chased with Coca-Cola with twist of lime and garnished with a sprig of mint.

The rum was wonderfully fragrant and the smell of it was layered with the freshness of the mint and the tartness of the lime, and although it was aggressive it was smooth, which made Cornelia drink it quickly. Soon, the lining of her mouth began to feel as if it had been trimmed with fur.

Rebecca stayed behind the bar to mix and pour. Anxious, she'd begun to drink the heady mixture at the rate of lemonade. She'd never touched a woman in the way that she was thinking that she'd like to touch this lovely girl—completely—as completely as the darkness that was clouding all her judgment from within. And she felt that it was wise to have the countertop between them in the moment that her feelings were unleashed. Saddened by her tragic state and loosened by the rum, she began to talk about her life.

Before this private moment, Cornelia barely had a passing

interest in the island's life. She'd begun her trip three months ago without ever having heard of it, and had only come because someone had told her of the beaches of the *back beyond*. Now, after learning more about the island from Rebecca, who over drinks had shared small chapters of her father's life—migrating from Lebanon, opening a shop below the house where St. William's mother used to live, returning to Amman to meet the stranger that his parents had selected for his bride—Cornelia felt as if she'd like to stay because it struck her as a place with layers that she could explore.

About herself, Rebecca didn't say a lot, but Cornelia gathered that she'd gone to convent school in Cuba, had gotten married very young, and held a harsh opinion of the States.

Once when Cornelia wiped some perspiration from her nose Rebecca leaned her head and said: "I don't like your country. And I don't like many people. How the hell do I like you so much? Why am I talking to you? I never talk about my life."

"You tell me."

"It's too obsessed with sex and race," she said, leaving Cornelia to discern that she was speaking of the States. "It needs to lighten up. I've heard about the things the racist people do. What do you call them again? Rednecks. How the hell can you kill someone for making love? How the hell can you incriminate a man for sleeping with a woman of another race? Why is sex a whole perverted thing? If they killed Carlitos for mixing, we'd all be good and dead. My father has a brother in a place called Dearborn. Do you know it? Doesn't matter, anyway. In nineteen thirty-six, when my father got the big store on the Queens, he went to Michigan to buy himself a car—the one that brought you here. He didn't want just any car. If that was it he would have bought it in Barbados. But all they had were little jalopies from England—Hillmans and Vauxhalls—humble little things. My father wanted something splashy, something that when the people saw it, they would see their biggest dream. And that is what the big store was when it opened—a place where you would see all the things you dreamed about from London and Paris and places like that. It had the first escalator in San Carlos, made by the same people that made the ones in Harrods, and Macy's in New York. Soda fountain too." Cornelia smiled with recognition on realizing that she'd bought her outfit in that very store. "So anyway . . . the car. I was home from Cuba for the summer and he took me on the trip. We flew the Pan Am seaplane to Miami, then a DC something to Detroit, and then my father's brother picked us up and took us to his house. We had a wonderful evening. I met cousins that I'd only written to, and met who's now my favorite auntie for the very first time. It was lovely. But by the very next day, everything had changed. . . ."

"What happened?"

"My uncle told my father not to worry if the salesman didn't shake his hand because sometimes they thought of us just like niggers."

"And you thought you were white?" Cornelia answered smugly.

"Well . . ."

"America is far away," Cornelia answered in a taut, dismissive way. "Can we forget it? It's very far away. Now what do you have against people?"

"Not everybody. Some of them."

"Okay, the ones you don't like."

"Which is most of them."

"Okay then," said Cornelia sharply. "Make the point."

"Most people are full o' shit. They want things from you but they don't just come right out and ask. They try to be your friend. I have so many so-called friends that I could make a bit of money if I sold them out."

"Are these your closest friends?" Cornelia asked her, making gestures to the house.

Rebecca held her drink above her head as if there were a hanging light and said, unsteadily, "Exhibit number one." As they laughed, she added, "Come around. There's something that you've got to see."

When Cornelia came around and was inside the narrow space behind the counter, though, she lost her nerve and said, "Oh God. I think I'm tipsy. I can't remember what it was."

"You were going to show me where you plan to pose for me," Cornelia answered, trying to get her way.

"Oh, leave it be."

"You have to let me shoot you," she insisted as she took Rebecca's hand. She shook it and they giggled, spilling drinks along their palms and wrists.

"Tell you what," Rebecca said. "I'll do it in five years. By then, the guys who made the pill will make another one that makes you young and fit again. You have no idea what it means to be around someone as young as you when you are old."

"You're one of the most beautiful women I've ever seen," said Cornelia as she took Rebecca's elbow in an act of admiration and support.

"I like you very much," Rebecca told her softly.

"And I like you too," Cornelia said with warmth.

"A lot of people like you. I am sure," Rebecca added after building up her courage with a cocktail taken in a gulp.

Cornelia said, "A few."

"A lot. I bet."

"Fewer than you think. What time is it?"

"You're making this so bloody hard," Rebecca said with spite. "A lot of people like you. You're the kind that people like. Don't act like this is news. Don't be a hypocrite about it. Just be who you are."

Cornelia put her arm around her shoulder.

"Did I just say something wrong?"

"Every woman in that room was scared of you," Rebecca said while working hard to stop herself from pouring everything that was fermenting on her mind.

"But what has that got to do with us?"

"They used to be afraid of me."

Cornelia slumped and pressed her shoulder blades against the bar, swirled the drink around her mouth and swallowed with a sigh as Rebecca pressed a finger to her collarbone and mumbled while she drank the over proof directly from the flask.

"There aren't as many of us as there used to be. As soon as there was talk of self-government a lot of people moved because they were afraid Xavier Joseph Jr. was going to win. San Carlos is a very tiny island. Good men are hard to find. There aren't enough of them for all of us."

"Who is *us*?" Cornelia asked with patience, realizing that her new, interesting friend was drunk.

"There is *us*," Rebecca uttered slowly, pausing in a grimace that revealed her upper teeth, "and there is *them*."

"They think I want their husbands?" asked Cornelia in a wry but sympathetic voice that matched her pouted lips in mood.

"They know their husbands want you. They know their husbands' habits. I know them too. I've slept with every one of them. I'm not ashamed to say it. For every one of them who's screwed my husband I've gone ahead and screwed their husband and their lovers in return. I saw the way that frigging Paula Chang was trying to study you, trying to size you up. Why the hell didn't you tell her to leave you alone?"

"But I don't want anybody's husband, Mrs. Rawle," Cornelia said efficiently. "I have somebody of my own."

Rebecca reached to take her face. Cornelia tried to move, but her reflexes had been dulled.

"You want my son," she said with menace. "Leave that boy alone."

"You already said he's not for me," Cornelia answered, brushing off her hands.

"So if you leave me here right now and go in there and he asks you for a dance, what are you going to do?"

Cornelia sketched a mental treatment based on her impassioned brief. In act one she told him yes and they danced. In act two she went outside for a walk and he followed. In act three she was alone with him behind the bar, right where she was standing now . . . and he was kneeling with his head beneath her hem . . . and she was high up on her toes . . . and he was lapping at the moisture being filtered by the fabric of her drawers.

There was a crack between two banks of clouds, and moonlight drizzled down and in this new illumination, which didn't last, Rebecca saw again the raw, compelling beauty of the girl, and felt a twinge of hatred for her son. Along her upper lip there rose a bead of perspiration. Through the fabric of her dress, her nipples showed.

"I must seem like some sort of idiot to you," she told Cornelia, whose lips were twitching as she focused on collecting all the pleasures dripping from her secret thoughts.

"You're a wonderful woman, Mrs. Rawle."

"What do you see when you see me?" asked Rebecca urgently. "All God's honest truth."

Laughing to herself, Cornelia said, "You may not want to know."

"Yes, I do," Rebecca said impatiently.

"We shouldn't do this kind of thing when we're drunk," Cornelia answered, as she saw the doctor slip his hands inside his pants and smear his taste around her mouth.

"I'm not drunk," Rebecca said. "Are you?"

"Perhaps."

"An intoxicated woman who screws a man is a whore," declared Rebecca, disappointed that she didn't have the skill or nerve to mount a full seduction of the girl. "Is that what you see when you see me?" she asked, as she made some more concoctions. "A washed-up old whore? I have a reputation, you know. I've had it for a very long time. I got it in my days at convent school and brought it home. I'm not a happy woman, you know. In fact I'm quite sad. But you can see that. That's not news. A drink?"

"Maybe not."

"Just one more drink."

"No. I'm getting drunk."

"Please . . . have one with me . . . please . . ."

"My head is gonna spin."

"Please . . . only drunkards drink alone. I'm not a drunkard, really. Don't make me feel like one. Just have one with me. Have a little spark. Have a little fun. Have a little damn consideration."

"I can't. I shouldn't."

Rebecca slapped her palm against the bar and said, "You must."

CORNELIA TOOK THE last drink very quickly and it put her in an introspective mood. Standing with Rebecca, leaning on the counter, gazing blankly on the shelf of spirits on the wall behind the bar, she thought, *Lowell and your frigging son are different but the same. Men whose parents rule their lives.*

As the rum began to seep inside her she began to argue with Rebecca in her mind. *You need to let that boy go, you know. If he wants to have me, he will. And the way I'm feeling now . . . free like this . . . if he wants to, I'll let him. Mrs. Rawle, I don't think you know it—but you've pissed me off. How dare you tell me to stay away from your son like you think I'm not worthy? What a goddamn awful thing to say. Do you think I believed you when you said it was for my own good? I didn't believe you at all. I know the drill, Mrs. Rawle. I know the drill. I wasn't even look- ing at your son. He was looking at me. I mean, I saw him. He's as* handsome as anything. But I wasn't throwing myself at the boy. And why're you minding his business, anyway. He is the leader of a country, for heaven's sake. He's your local Eisenhower. And you're gonna tell him who he's allowed to have? That is down-right disrespectful to his manhood. That's a low-down dirty shame. What kind of person would I be if I stood for that? When I get sober, I'm gonna go up to that house right there and take him to the side and let him know he can. I'm gonna tell him that it doesn't matter what his mama says, that he can do whatever he wants because he's Dwight goddamn Eisenhower. And do you really think I need to tell the man all this? He knows. And why does he know? He's charismatic. Lemme tell you something, Mrs. Rawle, I want to screw your boy until he calls your name instead of mine. I don't give a damn how many women he has or wants or needs. I just want that boy tonight. And you know why? I want to piss you off, Mrs. Rawle. I want to piss you off and I want to piss off my man because there's nothing better to do. I'm engaged to a man who doesn't really want me, Mrs. Rawle. He says he does. But you know what? I don't want him either. Screw him. You said that husbands want a woman with a little touch of color for a mistress, but never for a wife. Well, I just wanna be your boy's mistress for a night. I wanna see if he can make me feel like a *negrita*. Where I live, Mrs. Rawle, we don't have cute names like that. You're black or you're white. One drop and you're it. Spoiled like poison in the baby's milk. I know what it means to feel like a woman. But you talked up this *negrita* thing to make it sound like it's something else. And I need to find a something else because where I am is not a happy place. They would screw me but they wouldn't marry me. Well, look at that . . . but that's all right. I'll take a stranger who'll make me feel like a *negrita* over a fiancé who'll make me feel like I'm a nigger any day. Well, not any day. Tonight.

"Be honest," said Rebecca, interrupting her. "When you look at me what do you see?"

"Oh . . . it's too damn dark."

Rebecca lurched around and stood in front of her.

"Okay . . . take a guess."

"It's too damn dark, okay."

Rebecca tottered forward and Cornelia brought her hands toward her chest and held her breath as if she thought Rebecca would explode. Suddenly, the interaction felt untrue, intimate but shallow; invasive yet consoling and close. Nothing was clear or sure now. Only that the space behind the bar was small and that this woman was standing only inches from her face.

"Look. Tell me. Tell me. Please look."

Cornelia looked, but her mind was too blurred to see the evidence presented by the genes, especially the mouth—the fatty upper lip, the subtle overbite.

What did she see when she looked? Nothing that she hadn't seen before. But in searching, in peering, in roving with her eyes, she sensed a presence, a beckoning that had no name, an enigmatic openness, a magnetizing pull, a deep subconscious stir of interest that was not unlike the mystic calling of a song constructed on familiar chords.

Rebecca pressed her finger to Cornelia's mouth.

"In another life you could have been my daughter," she mumbled. "Will you drink to that?"

Cornelia barely raised her glass to make the toast. Rebecca took her hand and inched away.

"You have his mouth," Rebecca whispered, as if anyone was close enough to overhear. "His chin. His fingers too. I'm glad you're not my daughter, though."

"Incest is a dirty thing," Cornelia answered as she thought of all the things that she and her imagined brother would find the time to do.

"Naughty girl, how old are you?"

"Twenty-four."

"Even at this age I'd want to suckle you."

As Cornelia tried to pool her thoughts, Rebecca took her hands and placed them on her breasts.

"This is going a bit too far," Cornelia said politely, still a little guilty that she'd hurt her feelings by suggesting that she face the camera in the nude. "This is much too close."

"Let's go to where the land and water meet," Rebecca quoted, as Cornelia slipped away.

"No. I cannot do that, Mrs. Rawle."

"Yes, you can," Rebecca said and took her hand again.

"I don't like how this feels."

"Sshhhhhhhhh. Don't panic. I just want to show you a little thing."

Cornelia pulled her hand away. Rebecca laughed, then reaching round behind her back, undid the buttons on her dress and tugged the fabric low, exposing breasts that over-creamed the D cups of an underwire bra.

"What do you want me to do with that?" Cornelia asked her with a shudder that became a shrug. "They're titties. They're breasts. Did you expect me to be shocked? Well, I'm not shocked at all. I just think you should tell somebody before you think of doing something as crazy as that. Not that I care. They're yours. Not mine. I keep my breasts safe."

"But can you kiss them?" asked Rebecca in a voice that had a touch of mystery, which Cornelia in her state of haze accepted as a dare. "Or do you need someone to do the job?"

"And of course you know someone who can do this."

Rebecca answered, "Me."

Cornelia crossed her arms and leaned her head and giggled. Rebecca took the dare.

She reached around again and wrestled with the hooks and heavy breasts came down. Breathing deeply in enjoyment, she raised each one toward her face with all the reverence that a chef applies to choosing fruit, moaning as she rubbed them on her lips and cheeks. When she'd fondled them she placed their nipples in her mouth and took long sips like they were straws protruding from a water coconut.

"With all due respect, Mrs. Rawle," said Cornelia, "will you please pull yourself together and leave me the f——k alone?"

"Come," Rebecca said serenely, breasts carried in her palms as if they were refreshments on a tray. "Come, my daughter. Come."

Cornelia watched her, feeling something that she chose to call artistic interest urging her to step outside the boundaries that she knew.

"See, you're not so bashful," she prompted in a warm accommodating voice, "Who said you were too shy to pose? Not me. Not me. Not me at all."

"Do you want to see more?"

"It's dark here," said Cornelia, feeling out of kilter as she tried in vain to stop the flow of wetness that she'd accidentally turned on. "Show me everything when you're sitting. Right now, I can't see a thing. What would be the point? Whatever you wanna show should be kept for some other time. Right now isn't it. It isn't it right now. Let's get . . . dressed. It's getting late. The story of your father was really fascinating. Pity that . . . he never got a chance to meet my mother. She's a Turk. I mean . . . she's not Arab or anything . . . but maybe . . ."

"Do you want to shoot me?"

"Very much," Cornelia said.

"Then you must obey. Touch them. See if they're worth the Kodak and the time."

"Don't force me, though."

"I would never do that, darling. I just want to be nice."

As if she thought that they would burn, Cornelia reached out in the dark toward Rebecca's breasts, changed her mind and pulled away, then slowly stretched again. She stopped midway, compelled, confused, then Rebecca reached for her and drew her in a slack embrace.

"What am I supposed to do with you?" Cornelia asked her in a trembling voice belabored with reluctance and disdain.

"Shoot me, commandante," said Rebecca as she kissed her neck and touched her in a tender way. "Execute me. Put me flat against the wall and take my life."

"We're two sorry drunks," Cornelia said, trying to explain her feelings to herself.

"I'm not drunk," Rebecca slurred. "Are you?"

"I have to be. Your hands are in my underwear. You're kissing on my neck."

Cornelia stiffened when Rebecca's hand began to pull against her nape, and she submitted then resisted, then submitted once again, shifting, weaving, dodging, twisting, standing tall and fighting back, convincing like a boxer just before the dive.

"Why?" she asked when she'd removed her mouth. Her lips and tongue were spangled with the bitter taste of talcum powder mixed with perspiration and perfume.

Rebecca answered weakly, "I don't know."

"I'm not what you think I am, you know."

"Me neither."

"So stop."

"You're so exquisite," said Rebecca from a place of deep infatuation after backing off. "Hold me. I'm cold."

Cornelia leaned against the bar and crossed her arms. How did it get to this? she thought. And what about the urge to run? You're drunk, she told herself. You can't even think right now. You bitch. You bitch. You stupid bitch. You're a dumb, drunk bitch, Cornelia. How'd you ever come to this?

"What do I taste like?" asked Rebecca softly.

"Like menses mixed with shit?"

"I don't want to fight with you, beloved," said Rebecca, who was deeply hurt. "I only want to show you love."

"Stay where you are."

Rebecca disobeyed and came closer and Cornelia spat directly in the center of her face.

"Is that how you would treat my son?" Rebecca asked. "Is that what you do after playing with a person's heart? You spit on them and treat them like they're shit."

"You're nuts," Cornelia answered, glancing at the house.

"Oh yeah?"

"Oh go to hell."

"Is that how you would treat my boy? Tell him that he tastes like shit?"

"Please stop."

"Stop what?"

Cornelia dropped her face into her hands and said, "Confusing me."

"How could you spit at me, my darling," said Rebecca as she made a slow approach. Cornelia stumbled and she took her weight and wedged her in a corner of the bar against the shelves.

"What do you see when you look at me?" she asked. "Don't I look like him?"

"I don't give a shit about your son," Cornelia groaned, without lifting up her head to see. "I'm drunk."

With this, Rebecca pounced. In a single move she grabbed Cornelia, slapped her face and threw her on the countertop, slapped her on the other side and spat into the burn. Shocked, Cornelia didn't have the time to scream. It clotted in her throat.

"I will kill you for my f——king son," Rebecca, said and backed away. "Say whatever you want about the mother, but leave the son alone."

The shock had two effects on Cornelia—it cleared her head, and it convinced her that Rebecca had to feel some pain.

"Let me tell you something," she started, standing up and shaking out her arms while finding the power to laugh. "I'm gonna go into that house right now. And I'm going to screw your son. Now, isn't that lovely, Mrs. Rawle. I'm going to give him what you'll never have. You're over, Mrs. Rawle. You're over. You're done. I tried to comfort you before. But now I'm going to tell the truth. You're nothing but a soggy, wrinkled bitch. I didn't want to take a photograph of you. I was just trying to be nice. You're a sorry woman, Mrs. Rawle."

"I love you," said Rebecca, bursting into tears. "Don't you understand?"

"No, you don't. You love your son and you hate yourself. You're a damn unhappy person—which I understand. If I had tits like yours, I'd be unhappy too. There's nothing you can do but hide them, my love. They're yours for the rest of your life. You're a sorry case, you know. I've never seen it worse. You're gonna be a sorry bitch until you die."

"I can't take it anymore," Rebecca said, while slumping to the floor. "Oh stop. Please stop. You wouldn't understand. Oh stop. Please stop. I can't take it anymore."

"You're right," Cornelia told her, switching to a warm, supportive tone. "I should really stop. What I said to you was wrong. So wrong. Forgive me, please. Please forgive me. Will you forgive me? Come here."

"Oh, leave me alone."

"No . . . please. I need to talk to you."

Smiling to herself, Cornelia took Rebecca's nervously extended hand and helped her to her feet. Hiding all expressions of her true emotions, which were vile, she leaned against the countertop and held Rebecca tightly while she cried, savoring the buildup to the moment of revenge.

"I'm very sorry," said Rebecca while Cornelia rubbed her head. "I must have lost my mind."

"We're drunk," Cornelia said, working hard to focus on pronouncing in a sober way.

"No," replied Rebecca. "I'm crazy more than drunk."

"Oh, don't be so hard," Cornelia told her as she brought her other hand around her shoulders, right behind her neck, and used the other hand to stroke her face. "We all have our times. Don't worry. It's okay. But there is something I must tell you."

"Tell me."

Cornelia changed her grip around her neck and said, "I love to think about your son."

"Stop it," said Rebecca, when Cornelia caught her in a hook and bent her over. "Stop it. Let me go."

"I like to think about him licking me. Is that okay with you or do I need to write a letter of permission for that? I want to f——k your son, Mrs. Rawle. And I want him to f——k me. I don't want you or your husband. And I'm sure as hell not drunk. But most of all, I'm not like you. You got that? I'm not like you. I'm not like you. I'm goddamn not like you."

Cornelia felt a warm, delicious pleasure as they fought. In the dark, constricted space, the heat created by their bodies was contained, and hovered like a mist. Perspiration washing them, they spun and rushed and tripped and fell and rolled and struggled up on shaky knees, spitting at each other randomly—but always striking at the mouth; tugging at each other's clothes—but always in a way that wouldn't make a rip; and cursing at a level that was never quite a noise.

"That boy is not for you."

"You're such a greedy bitch."

"Leave my son alone."

"So you alone should have the two of us?"

"I'll get what I want."

"So you're willing to kill me, then?"

"I should have choked you when I had the chance and stopped your bloody breath. Don't spit at me. I hate the taste."

"You'll love the taste of this."

While allowing her a freer space in which to move, Cornelia closed her eyes and flopped with arms outstretched along the counter, toppling glasses to the floor. She saw the moon withdraw behind a bank of cloud; heard the sound of fabric rustling; smelled a musk uncurling when her panty crotch was torn; and felt a pair of sweaty temples opening her thighs.

"How do you feel?" Rebecca asked her meekly as they helped each other to arrange their clothes.

"I dunno . . . confused?"

## IX.

THE NEXT TIME they saw each other many things had changed. Nigeria was an independent country; Lumumba had been shot and Mobutu Sese Seko settling into kleptocratic rule. Kennedy and Fidel had scared the planet with their cockfight, and the bigger dick had won. Cheney was dead, Schwerner was dead, Goodman and Malcolm and Martin were dead. And four little girls in Alabama had gone to heaven straight from church in chariots of fire. Baldwin had published *The Fire Next Time;* the Voodoo Child had lit his ax at Woodstock; and gay people had revolted at the Stonewall Inn.

It was 1969. Ten years had passed since their meeting, and Cornelia, now a photo editor at *Life* magazine, was on vacation with her husband, Lowell Mason, who'd begun to dye his hair and ride a chopper, searching for his youth.

On the morning that they met again, Cornelia left him reading galleys in the kitchen of their rented house, which looked down on the beach from way up on a ridge that arced above the lower town, leafy rainbow streaked in shades of green.

They'd considered bringing the children—twins, Carmona and Jean-Paul—but had agreed that this, their first excursion to Jamaica, would be better spent alone.

In those days, Montego Bay was quaint; Rastas lived like hermits in the hills, and the harbor was a slush of marshy cays.

Cornelia was about to enter Doctor's Cave, a curving tusk of sand along a busy strip, that morning when she heard somebody call her name.

Looking up, she vaguely saw Rebecca leaning on a car across the street; behind her were the steps that led into the lobby of a small hotel. With the dreamy movement of a person in a trance, she waved at her, then paid her fare and passed into the hall that opened to the promenade and broke into a run.

With one hand on the banister, she weaved between the shifting gaps that opened in the crowd and took the stairs in twos and threes and raced across the sand, churning grit as white as salt across the oily flesh of tourists set in rows like chicken breasts slow-baking in the sun.

On the jetty, at the beach's eastern end, she sat with dangling feet above the water, spots of perspiration blooming on her dress, and as the memory of that distant night confronted her she cried into her hands, a throaty, body-shaking flush of deep emotion that left her feeling drained as if she'd just awoken from a night of throwing up.

"Leave me alone," she shouted when she heard Rebecca's voice behind her, coming closer, but still far away. "Don't talk to me. Just go away." She dropped her head between her knees and drew her arms around her head and closed herself as if she were a shell.

"May I sit?" she heard Rebecca ask.

"Why? What's the point? Why can't you sit somewhere else?"

"Because . . . because . . . I want to talk to you."

"I don't have a goddamn thing to say to you, okay? Just leave me the hell alone."

"It shouldn't have to be like this," Rebecca answered as she took a seat away from her and leaned against a heavy wooden post. "You're a big woman now. You're not a child. Why should I be chasing you? What's all this bloody drama? Why did you run away?"

Don't make her bully you, Cornelia thought. Straighten up. Ignore her. Eventually, she'll leave you alone.

She sat up straight and left her legs to dangle while she fixed her eyes out on the long horizon, where she saw a lonely boat. She could see Rebecca from the corner of her eye, some twenty feet away, but in a blur, and made out that she wore a purple dress and bracelets made of colored stones, for she was sitting with her hands around her knees.

To their left, beyond the beach, white birds with long, unhurried wings were floating low across the cays. As she watched them moving slowly, Cornelia pictured moments from a long, slow-motion movie of her life, bracing for the moment when her old tormentor's face would fill the screen.

While Cornelia sat in silence, Rebecca spoke aloud as if she were a writer making notes. And in the way that she recalled that night in 1959, Cornelia understood that she'd given it lots of thought, for everything was in its place—each name, each joke, the sequence of events.

When she faltered into silence, Cornelia made attempts to look at her, but found it hard. She wasn't sure how facing her would feel. And there were parts of her that didn't want to know. When she found the will to look at her she was jolted by how much she'd aged. Her hair was limp and silver, and was cut in what she thought of as a mannish way. There were deep sunbursts of wrinkles at the corners of her eyes. Her ears, it seemed, had grown. And every time she cracked her lips to speak and found herself without the words, a bag of skin would fold out of her throat.

Cornelia swabbed her hands along her dress then wiped her face, unsettled as she thought of what her mirror showed these days. Already, there were creases perching on her lips, and at certain angles, pleats along the tops of her twin-suckled breasts, flocks of them like vultures, traipsing all across her, pecking at her slowly, imprinting their crow's-feet.

As a woman who was old enough at thirty-four to have the fear of age, Cornelia saw Rebecca in a slightly different light.

"You changed my life," she said, surprising both of them. Neither one had thought that she would speak.

"For better or for worse?"

"I married Lowell. I got pregnant, had babies. We were going through a very hard time when I met you and I was sure that we'd separate. But that night . . . oh God . . . that horrible confusing night . . . I did everything to make things right between us. I was so damn scared."

"You were scandalous," Rebecca joked. "News got back to me. News travels in San Carlos very fast."

"I was," Rebecca answered, glancing up with watery eyes. "We were so embarrassed that we checked out in the morning and were on a chartered seaplane to Barbados in the early afternoon."

Cornelia turned her gaze toward the sea again.

"Are you happy?" Rebecca asked.

After thinking how to best explain, Cornelia answered, "Happiness is feeling safe. I feel quite safe right now."

In an urgent but respectful voice, Rebecca said, "I'm frightened for my life."

"Really," said Cornelia, shifting over.

"Do you know why I'm here?"

"Well . . . no . . ."

"I'm on a honeymoon."

"Congratulations."

Rebecca shrugged.

"No one new. I keep leaving him and coming back. On one level it's quite funny. On another one, insane. I saw you from our window. I was gazing out and he was working on another book."

"You threw me. I'm confused."

In a tired voice, the words emerged in trickles, which conveyed the feeling that she'd told the story many times. Rebecca gave Cornelia heirloom secrets. Now Cornelia knew about St.

William and Wilfredo and Estrella, and as much as Rebecca knew about her complicated feelings for her son.

When the telling tapered off, they sat together in an awkward silence that was often interrupted by attempts to speak. Jaws would open. Brows would raise. But nothing would come out.

"I have to go," Cornelia said, realizing that her children's life could be disrupted by her need to know and understand. She stood and took Rebecca's hand and pulled her to her feet.

On the promenade, which framed the beach, a microphone began to crackle and they turned to see a semicircle forming round a rumba band, which soon began to play.

"What happened to your book?" Rebecca asked.

"Which one? There've been a few."

"The one about beaches."

Cornelia chuckled with nostalgia for the days when she was brave enough to work on speculation.

"That one was never done."

"Maybe it could have been," Rebecca murmured. "It just wasn't meant to be."

"Perhaps."

"But let's not talk about it anymore."

"You are right."

"I have to go."

"So go."

"Should we shake hands or hug?"

Cornelia looked at her. Turned her head from side to side to size her up and said, "Damm it, girl. Let's hug."

She allowed the older woman this expression of her love, this moment of joy, and fought the urge to flinch when she felt experienced hands along her nape, long fingers searching through her hair.

It might have started as a gentle rock; perhaps it was a sway that had been hinted by the breeze, but as they hugged good-bye, their feet began to shift, and their bodies took the song, and at a speed inspired by the pace at which the earth revolves, they danced.

It was only when Rebecca whispered, "Now I can go," that Cornelia noticed that she'd lost her precious breasts, for she was pressing on her body closely and the breasts that she'd touched and tasted . . . well . . . they simply weren't there.

She didn't want to ask. She didn't want to know. And she was saddened even more when she caressed her through her clothes and felt how much her body had succumbed.

Don't ask, she told herself. You don't want to know. But you already know. What else is there to know? Ten years ago was ten years ago. Today is today. Leave her. Let her go.

She smacked her on the rump with deep affection, muttered something sentimental and controlled her breathing as she watched her limp away.

Rebecca walked along the jetty with the most majestic stride that she could manage in her latter days, and as Cornelia wept, she made a mental list of all the things she'd like to say—that she hoped that this time her marriage would be safe, that she hoped that St. William would be able to forgive her by the time she passed away, that by then she hoped that she would find a way to show some mercy too, that whether she'd forgiven him or not, she hoped that he would be her husband on the day that she was lowered to her grave beneath a wreath of flowers gathered from the garden of a house that had been built in 1800 by a doctor who'd fled the Haitian Revolution, the house where she was born and where years later an American tourist kicked her sister's dog, and the woman who had danced with her had slept and wept and loved.

Dear Editor:

I am hereby giving fair warning to the government of this country that I intend to file a complaint with the United Nations High Commissioner for Human Rights on behalf of myself and all the people of this island who are opposed to the removal of adult channels from the local cable system.

Article 21, section (2) of the Universal Declaration of Human Rights states that:

"Everyone has the right of equal access to public service in his country."

Seville Cable Company, like all media entities on this island and many companies in the fields of science and technology, are GLC's government-linked companies, profit-making entities operated by the government.

Technically speaking, the adult channels were part of a public service. If you should ask me if adult channels are an essential public service, I would respond that the standard for public service is not whether it is essential, or how often it is used. For example, we have a public bus service that is utilized by few. But does that mean that we should be complacent if the government unilaterally decides to take away some routes currently being plied by San Carlos Omnibus Service? Of course not. The issue for me is unilateral decision.

The removal of any channels from the cable service is disheartening. Up here in Mt. Pleasant it is very hard to get a solid signal with a satellite dish.

This is a very stressful situation for me. The pressure is building, and I am afraid of what might happen if it doesn't get released. It was many years ago when I considered starting up a revolution. Unless this government reviews its actions, I'm afraid that this course of action might be considered once again.

Yours, etc.

St. William Rawle

# REVOLUTION

EVERY FRIDAY, AFTER taking tea at four o'clock, St. William Rawle would drive downhill in his blue Ford Fairlane, dressed in a crushed white suit.

Tall and thin, with a belly gone to pot, he'd flunked out of Cambridge before the war and had returned to San Carlos to discover that fate had changed his fortune. A blight had swept the island and the family's coconut wealth was gone, which meant he had to work. With a high school education and a letter from the bishop and the commissioner of police, he was appointed headmaster of an all-girls' school, a position that he kept until a book by Graham Greene convinced him that he was a man of letters.

Since that revelation, he had published thirty books, a volume for each year, thirteen novels, six books of verse, nine books of science, a natural history of the island, a translation of the

New Testament in the local dialect and a primer on etiquette for ladies—all at his own expense.

He had been married four times, all of them to Rebecca Salan, the daughter of the island's richest Arab merchant, who had died beside him in her sleep four years ago, in 1971, while he asked the Lord to take him in her place. But to anyone who offered him condolences, St. William would reply that he was not bereaved, because Rebecca came to him at night in dreams with answers from the other world.

Every Friday evening at ten to five, St. William would sit on a folding chair below the statue of Admiral Nelson, face the public buildings that three-cornered the square and have a drink while shouting: "The leader of this country is a bloody ignoramus and as such he must resign."

The square had been renamed for him four years ago, and so it was with deference that the cops would execute their orders to arrest him, a man descended from the English general who'd seized the island from the Spanish in 1802 and razed the domed cathedral, erecting in its place a parish church whose spired clock was mute and arthritic.

On the morning that St. William heard the brick-and-plaster timepiece chiming for the first time in his life, he sat up in his postered bed and made a quick decision. For the last eight months his wife had been appearing in his dreams in army greens, her eyes replaced by watches.

And so it was, at the age of sixty-five, when he should have been gazing at retirement from public life, that St. William Rawle decided that history had invited him to start a revolution.

He lived alone in the Metropolitan Hotel, which everyone still knew as Mt. Pleasant—a plantation house on fifteen hundred blighted acres that hadn't seen a guest in three years. The floor planks were damp and the rafters draped with spiderwebs and the new extension that created what was advertised as "modern relaxation by the pool" had all the style and polish of the Bates Motel.

St. William was not a violent man, but in his soul there ran a subterranean stream of anger that erupted with orgasm into flood. An early riding accident had left him sterile. Still, he'd accepted from his wife and many mistresses a brood of eighteen children. The chief minister was one of them—the only boy—and he'd caused St. William great humiliation.

In a recent address on national radio—television would arrive in later years—he'd ridiculed St. William's plan to will the old plantation to the people of San Carlos as a national learning center: a library, a museum, a teachers college and an institute for the study of Atlantis.

The property had been in St. William's family for a hundred and fifty years. The chief minister, who was St. William's heir, had plans to use the land for public housing.

That f——king bastard, thought St. William, standing at the dresser, whose top was inlaid with mother-of-pearl and littered with old books, enamel bowls of melted ice and bottles of the finest Royal Standard rum. The last time we built them housing they were slaves.

"Estrella!"

By the time the footfalls had arrived outside his door, he was dressed in a khaki shirt, a baseball cap and knee-length water boots.

From his double holster hung a pair of silver-plated pistols that had once belonged to his grandfather, and slung across his shoulder was a bolt-action rifle with a wooden barrel and a clip that held six slugs.

His silver hair was parted and his oval jaw was radiant with the soft gardenia whiteness of an egg.

As he heard the turning knob, St. William swiveled to the mirror to appraise himself, resuming his stance to see at the door not his old long-suffering maid, but a young woman in a calibrated state of semi-dress—white string bikini loosely tied at the side and an unbuttoned vest in iridescent Indian silk that stopped just below her bosom and continued to her waist in a shower of delicate braided fringes hung with colored buttons.

Her hair, which was brown and curly, was parted in the middle and tied in a pair of poufs. She was holding a bouquet of roses. And in her state of shock her arm began to fall until the petals brushed the floor.

Her lips were dark and pouty, and below her eyes, whose lids were rainbow-shadowed in yellow, pink and blue, her long cheekbones resembled horizontal bruises.

"Get away from here!" St. William shouted in *sancoche*. The woman leaped backward, and he slammed the door and flung himself across the bed, where he pumped his surge of anger till it burst its banks, erupting in a flood.

Over a breakfast of jackfish and pounded plantains in a little room beside the kitchen, Estrella told St. William that the woman was a paying guest who had arrived the night before, an American with a New York address who was the lover of the man who had arrived at dawn that morning, hours after he had been expected.

The man was short and slim, described Estrella, and judging from his face and arms possessed a body that was tightly muscled. His hair resembled an explosion, and his voice was keen in pitch and edged with danger like a file against the blade of a machete.

The woman's arrival, Estrella gathered, was not in fact a rendezvous. It was an ambush, a surprise, for her voice had been timid when she requested to be notified the minute that the man called down for breakfast, her intention being, Estrella thought, to present him with something more delectable than bread.

"So why did she come to my room?" St. William asked as the clock began to strike again.

Estrella raised her brow to indicate that she was wounded still by choices she had made in the vertigo of youth, and muttered: "Like every other woman who has ever made that trip, she made a grave mistake."

That day, St. William kept watch through his window, which overlooked the pool, a palm-shaded puddle in a square inscribed by the back of the house and three wings of concrete extensions—row upon row of brown doors and glass jalousies and redwood railings stained black with rot and water.

How many revolutionaries, he asked himself, had been faced with such a monumental choice? If Toussaint had been faced with a woman such as this, would Haiti be French today?

The Spanish influence in San Carlos ran deeper than its name. *Sancoche* was based on Castilian. Old men still foraged for love songs between the wires of the cuatro; and Carlitos of all ages kept an almost sanctimonious faith in the virtues of siesta.

But at two o'clock, after using the pealing bell to mark the terraced descent to the hour of sleep, St. William did not go to bed. If he did, he knew, he would dream of Rebecca, who would admonish him for ignoring the call of duty. And disobeying her, the only person who had ever believed in his greatness, would be a monumental act of treason, surpassing in vileness the affair he had pursued with her goddaughter, a teenaged seductress who would entertain him by raising her tunic above her breasts, crossing her ankles behind her head and performing tricks of ventriloquy with the lips of her vagina.

At two-thirty, just as St. William's lids began to droop from habit, the woman appeared on a balcony, dressed in a full-length caftan whose neck and cuffs were trimmed in gold. Her hair was no longer in poufs, but had resumed what he assumed to have been its natural form, a style that he knew as a makeba.

She glanced over her shoulder and slammed the door and tipped up on her platform clogs and slapped it with her palm, shooting a remark whose answer was a burst of automatic laughter.

By the pool, she spread a towel on a slatted chaise beneath a palm and lay without moving. To observe her more closely, St. William watched through his binoculars, holding his breath as she withdrew her head and arms into the caftan, reappearing in a bathing suit whose color matched her skin, the evenness evoking foreknowledge of her body in the nude. On her inner thigh there was a mole that made him marvel. It was black and slightly raised, and in its center was a single copper hair.

The way the shadows striped her, the wooden slats that pressed into her flesh, the suggestion of her ribs through the fabric like gills, St. William felt the hunger rise inside him, and he wanted to consume her like a fish.

As he thought of this he heard a rusty hinge and changed his view and saw the man emerging through the door. He was wearing jeans with bell-bottoms and, when he raised his foot against the wooden rail, St. William saw a pair of zippered boots.

He was shirtless. In his mouth there was a conical extravagance of what St. William's hairy nostrils told him was imported marijuana; and he was holding a guitar, which he carried by the neck, slackly but with need, like a drunkard holds a bottle.

"Baby," the man commanded.

The woman did not reply. The man chuckled and disappeared inside the room, returning with a vase of roses.

"Baby," the man called out again.

The woman did not answer, and the man began to toss the blooms. As one hit the water he would toss the next. When the vase was empty he disappeared inside the room, leaving the door ajar.

When the clock struck three, St. William vowed to take bold action. He would send a note with Estrella. If the woman did not reply in his favor he would commence his revolution. If she did, he wasn't sure what he would do.

He invited her for tea at four o'clock. And when he arrived downstairs in the drawing room, she was sitting on a hassock trimmed in chintz beside a window whose translucent curtains softened the Antillean light.

Out of habit St. William was dressed in a crushed white suit. His shirt was blue to match his eyes. And he walked with a silver-handled cane that he did not need but which he carried, in case she was the kind of woman whose passions would disguise themselves as sorrow.

"Good day," he said as he stepped off the mahogany stairs onto a Chinese rug. "Welcome to the owner's tea at the Metropolitan Hotel. It is a long tradition here for us to cater to our guests, especially those that bring to mind the exquisite beauty of our local flora."

"I'm sorry for our rendezvous this morning."

Her smile, which on one side was clamped with a sarcastic tuck, was otherwise open and persuasive in a way that implied that he had been given accidental insight to her erotic mysteries, which were deep and dark and usually accessible only to those on the verge of undertaking a journey through the constricted passage that released the soul into the light.

"My name is St. William Rawle," he said in courtly manner, sweeping his hand to invite her to the table, which was set with dull silver and chipped porcelain and baskets of freshly baked scones.

"Felicia Morris," the woman said, passing her hand along her flanks before sitting down to prevent her dress from creasing.

"Have you been to the Caribbean before?"

"Yes," she replied. "Many times."

"And what brings you to San Carlos?"

"To be with a man who doesn't want me."

That isn't true, St. William thought. Such a man, I'm sure, does not exist.

He inhaled deeply as he had often coached young actors, and hoisted his chin, staring at her down his nose in a way that he believed communicated power. And as he appraised her, the cup dangling halfway between the table and her lips, she whispered that his nostrils were clumped with boogers.

"My goodness," she exclaimed. "How can you breathe?"

Before St. William could recover from the shock of her response, she was standing by his side with her elbows on the table, pressing his nose into a napkin and coaxing him to blow.

As if summoned by the honking, Estrella entered the room.

"I am fine," St. William grunted.

"You won't be when you hear this. Do you know why the bell has been ringing all day?" she asked in *sancoche,* sparing the guest from experiencing an anxious moment. "A band of idiots from Black Well tried to start a revolution. They used the bell as a sign. What kind of idiot would try that in San Carlos?" She raised her arms and showed her palms, which splattered on her thighs. "They tried to take over the radio station, I heard, but the police cornered them and they surrendered. I hope they get some licks with the pistle for their work."

"At least." St. William sighed; they had a plan.

"What's the matter?" Felicia asked, as Estrella left the room.

"Some fools tried to take over the country. But don't worry. They caught them. There is no excitement. All is well."

"And you were their fearless leader?" she joked.

She brought her elbows to the table and cupped her face. The tucked-in smile appeared again, and with her face framed by her hands, St. William looked anew and saw the freckles sprinkled on her nose, which brought to mind the memory of the mole, which he began to think of as a scar remaining from the scorch of his saliva.

"Your friend," he asked to change the subject, "what does he do?"

"He is a singer."

She told him the name, but he did not recognize it.

"And what do you do?"

"Floating around. Hoping to become a writer."

She slid her hands around her cheeks to hide her face; and he allowed her this moment of childish indulgence and held his breath through her re-emergence, forehead first, hands retracting like the hood that hides the clit.

"I am feeling very sensitive right now," she said, arousing his appetite for scandal with a sigh that caused her breasts to heave. "I need someone to talk to. I'm leaving in the morning. So it doesn't really matter."

"That is true."

"I left my husband for him," she said, leaning forward in a whisper, her eyes flitting from the doorway to the stairs. "And this is what I get."

"I saw him throw the flowers in the pool," St. William told her. "I was watching."

"Oh, you must think I'm such a fool."

"It depends. How long have you known him?"

"Today makes a week."

St. William tapped his tongue against his palate.

"And you followed him here and he doesn't want you?"

St. William found this fascinating, for she did not strike him as a woman who was weak. And although he had often been guilty of bad judgment, he instinctively believed in his instincts, which were urging him to offer her his help.

"Would you like me to say a word?"

"To who?"

"To him."

"About what?"

"About the two of you?"

"Well—"

"Remind me of his name again?"

"People call him Bob."

"I must tell you something," he whispered, gathering his thoughts as the clock began to peal again. "I am doing this because I want you, and I know I cannot have you. When you came into my room this morning I was going to start a revolution. But I haven't been able to think about anything since you came into my life. I laid down my gun and took off my clothes and touched myself as I thought of you. I watched you all day through my window. I need to touch you. Allow me, please. Can I touch you? Out of sympathy. I am old."

"You could be my father."

"I understand," he reasoned as she laughed, "but that is neither *yes* nor *no*. Do you know what you are doing? You are making me feel sensitive right now. You are making me feel old. I watched you and wanted you. He threw you away."

As he listened to himself, St. William was aware that his voice was rising and that his brave appeal had liquefied into a grovel.

But what he was too old to understand was that in those flagrant days of the sexual revolution, when women were still excited by the view from the top, an appeal from the bottom, wet with blood desire and the suggestion of tears, would soak and undermine a woman's will.

"I have to go to my room," she said with a dreaminess that he mistook for boredom. "Don't worry about dealing with this. I'll handle it on my own."

St. William nodded and, having lost his pride, confided that he hadn't had a drink all day and would be going to his room to be rum-suckled.

Ascending the stairs, he began to use his cane, although Felicia was not watching. His heart was filled with lamentations and his lungs filled with the dust that his repeated sighs had brought into his scoured nasal tunnels.

I have failed myself, St. William thought. He sat on the edge of his bed and gargled with the rum before he swallowed. Through the window he watched the man, who was sitting on the railing, strumming his guitar and singing softly what sounded from a distance like a psalm, his voice light but keen and edged with a profound sense of longing, as if it emanated from a hole in his heart; and as St. William felt himself being drawn into the mystery of that hole, he put away his bottle and walked to the window and pressed his face against the glass and felt the coolness on his forehead as the rage evaporated out of him into the gash from which that voice had come, that primal place of grief, that wound left behind when the first fruit fell away from the first tree and faced the conflict of survival, the unconquerable knowledge that it too would cause pain when it split the earth to set down its roots.

As St. William watched, Felicia climbed the stairs and the man put down his instrument and draped his arms around her as a bird would fold its wings around its young, and as she opened her mouth and the man's head dipped toward her, his hair like an ignited plume, St. William felt his bones reverberating as if they had been struck by a gong; and in a flash of clarity he understood why she had come this far this quickly to see this man—he had the charisma of the revolutionary, the capacity to embrace and rebuke without apology, which is rooted in the understanding that life is a cycle of regeneration, and that regeneration is a cycle of pain, and that the great leaders are those who can inspire people to face the coming pain with strength and grace and a vision of life beyond it.

That night Rebecca did not appear in St. William's dream. He dreamed instead of Felicia. In the reverie she lay across the bed and spread her legs, and he saw her lower lips, which were sealed and folded in a dusky line, glistening like a keloid that had overgrown a wound, and he slid his tongue along it to console her, to ease the remnant of her deep, abiding pain.

The next morning, he arose to the sound of a rooster—the chief minister had ordered that the mechanism of the clock be removed—and found outside his door a package and a note.

*Thank you for reminding me that I'm wanted. I almost slept with you. Yes, for a minute you could have stolen me, but I would have gone back to him. Accept this gift as a token of whatever, of two people, no, three people and a moment. It will be coming out this year. One love. Sorry that I couldn't make him sign it.*

What a fascinating name, St. William thought as he tore the paper: *Natty Dread*. His thirty-first book was a translation and discussion of the lyrics in *sancoche*. In his memoir, published at his own expense on the eve of the millennium, St. William would describe it as "my most important work to date."

Dear Editor:

Mt. Diablo is not extinct as we believe, and I am calling on the illegal government of this country to investigate it before it is too late. Otherwise, all the investments that have flowed into this economy will dissipate, all the engineers and technicians who have relocated here will simply move, and in shame we will return to what we used to be before we became enamored with progress and corrupted by an obsession with success—a small island abandoned to fend for itself after hundreds of years of Spanish and English rule.

I live on the slopes of Mt. Diablo in the house where I was born, in what we used to think of as "far away up there." For many years, our fifteen hundred acres was the only land for miles that wasn't forest. Now, everywhere you turn there is a house. It has gotten so bad that the other day I heard a trip to Mt. Pleasant being described as "a little trip to town."

Who chose to make this town? Who chose to not retain the mountains as "far away up there"? Every place needs to have a "far away," a place where the mind if not the body can elope for retreat. I did not make this choice. This choice was made for me. Because when this illegal government, which suspended the parliamentary system after independence for this perverted system of dictatorship called "guided democratic rule" that does not allow the people to elect their leader, decided to create that monstrosity called New Seville, they forced me to sell them fourteen hundred of those acres so they could build new houses for the people whom they moved. As soon as that happened, the land grab was on.

This morning as I walked on what is left of this property, I felt the anger of the mountain as it trembled underneath my feet. Today marks to the date a hundred years since the last eruption in 1903. Why do we think it won't happen again? It happened in

St. Vincent in 1979, and in Montserrat in 1995. It can happen here again.

We've built our wealth on technology and science. I've never been good at these things. But as a boy I used to use divining rods to find water. Call me *buckra massa* if you want, but in the old days people used to pay attention to the land. Now we pave it over.

What happened to the plans to enshrine the *back beyond* as a nature preserve? Who brought mass tourism to the cays? Greedy people. Craven people. People who lack vision, though they have a pair of eyes.

I don't know science. But I know earth. As my flesh withers away I am better at feeling things in my bones.

Yours, etc.

St. William Rawle

# HOW I MET MY HUSBAND

## I.

I MET HIM in San Carlos in the spring of '82.

In those days, before the island had been ringed and cuffed by all-inclusive chains, a twenty-year-old girl could stay for months in charming places built on sand as white as coke for less than it would cost her mother for a single term at Yale.

I didn't go to Yale, but I knew how much it cost. In the eighties everybody knew the price of everything. If something didn't have a price, it really didn't count.

When we met I had been living with Orlando Walsh, an architect who had a daughter from a marriage that had lasted for a year. He was in his early thirties but was still considered "older," and we spent a lot of time remodeling our loft above a loading dock on Crosby Street whenever I was there.

On dropping out of Penn I'd sued my mother for a portion of the money in my trust to buy the loft and start the Blue Line Trading Company—a simple operation. This is what I'd do.

I used to travel to the Caribbean with my luggage stuffed with rubbish purchased on Delancey Street. Knockoffs that I'd trade for true creations that were treated like stepchildren in their island homes.

In Dominica, for example, pleather loafers by a "Pair Cordon" could fetch a dozen bowls handwoven by a Carib Indian who was eighty-five years old. In Haiti, half a dozen jeans by "Kevin Kline" could get a painting done with chicken feathers by a living voodoo priest.

Buy low; sell high. That is what I did. I did it often and I did it very well. I had a special driver booked on every island, and on landing he would take me to the isolated districts where the old folk artists lived, usually along the most forbidding coast or up into the creases of cloud-misted hills.

But for certain kinds of things you had to go into the towns. Outside the areas rated fit for viewing by the tourist boards, along the paths that sprang like broken wires from the humming shantytowns, you found young people generating art that you could sell as "bold interpretations" of some common things. A chessboard made from beaded velvet fitted to a box would cost me seven dollars but would sell for maybe ninety-two. Model cars created from recycled cans of Pepsi could be had for thirty cents when purchased by the gross but sold at twenty bucks a pop.

Every island was unique, but every deal was just the same. You haggled till your lungs began to hurt, then you huffed and packed your things to go away. You reached the door at full momentum, pausing when you heard the whistle or the clap that came before your name. After this, you sat again and haggled in a quiet voice but kept the tension stiff until somebody sent somebody for the drinks.

The drinks would come and you'd begin to talk the way that people do whenever drinks are brought around—all cool and easy—till you looked up from your watch and raised your brows and made it known that it was way beyond your time. If it didn't happen now, somebody else would get the deal.

Now, you traded things like they were parting gifts—"Oh, my darling, take two more of that"—and you would leave the table feeling good about yourself until you turned to wave and saw the way they lived.

SoHo was a different scene. Once a month I'd drape the loft with yards of silk suspended from the pipes. In the corners, which were always dim, my girl Regina would create the "panty rooms"—camping tents with Indian rugs and cushions just for making out.

She was five foot ten with kinky hair, and skin that had the frosty unreflection of a Baby Ruth that had been left to harden in the fridge. She was slim and shapely with an elegant proportion to her bones, but she was fatty in the ass, which meant she couldn't model more than half the time. She made her college money tending bar . . . well . . . sort of . . . indirectly. Tending bar positioned her to get supportive fellowships from men.

At my parties, she would serve the Absolut across a sheet of ply. A secret ex would bring his band and spritz the air with atmospheric jazz. And at midnight, when the room was fully circled by the cats in suits who came with dreams of feasting on a buckskin hide, I'd cross my legs while sitting on a silver-plated stool, rest my drink against a stack of peeling steamer trunks and, in the manner of a singer doing cabaret, discuss my life and journeys, making moments come to life through accents and hand gestures, giving common objects greater value by infusing them with legends and mystique.

But by 1982, mystique was fading. The goods were getting stale. The crowds were getting thin. I started reading up on other places, started branching out. And this is how we met.

I MET HIM in Seville, a lovely town that climbed the hills around a small, steep-sided harbor that was blue and clean because it never made it as a port. The harbor was the crater of an old volcano that had shot its load and crashed, and now its rims were sloping arms of land that hooked around and almost closed, which meant that cargo ships would need a perfect navigator just to make it through. The arms of land around the harbor were tattooed with modern houses like the kind you see along the California coast—rows and rows of floor-to-ceiling windows and projecting sections with no obvious support.

But you didn't feel as if you were in California. The scale of things was more in line with what you'd see in smaller towns in lesser Europe, say a Portugal or Spain—a fine achievement in a country where most people had been slaves.

There was an old, impressive plaza by the harbor; and along the streets around it there were many small, tree-tufted squares. Some were cobbled; others paved; and some were lined with newish office buildings of a modest height. Nothing fancy. Functional, affordable design. The streets were lively and the traffic was a slow parade of tiny cars from Europe and Japan. And every corner had an orange garbage bin that people put to use.

It was a kind of Caribbean town I'd never seen: a well-proportioned, vibrant place without a tourist trade or gross extremes of wealth.

On coming in to land, I'd seen miles of naked beaches bathing in the sun, thighs of whitest sand just lounging by the sea. I saw farms—but none of them were growing sugarcane. Along the rough Atlantic coast I saw a big container port with gantries lifting freight from ships and factories puffing smoke. But what struck me most of all was Mt. Diablo.

I'd never flown above a crater, and I felt my stomach tensing when I saw the steam arising from the upper sulfur springs and all the lushness that embraced the crater lake. When you looked at it, you felt uneasy but you couldn't look away, as if it were a breast with all the mass around the tip removed.

I quickly learned that you could see Diablo everywhere.

Turn and it was right above your shoulder. Like your past, it always followed you.

It was watching when the taxi dropped me at the National Craft Market, where I thought I would begin; and as I stepped out of the car beside the harbor, a sky as clear as glass began to crack and I was splattered with a drop of rain.

With a copy of the local paper on my head, I rushed between the columns of the open gate while office workers who'd come to lunch along the promenade began to sprint the other way.

It was less a market than a shopping complex built around a square of grass—twenty wooden cottages in festive hues. Each one had a porch with lacy trim along the gables and a wooden sign that hung.

The rain began to ease and I began to walk; but seconds later I was startled by a thunderclap, and water crashed against me with the force of nails. I bolted for the door of Miss Estrella's Art & Craft—and English Shoes. It was the closest. This is really how we met.

I was standing at the counter, which was made of wood and glass. On the other side there was an opening protected by a heavy curtain made of beads. What lay behind it wasn't clear. It could have been a corridor . . . a cubicle . . . a nook.

I was looking at the beads with expectation, waiting for somebody to emerge, when I began to sense his eyes. I turned, glanced across my shoulder back toward the door and saw that he was there.

He was dark and long-bodied, dressed in Levi's, and a T-shirt with a navy trim, leaning in a corner, quiet as a broom.

When I said, "Good day," he nodded but he didn't change his stance. With his arms and ankles crossed, he used his chin to let me know that I was free to look around, then quickly drew away into his world.

Cold is not the word. I don't mean this in a slangy way. Although he was remote, he wasn't rude. About him was an air of reservation, a sense that he was holding back, a faint resentment. They don't have blizzards in the Caribbean. What they have is rain. A drop of that is worth four feet of snow. If I hadn't come he would be packing up to leave. But I was there.

He spoke as time went on, but only when a nod or flick or swivel wouldn't do. Then, his words emerged as if from hibernation, as if they had to squint to see.

"Do you make any of this yourself?"

"Hmmmm . . . no."

"You work here?"

"Hmmm . . . sometimes."

"Like it?"

"It's my mother's place."

"I see."

Tentative. That's how he spoke. Before he answered you, he'd pause or look away, which challenged you to make yourself a little more appealing. That, at least, is what it did to me.

I was about to break the ice by saying something funny about . . . gee . . . I didn't know . . . when the rain began to come with unrelenting force. Nails had muscled up to iron bolts.

Muttering, he went behind the counter, disappeared behind the beads and came out in a pair of orange water boots and yellow slicks and tramped into the rain. I watched him through the windows till he dropped the shutters to protect the glass, then waited by the counter in the dimness, wondering if I should have volunteered but also why a store like this would have a rack of shoes. In the Caribbean I'd seen all kinds of stock combined—candy stores that carried auto parts, and bars that had a little case of sporting goods—but never art and craft with Clarks.

He hung the slicks and dropped the boots inside an empty box beside the door, then heaved a sigh and chucked his gaze upon the floor. I'd left a trail of footprints in my wake. Grudgingly, he slipped his feet inside his running shoes and went into the void behind the beads, returning with a mop. And louder than I'd ever heard him raise his voice he whistled as he slopped away the proof that I had ever come into his life, scrubbing with sardonic effort, cheeky and sarcastic like an old pragmatic maid.

With the shutters down I didn't have sufficient light. The shelves began above my ankles and laddered up to where the yellow walls abutted with the roof—sheets of corrugated zinc supported by a frame of intersecting beams. From the center of this rack of wood there hung a fan that had a fixture with a pair of bulbs whose wattage was too low.

I decided he was handsome when I'd asked him if he carried necklaces and he'd returned from ducking through the beads with heavy boxes that he placed in rows along the countertop, inviting me to look.

No. This is not the truth. It happened when I asked him if he had a lamp or torch or other form of light and he had called out from the void behind the beads, directing me to feel beneath the counter's lip, where I would find a switch. Tipping now, and stretching over, I did as I was told—I thought—and killed the only light.

He exhaled with great impatience, and I felt defensive as I heard him coming forth. I watched his shadow looming, heard the jangle of the beads, then felt my breathing slowing as his scent began to stray toward me and I lured it through the dark.

It was a musky scent, smooth like unfermented sweat, the scent a body keeps when it is washed and rested overnight but not perfumed, the scent a woman always grows to love.

He uncrossed his arms, and when they fell I had a vision that they'd strayed to me. The notion was amusing, and I dropped my head as I imagined what his face would look like if he knew the flick that was playing in my mind. The counter shook each time he fiddled. On the other side I squirmed.

"So you're looking for accessories for yourself?" he asked me as my eyes adjusted to his closeness and the brightness of the extra light, which came by means of bulbs that had been built into the case.

Along my spine I felt a flicker then the humming of a cool fluorescent glow. With a single word a spot had been lit up. In the Caribbean, men who say "accessories" do not work in stores. He'd been doing all he could to barricade himself, and with this little crack a sliver of his private self had been exposed.

I began to think of him with deeper fascination, as a puzzle that would pleasure me to figure out. The way the rain was coming down, I reasoned, I would have sufficient time.

This is when I really looked. With my fingers strolling through the boxes I began to glance, and saw that he was leaning forward when before he had been easing back. His arms were spread, his fingers splayed, his stare indifferent but direct.

I noticed that his eyes were deeply set beneath a pair of girlish brows that gave his face a look of concentration. At its end, his nose was broad and softly rounded with the nostrils underneath, inspired by a lion's paw.

There was fuzz along his chin and in the scoops below his mounded cheeks; but there was so much space between the bristles that you'd think they had been markered on.

I took accounting of these hairs because they were the only ones that I could see. His dreads were wound up in a bolt of linen that affected me as if it were a bandage on a thumb.

"So what do you do when you're not here?" I asked above the rain. My voice was strong but soft in tone to comfort him, to give him some relief from what I had decided was a slow, corrosive pain.

"So what exactly are you looking for?" he asked me in an open-ended but constricted way. He caught himself and quickly moved away to settle in a state of agitation on a stool adjacent to the corner where he'd been standing when I'd come into the room, legs extended, ticking PUMAs pointed out.

"It's so much stuff," I answered, taking note of how my hips would love to stretch the space between his knees. "It's hard to say. I'm not so sure."

"Well, I have to pack up and go home," he said dryly. "There's no more business for today." He uncrossed his arms and put his hands against his knees. "Made up your mind or what?"

I cut my eyes and turned around to sort more quickly, annoyed that I was trapped by rain and couldn't leave. It was okay to be indifferent, but insulting? That was something else.

I kept my feelings to myself and tried to tune him out, but it was hard now that I knew his smell. I began to feel uneasy, awkward, irritated, self-aware. My clothing was a little damp. The smell of wet newspaper was arising from my permanently tousled hair. He was watching me. I felt it. Which made me want to look.

I never caught him staring. Whenever I would turn, I'd find him gazing into space, his fingers vaguely stroking at his chin.

You know what? I told myself. You should ignore him. And as I'd learned to do quite early whenever I was teased, I hummed my secret song:

> My name is Miss Carmona
> My mother is Cornelia
> You hate me 'cause I'm bet-tah
> So f——k the bitch that made ya.

I did it and it worked. When I pulled away from him, his childish counteraction was to come around to me.

He began expressing interest in the objects that I found, voting with a dull, robotic "Yes" or "No." It was absurd but quite amusing, this playacting that I *was* and *wasn't* there. When I began to look at him directly, he struggled then retreated then began to do the same, and with our eyes in contact, we began to be engaged.

If I liked a piece and he did not, he'd tilt his head from side to side to weigh our views, then use his hands to ask if I would slip it on. He'd raise his brows to vote for "Yes" and shrug to vote for "No."

Once or twice he used a wave to summon me; and just when I was sure that we were going to touch, he'd find a way to turn me at the proper angle solely with his eyes. Eventually, we did. He took a choker from my fingers and proceeded with the screwing of the clasp, his fingers working softly on my nape. Another time, with earrings, he appraised me while I leaned my face from side to side and swallowed loudly when I scooped away my hair. Later, with a long, five-stranded necklace made of speckled stones, he was a little bold, directing me with miming fingers to undo the second button of my blouse. I obeyed, but in a tease. Like a clock, the button took a half a day to turn. And in the midnight mood that I'd created I drew and pressed my collar in a wider spread and flashed a bit of cleave.

By the time he swallowed twice and muttered, "Come into the back. I have some things you ought to see," I was prepared to give it up. Dim light, hard rain and scent of man had cast their vote. My nerves began to buzz in referendum. The body politic had chosen. The panties would secede.

In those days my friends and I believed that feminism had become a crabby institution, a prison for the woman who did not believe that bad-behaving men would change because she didn't shave her legs. We thought the leaders of the movement were a little out of touch, that they didn't really feel it for the sisters who had choices—who *could* get a date, who weren't forced to grin and bear it while it hardened up.

We were feminists who chose the quick orgasm as our rebel yell. After more than sixty years of suffrage we believed that it was safe to be a broad again. Words like "slut" did not offend us. In fact we used to joke that if you scrambled it you'd only get to "lust," and what's so wrong with that?

So sleeping with a stranger didn't take a lot of thought. In any case I didn't see this as a time to think. I'd thought before and now it was the time to act. And *f——king,* I remembered, was a verb.

He led me through the beads, then turned the knob to crack an iron door. The little room was windowless and lined with shelves that sagged beneath their weight. He put a pillow on a wooden box and swept his arm to offer me a seat. While I waited for his move, he reached between two baskets on an upper shelf and came down with a canister in which there was a paper bag containing sprigs of aromatic weed.

He leaned against the wall and built a *spliff* with long, quick-moving fingers on whose shafts I noticed quills of hair. Absorbed, he drained along the wall into a squat. Now and then he'd peek at me above his work, eyes widening then averting like a nervous typist stealing glances at the object of her new infatuation as she slipped and turned a sheet of writing paper in the platen of her Smith-Corona.

Finished now, he held his work of art between his thumb and index finger, stroked his chin and made a presentation, cupped it like an offering of water. Daring him, I took it by the head into my mouth, then flicked it round.

By the time he struck the match to light it we'd accepted that a haze had formed between us, and his edge began to soften in the warm romantic mood.

In my travels through the islands I had slept with lots of men. People travel on their own for many reasons, but in truth there's only one—the animal inside our deep unconscious needs a break from rote domestic life. Sometimes it seeks a pack. When it wants to feel the bliss of getting caught it seeks a bevy or a herd. But like a tigress, it prefers to hunt alone.

Orlando had proposed. On leaving for my trip I'd told him that I'd give it lots of thought. I was a twenty-year-old woman on the verge of being chained.

"So who are you?" the man before me asked with fresh exasperation, putting me on guard. He was staring now with flaming eyes. The haze evaporated from the room. It was an awful look—the kind a man should only give a woman if he woke up in her bed with empties all around and after shaking out his head remembered that she was his touchy-feely aunt.

"I don't know a thing about you," he carried on, as if the fault were mine that he'd never asked. "You've been sitting here for how long now?"

"Gee, I'm smoking, I don't know."

"That is not the point. You've been here since, like, one o'clock and now it must be after six and I couldn't tell you if you're cat or dog. What kinda thing is that?"

Above our heads, a bulb was dangling from a wire like a snake. Water was exploding on the roof. And in a moment when I should have felt defensive, I was in a jolly mood. He was discombobulated. I'd made him lose his cool.

I stretched his gift toward him, thought he needed calming down.

"No," he said disdainfully. "What? Every Rasta has to smoke?" Softly now, he uttered, "Talk to me. Tell me who you are. I want to know."

With him, I found it hard to talk about myself. Well, what was there to say? I used to be a student but I'd lasted just a year? I sued my mother, now she doesn't talk to me? Buy-low-sell-high-that-is-what-I-do? I'm a girlfriend on the loose? I have a brother who is on his way to being a doctor—which is really great because he is my twin?

I talked about my travels and he listened with intent.

"And you?" I asked, when I was done. "Tell me anything you want about yourself." I thought it best to start him very slow.

He crossed his arms and answered, "Hmmmm . . . well, what do you want to know?"

"Well, anything you want to tell me," I responded in the

voice of the instructor who'd been stymied with the question "Miss, what should I draw?"

"Now is not the time," he answered vaguely. He said it twice, and it was flat the second time.

When he stood, I saw a model of his bulbous present printing through his jeans, and when he saw me gaping he began to shake imagined stiffness from his legs.

"Time is a funny thing," I told him, standing up as well. As he shook his legs I edged a little closer, hoping he would make the move.

"Oh yeah?"

"Oh yeah. It's a lot like smoke. It doesn't stay around. It blows away."

"Look, my brother Shooky might be coming by," he hastily explained. "What you want to do? I can give you an umbrella. There are taxis by the gate. Don't worry, I will pack up everything. You can come tomorrow if you want. My mother will be here."

"And you?"

He answered with a question.

"Tell me where you stay?"

"A little place. You might not know it. On the ridge above the big savanna. Grand Vue."

With a single hand, his elbow straightened out, he held me by the cheeks and drew his fingers with precision to the corners of my mouth, slid his thumb and pointing finger to the trembling center, paused, and quickly took the *spliff*, pulling on it deeply then exhaling it in streams across my face.

"So what time should I come for you?"

"Who's coming?"

"Hmm . . . Albert Dominguez is my name."

Dear Editor:

It is with great pleasure that I congratulate Mr. Shoucair Dominguez on being nominated for the Commonwealth Writers Prize. They don't give those things away. They're earned. Also to be congratulated are his mother, Miss Estrella Dominguez—née Thompson—and his late father, Wilfredo Dominguez, who made the bed from which this letter is being penned.

I must admit that literary success is something that evaded me in my time. I am forced to admit it because the people of this island are so uncultured that perhaps they may be unaware that Mr. Dominguez is not the first person on this island who ever dared to write. Of the sixty-seven books that I have written, every single one of them is technically in print.

As the most important investor in my career, I've preserved every one of my plates. So if there are some of you who would like to get a copy of any of my titles, please send a letter with a check. You know where I live, so there is no need for me to include an address.

Young Dominguez, whether he wins the prize or not, should receive a national honor. However, this will be difficult, as such an honor does not exist. As a service to the arts in this country, I would like to offer the government fifty thousand dollars toward its establishment, and of course, a name.

Yours, etc.

St. William Rawle

# POETIC JUSTICE

**I.**

KENDALL POWER IS the worst kind of man—the kind who should
be locked up in a cell in drag with members of a prison gang before he's burned alive. When he goes to hell, the Prince of Darkness should ignite the special furnace that he minted after
crisping all the founders of the Klan. I would love to watch a
demon feeding on his c——k. I would love to watch him die.

Stop it. Don't feel sorry. You don't know him as I do. He's a
really awful poet—the kind who makes you want to take the side
of autocrats who lock up writers in the name of public good. But
his writing isn't why he has to suffer. Or why he needs to die. I
just discovered something—he used to stretch my girl.

*Stretching* is an optimistic slang that, truth be told, I haven't
earned the right to use. But that's another story for another time.

Reg and I were leaving Campbell's in the Galleria when she
said that Kendall Power would be reading at McSweeney's
Books on Thursday night. Since the boom, we Carlitos have

adopted habits that I wouldn't have predicted when I went away to study many years ago. One of them is buying books . . . books we never read. We're rich. We shop—I'm glad . . . I write.

"Kendall Power?" I replied while giving her a smug, ironic look. I'm five feet seven with a bony frame, so shopping with a former model who's taller by a half a foot was equally exciting and embarrassing to me. In Campbell's, while Regina stroked my arm and I concealed my hurt and acted jolly and amused, I'd fitted jeans and khakis in the section marked FOR BOYS. So when she mentioned Kendall Power's name, she stirred my fundamental need to garner victories over taller men.

The last time that I'd seen him I was signing at the B&N in Union Square and he was posted at the information table, taking jobs away from people who'd gone to school at night to get a GED, his hair and goatee cut to look like Malcolm X. He complimented me, but when I turned around to smirk at him in secret, he was giving me a disapproving look.

He was a smug, self-righteous member of the cult of Madhubuti and Baraka, whose poems, like a lot of those composed by his *orishas,* had the kinds of blatant messages that speak to men who fall in love with reading late in life while passing long, unstructured days in jail. And as such, he disregarded any kind of writing that was not inspired by the darker parts of life.

We met in college, where we each pursued an MFA. I tried to get to know him, but he didn't take it well and our conversations when they happened always ended in a stall.

He didn't like to talk; he liked to argue. He didn't like to chat; he liked to teach. As if he had a platform in his shoes, he spoke like he was up and you were down, and had the habit of explaining common references as if he thought that he was pitching way above your head.

He was the only person on his block to go to college, and as such was used to certain perks, including plain regard, which at school he worked assiduously to get. When it didn't come by reason, he began to hustle with his point of view: always on the radio station, always in the campus news, always sitting in, taking up the call to lift the race by any means—except, it seemed, by writing poems as interesting and exquisite as we know ourselves to be.

In short, he was a prick—six four and self-inflated, with the kind of lean, athletic look that many women like.

"He's hit the *Times*," Regina told me as we walked toward the car, a scarlet MINI Cooper made in '72. "Where've *you* been?"

"Hit the *Times* with what?"

"A book. A memoir in verse."

"He flung it at the door?"

"You're so silly. I'm not playing. The brother has a book."

"Oh, shit. I didn't tell you. I've been drafted by the Knicks."

"Come on, Shooky. I'm serious. No joke . . . FSG."

A horn surprised us, and we stepped out of the lane and leaned against a white Accord whose trunk, like many more around us, bore a sticker of the flag of India—horizontal bars of saffron, green and white.

Was Regina pulling my dick?

It was hard for me to tell. Although I'd known her on and off for years, our love affair was new. I'd met her indirectly through my younger brother Albert, who is married to Regina's closest friend.

Too fatty in the hips and ass to make it big in fashion, she'd returned to college in her middle twenties and had gotten her degree. She lived in Brooklyn and taught English at a private school near Central Park while writing soberly insurgent novels in the vein of Alice Walker. It was a difficult time for her to write, an era when those kinds of books were hard to sell. She knew this, but she wrote.

"You know that all you need to do is write *the book*," I used to tease her. "You're living in the ATM. And after Terry McMillan, babe, the constitution of your country says that there is a book that every negress has to write . . . four sister-friends in Atlanta, D.C. or L.A. Places where they get to drive expensive cars. One's a corporate workaholic—single and divorced. One's some kind of artist who just cannot keep a man. Give one of them a doting husband with a secret double life. Round it out by making one of them completely sweet and fat. She must be the dark one and the one who didn't finish school. There you have the recipe. Go cook the people's book."

But that day, standing in that parking lot among the Beamers and Accords, the official cars of progress in a country where the superstars were bankers and computer engineers, the fortunes of a writer weren't funny anymore.

I was the most accomplished writer that the island had produced, and although I'd been reviewed in all the better places, well, I'd never hit the list.

## II.

WE ENTERED TOWN along the motorway that linked the city to the factories and the gantries of the big container port that dominated what we used to call "the far" Atlantic coast. With suburban sprawl behind us, spreading high into the slopes, we had turned into a fragment in a hot metallic sludge. It was a weekend when a tech convention and a music fest were going on, and we were caught between a flatbed and a shuttle bus with minivans on either side. Windows down, radio on, shopping bags behind our seats, blind to all that lay ahead, we'd settled in our own respective worlds.

"What kinda book is it?" I asked her as the shuttle bus began to move again.

"Are you still on that?"

She wiped a film of perspiration from her smoothly tapered head.

"I'm not on anything," I answered, smiling.

"What about my case?"

"Well, what's it called?"

She leaned against her door and dropped her chin to look at me with laughing eyes above her silver shades. Framing her outside the car were shafts of steel and glass, the new convention center and its satellite hotels, which had been built along the harbor front along the promenade.

"Don't laugh," she said. "You promise? *Recognize I'm Real.*"

"Why didn't he just call it *Pinch Myself and Wake Me from My Dream?*"

"You have a really evil side, you know."

"So said my better half."

Staring off, she muttered, "And I heard he got a chunk o' change."

"So how do you know all this?" I asked, believing that I knew what she would say: *Blah blah blah saw blah blah blah at blah and said blah blah. Then the other day blee blee was having drinks with blah blah at bloo bloo and heard it too. But it wasn't until bling bling brought it up that I began to pay it any mind.*

Her actual answer brought a feeling that I'd never had before—a shriveling of the scrotum in hot weather, a deep testicular quail, which caused me to reflect on how the sack that holds the future, when contracted, bears a likeness to the brain.

"He told me," she said, laughing by herself.

"Oh, you know him?"

"Yeah. We used to be friends."

"You've never mentioned him before."

"I don't talk to that idiot anymore."

"Why not?"

"We broke up really badly."

I couldn't turn around to look. Welded by the shock, the bones along my neck had fused. By the time I'd left the boulevard and turned into the narrow streets of Old Seville, I had discovered that the man I hated and the woman that I loved had been together on and off for seven years, that they were high school sweethearts in New Brunswick, that they used to live together for a year, and that for some of this I was his classmate in a writing program in New York.

In town, along the boulevard we call the Queens, we stopped at Cup & Chaucer, where I hoped to get a pick-me-up. My preference was a greeting from a fan, but I would settle for a Zip (four espresso shots with honey and a drop of condensed milk).

The Queens was lined on either side with mansions from the Spanish time, sweet confections made of coral stone with iron balconies like lacy bras along the upper floors and columns like the thighs of strolling *señoritas*.

When I was a boy, this was the place to shop; but now it is the place to eat. And of all the coffeehouses, Cup & Chaucer's was the best. They got their coffee from Havana. They had a good live music scene. And with its former living quarters now accommodating wooden shelves, it was the most exquisite space in which to buy a book.

As I put the little car into a parking spot where nothing else could fit, I felt a blend of dark emotions seeping out. My heart was like a tea bag, my body like a mug.

"When was the last time you and him talk?" I asked in island English. This was not a choice. It was the way the words came out.

"Not since we broke up."

"So how he get your number then?"

My hands were still at three o'clock along the steering wheel, although the car was parked.

"From Joan."

"If my agent do that, I would fire her to *rass,* 'cause that ain't make no sense."

"She's his agent too," she said consolingly while reaching for my hand. "I didn't know that she'd signed him on. It's not a . . . you know . . . conspiracy. Like you, I was surprised."

"Makes sense. She's a talent agent, and he doesn't have the goods."

She leaned her head against the window, sucked her teeth

and closed her eyes, her nostrils flaring as she throatily exhaled. She was biting on her teeth. I saw the clenching in her jaw, which caused the silver hoop that dangled from her ear to twitch. Through her dark French-roasted skin, a vein began to show along her neck.

Sometimes her beauty shocked me. And in times like these I felt a need to reappraise myself. I'm not what you would call a handsome man. In fact, the opposite is true. Acne was the terror of my youth. My cheeks and jaws are rough like orange peel. My bulbous nose is shiner than a grape.

"Shoucair," Regina whispered tightly, trotting out my proper name. "I don't wanna talk about another man right now. I only have one man, and that is you. I'm sorry if I hurt your feelings, baby. But you're gonna treat me like a woman. Not a girl. Before you, I had a life. Before me, you had one too. Don't upset me with some unimportant shit that happened long ago."

"It's not that long ago," I mumbled.

"You left New York in *ninety-two*."

"I just can't stand that f——king guy."

"Well, maybe he's different now."

"He has creative eczema. He cannot change his spots."

"A lot of time has passed," she said astringently, and cracked her door. "Maybe he's turned into a decent poet. Maybe he's been decent for a while and like some folks I know just couldn't get a break."

I held her arm so that she couldn't leave.

"A decent poet? A decent poet? That's like saying someone's a decent short-order cook. Look, Regina, anyone can be a poet nowadays. All they have to do is make a list. *I am strong. I am bright. I am black. I am proud. I am.* There's a poem right there. Do you want another one? I'm hot right now."

"No thanks."

She got out of the car and quickly merged into the stream of people walking up and down the street.

"Don't complicate it, Reg," I said when I'd caught up to her. "I'm serious."

She was walking very quickly, shoulders swinging like the ass that dangled from her waist and gave a fruity splendor to her twiggy frame.

"If I were you," she warned, "I'd leave this girl alone."

"Look, this is serious. Say anything. Go on. Anything. Anything you want."

She stopped and crossed her arms.

"What do you mean?"

"Just say something. I don't care. Whatever comes to mind."

"Fine—I thought I was on the way to spend a lovely afternoon with someone who means a lot to me before we went to jazz tonight. I was wrong, I guess, 'cause now I'm being harassed. Look—I'm just too goddamn grown for this."

"Is that a poem?"

"No. It's not."

"And that's my point. In Kendall Power's world it could be. Now hear me out. Doesn't this sound like him?"

*I thought*
*I thought*
*Oh, yes I thought . . .*
*I thought I was on the way to spend a lovely afternoon*
*with someone who means a lot to me*
*before we went to jazzzzzzzzzzzzzzzzzzzzzzzzzzzzzzzzzzzzzzzzzzzz*
*tonight.*
*Coltrane jazz. Soul train jazz.*
*I was wrong I*
*guesssssssssssssssssssssssssssssssssssssssssssssssssssssssssss*
*'cause now I'm being harassed*
*like Rodney King, and Martin Luther King,*
*I'm the monkey man King Kong.*
*Look—I'm just too damn grown for this*

*For this . . .*
*For this . . .*
*For this . . .*
*White America where a black man is an ape.*

"Don't patronize me, Shooky."

"I'm not mocking you. I'm mocking him."

"Envy doesn't suit you."

"Envy," I said as we began to walk again. "Envy? Envy who? Envy him? Gimme a break. I'm a novelist. I write symphonies. That idiot scribbles greeting cards for folks whose teachers should have kept them back."

"You're jealous. Just accept it. Accept it and deal with it or move on."

We were in front of Cup & Chaucer, standing on the pavement right below the crowded steps where tourists and Carlitos roosted, sipping as they talked from paper cups with printed illustrations from the *The Canterbury Tales*.

"Jealous," I said. "Of who?"

"Of him."

"Of Luke Cage Power Man? I'm jealous? Did that just come out of your mouth? Well, what are you gonna say next, that the world is round?"

"F——k you, Shooky."

"Baby, wait," I answered as she flashed her arm and picked her way between the people on the crowded steps. "That was supposed to be a joke."

III.

OLD BOYFRIENDS SHOULD be treated like old condoms—either dumped in the garbage or flushed. But women always find a way to keep them. Rummage through a woman's dresser and you're sure to find the proof—a shirt, a note, a ticket stub, an arbitrary list. They even keep defining phrases from their speech. (You know she had a boyfriend from Jamaica if she rates a great experience as "de boom.")

In the female mind an ex is never just an ex. In addition he's a *why*. Why the hell did I go there? Why did it have to end like that? Why didn't he commit? Why did I lend him that money to straighten out his life? Why? Why? Why? Why? Why? Why? Why?

They keep in touch because they want to know.

Men forget their exes. We keep nothing that belongs to them. We treat them like a math equation written on the board. When the teacher leaves the room, we wipe them off. Blank the slate is what we do. If the problem disappears, we say it's solved. Go ahead and fail us if you want. *Ex* plus *why* is naught.

Of course this isn't true. The proof comes at the sighting—the first occasion that you see her with another man. It's never fair. The scales are never even. You're always looking like a man who's spent a month of reading nothing but the most depressing works of Dostoyevsky, and she's always beaming in an outfit that displays her figure in a way that gives it all the envy-stoking glamour of a check made out for royalties to Stephen King.

You're always tepid, 'cause you don't know what to make of her, and she's always either hot or cold. The best—or worst—of them can switch between the two as if each mood is fed by different plumbing like a pair of faucets in a British house.

The way they look will always get you. But the thing that really gets you is their tendency to pull your name—"Miiiiiiiichael! Richaaaaaaard! Pauuuuuuuul"—reminding you of all the lengths of rope you used to hang yourself.

Their date is always introduced as "Blah-blah-blah-blah, my friend from so and so," when you know his rightful name is "Blah-blah-blah-blah, the-man-I'm-sleeping-with-to-purge-myself-of-you."

You of course are introduced by nothing but your name—Michael . . . Richard . . . Paul—the lock of hair she cut away . . . the foreskin that was clipped.

## IV.

IN THE NOISY courtyard with its painted field of floral tiles, a crew from CNN was interviewing Ziggy Marley while a local band was setting up their back line on the music stage.

Since the boom, San Carlos had become a city-state of sixty thousand native-born and half a million "special guests"—professionals from overseas recruited by agents of the PPP, the bring-your-own-business party of dictator Dr. Don Octavio Rawle, a Cambridge-educated surgeon who'd advised Fidel and Clinton on the subject of cigars.

To one, he said, "You need to quit or you will die and they will overthrow your revolution." To the next: "You wouldn't be concerned about a cold sore if you'd carried two and found a way to slip the dry one in your mouth."

Upstairs, along the balconies whose flowered rails were lined with tables with a view of all the action in the courtyard below, I made a slow but satisfactory progress through the crowd. Everyone I spoke to seemed to like me. Everyone who jabbed my side or took my hand or poked my shoulder so I'd turn around and fall into a hug conveyed the feeling of a friend. All the women who said flirty things through lips pressed lightly on my ear while trailing fingers through the thinning brush that gave uneven cover to my head evoked a future filled with nights of passion to excess.

But outside now, sitting by myself where Reg had left me on the steps, a Zip in either hand, I felt abraded, like I'd spent a half an hour crawling through a hedge. There was something pricking me beneath the skin—the thorny issue of my brother's name. Everyone I'd seen had brought it up. He was the minister of security and finance—at thirty-six, the rumored heir apparent of

Octavio Rawle. He didn't socialize, and often traveled overseas, which placed him out of reach. So people, women mostly, tried to get to him through me.

Waiting for Regina, feeling all alone, I felt a slack, disorienting sense of loss. Life became a blur, the trees in the median, the facing buildings from across the street, the people moving up and down the sidewalk, softened to a smear, congealing in a long, amalgamated, multicolored streak.

Kendall Power and Regina. Kendall Power and the *Times*. Which was worse? I wasn't sure.

As I sat there contemplating this, a voice began to penetrate the sonic blob, and I regained my focus in the presence of an old white man in khakis and a polo shirt, one leg forward, one leg back, elbow resting on his knee. Nervously, he glanced across his shoulder down the steps toward the pavement where a lady with a camera smiled politely while her body language pressured him to speak.

"Are you who I think you are?" he asked. "I didn't mean to interrupt."

"Well, it all depends," I said.

"Dominguez," he said brightly.

"Yes."

"The one who wrote that book?"

"Yes. *That* book," I answered warmly.

"My wife's your biggest fan," he said. He turned to her. "It's him."

She was a frail, soft-spoken woman, polite and full of grace, and I pulled my knees toward my chest and wrapped my arms around my shins as we began to talk.

"So you're here for the convention or the music fest?" I asked her as I felt a vital force return.

"Yes," she said from where she sat beside her husband on the step below. "The music fest. You too?"

"No. This is where I live."

"I saw you on TV," the husband said. "You made me laugh."

"I hope with good intent."

"It was a lovely book," remarked the wife. She was a handsome woman with blue eyes and blond hair whose roots had whitened in the front. Her cheeks displayed a rosy tint, and when she spoke, I saw the way her bottom row of teeth was out of kilter like a picket fence constructed on a curve along a road where drivers like to speed.

Touching her as if to ground himself, the husband said, "At first I didn't like it, but she made me stick with it and she was right. Because it grew."

"Fred, maybe you should take our picture while I get a hug?" his wife suggested.

Beaming now, I answered, "That's all right with me."

I slid beside her and the husband stood below us and we held each other tightly till we heard the click.

Although I didn't know which book they'd read, I'd been a writer long enough to answer everything they asked . . . oh, the idea just came one day . . . a composite of various people, but no one person in particular . . . there's always something in the pot, but not that I can talk about . . . as long as I can remember . . . let's see, Rushdie, Twain, Márquez, also Naipaul in his younger days . . . there are a lot of good books out there now, but I'm not reading anything at the moment . . . if you put it that way, I'd have to say I'm black *and* Caribbean *and* a writer to boot. . . .

"And what about an ass?"

While the couple stared at me, I watched Regina walking down the steps.

"Is everything okay?" the husband asked.

"Not really," I replied, while standing. "A little thing came up."

I bounded down the steps toward her, quickly catching up, but just as I was going to rest my hand against her shoulder and apologize, she stopped abruptly and I found myself about to knock her flat.

Already in mid-step, I twisted to avoid her only to discover in my path a woman, sharing cookies with a child, who saw my shadow looming, looked up and began to scream. If I didn't jump or turn I would've shattered tender parts of her, and if I twisted back I would've knocked Regina down.

And in this slowing of time in which I had to make a choice, it crossed my mind to catapult myself above Regina's head, reasoning quite fallaciously that I was moving very fast. How fast was I moving? Just enough—just enough to be unable to retard myself. On instinct, though, my hand began to reach for her, to hold her arm in passing, just to stabilize myself, enough to vault above the screaming girl. But, as my fingers were about to touch her skin, Regina, in oblivion, leaned away from me to get a lighter from her purse, and when I touched her arm she was unstable and I swept her off her feet.

"Oh, shit," I said when I had cleared the diving. "Reg, are you okay?"

As I kneeled beside her, shadows crossed me as a crowd began to gather round. She had fallen on her shoulder but had rolled onto her back, and she lay there in a kind of daze just staring past my face into the sky, her arms behind her head.

"Can you move?" I asked. "Is anything broken? Does anything hurt?"

"Just leave me," she responded dryly.

"Darling, can you move?"

I realized that Regina thought I'd pushed her only when I tried to slip my arms around her back to help her to her feet and she shot up straight and slapped my face and flailed. With my elbows up to block my face, I took the scratches on my arms and rolled away.

"You cut me," I said, pointing to a filament of red along my wrist. "Here and here and here."

"You pushed me, Shooky. Get away from me. Don't touch me. I'll stand up on my own."

She stood up on unsteady legs and looked at me, then used her hands to cup her face.

"It was an accident," I said naively as she stooped to get her shades. I turned toward the crowd with open arms, demanding their support. "Ask anybody here."

"It's him," somebody muttered.

Another person whispered, "Did you see what he just did?"

"Are you happy?" said Regina, sharply pointing at my face.

"Look. I didn't do it. I know what you might think. I was trying to talk to you and when I reached for you, I lost my step. I slipped. I didn't push you. I slipped."

She put her arms against her lips and looked me up and down, then crossed her arms across her breasts and fixed me with a narrow-eyed, accusing look.

"All of this for something that occurred so long ago," she said with disappointment. "How could you stoop so low?"

"Look . . . I don't know what to say right now," I told her as the crowd began to drift away. I glanced around to see if I could find the woman who'd been sitting with the child, hoping that her point of view would help to clear my name.

"You're so goddamn full of your frigging self," Regina said beneath her breath. "You're not the only person who deserves success, okay," she said a little louder. "A lot of people struggle for a very long time. Be happy when they get what they're due. I don't deserve this, man. I don't deserve this shit at all. All these people watching. All these people looking on and just shaking their heads. Fighting with my man in the street. This is some Tina Turner shit. How did it get to all this, Shooky? What's next? A stomp? A kick? A pimp slap? A beat down? You know what, Shooky . . . you're a punk. That's what you are. You're a punk ass, Shooky. Shooky, you ain't shit. You ain't shit, Shooky. Shooky, you're a bitch. You're a motherf——king, p—ssy ass bitch."

Her lips were shaking. If she said another word, the tears that had been clinging to her lids would lose their nerve and jump.

"Let's go home," I said. "I need to be alone with you. I need to talk to you. We need to work this out."

"I'm not going anywhere with you, Shooky. You're out of your mind."

I moved toward her slowly, trying to gain her trust, postponing any effort to convince her of the truth. I'm not by nature an aggressive man. But alas, a man I am, which means that I must not be called a *p—ssy* or a *bitch,* and she had called me both.

"Believe me, Reg," I said contritely, shaking out my fingers, which were forming into fists. "Have I ever done a thing like that?"

She was about to answer when somebody intervened—the lady who'd just posed with me. Instinctively, I was relieved. If she'd been watching from her vantage point, I reasoned, then she would have clearly seen. And even if she hadn't, well, our conversation obligated her to side with me.

"Don't move," she said, arms raised as if she were confronted with a beast. "You're not gonna get away with this. My husband is a coward. But I'm not. I've seen my sister go through this." She leaned to speak around me. "Honey, go find a cop."

By now we were a sideshow and as such we were allowed to carry on like freaks. We'd gone beyond the point where people felt they ought to intercede.

"You don't understand this, ma'am. With all due respect, this is something between the two of us and we might be struggling right now, but we're going to work this out. And so I'm asking you nicely, please sit down. Please relax. You don't know what is going on. I need to talk to her, and you're in my way. And if I have to move you, I will."

"My sister's husband used to beat her all the time."

A crowd began to circle us again.

"Ma'am, I need to speak with her. Please get out of my way."

"You're not listening, are you? Fred, did you get the cop?"

"Cop? What cop? Why f——king cop? Where you think this is? What you take this for? Regina, can you talk to her? She's getting on my nerves."

Regina doubled over and began to laugh. I moved toward her and the woman took a forward step and pressed her palms against my chest. Instinctively, I grabbed her arms. She twisted, and I tensed my grip. She kicked my shin. Her husband lunged at me. I did a really awful thing.

## V.

THE NEXT MORNING, as I lay across the bed, my agent, Romello Thomas, called me from New York. I lived alone in New Seville, or, as some people called it, "Ningapore"—the ten square miles of dense, sky-reaching towers whose construction meant the end of Black Well, a shantytown that traced its roots to a settlement of former slaves along the banks of a lagoon.

"Shooky, what the hell is going on?" Romello asked.

"Depends on what you mean?"

"Go to CNN."

I did as I was told and saw a man who looked like me and shared a name with me reacting to an unexpected kick by doing a really awful thing—he sharply turned a lady's wrist. The lady's name was Thelma Olsen and her age was sixty-one, and she'd won a trip for two from Bagley, Minnesota, where she'd once again been chosen Teacher of the Year.

Cut to witnesses. Now cut to Reg. Now play the scene again.

"Oh, shit," I said to Rommy. "It doesn't get worse than that."

"Well, it does. Look what comes after the second loop."

On the screen now, in reaction, from a street in Harlem, was a man who should be locked up in a cell in drag with members of a prison gang before he's burned alive—making an audacious threat: "Shooky Dominguez, wherever you are, I want you to listen to this. Women are not punching bags. Women are queens. If you want to fight someone, well, be a man about it. Fight me.

Let's get in the ring and really see who's the man. This is no joke. This is serious. Let's do it in the ring. Mano a mano. Toe-to-toe. This is about respect and honor. I'm not a man of violence. But Regina Walker is close to my heart. You attacked her from the back just like a little punk. We'll see what happens when we get together face-to-face. I'm not playing. This is not a joke. You better recognize. I'm real."

"What the f——k is his problem, Rommy? Can you believe that shit?"

"He doesn't have a problem, Shooky. Not compared to you. Thelma Olsen's people want to sue you for the wrist."

"It's broken?"

"No. But badly sprained."

"Oh, shit."

"You're sitting down?"

"Just tell me."

"This is hard."

"Just . . . what?"

"They're asking twenty mil."

"For a wrist? What did she teach? How to jerk people off? That's crazy. Who has twenty million dollars?"

"It's not the hand, my friend."

I drew the blinds and opened up the sliding door and went out on the deck. The ground was far below, but surely not beyond my reach.

"It's pain and suffering," said Rommy in his breathy, therapeutic way. "Emotional distress. Public humiliation. The woman is on CNN."

"I don't have that kind of money. What are we going to do?"

"Settle for a hundred grand as they expect."

"A hundred grand? Who has a hundred grand?"

"Your condo's worth a half a mil."

"Don't f——k with that. There has to be another way, Rommy. This is where I live."

## VI.

REG WAS STAYING at my brother's house, which added to the depth in which I'd found myself in shit. My brother, as I've mentioned, was the husband of her closest friend. As such, he welcomed her arrival with the kind of glee that brides reserve for menses that arrive without a warning on their wedding night.

My brother hardly speaks. When his words emerge, his eyes assume a queer, distracted look, kind of a cross between embarrassment and shock, as if he's trying to keep the conversation going in the presence of an unacknowledged fart.

He's an economist. By temperament and training, he's inclined to take a watchful stance. His instinct is to pull away to take the longer look.

But this morning when he came to see me, though, he got up in my face.

"What kind of f——king thing is that?" he asked me through the door.

"Don't start with me."

"Just open up."

"Have you heard my side?" I asked him as he dropped his briefcase on the carpet in the living room and slid away the double doors that opened to the deck.

We look alike, but indirectly. He implies me in the way a horse implies a mule. In looks, he's certainly the better draft—taller, with the kind of shoulders built on which to hang an English suit. He's younger, but has always gotten more respect. He's always been my mother's prize, the one who, on his holidays from college, would return to work behind the counter in her tchotchke shop, especially in his Rasta phase. He's my only sibling. But my rival he's not. He's way ahead of me these days. He's won.

"Shooky, do you know what it's like to be in a house with two angry Yankee gals?" He was standing with his back toward me and his hands along the rail that ran around the deck. "Man, just push me now. They beat me down so much, I don't even have the strength to blasted jump. Do you every think of me? You must have seen the camera from CNN. People told me that you were inside the blasted spoon and porridge or whatever you want to call it, profiling and all. Shaking hands like you want to enter politics. As usual, going for the limelight. Well, you're in the limelight now, my friend." He spun around to face me in his double-breasted suit. "Because of you I have no voice in my own damn house. As soon as I open my mouth, they just get loud. I'm in line to be the leader of this country when the doctor steps away and I can't even voice my own opinion in the house that I built? You have f——ked up my life. My wife is changing right before my eyes. The woman who told me that she understands that voting and democracy are two different things is now saying that there will be no dictator in her house. Throwing words like that. I want to ask a question or clarify a point and they drown me out. I try to speak above them and they turn into a mob. Are you hearing me? Remember how it used to be after independence back in seventy-nine when the doctor said the parliamentary system in a place like this would only cause a lot of strife, and he unified the country under him, and backward, nonprogressives used to demonstrate and say he was a despot who would take away our freedom with a single-party state? Well, I'm living that right now. If I say a word in opposition, I'm Baby Doc."

"Well if your leader is so great, and seeing that you're so great, then why don't you go back to your house and do what he did? Turn them out and separate them, raze the house and build expensive towers on the real estate."

"Look. They got much better houses than they had before."

"Houses, friend. Not homes."

"They own those houses now, houses they can sell. They have something most black people on this planet never see—and that, my friend, is wealth."

"Fine. You bought them out."

"And fine. You f——ked me up."

I put my arm around his shoulder, tried to calm him down.

"Don't believe what they're saying, Albert, especially the foreign press."

He went inside and lay across the bed.

"So what," he asked sarcastically, "this whole thing is a lie?"

"It was an accident. I was going toward her and I tripped, and knocked her over. Now everything is f——ked."

"You don't look as if you give a shit, to me."

"Well, look again."

He propped up on his elbows, shook his head and said, while struggling with a smile of ambiguity, "Well, maybe everything isn't f——ked, not f——ked as yet."

"Well, tell me what you mean."

He got up off the bed and made his way to me.

"She won't be left unf——ked for long, my brother . . . if you know what I mean."

"What is there to know?" I asked him coolly, holding in the hurt.

He crossed his arms and stroked his chin.

"You should know that she and Power are in touch."

"How do you know?"

"How do I know anything I want to know?"

"Okay. You tapped her cell phone."

"The words are yours, not mine."

"So is there a possibility that there might be something somewhere like . . . let's say . . . a plan?"

"He wants to see her and she's angry and that's all that I can say."

"Come on, Albert. What's the rest?"

"I sent her sixty roses in your name. That means you owe me. Call her in half an hour at the house."

"So on top of everything," I said, "he's trying to stretch my girl?"

"It's a little worse than that. He's getting into town tomorrow afternoon."

"His reading's not till Thursday. That doesn't make any sense."

"Oh, yeah? She wants revenge."

"Not in my face, Albert. Not in my backyard. Do you know what he's doing? He's calling out the beast."

"Whatever you do," he cautioned, "don't embarrass me."

"I don't give a shit."

"Don't go to jail for this."

## VII.

I DIDN'T DO as I was told. Instead of calling Reg, I turned on my computer and began to type . . . at first a word, then two . . . my fingers moving slowly but with deep intent . . . stealthily like paws. . . .

## VIII.

I CALLED HER two days later after dodging many calls—family, friends, Rommy, the press.

"Hello."

"Shooky?"

"Yes. It's me."

I was in the bedroom, padding back and forth, sipping from a water glass.

"What do you want?"

"To tell the truth—"

"You don't know anything about truth, Shooky. Everything you're about to say is a lie."

"Will I ever get a chance to even speak?"

"If you're gonna be belligerent, I'm hanging up."

"I didn't call to speak to you, Carmona."

"Well, why'd you call my frigging house?"

Carmona was my brother's wife. When they met she was a curvy butter sculpture. After years of loving in the tropics, though, she had begun to spread.

"It's your house but not your phone, okay. So give the cell to Reg."

Carmona was especially upset with me because she'd created the opportunity for me to sleep with Reg. Friends don't let friends drive drunk! Well, friends don't put their tipsy friends in a car with their horny brother-in-law.

Reg was drunk. That's how we started. But this is why I think she stayed: she was so embarrassed in the morning that she had to stay, she had to bring it off, she had to make it seem as if she had the kind of deeper insight that it took to see something compelling in an okay guy like me. I was a guy. She was a babe. In fact, she was a babe deluxe, a former model with advanced degrees. And look at me? The guy who comes to mind when women raise their hands and swear, "I'd have to be f———cked up out of my mind . . ."

Through the phone I heard the women trying to whisper, hissing like a ball of snakes.

"I'm sorry, Reg," I started when she took the phone. The voice that I had sought and found was something of a purr. "Baby . . . can we talk?"

There was a long intake of breath.

"Well," she said, a little hoarsely, "well . . . it all depends."

I stood and crossed my arms and paced again.

"I'm sorry," I said with true regret. From her voice I knew that she'd been crying, which brought on me a new awareness of how much she had been hurt. And so I spoke as if the ring of holes in the receiver were a patch of prickly wounds. "I love you too much to hurt you, babe. It was one of those strange moments in time where everything just works out for the worst. If I were an engineer like every second person on this island, maybe I'd know enough physics to even try to guess how certain forces work. Whatever they are and however they work, they worked against us, babe. Have I ever done anything like that to you? Gimme some credit, Reg. I'm a better man than that. I know you're hurt. I know you're pissed. But can we work this out?"

There was a lengthy silence amplified by bits of sound the way that clouds of dust add body to a stream of light.

I cast my mind toward the house in Mayfair Gardens and, padding back and forth across the lion-colored carpet, used my ears to track Regina's movement through the house.

She left the kitchen through a set of swinging doors that opened to a narrow passageway, her sandals slipping slightly on the marble tiles. At a heavy door, she jostled with the lock and stepped into the light, and walked around the pool, passing on the way the humming pump, the toucan cage, and settled pertly on a chaise beneath the rustling mango.

"Thanks for the flowers," she said cagily. "They were really nice."

"Don't mention. They're nothing. But you're welcome. Okay?"

"This has all turned out so badly," she responded in a verbal heave. "Now Carmona knows."

"It's okay."

"But I felt I had to talk to her. Do you know what I mean?"

"I guess. I mean . . . well . . . sure."

"You don't get it, do you?"

"I just want to know if you're in love with me?"

"Don't put me on the spot."

"I'm not trying to twist your arm, babe. I mean . . . it's important. I just want to know."

"Shooky . . ."

"Is she there?"

I leaned my head from side to side to drain the stiffness from my neck.

"No," she said defensively. "I'm here alone."

"Okay, babe. It's me and you now. No one is there to get involved and come between us. Let's talk. Just you and me."

"Shooky . . . look. This feels unfair. You're making me feel like I'm a traitor now. I don't wanna go behind her back. She's really pissed with you."

"She's pissed with me because of you. Because of what you said. She wasn't there. Maybe I should call you later or something or leave it in your hands to call me back. Maybe I'm trying too hard or forcing something. Maybe this is not the time."

"No. Don't."

"Don't what?"

"Don't call back. You'll only get her. I'm not answering the phone. CNN has called me once or twice. Then there's FOX and MSNBC. They want to drag this out." After pausing, she became a little strident now. "And Kendall has been calling me as well."

As rehearsed, I answered with concern and open-minded reservation when I got the news.

"That's nice of him."

"Don't be a shit."

"Look. I have a more accommodating mind these days. I know what it's like to be wrongly judged, for folks to read all kinds of evil in your best intent."

"I guess."

"So . . ."

"So what?"

"So . . . what did he have to say?"

"I don't want to get into it."

"What did he say to you?"

"Oh, he's so full o' shit."

Like you, I thought. Like you.

"So, he calls you up . . . ," I prompted, putting down the water now and gesturing with my arm.

"Everything about him that I used to hate has all come rushing back. Did you see the shit on CNN?"

"Well . . ."

"What am I thinking? Sure, you have. He's such an opportunist. Now he wants to fight you. Now he wants to rescue me. Now he wants to put himself up as this guardian of my honor. He's trying to act like he's my prince, but when we were together we would have these fights because I wouldn't let him tie me up and spank my ass and shoot it on my face. Who's he trying to fool?"

As the fingers of my free hand formed themselves into a gun, I told her calmly, "I think I need to talk to him. I'm the one who got us into this, so I'm the one to get us out."

"Oh, leave that shit alone."

"Avoiding it won't make it go away, babe."

"Drop it, man. It's done."

"Is there a reason why I shouldn't talk to him?"

"What are you trying to say?"

"I'm not trying to say anything. I'm trying to get some answers, and you're not cooperating. You're blocking. You're stalling. You're holding back."

"I just don't want you to deal with this."

"Why? So he can keep calling you? So the scandal can keep going on? So he can use your name to get attention? This man you say you hate? Look. I want to put an end to this. Things aren't sorted out between us, and unless they're solved, well, things will never be. And from the way you're acting now, I can't tell if they're going to get solved for good. Maybe they'll get solved and we'll just kiss good-bye and go our separate ways. 'Cause you don't want this, Regina. This whole thing is a burden to you."

"Why is this so important?"

Her voice was steady and direct. If I took too long, I knew, then all that I had worked for would be lost. She expected me to back away or stumble while I tried to overwhelm her with rhetoric, but instead I took her side.

"Closure," I said, evoking dreams of that elusive thing that women seek but never find with exes, the thing that marks the *exes* from the *whys*.

"He's staying at the Sheraton Marina," she conceded. "Second tower. Suite 1132."

I knew better than to ask her how she knew.

"Just . . . no more trouble," she said pensively. "And if it isn't handled right, I'll deal with it myself."

"What are you doing tomorrow night?" I asked her, switching tone and subject quickly like a double-sided coat.

"I don't know."

"Let's have dinner. We need to talk. If you don't know if you love me, then we need to solve *that* thing. What time should I pick you up?"

"Carmona's gonna get all freaky if you come for me. But that's for me to straighten out."

"You need to tell that girl the truth."

"I don't wanna get into more than I can deal with right now."

"Okay. Seven at Miranda's. If you think it is important, you'll get there on your own."

"I wanna ask you something."

"What?"

"You really didn't mean it, right? You're not a brutal kinda guy."

I told her, "No," while smiling at the papers scattered on my bed, my most important work, every single mention of the prey—as I'd begun to think of him—downloaded from the Web.

My senses taut like any stalking beast's, my index finger leading like a lowered nose, I'd tracked through every line. Sometimes I'd think I'd caught something important, then it would unravel like a rotten thread; sometimes a trail would lead in circles, back to things that I'd already known—his parents' separation; his belief that poetry had saved his life; his view that Tupac was a martyr and not a selfish, charismatic thug.

True, a lot of it was useless, but by stalking through the underbrush I'd found what I had sought, which was the most humiliating way to get my just revenge. In an interview in something called *The Chronic* back in 1991, the prey had shared his greatest fears: "Failure, mediocrity and mice. In the projects, there had been lots of them. I used to go to bed afraid that they would bite me in the night."

How do you get a bag of mice?

1. You don't go to a pet shop. Gerbils and hamsters won't do. And don't ask your friend who teaches bio. You'll get the mini polar bears that used to make you wince each time you had to pin their sleeping bodies to the corkboard in the lab.
2. To get the big brown ones that look like beavers with a shaven tail, well, this is what you do. You find a seedy area. There, you find a drunk. You ask him what he'd like to drink. You put the money down and listen while he talks.
3. Gently probe until you find his goal in life. If he doesn't have one anymore, then find out what it used to be. You sympathize. You touch him with your hand. You tell him that you want to help him out. You offer him a job. You keep its nature secret while you get a gauge of what it costs to keep him tipsy for a week.
4. How you frame the job is crucial. You must do it in a way that makes him see you as a guy who's doing well, but who is really down and out. Brotherhood. That's what it's all about. The little guys against the big.

Do as I've instructed, then, and this is what he'll do. He'll tell you where to find the kind of mice you need—the trash behind the KFC or Burger King.

Tips:
1. Don't give him all the money.
2. Give him 10 percent to start. Give him ten more when you meet before the mission and he shows you all the rodents in the bag.

3. Lastly, never pay a penny of the balance till he's done the job—delivering the goods.

Private embarrassment is better than public—if you're the prey. At seven o'clock this evening, Power will be shamed in a most spectacular way.

## IX.

"POWER SPEAKING."

"Hello, Kendall. How's your room? Do you know who this is? Shooky . . . Shooky from NYU. Welcome to San Carlos, man. Whassup?"

" 'Sup, Shook," he answered guardedly.

"Nothing much. Just thought I should check in. I heard you were in town."

"This shit is crazy, yo . . ."

"Nothing to worry about."

"Look, I don't have any beef with you, okay."

"I'm cool, man. That was all a big mistake."

"Look, I know what you might be thinking after all the stuff that's been going around in the media, but I just want you to know that a lot of what I said was taken out of context. You know how they always do. I was dealing with it on the level of the hip-hop esthetic, where battling is not physical per se, but a match of wits. And all I was trying to say was that the two of us should work it out with words—as an example to the youth. But they cut that part out. But you don't need to hear no shit like this. You know the way they do."

"Well, now that you've explained it, well, makes a lotta sense. Honestly, I was, like, 'What's my man doing? Why's he coming at me like this?' But now I get it. Now I understand."

"So did it make it on the news down here?"

"Nope. It's like it never happened. Not a word."

"So, do you think folks are gonna come out to the reading?"

"The whole reading thing is funny down here. It's hard to say."

"Well, is there anything that we could do?"

"Like radio or something? Interviews? That kinda thing?"

"Anything, man. I just wanna get the word out."

"I'm sure there are a few things. Don't worry. We'll hook it up. So you've got a new book. Congratulations. I heard it's doing well."

"Thank you. I . . . uh . . . read your last book . . . the one about your mother . . . *Miss Consuelo*—"

*"Miss Estrella Thompson, If You Please."*

"I'm not that good with names," he said defensively. "But, yeah . . . I read it. It was good."

"Thanks. You read my book. That's very cool. It means a lot. I haven't read yours yet. But it's right there on my list."

His silence slammed before me like a gate.

"Don't sweat it, man," he answered seconds later, when he'd opened up again. "Brothers need to get out of that tit-for-tat thing, that capitalist mentality that says, 'I have to do for you *because* you do for me.' I didn't read your book so you could read mine. I read it because you're a successful black man and although we've had our differences in the past, I still respect what you do."

"Look, I don't get around to reading much poetry . . . these days . . . but I'll get around to it."

"Hey . . . whatever . . ."

"Can I say something to you?" I said to re-bait him, as the conversation slipped. "It's not a big deal . . . just something I've wanted to tell you for a very long time."

"Speak your mind, brother. Communication—or the lack of it—is something that has always kept our people mentally and economically enslaved."

"What I want to say is that I need to hand it to guys like you—"

He interjected, "In order for me to process what you're say-ing, first you need to define what 'guys like you' means."

"Poets, you know . . . poets of the people . . . guys like you who studied Walcott and Rilke and Lorca and Hopkins but write poems that feel more like something that just flames right off the tongue of a Baptist priest or a guy just talking smack inside a bar-ber shop. When I read this stuff it feels so . . . real . . . like real lan-guage that people use every day . . . but just with shorter lines. You guys are the true artists of this writing thing. I just had to say that. It's a kind of magic thing that you guys do . . . to take the language that people speak and put it in a poem and send it back to them like nothing changed. I once heard someone describe it as poetry by stealth. The poem just finds a way to fit in with everything around it without scaring folks by calling attention to itself. That's power, man. And that kind of power intimidates."

I'd been pacing back and forth before, and now I broke into a little dance.

"I don't know what to say," he said while chuckling, amused by what I'm sure he thought of as an interesting turn of events. "We just do what we do. But what we do is connect with the people on a daily basis. And since you and I are being honest, I think it's fair to say that I didn't always see you as a brother who really wanted to connect. And I'm not trying to judge a brother. I'm just saying that I've always seen you as a brother whose tal-ents would be so useful to the struggle if he only changed his frame of mind."

"You're right," I mused. "You're right."

"Hey, man . . . I know."

"I'm proud of you," I added pensively. "You stuck to your be-liefs and here you are. I've always admired that part of you. I was talking to Regina about that one day before this whole thing went down. I was, like, 'Kendall is the kind of brother man we need to take the weight.'"

"Well, to be honest, brother . . . and I'm not talking behind a sister's back . . . but, that's not the impression that she's given me."

"Well . . . you know . . . people misinterpret things."

"I give it straight at all times. So if I'm saying that I used to have another impression, that's the truth."

"She's here, you know."

"Oh, really?"

"Oh, yeah. You didn't know?"

"I just got into town, brother."

"Well, she is. Her U.S. cell works here. Give her a call. If you need the number, I'll give it to you."

"Hold on. Lemme get some paper."

"Women are funny," I observed while he played at taking her number. "Maybe there's a part of her that doesn't want us to be friends. Maybe she thinks we'll compare notes or something. You know how women are."

"Yeah. We know how sisters get."

"Ooooh . . . what time is it? Shit. I have to run. But check this, we have to have dinner tonight. It's an island custom. Reg and I are having dinner at Miranda's. It's along the promenade. If you step outside your hotel and make a right, it's there. A ten-minute walk along the water."

"I'm not sure if I'm ready for Regina," he replied. "How does she feel about all this?"

"Ask her when you see her."

"I think I wanna chill."

"Come on, man. Let's break bread. Plus, I have a hookup at a local channel that supplies a lot of stuff to CNN. I think if they came down and did a little something, it could air."

"Here, or there?"

"Both, I think."

"Lemme see. What time?"

"Seven."

"Seven . . . seven . . ."

"Yeah, man. Seven."

"Check it. My reading is Thursday. Why don't you come to that?"

"Well, can I be honest? I was so convinced that you would do this, I put some things in play."

"Okay, Shooky. You da man."

"It's the least that I could do."

"You're a genius, motherf——ker."

"You're the poet, man. That's you."

"Miranda's? Seven. And you'll be coming with that fine ass girl?"

"Regina will be there."

"Is she still kinky? Still a little freak?"

"Not that I could see."

"Hmmm. Guess she must have changed."


## X.

It was a humid evening, and the lapping water of the harbor shimmered with reflected light. Light swirled around the globes along the railing of the promenade that curved around the waterline, floated like confetti from the windows of the large hotels, and you could see it in the hair and on the shoulders of the tourists and conventioneers who sauntered by.

Miranda's was a lively place with gracious service on a patio with taupe umbrellas and the most exquisite wicker chairs you've ever seen. It opened out directly on the promenade, the way that restaurants in Spain expand into a plaza or a street. It was a lively night. The place was full. And in a gauzy shirt and linen slacks, I thought I blended in.

I surveyed the promenade for my accomplice while a P.A. gave a hasty brief. I should be warm, but not gushing. No broad gestures with the hand. They want some easy sound bites. Nothing heavy. Nothing controversial. To quote: "You know . . . informative but feel-good . . . light . . . with a bit of breeze and, for want of a better expression, fluff."

Up until this time, I'd felt as if I'd covered everything, that nothing could go wrong. But now I had the disappointing feeling that nothing would be right. Before I left the house I'd double-checked with Albert, who assured me that his operatives had jammed Regina's phone, which meant that she could not receive a call. He'd given her tickets to the music fest and told her she could use his car, so getting here was sorted out. I had checked in with the prey, who'd told me that he'd chatted with the news producer. But I hadn't thought beyond this point, hadn't thought of what to do in case the drunkard didn't come. He had to come. He had to or he couldn't get his pay.

When I had been put in place and lit against the railing, the sea behind me, people moving, hotels left and right, the reporter opened with a simple question.

"How do you feel about what happened at the Cup & Chaucer? The fight?"

"There was no fight," I said firmly, while holding up a smile. "There was a misunderstanding, as Regina will tell you as soon as she comes. I was about to ask her something and I lost my footing. I reached for her and crashed into her body from behind."

"Well, what about Thelma Olsen, the lady who is suing you for breaking her hand?"

"I didn't break her hand. Let's make that clear. All evidence will show that she assaulted me and that I exercised considerable restraint. Second of all, her wrist is sprained. There's a difference. But with all that being said, I hope that Ms. Olsen is recovering well. It was a very unfortunate accident. She's old. She could have damaged her wrist at any time. She could have slammed her fist to make a point. Bam! Or clapped her hands together as she laughed. Pow! She's a very lucky woman."

"Would she agree?"

"She would if she considered that her misfortune happened in a country with one of the most well-developed health care systems in the world, thanks to all the progress made by our leader Don Octavio Rawle and the PPP. If it had happened in another place, let's say the Virgin Islands, it would have ended in a national disgrace. And that is why the country needs to stand with me in this crisis. To save our country from international disgrace."

"Is Regina fine? Is she okay?"

"She is wonderful, and we are great. In fact, she will be joining me tonight."

"There are rumors that she's left you. Are they true?"

"As I said, she will be joining me tonight."

"You spoke to Mr. Power, earlier. This is what we've been informed. What did you talk about?"

"How much we admire each other's work. It's amazing how much his work has always meant to me and vice versa. We'd just really never had the chance to talk."

"Were you ever tempted to accept his invitation? Did it ever cross your mind to step into the ring? He's much bigger than you are. Even a little . . . were you scared?"

"I deplore all kinds of violence and intimidation. Boxing is certainly violent, and although I would have been concerned about his weight advantage in the ring, I should remind you that boxing is a lot like writing in terms of its reliance upon technique. Fighting him would have been useless. So he ends up on the canvas and I stand victorious and then what? Of what would that have been the proof? That I can do to him with my body what everybody knows I can do with my mind? Do you know what? Let's not go there. Just talking now I smell the blood."

When I was through and seated, waiting for the woman who betrayed me with her ex, I looked out on the promenade, across the bobbing heads, and there, beneath the lamp where he was supposed to be, a bag across his shoulder, was my accessory. No. My hero. No. My friend.

I nodded, but he didn't see me, so I stood and slapped my pockets in the way that you would do if you were searching for a pack of cigarettes. To show me that he noticed, he began to swing the bag from hand to hand before him, giving me the sign that we had prearranged to indicate that everything was well.

With a sense of satisfaction, I sat back and had a drink, beaming like the playwright who was sitting in the audience with superior knowledge of the actions and reactions that would draw our deepest feelings from our bodies and invest them in the action on the stage.

I had a frozen daiquiri, and as I sipped it I became aware of how my breathing burned the frosting on the rim around the glass, how a single, concentrated spurt could perhaps make the frosting go away, and I began to wish that I could burn away my feelings for Regina just like that.

I had loved her for a very long time before that night when I'd driven her home. I'd admired her for years. I was not quite good at love, and as I did with things in which I could not dominate, I stayed away. I stayed away from love for a very long time, which wasn't all that hard—love had always stayed away from me.

When did I fall in love with her? I do not know. I couldn't pick a moment or a time. For loving her had been transformed from an experience into something higher—a fundamental truth, a premise, a dogma, an omniscient point of view.

What if she hadn't been a model? If she didn't have the skill to write exquisite books? Would I have felt the same? Of course. I loved her because she made me love again. Loving her renewed my faith. Through her I was redeemed.

But as soon as this was said, another voice arose.

*F——k her, Shooky. She's a bitch. If she was any kinda woman she woulda take your word. She wouldn't disgrace you in the street like that. She woulda never let certain words come out her mouth. Calling you p——ssy ass bitch and all them things. What kinda person is that? She ain't respect you, Shooky. She ain't respect you at all. And she ain't love you, neither. You ask her plain-plain on the phone yesterday if she love you, and she never answer. And look! Braps! A little thing happen between the two of you, and look she run gone talking back to her old-time man.*

*No matter how she say that Power harassing her and that he full o' shit, your own brother tell you that she and him was having secret talks. If you was another man, in truth you woulda put on two lick on her right there in the street. Wilding up herself! Slapping up your face! Scratching up your arm!*

*And when that old white lady rush at you, what she do? Nothing. When the lady send her husband for police, what she do? Nothing. Nothing but laugh.*

*She take you for a laughingstock, Shooky, and you ain't need no f——king woman like that. You need a woman that have your back. She's a blasted traitor, man. She ain't treat you special. She treat you like everybody else. On principle, she shoulda take your word 'bout what happen, seeing as she ain't know you as a man that do them kinda things.*

*Shooky, you is a p——ssy, in truth. If you was any kinda man you wouldn't even be doing them cat and rat things. You woulda just go by your brother house and try and reason with her and if she carry on with any stupidness in front of Carmona just to show off and show you up, just bust her ass one time. Give her back at least what she give you in the street, for she ain't have a right to bitch you like that and p——ssy you like so.*

*And after you bust her ass now, here is what you do. You go by Power reading at McSweeney's and beat him too. Just walk up quiet while the f——ker reading and just pop out the mike and start to lick him with it. And you know it going sound nice and loud with the echo and reverb.*

*They think they f——king know you, Shoucair Dominguez, but they ain't know you at all. But you know them. That's why you is a step ahead and they is a step behind. That's why they going to fall into the trap you set tonight.*

I was finishing the daiquiri when she arrived. It was red and still cold, and as cold things often do, it passed along my throat as if it were a stream of liquid silver, or what I thought that it would feel like if someone had found a way to make a metal into something you could drink.

"How are you?" she asked me from behind.

"Me? I feel like shit."

"Got eyes in the back of your head?"

"I need them these days."

"Is this the way to start?" she asked.

"It's a damn good way to end."

A chill ran from my brows across my scalp and down my shoulders as I rushed the balance of the drink and I shifted in the seat.

"Did you invite me out to be a sourpuss?" she asked me when she'd sunk into a squat so that her face was level with my neck. I couldn't see her, but when she spoke I felt the streaming of her breath against my ear and nape.

"I don't have it in me to be sweet," I told her. "Not tonight, at least."

"You're on edge."

"I'm unloved."

"Look. I better leave."

"Have a good life."

When I thought she was gone, I turned around to look and caught a glimpse of her unhurried progress to the bar. She wore a short white dress with straps that trailed across her shoulders down her back like streams of milk.

"So why'd you come?" I asked her when I'd followed her, and slid beside her, joined by the hip to her stool.

She'd ordered me a frozen daiquiri, gambling that I'd come, and now she dipped her index finger in the frappé top and said, "Let's make a toast."

"To what?" I asked.

"To anything. To nothing. I don't know."

"To everything and nothing," I said grumpily. "To all and sundry."

She flashed a timid smile. "You said you wanted to talk."

"I thought so at the time."

"What do you want to talk about?"

"Forget it. It's too much. Your dress is nice. Your necklace, too. What are those? Pearls?"

"Cow bone."

"They look good. You look good."

"Yeah? But I feel like shit."

"Do you want to eat? I'm not so hungry anymore."

"There is something that you want to ask me. Go ahead."

"I've asked you everything there is to ask."

"You're not telling me the truth."

"It doesn't matter what I say these days. You'll believe what you believe."

"Shooky, that's not—"

"Do you love him, Reg?"

I peered into her eyes, whose lids were softly tinted powder-blue.

"I don't know how to answer you."

I passed my hand across the downy smoothness of her closely shaven head. The lights picked out the sheen. As she looked, I brought my fingers to my nose and pulled deeply on the scent. She'd rubbed her scalp with olive oil.

"No bullshit," I told her. "No avoidance. Just speak the f——king truth."

With eyes averted she began to speak, her voice shimmering and low beneath the chatter and the music and the other sounds, cloudy like a vision of a fish in brackish water. My temples pounding, I drew closer, slipped my arms around her shoulders, put my foot against the rail, held my breath and bit my tongue and huddled in.

With her elbows on the wooden bar, my arteries feeling like they were transforming into stone, she bowed her head and spoke.

"He's a shit. He's an ass. But I've known him for a very long time, and I mean . . . that has to count. History isn't something that you waste. I have a lot of history with this man. And I cannot let it go. You might think we're not an easy fit, but it really isn't up to you. I love him. And my second chance is here. I screwed it up the last time. I'd be really stupid if I let him go."

"I see."

"Well?"

"Well what?"

"That's all you got? *Well?*"

"Reg," I said, my voice cracking. "Look. I don't know what to say."

"Just say you love me, baby. Just say I'm not a fool. Just hold me tight and kiss me. After that, please take me home."

"So you love him that much. Oh f——k."

"You little shit," she answered lovingly, "I'm referring to you."

## XI.

I COULDN'T TAKE her home as she had asked. Something had been set in motion that I had to urgently undo. With her revelation had arrived a deep awareness of the ways in which my search for vengeance could affect our lives. The simple shock of it—it wasn't going to be a pretty sight; then there was the heart of it, the core of what it would ultimately come to mean—if the mission failed and my role was known, it would be hard for me to orchestrate theatrical revenge against another ex. In other words, I'd lose the advantage of surprise.

As I considered this, the P.A. who had briefed me now approached.

"Excuse me. Mr. Dominguez, I don't mean to bother you,

but there is a rum head by the railing who's harassing everybody to come and ask if you could be a sporting man and treat him to a drink."

From the bar I could see clear above the heads of all the people who were sitting down and I scanned the crowd that moved along the walk.

"Which man?" I asked. "Can you point him out?"

"Oh. I don't know where he turned."

"Just tell him no, okay? Tell him no, and that I hope he'll understand." I glanced at Reg. "Tell him that I'm on a date tonight and cannot be disturbed."

"What is all of that?" Regina asked me with new interest when the P.A. walked away.

"All of what?"

"Cameras and stuff." She pointed. "Over there."

"I don't know."

"I don't want to be around any cameras for a thousand years," she joked while pulling on my arm. "That's a sign if I ever saw one. I think it's time to go."

"How'd you get here?"

"Albert's car."

"So why don't you take it back to Mayfair Gardens and I'll pick you up?"

"Drive behind me and we'll just make it one thing."

"Carmona," I remarked with worry.

She shrugged.

"She'll get over it."

"Look," I said indulgently, "I need to find that guy. I don't want people to start saying that I'm some kinda pig, you know what I mean. He might take it the wrong way. This is a small island, and everybody knows everybody and everybody knows everything. Plus, tonight I've been blessed. My woman has come back. I should really tithe."

"Okay," she answered, misty eyed. "In the meantime I'll run

to the powder room. Drive behind me to Mayfair. I'll drop off Albert's car and then we'll go." She kissed me on the cheek and squeezed my hand. "Meet you at the door in five."

OUTSIDE ON THE promenade, I broke into the P.A.'s conversation, took her by the arm and marched her to the side.

"Tell me. Where's the man?"

She swiveled left and right and flexed up on her toes.

"He was here a little while ago. I don't know where he went."

"I'm going to look for him, okay? If you find him before me, tell him that these cat-and-mouse games can't work, and that he needs to check with me later 'bout this thing so we can make another plan."

"If I see him I will tell him, but I can't do that right now. The other guy is here."

"I can't do my part," I said, a little panicked. "A family emergency. Something has come up. Tell Kendall that I had to go, and wish him lots of luck."

"But we need to have the shot of when you meet and greet."

I took her by the shoulders and looked her straight in the eye.

"Look. It can't be done."

"What can't be done, my brother?"

Jesus. It was him.

In heavy boots and baggy pants, as if he were a kid—his shirt, of course, Versace silk—he tried to pound me, while my instinct was to shake his hand and so we grappled and slipped. His clothes offended me. I'd never seen a pair of boots so clean. They were absurd, like pit bulls coiffed like poodles, like thugs on the down low.

As they lit him I withdrew toward Miranda's, glancing back across my shoulders every now and then while peering at the faces in the crowd that streamed around me, searching with intensely focused eyes.

"So Mr. Power," began the interview, "welcome to San Carlos and our capital, Seville."

"Thank you, my brother. It's always good to be in a prosperous black country such as yours. I'm amazed at the infrastructure and just the general sense of purpose that I see here. There is a lot of positive energy here. This is what Garvey was talking about. Black businesses. That is one of the things I talk about in my book *Recognize I'm Real*—the connections across the diaspora. They've been trying to separate us for centuries. But our destiny is to be a glorified and unified people."

"Is Shooky Dominguez now a friend of yours?"

"Everyone is my friend. That's what my work is all about, friendship."

"Your work is most often described as being about the black experience, though. Are you saying that your focus has changed?"

"Blackness is friendship. Just think—when it's pitch black, dark, like during a blackout, we can be inspired to fear or friendship."

"What does that mean?"

"What does it mean? Poetry for me is a mystical thing. *Recognize I'm Real* is all about the mystical journey that the black man has to take. The ghetto is a mythical place. Where I came up in the projects every day was a battle of good and evil like in the days of Mt. Olympus and the Greeks. Do you know what I mean? Looking at you now, I can see that you don't. But if you come out to McSweeney's this Thursday at seven-thirty, a lot of this will be explained for real."

Glancing back across my shoulder, I observed Regina, tall and dressed in white, approaching with her hands against her hips, her elbows jokingly projected to the side.

"What is this?" she asked suspiciously. A thought was crystallizing in her mind.

"Ask him," I said blankly. "I know as much as you."

She looked at me, then looked at him, and when he noticed

her, he dipped and made a little pistol with his hand and fired from the hip.

"What is that supposed to mean?" I asked, my nostrils flared.

"That what?"

"That phallic thing . . . that shooting thing."

"Shooky, I don't know. Baby, please don't."

"I just want to know."

"Baby, let's just leave."

"I can't, babe. I can't. If I were you, I'd go. Just go. Please go. I'll meet you in Mayfair or something."

"Or *something*?"

I began to scan the crowd again.

"Yes," I said vaguely. "Something. Something like that."

From the sea of bobbing heads, I noticed one that had a slightly different float, and I waited tensely as my accessory, friend and hero drifted side to side and into view, his bag of mice across his back. With a hand across his brows to shield his eyes, he passed six feet in front of me while gazing at the man who was the focus of the camera and the lights.

"I'm not going without you," said Regina.

"Just a minute," I replied while admiring the drunkard's sly approach.

Sensing something, Kendall turned around and saw him standing there, the hand across his brow resembling a mock salute.

"Whassup?" said Kendall Power.

The drunk did not reply.

"What the hell is going on?" Regina asked.

"I think it's time to go."

In the moment that I turned to say this, something happened. The truth is that I didn't see. But like everyone from here to southern California, I heard the girlish scream.

Dear Editor:

The rumors that I've passed away are untrue. I am in the pink of health. "Vim" and "Vigor" are my middle names. Reports to the contrary are fabrications designed to sully my name. Rather than writing letters to you expressing my opinion of the country's progress, I have been trying to finish a book.

After working at my craft for over half a century, I have finally received a contract from a publisher—"a deal," as young Dominguez calls it—for the story of my life. They intend to publish it when I'm a hundred years old—which means I have five years to go.

All memory is fiction. History is the arrangement of events to fit a plot. Don't expect the truth. Expect what I wish had been. This does not mean that truth is not my ambition. It is. But as I am discovering more and more these days, flesh is fallible. Flesh corrupts. I am just a man.

I know what drew them to my story—the bounty of my life and loves. But I am not sure if that is the story that I'd like to tell. I want to tell the story of my passing, of pretending that it was of no importance that my father, Eddie Blackwell, was half black, that my mother, Eugenia Campbell, was a quarter so, but that I chose to live as if I were white. What does it mean to be white? I do not know. It is something that I have never been. Something that I hope this writing will help me find out.

In between writing I have been working out with weights. Young Dominguez in his inimitable style assures me that I'll be a magnet for what he calls "the babes." He's a flatterer, that one. But "black is beautiful," they say.

Wishing you and yours a happy life and lots of health and strength.

Yours, etc.

St. William Rawle

# JUDGMENT DAY

SHE KEPT GLANCING out the window while she waited for the tea, as if she hadn't grown accustomed to the changes in the light. She was blind in one eye from glaucoma, and her left side, though unbending, still moved.

In a skirt suit and dark stockings with a seam, in butterfly shades whose wings were barely wider than her cheeks, she would have been a little overdressed if she were white. But she was an old black woman in the big plantation house where she'd worked and had her children and had plunged herself into a long affair that had begun when she was barely older than a child.

And now, at seventy-five, she'd dyed her hair and plucked her brows and come to say good-bye.

Mt. Diablo had erupted. Four hundred thousand people in Seville were now at risk. And like half of them she planned to leave until the tremors and explosions had ceased. The first eruption in a hundred years had happened seven weeks before—a quiet venting of some steam. Since then there had been mud-flows and spurting streams of rocks embroiled in superheated gas. But three days ago a large explosion had released a mighty cloud of ash.

Her son, Albert Dominguez, a quiet man who'd been named as president and party leader by the charismatic Dr. Don Octavio Rawle, had sent her in a car with an assistant who'd been charged with making sure that her appointment would be brief.

Glancing through the window, sipping on the tea, Estrella wondered what St. William Rawle would do in this eternal night. Perhaps it would be good, she thought, the ash had partly blocked the sun, and maybe all the cancers that had pocked his skin would heal. Praise God.

"So you running too," St. William offered when he'd made it down the stairs, supported by the maid. He was leaning on a cane, dressed for the occasion not in his pajamas, but a crushed white suit.

As it often did these days, Estrella's memory failed, and she removed her shades to look at him anew. Her mind, which had resumed its childish fascinations, was distracted by the patterns of the chintz.

"Who are you again?" she asked him when a fleeting sense of purpose had returned.

"It's Willy Boy."

"Yeah? I thought you dead." She shook her head and drank her tea and put the saucer in her lap and rocked from side to side.

"You know who that is?" he asked, pointing to a painting with his cane. "That is you with Octavio when he was small. Remember Octavio? My son?"

"I ain't really sure. The head go and come these days." She laughed. "My mind don't like to concentrate."

"So where are they going to take you, then?" he asked her through a phlegmy cough.

"For ice cream, I suppose."

St. William had been old for a very long time and was no longer sentimental about matters of decay. He was frank about his putrefaction. To climb the steps without depleting earth of oxygen would make him feel amazed. But to see Estrella Thompson disappearing in herself, to witness her misplacing thoughts like bunches of redundant keys had opened the vat in which he kept his aging tears.

"What you crying for?" she asked. "Come here, child. Come here."

He sat beside her, and she helped to ease his creaking weight into her lap. He wasn't heavy, but his limbs had lost their full control.

"Albert," she said softly, as a memory met a sentiment and multiplied into a name. "You ain't have to cry because your mother gone. I ain't gone for no long time. I gone to come back."

St. William swallowed hard and answered, "I might not be here."

"You ain't supposed to be here, when I come back," she said while scraping through the remnants of his silver hair with dark arthritic hands. "You suppose to be gone away to school. Son, is plenty things you ain't really know. I hate this place, you wouldn't understand. Mr. Rawle might be a nice man to you, but he ain't such a nice man to me. Is plenty things I know that he ain't know that I know."

St. William, who by then had written seventy books, only one of which he had not published by himself, had grown addicted to suspense. The very chance that he might uncover something secret made his body tense, and so he asked, "Like what?"

"Octavio is your big brother," she whispered in the rarely uttered Spanish dialect called *sancoche*, which education had diluted out of common use. "You father and his father is the same. It ain't Mr. Rawle. When I was a young girl, my son, I fall in love with Mr. Rawle, and I do certain things that ain't make me feel so proud. But I give that man all my substance and every time he let me down. Mrs. Rawle, as pretty as you see her there, she was a little whoring gal who use to always have another man, and because she know I know and because she know how I feel about Mr. Rawle and Mr. Rawle use to feel about me, it cause contention in this house. And one day she do me something and you know what I do? I say I going to show her something and I went and make friends with her man and make two children with him quick time."

"I know that story," said St. William tightly. "You married him. It didn't last. Wilfred was a drunk."

"Oh," she said vacantly, and ran her hand beneath his jacket, down his deeply corrugated ribs. "Sometimes the head come and go and I forget. But I won't forget you though. I going come back."

The assistant, who'd been waiting in the kitchen, cleared her throat and came into the room.

At the door, St. William hugged Estrella close. She'd replaced her hat, a man's Fedora. Her face was covered with a surgeon's mask to keep the ash from spreading to her lungs and throat, and on her feet were tooled, expensive English shoes. Behind her, through the door, the details of the world that they had known had been transformed by ash into a pointilistic scape of grays, a dot screen that made it seem as if it were a scene cut from the news and magnified or held against the nose to be perused by unbelieving eyes.

"Did you love St. William, Mr. Rawle?" asked.

She took his face and said, "Oh, boy."

"Is that a yes or no?"

"They ain't have no word for that. But when you see him, tell him I gone. Tell him that the last time I see him he wasn't looking so good. Tell him to eat liver and kidney to strong up his blood. Tell him I ain't forget all the things he do for me in life.

My first shop I had is he lend me the money and all the offer that I offer him, he never want to take it back. Tell him that that girl he have working for him now can't wash white suit. Tell him to tell her go get some Blue."

"I will."

"You looking sad."

"I don't know how I'm going to live when you're gone."

"Come, lemme bless you."

He bowed his head, and she spit in her hand and streaked it in his hair for his anointing, palmed his head and closed her eyes.

"God of Abraham . . . God of Jacob . . . God of Moses . . . bless this child that grow in my hand, that nurse on my breast, that play at my feet. Give him strength. Give him health. Give him life. Bless him that his days will be long. Bless him that his heart will be true. Bend him from his crooked ways. Forgive him of his sins."

Dear Editor:

    I am writing to express a grave concern about the way in which the government is conducting this island's affairs. Am I the only one who thinks the president is just a bit too much?

    When the annual St. William Rawle Award for Literature was instituted three years ago, the president explained the paltry cash allowance for the prize in terms of all the costs incurred in the recovery from the eruption of Mt. Diablo. Since then, prosperity has returned to San Carlos and each and every one of us has recognized that our situation is quite similar to that of California, where, despite the fact of earthquakes, people go about their lives.

    If St. William were alive today, he would promptly request that the prize be withdrawn or at least lobby for the removal of his name. This year, my novel *Rats* is in the running and I have to say that winning thirty thousand dollars won't really change my life. Based on our nation's cash reserves, the value of the prize could easily be raised. If I remember rightly, an award of half a million dollars is the sum that Mr. Rawle had been talking about.

    On my mother's grave, I swear that I am sure the funds would have been found if this were a prize in the sciences and not the arts. I am not the only one who believes this. All the other nominees, including my wife Regina Walker, fully agree. The best is ahead of us. The worst is gone. Open up the pipes and let the money flow. What are we hoarding it for? We can't take it with us. And who knows when life is going to end. We're not here forever. We're all just passing through.

Yours, etc.

Shooky Dominguez

COLIN CHANNER is the author of the national bestselling novels *Waiting in Vain* and *Satisfy My Soul,* and the novella *I'm Still Waiting.* In 1998, his influential debut novel *Waiting in Vain* was selected as a Critic's Choice by the *Washington Post Book World,* which described it as a "clear redefinition of the Caribbean novel." *Waiting in Vain* was also selected as Book of the Summer by *Time Out New York* and excerpted in *Hot Spots: The Best Erotic Writing in Modern Fiction,* which placed Mr. Channer in the company of writers such as Russell Banks, E. L. Doctorow, Don DeLillo, and David Foster Wallace.

Described as "Bob Marley with a pen instead of Gibson guitar" by award-winning poet and critic Kwame Dawes, Mr. Channer was born in Jamaica and lives in New York. He is the founder and artistic director of the Calabash International Literary Festival (calabashfestival.org), the only annual international literary festival in the Caribbean.

Mr. Channer is the bass player in the reggae band Pipecock Jaxxon and has taught fiction writing workshops in Jamaica, London and New York.

For more information visit colinchanner.com or write to him at colin@colinchanner.com. He answers all his mail himself.